THE
LEVIATHAN PRINCE

Book two of the Roanfire Saga

CK Miller

DEDICATION

To my three precious little boys, Riley, Carter, and Jesse.

ACKNOWLEDGEMENTS

First off, thank you so much to my friends, family, and fans who have embraced my love for writing. Truly, without the support of important people like you, this would not be a possibility.

A special thank you to Marlow York for helping me with some issues in book one, and her support as a fellow author. Thank you to my friends at Castle Rogue! And to Richard Paul, a genius poet and bard for coaching me in the WARDENTSONG on page 175.

A very special thank you to Amber Kizer – her constant enthusiasm for the story and the characters has driven me to finish this book, and I'm sure she will be hounding me to complete book three as soon as possible. Her energy is contagious.

Last, but not least, thank you to my husband, Matt Miller, for giving me the time to write, for supporting my goals and helping me reach them, for giving his time (and money) to help propel this dream along, and for sitting with me to brainstorm through plot issues!

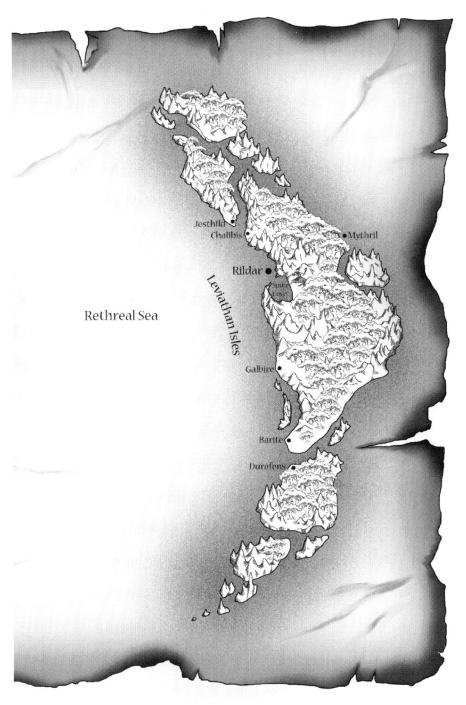

CK Miller

1

FALSE HERO

It had been a fortnight since the attack.

The wooden frame that held the warped glass panes of the window creaked open. Morning light seeped into my chamber, clinging to a poisonous hazy glow in the sky. The stench of smoke and blood festered in the air, and the sickly caw of three crows perched along the damaged walls of the Meldron Castle, grated on my heart. Like the remains of a burnt-out fire, gold and brown leaves swirled inside the decimated courtyard below.

The lump in my throat tightened as I pulled the window closed and drew the curtains to hide the terrible scene beyond. Roanfire may have won the fight against the Leviathan Pirates, but as the defeated pirates fled, they had burned whatever autumn crops remained in the fields and frightened most of the wildlife away. Roanfire was now faced with a new threat: starvation.

My hand absently wandered up to the jewel that hung about my neck. The warmth of the newly transformed sapphire stone radiated through the tips of my fingers like a beacon of hope. But it did not ease my pain. My battle against the Phoenix Witch had only begun. The memory of Ikane struggling for breath as I held him in my arms was still strong. He still hadn't roused from his coma, but I knew Rion would not allow him to die. Not yet.

Deliberately, I looked at my sword which lay upon the small, wooden table to the right of the window. I had polished, cleaned, oiled, and sharpened my weapon every day since the dreadful battle, and yet I thought I could still see the copper stains of blood hiding in the delicate notches and grooves.

My fingers trembled as they brushed across the hilt of it. I wasn't sure that I was ready to wield it again. My hand curled around the leather-bound grip and I lifted it from the table. My body still ached from the aftermath of war, or perhaps it was the fear in my mind that caused the pain to linger. What good would I be to my king if I could not fight? I was a soldier of Roanfire, after all.

With a practiced twist of my wrist I spun my sword across my body, as I had so often done, to loosen my muscles. The sword flourished across my frame twice before my hand lost hold of the weapon. I flinched as it flew across the small room, collided with the heavy wooden door, and clattered loudly to the stone floor.

Almost immediately I heard the click of the lock on the wrought-iron door. I had become well acquainted with the elderly soldier who had been assigned to guard my 'prison' over the past few weeks. His name was Wellam Thraner. There was something about him that always struck me as odd. He was unusually kind to me since the battle with the Leviathan Pirates. He knew, as well as anyone else in Roanfire, that I had befriended a Leviathan Pirate... a prince, no less. The traitors' brand of a phoenix and serpent locked in battle upon my shoulder constantly reminded me of that. It smarted even now as the fabric of my shirt brushed against my healing skin.

Thraner's bald head pushed into my chamber, bringing to mind the top of a polished helm.

"Brendagger?" he asked as his eyes scanned my chamber for the source of the noise. His thick, white brows furrowed when he discovered my sword lying on the ground. "Are you well?"

I pursed my lips as I stooped to pick up my weapon. "Well enough. Is that still necessary?" I motioned to the key still stuck in the hole on the door. "I am not a prisoner of war. Why does King Sander order that I be locked away as though I am a threat?"

Thraner shrugged, causing his crimson tunic to rumple around his slightly rounded belly. "I am only following orders. You look well rested today. Sleep is quite important for a young lass your age."

I barely listened to him as I grabbed my belt and scabbard from the post of the small bed in the center of the room. He had a tendency to ramble anyway.

"You know, I have a daughter who is your age," he continued. "I just got the news that she is well and safe in Pedre with her husband. She lived in Shard for quite some time, but when the Leviathans made their way up the Karn River, she and her husband fled. Did I already tell you that she's expecting her second child? I haven't seen her in several months."

Buckling my scabbard to my slender waist seemed tedious as he spoke, but it was the weight of my sword that caused a slight tremor to arise in my chest. The heaviness of my sword bearing down against my left hip felt like a sack of rocks designed to drag me to my death.

"Where shall I inform the king that you've gone today?" Thraner asked when I didn't respond. "The kitchens?"

I frowned. "You know where I go every day."

His eyes hardened. "The Leviathan," he said with unmasked disdain. "Why do you care for him so? He betrayed you, attacked our home, and—"

"You needn't remind me," I cut him off and pushed past him. "Inform King Sander that I intend to train with the soldiers this morning."

Thraner's eyes widened. "Are you sure you are well enough for that?"

I didn't look at him, fearing that if I did, my resolve would waver. "Yes," I said firmly, and placed my trembling hand on the hilt of my sword. It was cold and hard.

The older soldier nodded. "Do not be ashamed if your body does not perform as well as you'd like. War changes people."

I already knew that. My failed attempt at flourishing my sword was already an indication of how difficult this would be.

I made my way through the labyrinth of the castle. The sullen glances of refugees huddled against the walls bore into my mind the grim reality of what Meldron had endured. The people were filthy, broken, and hopeless. My heart rate quickened as I noted the stains of tears upon their soot-smudged faces. By the time I reached the heavy wooden door leading to the courtyard, my entire body reflected the quivering fear, dread, and hopelessness of the refugees. On my first try to open the door, my hand completely missed the lever. Desperate to flee the darkened hallways of gloom and despair, I clamored at it again and finally stumbled into the cold brightness of day.

My lungs gulped the chilly air as my eyes adjusted to the hazy light. Why was this so unbearable? Why, after so many years of training and battle, did my body tremble like the dead leaves upon the autumn trees? Was I unfit for this? Was I no longer suited to be a soldier?

My eyes lifted to the walls of the castle, taking in the mutilated plethora of black and red scars upon the pale gray stones. Perhaps Thraner's observation was indeed true. I was as changed as the castle. Where the front doors of the citadel once gleamed bright, they now drooped with lethargic stains of cold oil.

I shut my eyes against it all. I did not want to see anymore.

It was then that my senses were able to discern the familiar noise of weapons clashing in friendly sparring and the grunts of exertion from soldiers. Fond memories of training with the armed forces in Daram returned.

I gathered another deep breath of the bitter, rancid air, before opening my eyes again. The training arena was filled with soldiers that sparred in scattered pairs across the dusty ground. But they moved slowly and methodically. The battle was as leaden with them as it was with me.

Removing my cloak, I draped it over the edge of a nearby rain barrel. An eerie silence stretched across the training arena as every single one of the soldiers paused from their calculated sparring. Men and women turned to gaze upon me, their soundless breaths hanging in the frigid air.

I bit my lip and shifted uneasily. I hadn't sparred with the soldiers since the great battle.

A soldier moved in the distance. As he approached, the others parted to allow him passage. I recognized the man at once and discreetly gripped the hilt of my sword with a cautious step back. It was Commander Tamian.

Before the great battle with the Leviathan Pirates, I had been his prisoner. In his anger, this man had cropped my hair short as a symbol of treason for befriending a Leviathan Pirate.

My body tensed as he drew near. To my astonishment, the commander tipped his head in a respectful bow, as if I were some formidable noble. My brows furrowed.

"We are indebted to you, Keatep Brendagger," he said. "Your power alone has spared us. We know nothing of what magic you used to defend Roanfire from the Leviathan Pirates but defend us you did."

The crowd of soldiers nodded and murmured in approval behind him.

I swallowed hard and tried to hide my grimace. Was this the reason they revered me so? Was this why Thraner was so kind to me? It had been said from eye-witness accounts that a magical sphere of power had burst from my unconscious form on the battlefield. The raw power had drained energy and life from the Leviathans, felling them in the form of a mighty scythe to wheat. But it had been Rion's power, not mine. And it was not something that should be honored.

He pressed his hand to his heart. "Forgive me, Keatep Brendagger. I misjudged you." His voice was hushed with shame as he cast his eyes to the ground.

I swallowed hard again and cleared my throat. "I will not deny that I have befriended a Leviathan Pirate."

Tamian did not look up at me, but I could see his jaw tighten, even beneath his thick beard. "The one who defended you in battle?"

That too was an account of the spectators, for I recalled none of it. "Yes."

Commander Tamian looked up at me. "I cannot bring myself to trust a Leviathan, even if he did spare you. However, you have shown your loyalty to Roanfire. No man can deny that."

I did not know how to reply, especially when the entire Meldron Army looked to me as if I were some sort of goddess. It suddenly dawned on me how furious Rion would be if she knew how the soldiers revered me for her powers, for that was her goal.

"Would you care to spar with me this morning?" I asked, breaking the reverence.

A solemn smile spread across his thin lips. "It would be an honor."

Perspiring, mentally energized, and physically drained from the drill, I made my way from the training arena to the warm kitchen. The spacious stone chamber was alive with clatter and noises of soldiers gathering for breakfast. Hopelessly, I searched the chaos for my dear friend and mentor, Mayama. But the friendly, plump cook was not here. I knew she wasn't. She had never set foot in Meldron.

In spite of the fresh roasts in the oven, and the wafting aroma of rabbit stew steeping in onions and herbs, it smelled terrible. Hundreds of people gathered here daily, and since the castle had taken on the care of the refugees, it was more crowded than ever. The thick stench of body odor was overwhelming.

I barely glanced at the cooks and kitchen aids as I gathered a tray and loaded it with two bowls of spiced squash soup and a pair of crusty slices of bread.

The guards standing by the door – who would surely be reporting my ventures to King Sander - nodded to me as I made my usual path to another room in the castle on the fifth floor of the spiraling staircase. The hallway was narrow and barren, with few torches lighting the dank servants' quarters. Two soldiers stood guard by one of the small doors, and one moved to produce a key when she spotted me coming down the hallway.

"Is he awake?" I asked her.

The redheaded soldier turned the key and unlocked the door while the other glanced at the tray of food in my hands.

"Why do you insist on dining with that man? He has yet to wake." Her tone was brittle and harsh.

I returned her discrimination with a glare of my own. "He is my friend."

The soldier clamped her mouth shut as the redhead opened the door. Without another word, I stepped inside the darkened chamber.

The claustrophobia didn't set in until my eyes adjusted to the darkness and the door locked behind me. The only light in the stuffy chamber came from a single crevice near the topmost corner of the wall, and it did little to relieve the festering smell of death.

With my back pressed up against the cold wall, I inched my way to the little round, wooden table sitting by the head of the uncomfortable looking cot. The man lying upon it barely stirred at the noise of the tray as I set it down beside him.

His thick brows held a subtle furrow above his closed eyes, hiding the unusual colors of his irises. Unlike the first day I had met him, his long raven hair was matted and filthy, and his bare torso was mutilated with the pale color of bandages that were stained with his blood. My eyes strayed to the black tattoo of the Leviathan Pirates upon his broad shoulder, but it no longer made me shudder with the inbred hatred that I once clung to.

Gently, I sat on the edge of his bed and allowed my fingers to trace the scar upon his left cheek where his thin beard refused to grow. A new injury, that would surely scar, trailed across the bridge of his well-formed nose to form an uneven 'X' upon his cheek.

His attractiveness was not dampened in my eyes.

"Ikane?" I whispered, holding out hope that he would finally wake. When he didn't rouse, I sighed and took my bowl of soup from the tray nearby and ate in silence.

The cynical healer had informed me days ago that Ikane had slipped in and out of consciousness for the past fortnight. It was a miracle that he still lived, for the injury dealt to his chest was mortal. His suntanned skin was still hot to the touch as a raging fever burned through his lean, powerful body. Deep inside, I feared for him. I knew what evil kept him alive. I knew what would haunt him when he woke. But I did not know if he would wake as my friend, or as a man possessed by the Phoenix Witch.

Having lost my appetite, I swallowed the mouthful I had taken and set the bowl back onto the tray.

"I'm sorry," I whispered to him, then bent down and kissed his feverish forehead. "I'll come visit you again."

With that, I stood, gathered the tray, and knocked on the door to be released.

Thraner was not guarding my door when I returned. And that worried me.

My hand gripped the hilt of my sword as I cautiously neared the heavy wooden door. The key was still inside the lock. Carefully, I turned the lever and the door swung open.

Startled, three men whirled. The heavy tension within crashed into me before I had even stepped over the threshold.

My guardian, Eamon Brendagger, stood by the foot of my rough cot. His cheeks were flushed, and a deep crease sat between his thick, graying brows, indicating that he had been locked in a heated, but hushed discussion with none other than... King Sander!

I bowed deeply in his presence. "My king."

The kings' garb may have been simple, and he did not sport the golden crown upon his head of deep auburn hair, but there was no mistaking this tall man with chiseled features for anyone else.

"Hurry inside." The king's servant, who rarely left Sander's side, nearly sprinted across the room to shut the door, pushing me inside. He peered around the frame as if to be sure no one had seen them.

"Kea," Eamon said as he broke away from King Sander and came to stand beside me. When he firmly gripped my arm, I knew something was wrong. His brown eyes were laden with worry.

I was about to speak when my eyes fell upon another figure leaning against the window frame behind the king. I hadn't noticed him. It was obvious that he had been there for quite some time, since he had abandoned his attention stance. His arms were folded casually across his chest as he gazed at the destroyed landscape beyond the frame. His eyes turned to me when Eamon spoke my name and his strong jaw, adorned by a thin patch of a fiery-red beard upon his chin, clenched.

I ached for his friendship again. Ropert may not have been my blood brother, but he was family to me.

"Keatep," King Sander stepped forward to claim my attention. The deep blue of his eyes bore into mine as he spoke. "I wish to proclaim you to the court as rightful heir to the throne of Roanfire."

I barely comprehended the statement. Ropert continued to glower at me with ice cold eyes that used to shine a warm blue.

"Again, sire," the king's servant interjected his concerns. "I strongly advise against this. Princess Lonacheska will not accept an illegitimate child as her heir. Her offspring is rightful heir to the throne, and this will put our alliance with the Glacial Empire in jeopardy. It may even be grounds for annulling the wedding entirely, and you know how much Roanfire needs aid. Especially after the battle."

I glanced at the servant, stunned at how freely he addressed the king.

The king whirled to face him. "Keatep is my daughter and I'd like to treat her as such. I was denied my right to be her father by my own. King Myron no longer controls every aspect of my life. Now that he is dead – may he rest in the blessed realm of the Phoenix - I wish to claim her. Is that so wrong?"

"Not at all, your majesty," Eamon said boldly. "However, we must consider the emotional strain this will place on the princess and her people. You've been betrothed to her since childhood."

"Do you think so little of my bride's people?" Sander said hotly. "A war would not ensue because of this."

"I am not suggesting that it would," Eamon said. "But it will most assuredly cause tension and the annulment of the marriage. And we need their support if we are to recover from this battle with the Leviathan Pirates."

A flurry of hushed arguments erupted as the men completely ignored my presence - clearly, this was the way Ropert had felt when I first arrived. We were simple soldiers. We obeyed commands and waited patiently to receive them. Until the argument settled, there was nothing more we could do.

Ropert ran his hand through his hair to brush the soft waves away from his face. His once long tresses of strawberry blonde hair had been cut just below his shoulders, making it difficult to tie back into a warrior's tail.

I gathered courage and approached, sneaking past Eamon and the foot of my bed to do so. He pushed himself from his casual position against the wall and stiffened.

"You look well, Ropert," I said to him, forcing my smile.

I watched the muscles in his jaw move. "You do not deserve the title of a princess," he said through his teeth.

My heart sank at his tone and it took every ounce of strength to hold the burning tears at bay. If he noted the slight quiver of my lips, he didn't acknowledge it. He folded his arms across his chest again and turned his gaze back to the thick window panes that warped the scene outside.

"I don't even know why I am here," he mumbled to the glass.

"You are here because you know of Keatep's heritage," King Sander stated as he took three short strides to cover the distance of my small chamber. The back of my legs bumped into the frame of my bed as I moved to make room for him.

Ropert, like a good soldier, immediately saluted the king.

"You have proven loyalty to the crown by keeping Keatep's identity secret," the king continued. "I have a special task for you, Ropert Saded. I would ask that you consent to be her bodyguard."

My jaw dropped at the magnitude of this request.

"You trust that I would protect her?" Ropert asked, making no effort to hide his disdain for me.

King Sander's expression was that of pure conviction. "I do."

The tenseness of Ropert's jaw eased at the king's confidence. Ropert then bowed respectfully. "Then I shall do as you ask, my king."

"As for you," Sander placed his hand on my shoulder, "we must determine what is best for you and for Roanfire."

"I am your faithful soldier and feel it best that I remain such," I quickly said.

Sander tilted his head in confusion as his eyes squinted at me. "Do you want to remain a mere soldier?"

I was surprised by the question. "It's a good life."

Ropert cleared his throat for attention and Sander gave him a quick nod, granting him permission to speak.

"Keatep Brendagger is hailed among the soldiers for her arcane magic," Ropert began.

I wanted to stop him then and there. The magic was not mine, but Ropert pressed on. "We won the war against the Leviathan Pirates because of her. It's all they talk about in the mess hall and the training field. As is custom for a wedding, you may pardon a subject."

"What a brilliant suggestion," the servant chimed in, crowding into the corner by the window. "This will allow you to dote on Keatep like the daughter you so desire without annulling the alliance with the Glacier Empire."

I scrutinized the middle-aged man that appeared to be King Sander's servant. He was neither thin nor bulky, tall or short, handsome or unsightly. Wrinkles creased his vigilant amber eyes. His graying hair was thinning at the top of his head and fell down to his shoulders in a graceful wave. He appeared harmless, but the scars across his hands and under the trimmed beard on his face betrayed his weakness as a servant. He was more dangerous than I cared to know. And I began to suspect that he was more than just King Sander's servant.

"I suggest that Ropert also be pardoned and receive an esteemed title in your army as well," the servant continued. "After all, he is innocent, and his efforts to save Meldron during the battle should be honored."

Ropert's frown softened with hope.

"Keatep." Sander took my hand in his. "I know it isn't what you deserve. You are royal by blood, but it is the best I can do to appease my counselors and my bride. I trust you understand. I simply wish to care for you like the father I should have been all these years."

I was not pleased with the arrangement, but I was loyal to my king. "As you wish."

He then leaned forward and pressed his warm lips against my forehead in a tender kiss of a father. "You are worth more than you know, little princess," he whispered.

My brows shot upward. I had never before considered myself worthy of that title. Nor did it feel right.

The king turned away and waved to his servant. "Come, Chanter. We have work to do."

The servant nodded and cautiously opened the door. He peered around the corner for a moment. After deeming the hallway void of unwanted eyes, he nodded to the king and they silently slipped away.

Ropert didn't wait another moment. He pushed past me to exit the small chamber, deliberately bumping into my shoulder in the process. I stumbled aside as he disappeared into the hallway.

Eamon noted the cold behavior and stepped forward. He placed his warm hand on my shoulder and I gripped his wrist in return, as if he could somehow lend me the courage to accept King Sander's wishes.

"Why can he not see that I am not a child? I do not need him to be a father to me. I have you."

Eamon's grip tightened on my shoulder, then dropped. "I am honored that you think of me as such," he said cautiously. "But he is your rightful father and we must respect that."

A harsh knock on the open door claimed our attention. Before we had even turned to see who it was, Thraner leaned in with his bald head and thick brows.

"He's awake," the soldier panted. "The Leviathan has roused."

My eyes widened.

"Go," Eamon urged me, knowing.

Without waiting for another invitation, I sprinted from the room.

A disgruntled voice echoed down the hallway as I reached the top of the spiraling staircase.

"I will not toil on healing that man any longer!" He hollered.

It was not hard to discern that the elderly voice spoke of Ikane. Knowing that Ikane was surrounded by those who wished him dead, my pace quickened. As I turned the corner to the narrow corridor, I saw the familiar white-haired man garbed in the robes of a healer. A young girl stood in his shadow, obviously his apprentice. She struggled to hold the healers' thick satchel in her wiry arms.

The old man folded his arms across his chest in defiance. "He is a Leviathan. Let him die like the slimy, pungent snake that he is."

"Leviathan or not, you've been ordered by King Sander himself to tend to that man," the redheaded soldier retorted, raising her voice to match that of the vexed healer. "Do you intend to defy the king's orders? That is a felony punishable by death."

The old man snatched his satchel from his apprentice, sending one of his potions flying. The vial clattered loudly against the stone floor, then left a small tinkling noise in its wake as it rolled between the boots of the soldier. The apprentice scurried to retrieve it from the ground.

"I said nothing of the sort," the healer hissed and pushed past the soldier and into Ikane's chamber.

By the time I drew near, the girl had followed the healer inside. I paused beside the soldiers who had grown accustomed to my visits.

"Why has the healer been summoned?" I asked, arching my neck to see inside the small prison.

"The Leviathan woke with a headache," the ginger haired soldier replied. It was no surprise that the soldiers refused to acknowledge that Ikane had a name.

"The healer assumes that he may have some sort of head injury."

Worry slammed into my chest more forceful than a battering ram.

It had begun.

"The healer can do nothing for him," I said.

Without waiting for a reply, I pushed my way into the tiny chamber. The healer had just skirted around the edge of the cot where Ikane was rocking, fiercely digging his fingers into his scalp to the point of pulling out his raven hair. He groaned quietly, seemingly unaware of the people crowding into his prison.

The old healer scowled up at me and paused from pulling his varying herbs, tonics, and salves from his satchel. The apprentice's head shot up. With wide eyes, she looked at the healer and then back at me. She was obviously startled that anyone would dare challenge her master.

"What do you want?" the healer demanded in a tone that would have sent anyone less devoted to the Leviathan scurrying.

I did not take my eyes from Ikane as I addressed the healer. "Your services are not needed."

The old man rounded on me, shaking a vial of brownish liquid in my face. "Who are you to say what I am capable of? I am the king's surgeon! I have more skill in my little finger than you do in your entire body! Let me tend to this Leviathan filth as ordered!" He spat on the ground.

I resisted the urge to draw my sword and chase him from the chamber. "You can't help him," I retorted through clenched teeth. "You may tell King Sander that I am to blame for your noncompliance."

"Gladly!" the healer snapped and slammed his items back into his satchel. Without another word he stormed from the chamber with the startled apprentice on his heels.

Before the door had closed after them, I fell to my knees beside Ikane's bed. I barely noted the noise of the healer barking something about my behavior to the guards as I reached up to Ikane and placed my hands over his, trying to still his rocking.

"Ikane," I whispered fiercely. "Ikane, can you hear me?"

He looked at me with red pain radiating through his mismatched eyes. I was troubled by the fierce glow of his left emerald iris. I had come to expect its burn when he was in heated battle. But not here. Not now. He was fighting something.

"Kea," he groaned, pressing my hands against his head as if my touch could ease his suffering. "What is happening to me? My head is on fire!"

I knew his pain. I understood the intense burning sensation and the redness that crept in on his vision. I knew precisely the fire that sweltered through his mind, and soon enough, his nose would begin to bleed at the intensity of it.

"I am so sorry, Ikane," I whispered, trying to keep the lump in my throat from distorting my voice. I stood and embraced him, pulling his head to my abdomen. His groan was muffled as he clutched my waist in return, driving his head against my body to try and ease the pain.

"This is Rion's doing," I whispered.

Seeing as I could not provide him with the relief that he needed, he released me and dug his fingers into his scalp once again. As predicted, his nose had started to bleed, and the redness was already all over my tunic.

Blistering anger flared through my blood, and my fists clenched so tightly that I felt my fingernails digging into my palms. The full realization of what had happened to Ikane struck me like the harsh zap of lightning rending the sky.

"Rion." I wanted to scream her name. I knew she could hear me in spite of the hushed growl through my teeth. "What purpose does it serve you to waste your precious power on him this way? Do you intend to kill your host before finding a new one?"

In response, Ikane groaned, but his cry was cut short as the heat of her torture seared his lungs and pulsed through his skull. His body collapsed onto the bed in a fetal position as blood dripped from his nose and ears. Even his tears had turned red.

"Rion!" I cried, feeling hot tears burning in my own eyes. My hand gripped the hilt of my sword out of reflex and anger. I wanted to fight. I wanted to slaughter her, but I knew I could not battle her with steel. I needed my mind to connect with hers.

As suddenly as she had seized him, she let him go. She wanted me to know that she was in control. Ikane's fists grew slack as he gathered a deep breath of relief. Trembling in the aftermath, he pushed himself upright and looked at me with his familiar, charming, mismatched eyes. His green eye no longer burned the foreign jade that sparked fear into one's soul, but the fear lingering behind it was telling enough. He wiped the blood from his nose with the back of his hand, and his eyes darkened as he looked at the crimson blood on his skin. He knew.

"Kea..." he breathed. "You know I do not have the power to fight her."

I sank to the bed beside him and wrapped my arms around his neck, helplessly wishing that I could simply wring the Phoenix Witch from his form.

"I'm so sorry, Ikane." I hadn't intended to weep, but the tears burned down my cheeks nonetheless. The power to defeat Rion was the birthright of the female heirs to the throne of Roanfire. Not a Leviathan Prince.

I did not deserve the embrace that he returned. The warmth of his strong arms did little to ease my trembling as he buried his face into the nape of my neck. Only then did I feel the quaking of his own body.

What we faced was beyond anything I had ever encountered, and I knew that I could not defeat Rion without help.

"The White Wardent," I whispered into his black hair.

I felt him nod.

My search for the White Wardent had been interrupted time and time again. If I had found him sooner, perhaps Rion may well have been defeated the first time.

In time, we dared to release each other. I searched Ikane's different colored eyes earnestly, finding that my lip began to tremble with rage when I took in the tears of blood on his cheeks.

"Calm yourself, little Brendagger," Ikane said quickly as he stroked my hair back and cupped my face in his hands.

I gripped his wrists firmly in return. "This shouldn't have happened. It should've been me."

Ikane shook his head. "No, Kea. If it were you, Rion would've succeeded, and you know that. It is better this way."

My teeth bit down on my bottom lip. "The White Wardent. I need to find the White Wardent. But I will have to wait until after the wedding of King Sander to Princess Lonacheska."

Ikane released my face with a gentle nod. "The Glacial Empire then. That is where we must go."

"Ikane... you can't leave."

His eyes scanned the thick stone of his confined chamber and his mouth pulled to the side. "I'm a prisoner of war, then?"

I gave him one quick nod.

"What is my sentence?"

"It is undecided. You are a Leviathan Pirate, one of the princes nonetheless, and you did lead an army against us to war, even if it was under duress. But you also defended me in battle. It was witnessed by many Roanfiriens."

He rubbed his chest for a moment in memory of the fatal wound he'd sustained there. There was no mistaking the affection in his eyes. "I would do anything to protect you, little Brendagger."

I felt the heat of a flush rising in my cheeks, but I stood before he could notice. "Are you hungry?"

His face lit up. "Famished."

"I'll grab a meal for us then," I said.

I took two small steps to the open door, then paused to look back at him. "I will not abandon you to her, Ikane. I will find a way to free you."

"I know you will," he said with a grave smile.

2

LADY BRENDAGGER

The battered castle was decorated with the meager remnants of war. Instead of a white carpet cascading down the marble stairs and across the expanse of the dance hall, dry reeds, scented with lavender and rosemary, had been strewn across the floor. Thick pine branches, wrapped with faded white ribbons, adorned walls and windows. Even the candles were variegated, many of them broken or half spent, since no candle maker had the means to produce new wax.

Game in the woods was scarce since the marauding pirates had nearly hunted the forests clean. What they hadn't caught for food, they frightened away with their army. A few roasted hens and rabbits were the main course, while some smaller pastries filled the remaining gaps on the long stretches of tables.

It was obvious that the kingdom was severely suffering after the great battle. Knowing this made me uncomfortable in the new gown King Sander had ordered for me. Ropert too, had been garbed in similar fashion, with colors of faded red and cream. How was the king able to justify spending money on new clothing for us? Then again, it was good income for the seamstress.

We stood to the right of the grand stairway as King Sander and Princess Lonacheska exchanged vows at the top for all to see.

The Glacial princess's silky white gown, embellished with rich lace, trailed down the steps as she knelt beside King Sander. Her golden hair rippled down her spine like sunbeams, interwoven with little white pearls, ribbons and late-blooming bellflowers. Sander's white tunic and golden trimmings complimented the gold and white of the princess beautifully.

The clergyman, garbed in custom red and gold of the phoenix, stood before them. The long-winded oaths had the guests restless, especially with the heavy smell of food waiting to be consumed.

I barely heard them myself, but as King Sander and the new queen arose and turned to face us, a cheer erupted. Lonacheska smiled, her lovely face beaming down at her new subjects.

The ceremony was followed by music, dancing and feasting. During this reception, Ropert was knighted and granted the title of 'Sir'.

Then the clergyman pounded his golden staff on the stairs, calling me forth. Ascending those steps seemed a longer journey than scaling a mountain. Eventually, I reached the top where King Sander took my hand and turned me to face the crowd below.

"Keatep Brendagger. On this historic day, upon which the Glacial Empire and Roanfire have united, I hereby pardon you of all charges against you, and declare you Lady Keatep Brendagger of Meldron for your act of repelling the Leviathan Pirates from our kingdom. May you achieve victory against our enemies and serve Roanfire faithfully forevermore."

Numbly, I listened to the cheer of the guests. I had endured the wait to search for the White Wardent until this day, watching Ikane suffer with Rion's burning headaches for the past week. I simply wanted this event to pass.

The clapping waned as Ropert and I ascended the steps together and soon music overtook the cheering. The guests turned to each other and resumed their light-hearted conversing.

Ropert and I stood awkwardly beside each other at the bottom of the stairs. I tried not to fiddle with my dress as he cleared his throat.

"Would you like something to drink?" He didn't look at me as he spoke.

I nodded once. "Anything but wine," I said.

Even though Eamon was now sober, Ropert knew that I detested the stuff. The smell alone made my stomach churn.

"I'll return in a moment," he said stiffly.

I was not left alone long. As soon as Ropert stepped away, a young nobleman approached, entreating me for a dance. He introduced himself as Lord Didrich Everguard, son of the Duke of Kaltum. His attire was simple, yet refined, and his firm grip on my hand and waist affirmed that he was not a stranger to combat.

"It is an honor to meet you in person, Lady Keatep," he stated as we danced. Soft brown curls hung over his forehead, shading his dark eyes.

"Kaltum," I said, trying my best to make pleasant conversation. "That is the great fisherman's city that stands beside Glacier Lake, is it not?"

A warm smile spread across his full lips that did not, in any way, detract from his masculine jaw line. "Aye, it is. Has my lady visited Kaltum before?"

"No, I have not had the opportunity to travel there."

"Then you must see it!" His enthusiasm paused our dance. He took my hand in his, and his eyes brightened. "It is a glorious sight to behold when the fishermen launch their ships in the morning. The rising sun burns a godly orange across the Gyhro Mountains and reflects across the water like fire. And the afternoon storms... oh, they are spectacular!" His hand gestured as he spoke. "Lightning dances across the gray clouds and the rumble of thunder echoes across the lake like the invigorating beat of drums. It would be a pleasure to take you there. Kaltum may not be the most refined of cities, but it is prosperous and indispensable to the survival of Roanfire."

I smiled at his passion. "It sounds extraordinary, Lord Everguard."

"Please, call me Didrich," he quickly said.

I did not have time to comprehend his informality before another nobleman touched my arm to claim my attention. This man's deep blue eyes met with Lord Didrich's in a competitive manner that I didn't quite understand. His brown hair was stiff and slicked back into a silky black ribbon that complimented his regal attire. He tipped his tall frame in a rigid bow to us.

"Lord Everguard," the new man droned as one of his dark brows rose in a judgmental way. "I'm sure you won't mind if I steal Lady Keatep for a dance. It seems you've lost your rhythm."

I was immediately put off by his assuming nature. I had actually found Lord Everguard's casual exuberance for his home refreshing.

Without waiting for my consent, the nobleman took my hand from Didrich and forcefully pulled his arm around my waist to resume the dance.

"Such an unrefined lord, that Didrich Everguard," he scoffed. "You needn't entertain his crude ways. His rustic lands are no place for a beautiful lady such as yourself. I am sure you've heard of my lands. I am Lord Valdemar Sternrod of Oldshore."

"Yes," I said simply. His arrogance was disturbing. "Oldshore is known for its fruitful lands. How have your crops fared this harvest season?"

He shrugged. "The Leviathans have destroyed much of it. But let us not speak of that. I must say, for a warrior with your reputation, you are a lovely specimen."

I bit my tongue as my jaw tensed. Was this flattery? Why?

Abruptly he halted the dance. "What's this?" he asked, placing his gloved hand under my chin to force me to look up at him. "You needn't be ashamed of beauty. It is rare to hold both loveliness and strength. I implore you to not risk tainting your beauty further by wielding a sword. All you need now is your reputation. Think on it, Lady Keatep. The Leviathan's wouldn't dare set foot on our fruitful lands should you choose to settle down there and live a life of luxury and peace as Lady of Oldshore."

My body went rigid. "What?"

The presuming noble released my chin. "Eamon Brendagger is your guardian, is he not? I shall speak with him this evening for your hand."

Either he did not observe my visible shock, or he did not care. And I assumed it was the latter. My eyes narrowed as I realized his intentions.

"Lord Sternrod," I said his name harshly.

"Call me Vald—"

"No," I snapped, holding up my hand to silence him. I cared not if I offended this man. He was arrogant and used it as entitlement to anything he desired. "I may hold the title of a noblewoman, but I can assure you that my soldierly attributes are no less with that name. I will not be bullied into a courtship."

He pursed his lips as his chin jerked up. "Is that a threat?" he demanded.

My eyes narrowed. "Not at all."

I turned on my heel and marched towards the refreshment table, wondering what was taking Ropert so long. But before I reached it, two more noblemen accosted me. They covertly insulted one another as they vied for my attention. Three more young aristocrats approached, taking advantage of the tension.

My patience evaporated when one of them gripped my wrist and drew me to him as he argued with another. I prepared to jerk him forward with a punch to his elbow that would force him into an armbar. He was fortunate that Eamon pushed into their midst at that moment.

My guardian's deep brown eyes glowered at them with the authority of a king. Alarmed and humiliated, they retreated from me, realizing their costly error. Without a word, Eamon extended his thick arm to me. Gratefully, I slipped my hand into the crook of his elbow.

"You look pale," he whispered as he guided me away. "Are you well?"

My heart was throbbing so loud I could hear it in my head. I glanced back to the collection of young men, each eyeing me with pining significance. My instinct to fight dissipated as the urge to flee became stronger.

My body was trembling. "No."

Eamon grumbled something incoherent and patted my hand that clutched his arm tightly. "I anticipated this, but King Sander chose to ignore the issue. With the noble title, you've become a prized asset to other provinces."

"A title does not change who I am," I said fiercely. "Where is Ropert? I want to leave."

I strained my neck to search for him among the throng of finely dressed guests. Spotting my new bodyguard in the distance, I eagerly steered Eamon towards him.

In my haste, I nearly collided into a young man dressed in exotic attire. Although he was rather dashing in an outlandish way, I would have immediately rebuffed this man if King Sander himself had not accompanied him. His dark skin contrasted with the sleeveless cream-colored coat that hung to his knees. Red fabric wrapped about his slender waist like a belt, and his unusual style of wide trousers were tucked into leather boots that harbored a peculiar curve at the toes. He seemed startled at first but smiled warmly. His bright, honey colored eyes, shadowed by thick, black brows, studied me fervently.

This man was from the kingdom of Toleah.

"Lady Keatep," King Sander began. "I would like to introduce you to Shazadeh Leander Polusmed from Toleah."

"Lady Keatep Brendagger, the young man addressed me with a thick accent and tipped his head in greeting. A vibrant blue cloth, held secure by a multicolored headband, sat upon his brow, framing his slender face. His black beard was groomed immaculately – almost harboring pointed edges that made his jaw seem unreasonably perfect.

"I am pleased to meet you. Will you honor me with a dance?" He held out his dark hand, embellished with golden rings and bangles, for me to take.

I had my fill of dancing for the evening, but he seemed important to King Sander, so I nodded respectfully. Eamon folded his arms across his chest and narrowed his eyes at King Sander as the Tolean aristocrat guided me to the dancefloor.

Not accustomed to our music or our style of dance, he stepped on my foot twice before he finally halted and laughed at himself.

"I'm not making a good impression with dance, am I?"

I forced a smile and shook my head in agreement.

"Come," he said. Without giving me a choice, he gripped my hand tightly and pulled me from the great hall to the balcony just beyond an arched doorway. Here, other couples were relishing the clear air that wasn't tainted by body odor and wine.

"Do you like being a soldier?" he asked as he walked to the stone railing and gazed out at the thin clouds veiling the pale moonlight. It cast a melancholy glow upon the devastated landscape below.

"I fight well, if that is what you mean," I answered as I stepped up beside him.

He nodded and toyed with an emerald ring on his finger. "I've never learned to use a sword," he mused and casually rested his elbows on the railing and laced his fingers. In spite of the way "d", "t", and "th" in his speech were very pronounced, his hold on sentence structure was perfect. "My learning has mainly consisted of diplomatic subjects. Language, arts, mathematics, alchemy, and Ridarri martial arts... but little in the way of weapons."

I repressed a frown. He was making light conversation and I was not interested in it. I wanted to leave.

I clasped my hands at the small of my back to keep from looking impatient.

"Suppose you could teach me someday?" he asked as he turned his head to look at me with his bright, honey-colored eyes. Against his brown skin, they were stunning.

My brows furrowed at the insinuation of having contact after tonight. "I'm not sure I understand."

He stood upright, straightened his unusual tunic, and smiled warmly as he turned to face me. "Do you know who I am?"

Something about his presence made me feel small, even though he barely stood two inches taller than me. I took a cautious step back and shook my head gently, abashed by my ignorance.

He nodded in understanding. "I am Shazadeh of Toleah. Or how you say it, Prince of Toleah."

I felt as if a blacksmith's hammer struck my chest.

"My father has heard of your power and strength, something that should be honored above your station as a simple Roanfirien soldier. Now that King Sander has married a Glacier Princess, you could broaden that unity as Ameera of Toleah..." He paused. "Pardon me. You would be the Princess of Toleah."

My jaw dropped along with my hands.

The prince, noting my state of shock, withdrew something wrapped in a finely crafted kerchief from beneath his embroidered robe.

"It is customary to present my future bride with a gift," he said in a soft, but confident tone.

My hand came up too slowly for him, so he took it and pressed the gift into my palm. I swallowed hard, grounding my feet in an attempt not to flee. His bright honey-colored eyes smiled warmly as he nodded to the kerchief, expecting me to open it.

Obediently, I pulled the corners of the fabric away, revealing an armlet unlike any I'd seen before. From the way Prince Leander's clothing and jewelry glimmered with detail and gold, I was surprised to find that no intricate details were etched into the metal. Rather, its smooth surface was meticulously polished, revealing metallic colors of a rainbow on the glossy, silver surface. It almost resembled a piece of armor.

"You are not a delicate creature," he said. "You are strong and beautiful. I wanted this piece to reflect who you are."

My heart palpitated as I glanced at the gift, and my legs grew weak – a feeling I had never encountered before, and it terrified me. "I... y... you should speak to Master Eamon Brendagger."

"King Sander and I have, but he refuses to consider it," Leander said. "I ask you to speak to Master Eamon. Roanfire and Toleah may have differences, but this unity is for the good of both of our kingdoms."

"Why?" I asked. "Why would Toleah do this for me? What have you to gain?"

If he was offended by my bluntness, he didn't show it. His smile was sympathetic, as if I was a child who didn't understand what was at stake.

"I will not lie," he said. "You are a formidable weapon, and Toleah would rather not fight against one so powerful. We would prefer to have you on our side."

I swallowed. The power and strength he saw in me was a lie. I was no more powerful than Ropert, or any other soldier of Roanfire for that matter.

He reached out and gently trapped my hand, that still held the armlet, between his dark ones. His skin was warm, something that caught me off guard. I suppose it was the fact that I thought anyone who owned slaves couldn't be anything but cold. Toleah had slaves in abundance... and I was about to become one.

"Lady Brendagger," he said my name softly, the sharp click of the "d" in my name emphasized by his accent. "The Leviathan Pirates have destroyed your crops just before harvest season. You know that Roanfire will not survive the winter without help. Toleah is rich and fertile with food, but we cannot give without receiving something in return. My father, Shah Milak, has promised provisions that will help Roanfire survive in exchange for your hand in marriage to me."

I looked up at him. Something about the way he spoke about his father made me think that he was just as unhappy about the situation as I was.

"Think about it," he told me and squeezed the armlet in my hands. "If you choose to accept my offer, wear the gift. I will watch."

"When..." my voice broke and I cleared my throat. "When do you need an answer?"

His smile was weak, and his brows arched slightly with empathy. "You've about a month before Roanfire will be killing each other over scraps," he said. "Two weeks. That's all I can give."

My mind reeled, but I nodded anyway.

"It was a pleasure meeting you, Lady Keatep Brendagger. I am pleased to discover that your strength and beauty were not fabricated stories," he said. He turned my hand over and bowed slightly as he pressed his lips against the back of it.

Once again, the warmth of his lips caught me off guard and I involuntarily shuddered.

He didn't flinch in the slightest. "I look forward to seeing you again," he said. With that, he dropped my hand, tipped his head respectfully, and retreated to the celebration.

I sprinted to the deserted training arena. The delicate shoes I had been given to wear kicked up dust as I skidded to a halt. After carelessly tossing the armlet wrapped in the lavish kerchief on the small workbench, I snatched a sword from the row of pristinely arranged swords hanging on the wall of the weapons hut.

White knuckled and fuming, I whirled to face my imaginary opponent. The sword danced across my body in a flurry of blocks, parries, and deliberate star-patterned slashes until sweat clung to the collar of the beautiful gown King Sander wanted me to wear. It became clear now, why. It wasn't for the people. To them, I was a soldier, and my uniform would've sufficed. But King Sander wanted my appearance to be flawless when he presented me to the Tolean prince.

I roared at the deception and arched my sword in a side-downward stroke at the corner post of the weapons hut. The impact rippled up into my shoulders as the sword lodged into the wood. Blood boiling, I jerked my sword from the post, and struck it again... and again, and again. My arms, shoulders, and back burned from the exertion.

Vision hazy with hot tears, I didn't see the metal. My blade slammed into steel with an audible clang and rebounded harshly, breaking my pattern.

My eyes shot up to see the long metal blade of a broadsword. It had spared the hut any further abuse. My lips pulled into a deep frown upon seeing it's wielder. Ropert.

"What did the weapons hut ever do to you?" he asked with a crooked smile that I had once adored. Now it just irked me.

Breathless, I turned away from him, not wanting to give him the satisfaction of seeing my tears. "What are you doing here?" I growled, wiping furiously at my cheeks.

"I am your bodyguard," Ropert said simply.

I groaned and rolled my eyes to heaven as I whirled back to face him. "I am in no danger here."

He chuckled. "The weapons hut certainly was." He patted the splintered wooden post of the shed as if it were an old friend.

My hand tightened around the hilt of my sword. The anger building up inside of me needed a release. I wanted to hit something. I wanted to feel the rippling of pain in my arms to reassure myself that I was still alive. Ropert had stopped me.

"What do you want?" I demanded, jabbing the tip of my sword at his solid abdomen.

He took a small step back to keep from being pierced, and gently brushed my sword away with the steel of his own. "Perhaps I would like to spar with you," he said with a shrug.

If he wanted a spar, then I would oblige. My sword flew up at him in a deliberate angle that forced him to step back. He evaded it easily, but not without a surprised look crossing over his face.

As my blade flew past, my entire body spun to keep the momentum going. My next blow was even stronger. This time he blocked my sword with his own, sending a terrible ripple through my arms as the unpleasant clang of metal rang through the deserted arena. Instinctively, I stepped in, rendering the range of his sword ineffective. Without a second thought, my elbow flew up and slammed into his jaw. I heard his teeth knock together as his head rocked back.

He stumbled away, then turned to me with eyes wide and mouth agape.

"I am not your enemy!" I roared.

He rubbed his chin. "Nor am I yours," he said. "What's going on with you, Kea? Why are you so upset?"

His sudden concern for me stung like a scalding knife in my heart. Why was he so worried now? Ever since we were children, we had been together. We trained together to become the best soldiers in Daram. As younglings, we hid together during pirate raids, played, brawled, and squabbled like siblings. We fought many battles side by side. Nothing could separate us.

Yet, after I was accused of assassinating King Myron, Ropert had been branded a traitor and sent to Pedre's quarry, a penal colony, to labor. Archduke Goldest had seen to every aspect of framing me for the murder of the king, even to the extent of arresting and killing innocent people. How could Ropert even fathom that I took part in any of this?

"All I've ever wanted was to be a soldier and serve Roanfire!" I cried and my voice broke. Tears burned down my cheeks now and I didn't bother to wipe them away. Let him see. Let him see what he has done. "I am loyal to Roanfire."

Ropert's brows softened and he lowered his weapon. "I know you are."

I sobbed. "Then why do you hate me?"

He sighed and slid his sword back into the simple sheath at his hip. "I would think that you'd know."

"I don't! I don't understand why you despise me! You know where my loyalties are, and you know that I would never do anything to purposefully harm you! Yet, instead of supporting me in trying to maintain my position in Meldron's army, you give King Sander the incentive to raise my station! Lady Keatep Brendagger is now being hounded by noblemen seeking to fortify their lands!"

I glowered up at his pale blue eyes and I felt a spark of satisfaction when worry flickered across his face. I wanted him to feel profound guilt for what he had done.

"Kea..."

I didn't want to hear him say anything. I slammed the palm of my hand into his solid chest, forcing him to take a step back.

"The Prince of Toleah has just asked for my hand in marriage!"

Ropert's face paled like sheets hung out in the sun to dry. His eyes widened, and I saw his chest heave as he gathered a sharp intake of breath. I almost felt pity in seeing this stalwart man become so frail... almost.

"H... has Eamon given his blessing?" Ropert stammered.

My scowl deepened as my eyes took on another wave of dreadful tears. Prince Leander had made it clear that Roanfire was in dire need of Toleah's help. King Sander would make the arrangements at all cost – of that I was certain.

I tossed my sword at Ropert's feet, and a satisfying thunk rang through the training arena. Dust swirled around it, then settled on his boots and the polished steel.

"You've made me a slave," I hissed.

Turning on my heel, I marched back to the castle, leaving Ropert to ponder his reckless suggestion to the king.

But making Ropert feel shame and guilt didn't make me feel any better. In fact, I felt worse. My eyes burned so fiercely that I could barely see the blurry shadows in the darkened hallway that led to my 'prison' chamber. The lump in my throat grew to the point where I couldn't even instruct Thraner to leave me in peace. I rudely pushed by him and pulled the door closed after me.

Only after hearing the reluctant turn of the key did I allow the tears to burst forth. I crumpled to the cold, stone floor beside my bed and mourned the loss of my freedom.

3

RION

The silver-white globe of the moon hung in the sky, illuminating the snow cloaked landscape with a hostile grayness that leached all warmth from the world. Bright reflections of silver light curved around the fringe of roiling black clouds, silhouetting a snow-covered hill and a lonely tree. The weight of innumerable obscure creatures, clinging to the branches, pulled at the tree's fragile limbs until they hung to the ground.

A distinct howl of a wolf penetrated the thick night. At the sound, the creatures clinging to the tree, unfurled wings of black leather and leapt off the branches. Black arrows darted, spun, and circled through the air in a whirlwind of chaos. The beating of their leathery wings flailed against my arms raised to shield my face.

In savage fury, they ripped their talons into my skin, shredding it like an old piece of cloth in the wind. Frantic, my arms flailed, trying to fend off the torrent of beasts as they drove me to the snow.

The wolf howled again, and the shadow-bats scattered, leaving me for dead. And then a beast approached, walking *upright on his hind legs like a man. His ears lay flat against his head and the dark fur on his back bristled as he crouched over my limp body.*

Blue green eyes stared down at me.

My body jolted awake. Adrenaline pumped violently through my veins and I gasped for air that wasn't thick with leathery wings of bats. I groaned, realizing that it was only a dream, and rubbed the back of my aching neck. I must have cried myself to sleep at the foot of my bed, for I was still sitting on the floor, dressed in the red gown that King Sander had adorned me with.

Even though I knew it was just a dream, my heart throbbed with the aftermath. I stood, using the bedpost for support and flinched. Strange pain seared my skin where the wraith-like bats had slashed me with their talons. Pushing the long, delicate sleeves away from my forearms, I half expected to see gashes – or even welts - across them. But there was nothing.

The mismatched eyes of the wolf looking down on me burned into my mind. My anger immediately turned to Rion. She had something to do with this, of that I was certain. But why? What was she doing? What did she have in store for Ikane now?

The air still felt thick and I stumbled to the window, threw the curtains aside, and opened the frame. Wintry air burst into my chamber, soothing my skin and filling my lungs with crispness that made me feel alive. The bright moon cast a silver glow on the ravished landscape, indicating that I hadn't been asleep long.

In time, the dream-induced pain diminished into a memory. Rion's nightmares had caused my body to burn and blood to drip from my nose in the past. I had feared to sleep. Now that she was cowering inside of Ikane's mind, I thought I would be spared her nightmares, but I was obviously mistaken.

Would it ever end?

The cold from outside became too fierce and I closed the window against it. Just as the frame squeaked shut, an unexpected knock sounded at the door.

Surely no one would be awake at this hour.

I brushed my hair from my face and listened. The knock sounded again.

"Who is it?" I called.

"It's Ropert," came his muffled voice through the door.

My shoulders drooped as a frown pulled on the corners of my lips. I didn't want to see him.

When I didn't answer, he spoke again. "Ikane wishes to speak with you."

"Kea?" Ikane's voice called through the door with an urgency that made me worried. "Please."

My anger towards Ropert could not keep me from helping Ikane. I stepped around my small bed and worked with the flint and oil-laden fabric to light the single candle in the room. "Let them in, Thraner," I said through the door.

The wick caught, and a small flame flickered to life, but it did little to illuminate the small dark chamber. The cold moonlight coming in through the window was far brighter.

The lock on the door clicked and swung open, causing the flame from my freshly lit candle to flicker. I turned to see Ikane standing between Ropert and Corporal Thraner with his wrists shackled. The deep 'v' of his cotton shirt revealed the pink remnant of the healing injury on his chest. He looked well, but troubled.

Ropert's lips pulled into a sympathetic frown when his eyes fell on me. I'm sure I looked terrible, but I wasn't ready to speak to him.

"What's wrong, Ikane? Is it your headache?" I asked him.

He shook his head. "Something else..." He tapped his temple with one hand to indicate Rion. The thick chains on his wrists rattled loudly with the movement.

I stepped aside and motioned for Ikane to enter.

"Are those really necessary?" I grumbled to Ropert, motioning toward the heavy shackles on Ikane's wrists.

His chin rose, and his jaw clenched. "He is a Leviathan Pirate. I will leave you to talk in peace, but he will remain in iron."

Ikane nodded in agreement, but I folded my arms across my chest and glowered at my newly appointed bodyguard.

"Let it be Kea," Ikane said. "Ropert is doing his duty."

If Ropert was caught off guard by Ikane's compliance, he didn't show it. He simply ducked out the door and closed it behind him.

Ikane didn't waste any time. "What sort of dreams tormented you while facing the Phoenix Witch?" he asked. "I recall you waking with blood dripping from your nose on the ship from Daram."

"Are you experiencing nosebleeds?" I asked.

"No," he admitted. "But dreams... well, one dream in particular, I suppose."

I rubbed my eyes and pushed my hair from my face, feeling somewhat drowsy again. The adrenaline was wearing off and my eyes still hurt from weeping.

"Are you certain it is Rion?" I asked. "Over half of the soldiers are suffering from nightmares since the battle."

"Call it what you will, but this was no ordinary dream." He sank down on the edge of my bed and turned to face me. "There was a tree littered with bats, and a woman standing nearby. She seemed terrified, and then a wolf..."

I barely heard his voice as my mind replayed the terrible nightmare that had woke me but a few minutes ago. It was the same dream, but from his perspective!

"I approached – but I wasn't a full wolf, and neither was I a man. When the bats scattered, I saw the woman lying in the snow. It was obvious that she was dead." His voice faltered as he looked up at me with an expression near to horror. "When I looked at her face..." he shivered as if something cold ran down his spine. "Kea... It was you."

My body froze as I watched the meager candlelight dance across his face. His blue and green eye watched me intently.

"You had the dream too, didn't you?" he finally said.

I nodded slowly.

Ikane leapt to his feet, the chain linking his hands rattled loudly in the movement. "No," he said. "I won't let this be."

"Ikane," I said. "It was just a dream."

"Was it?" he asked as his eyes frantically darted between mine. I could tell that he hoped I could somehow dispel that fear, but I couldn't. He was right. Something about this dream felt real – and dangerous.

I tugged on the sleeve of the red dress. "This dream came to you because of the link we share. I don't think it was for you to see."

"But I did, and it worries me, Kea. What if I am your undoing?" He raised his hand and gently touched my cheek with the back of his fingers.

I grabbed his hand in return. "Don't think that way. Now that the wedding is finally over, I can search for the White Wardent. Besides, you wouldn't hurt me."

"Not intentionally, but with the Phoenix Witch inside of me..." He rubbed his temples and growled. "This blasted headache is getting worse."

I bit my lip. I knew the pain in Ikane's head. Each time Rion struck, red heat sparked behind his eyes. It throbbed like the mighty blows of a blacksmiths hammer ringing against a glowing rod of iron. It was debilitating.

"She's making herself known," I said.

He nodded. "You've tried everything."

I stepped around the bed and sat down beside him. "I haven't tried to use my power since she fled into you... your mind." There was intense shame that flowed with those words, and I didn't dare to look at him as I said it. "But if she was able to reach you through me, then I should be able to reach her through you."

He flexed his fingers. "Try it."

I had hoped that he wouldn't ask. But it was my responsibility, and he was suffering the pain that was meant for me. I needed to try something.

"I suppose... it was the kiss we shared that linked her to you," I said, trying to find a way to use her own power against her.

He nodded.

"Perhaps you simply need to open your mind to me." My hand reached out to touch his, but in the instant our fingers brushed against each other, his green eye flashed. He flinched as if my touch had scorched his skin.

I was startled by the reaction of his single green eye. When he was in battle or in a heated argument, it brightened and flared with otherworldly light. But now it flickered and sparked like green lightning bolts.

"Something isn't right," he said softly, and pulled his hands away. He rubbed his temples fiercely. "I can't... When I open my mind, it's like... like I'm being pushed... pushed away..."

Invisible, desperate anger pelted against my mind like ice in a hail storm. I recognized the essence at once. Rion had waited for this exact moment, when Ikane was ready to submit to my invasion of his mind. She was driving him back.

"Don't you dare," I hissed at her. I gripped Ikane's hands as if my touch alone could protect him from her overpowering presence. "Let him go!"

His eye went dark – lifeless - giving way completely to Rion. A hint of redness overtook the emerald glow of his eye, causing it to go black. In that instant, Ikane's hands shot forward and grabbed my wrists with such force that the blood to my fingers was promptly cut off. With all the force in his muscular frame, he shoved me back so that the small of my back struck the edge of the bedpost – colliding with my old arrow wound. The pain flared through my lower spine and rippled down the entire length of my left leg. My body tumbled over the edge, throwing the hem of my dress to my knees as I crashed on my stomach beside the small table.

I hadn't recovered before Ikane leapt over the edge of the bed and gripped my hair. Instinctively, my elbow came up and slammed into Ikane's nose. I rolled to face him as his head rocked back and rebounded off the wooden bedframe.

I had nearly forgotten her hatred, anger, lust, and power-mad greed that roiled within her. And now these horrific traits ensnared the mind of a man I deeply cared for.

Let him go, Rion! My mind cried out. With my leg still numb from his initial blow, I scrambled back until I hit the wall. Using it for support, I staggered to my feet.

He is mine! Her choir of voices hissed in return.

She penetrated my mind so easily. The force of her words slammed into my thoughts like the blunt end of a battering ram. All breath burst from my lungs, and searing heat blurred my vision, as Ikane lunged across the room with the power and bearing of a predatory wolf. His hands wrapped around my throat, driving my head against the wall behind me. The muscles in his forearms flexed as he crushed my neck. Desperate for breath, I clawed at his hands to pry them off.

Finally, I have the means to kill you. Rion boasted. *I never imagined it to be this easy.*

My head throbbed from the lack of oxygen and I could feel the heat upon my face as my blood burned for relief. With a final conscious effort to defend myself, I clasped my hands together and allowed them to fly up between Ikane's arms. My clubbed fists collided with his chin as I did so. He groaned and flinched momentarily but did not release me. With all the force I could muster, my elbows slammed down into his, causing his hands to break free of my neck, and his head to jerk forward. My forehead crashed into his nose.

Blessed air filled my lungs.

Giving him no time to recover, I drove my knee into his stomach, and thrust him away. He stumbled backwards, toppling over the small table, and landed hard on his back in the narrow space between the wall and my bed.

Let him go, Rion! It's me you want! I roared to the witch as I tried to catch my breath.

Hah! You simply fear that I have finally found the means to destroy you! And you should be frightened. I have within me centuries of combat knowledge and skill. All those warriors that I've consumed feed me with unprecedented knowledge! She forced Ikane to his feet. Blood dripped from his nose where my head had struck him. His dazed expression made his attack all the more unexpected.

With a quick step to the side, he sped right past me. I darted towards the door. I hadn't anticipated Ikane's quick reflexes as he rebounded off the wall and flew against my back. The force caused me to pitch forward and collide into the stones that created the frame for the heavy wooden door. Something cold and hard lashed over my face.

"Ropert! Thra—" My hands barely gripped the cold metal before I realized that Ikane had flung the chain from his shackles around my neck.

Using my foot to shove us back from the wall, we both stumbled toward the overturned table and crashed over it. But Ikane's hold on me didn't ease. No matter how hard I tried, I could not find the leverage to untangle my throat from the cold iron.

The corners of my vision blackened, followed by starbursts flaring across my eyes. I barely heard Ropert call my name as he and the guard burst into the room.

Ropert's fist flew over my head and collided into Ikane's jaw. Ikane's whole body rocked to the side, and the chain loosened. I clawed at the metal as Ropert grabbed Ikane's arm and flipped it over my head. The chain whipped from my neck.

I collapsed to the floor, trying desperately to breathe.

The horrible thud of a punch echoed through my ears that were slowly regaining the ability to hear. I turned in time to see Ropert slam Ikane's head into the nearby bedpost with such force that I heard an audible crack. Ikane slumped down, but Ropert proceeded to pound into the Leviathan with his solid fist.

"Ropert, stop!" I called, but being strangled twice took a toll on my voice. It was barely audible. I grabbed Ropert's arm instead to stop him from striking Ikane again. "Ropert!"

Ropert's nostrils flared as he stood, his face red with fury. He glowered at the Leviathan on the ground. An alarming amount of blood dripped from three cuts on his face.

"I told you he couldn't be trusted!" Ropert growled, shaking out his fist. His knuckles were already bruising.

"It's not his fault," my voice rasped. "He's possessed."

I crouched down to check on Ikane's injuries. Just as I touched a deep gash on his forehead, Ikane's eyes flew open. I fell against Ropert's legs as the Leviathan leapt to his feet and darted for the window. His body crashed through the glass, shattering the crosshatched panes with a brittle sound.

I rushed to the window, with Ropert on my heels, in time to see the Leviathan scurry across the snow in an unsteady jog.

Ropert glanced at Thraner, passing a silent command to hunt down the fugitive. Nodding, the old soldier rushed from the room. As soon as he was out of sight, Ropert grabbed my arm and jerked me to face him.

"That?!" He pointed out the broken window. "That is what you're so infatuated with? He's a monster!"

I jerked my arm free of his iron grip. "It's not him," my voice croaked with pain. I was sure yelling at Ropert was doing nothing to help it recover. "He did not want to kill me. The Phoenix Witch was doing it!"

Ropert threw his hands into the air. "You're mad, Kea! There is no such thing as an evil queen from the past! Ikane is a cold, bloodthirsty Leviathan and always will be!"

I stiffened. "He risked his life for me. He stood by me when no one else would. He turned against his own people to defend me in battle. I can't say the same for you."

Before Ropert could reply, another voice broke in.

"What in the name of the Phoenix is going on in here?"

Both of us turned to see Eamon, dressed in his night shirt and trousers, step into the room. His brown eyes flicked across the shattered window and overturned table, then his eyebrows rose. "Don't tell me you two did this."

"No, sir." Ropert answered quickly, folding his arms across his broad chest. "It was the Leviathan prisoner, Ikane Ormand."

Eamon looked at me. "Where is Ikane now?"

Ropert jerked his head towards the broken window.

Just as Eamon stepped forward to investigate, another figure appeared in the doorway. King Sander's servant, Chanter, scanned the room with his old eyes. Without a word, he walked to Eamon and whispered something into his ear.

Eamon nodded, and Chanter disappeared.

"Follow me," Eamon ordered us. "The king wishes to speak with you."

"Now?" Ropert and I asked dubiously at the same time.

"Now," Eamon confirmed and turned on his heel.

We had no choice but to follow.

4

BLOODLINE

The décor in King Sander's council chamber was minimal. A large, stone hearth stood at the head of a lengthy oak table, surrounded by ten cushioned chairs. A heavy, deep velvet curtain that reached clear to the floor, hung against the wall beside the hearth.

Eamon motioned for us to choose a seat.

I barely noted the glint of golden threads that created the crest of the firebird in the fabric as I jerked the back of my chair away from the table. I slumped down on the red cushion. Ropert deliberately sat across from me.

I scowled at the wall behind him where three tapestries covered the shuttered windows. The first tapestry portrayed an image of a king I did not recognize. The second, depicted King Myron. The third, I recognized instantly. It was identical to the stained-glass window on Meldron's Library. It was Queen Damita, the last female heir to the throne of Roanfire. Even the glow of the ruby hanging around her neck had been perfectly captured.

Eamon sat down beside me, glowered with disappointment at Ropert, and thrummed his fingers against the polished wood of the table.

"What is going on with you two?" he demanded. "You are acting like children."

"Ikane didn't mean..." I began.

Ropert tried to speak over me. "She is so delusional!"

"That's not—"

"She can't see that he is nothing but a viper—"

"I trust him! It's Rion that -"

"You blame everything on that witch!"

"ENOUGH!" Eamon roared and slammed his fist down on the table. The thud echoed through the minimally furnished room and into the fireplace.

Ropert and I clamped our mouths shut.

"Ikane has escaped. Keatep has been attacked. And Ropert neglected his duty to protect her," Eamon said. "These are the facts at hand."

The door to the chamber opened and King Sander entered, followed by his ever-faithful servant. Although the king was dressed in an embroidered red robe and a simple nightshirt, he still looked regal. He took the chair at the head of the table and brushed his fingers through his auburn hair before looking at us with tired eyes.

The servant took the seat to the right of the king's chair.

My brows rose in question. Why was this servant so bold? Surely, he was more to the king than just that.

King Sander noted my expression and briefly clapped the servant on the shoulder. "I see you are wondering about my servant. Master Chanter is not just a servant," he said. "He is my most trusted advisor, spy, and bodyguard. I see things through his eyes that would normally go unnoticed by a king."

Master Chanter tipped his head to me in greeting upon finally being introduced.

"Now." Sander placed his elbows up on the table and laced his fingers together. "Why have I been pulled from my bed on my wedding night?"

I groaned within. This was supposed to be a special night for him and his bride.

"It was Ikane Ormand," Ropert said, too eager to place the blame on someone. "He insisted on seeing Kea in the middle of the night and proceeded to attack her."

Sander looked at me with furrowed brows. "Is this true?"

"Just look at her neck," Ropert pointed out. "It's already bruising."

I scowled at Ropert and absently covered my neck with a hand. "Ikane's been possessed. He was not responsible for his actions."

Ropert groaned openly. "She's too delusional to see that he is dangerous."

I jumped to my feet. "I am not..."

Eamon slammed the palm of his hand on the table again. The loud crack brought me to silence.

"Need I remind you both that you are in the presence of the king?" Eamon said.

I clenched my jaw and sat back in my chair, folding my arms across my chest. Ropert simply glowered at his bruised fist.

"What prompted the late-night visit?" Sander asked.

"It was a dream," I said, still trying to unclench my jaw.

"A dream?"

I knew they wouldn't believe me, but I told the truth anyway. "We both shared the same nightmare."

"Dreams are merely fears manifesting themselves in our subconscious," Master Chanter said.

"My dreams are more than that," I snapped. "I witnessed the destruction of the Fold Garrison in a dream. I saw Queen Damita, the last queen of Roanfire, tear the Phoenix Stone from her neck four hundred years ago in a dream. I recovered that very stone in the exact place I'd seen it fall in the dream.

So, believe me when I say that Rion is real and my dreams are not childish fears."

Chanter clamped his mouth shut but did not take his eyes off me. Ropert openly rolled his eyes to heaven and Eamon shot him a warning glance.

"Your dreams are not the issue here," King Sander said. "Ikane is a Leviathan. A Leviathan Prince. He is dangerous. By fleeing the castle and assaulting you, he has chosen his fate."

"That is not what happened," I countered, pulling the sapphire jewel from beneath the gown that I had yet to change from. I held it out for them to see. "Do you remember the curse upon the Noirfonika family? The Phoenix Stone?"

Sander nodded slowly.

"I did not defeat the Phoenix Witch," I said. "She fled into Ikane's mind during the battle, taking thousands of souls hostage. She has possessed him. Those Leviathans that died? They are all a part of Rion now!"

Ropert's eyes widened at that statement, but Sander rubbed his temples with a sigh.

"I want to believe you, Keatep. I really do."

"Then please. Let me go after him," I persisted. "Your obligation as king is to protect the people and help them rebuild. Mine is to fight and conquer this curse against the Noirfonika family. If you've studied the White Wardent's writings, you know that Rion's magic has become twisted and dark. If I do not go after Ikane, she will grow stronger and become a greater threat. Not only to me, but to your children."

He leaned back in his chair. "Why is it that you must be the one to face this foe? It should've been me."

"You know that this curse only affects the daughters of Roanfire," Chanter said.

Sander nodded and tipped his head back as if he were trying to blink away tears.

"How could you?" A new voice broke into our conversation. The red velvet curtain swung aside with such force, I thought it would rip from the curtain rod. The creature that emerged was no less stunning than she had been during the actual wedding ceremony. Her silky blue robe contrasted beautifully with her golden hair. But her fists were clenched with rage.

King Sander leapt to his feet in alarm. "Lona!"

"Did you think I didn't suspect?" she cried. "She has your eyes! All this time I've kept myself pure for you!" Tears began to run down her flushed cheeks. "Was I not good enough?"

"Don't ever think that!" Sander nearly shouted as he grabbed her shoulders. He searched her face earnestly. "I was a fifteen-year-old boy when my father sent me to your kingdom. I was young and naive. I am so sorry for hiding this from you."

She shook him off. "You are only sorry because I caught you!"

I stood and bowed. "My queen. Sander was ready to tell you before the wedding. I asked him not to."

She blinked at me through her tears and then her face hardened. "You dare to speak to me, whelp?" Her beautiful voice was tinged with so much venom I could almost feel it in my blood. I bristled slightly.

King Sander tried to take her hand again. "Keatep Brendagger did not know of her lineage until last winter. Do not blame her. She only wants our happiness."

The queen jerked her hand away from his. "You've lost all chance of that."

Lonacheska then clenched her jaw and angrily lurched one of the chairs from the table. She sat down and folded her hands on her lap in a perfectly poised manner.

"Now gentlemen," she began in a softer, yet formidable tone. "Roanfire shall no longer keep secrets from its queen. I shall henceforth be present at every council meeting, beginning now."

Sander stood numbly, his heart clearly aching.

60

"Let us begin," she declared and leaned forward, tipping her head towards me. "What is this curse upon the Noirfonika family?"

I glanced at King Sander as I sat back down in my seat. "Perhaps it would be best to summon your scribe and allow the queen to read for herself what we've discovered," I suggested.

King Sander numbly sank back into his chair and nodded. He whispered something to his advisor, and the old man slipped out the door on an errand.

"I suppose that would be sufficient, but I should like to hear your account," the queen stated.

"Now?" I asked.

She shrugged her delicate shoulders. "What better time? We are all awake."

"As you wish," I said and straightened out in my seat. "Rion Noirfonika was the founder of Roanfire. She was a mighty and persuasive queen who brought the tribes together under her rule. It was said that she slowly became obsessed with youth and eternal life, and eventually persuaded the White Wardent, Yotherna, to stow her soul within a ruby known as the Phoenix Stone. It became an heirloom of the Noirfonika family. The intent was for Rion to garner life force from her posterity in order to be reborn, and she was ordered to be long-suffering. However, she became impatient and the absence of her own body caused her to lose all respect for life. She began to drain energy from her host before their time.

"Rion could only use life essence from her female posterity. For this reason, Yotherna administered a tonic to the king, rendering Roanfire barren of female heirs to the throne. He knew his plan wasn't fool-proof." My voice faltered as I looked at King Sander, and he averted his eyes. It stung more than I thought it should have.

"I am the first female heir to the throne of Roanfire in over four hundred years," I whispered, lowering my eyes as well.

I could feel Lonacheska's burning gaze. "And why has this 'Rion' not claimed *your* life?"

"She tried," I answered. I untied the cord that held the sapphire jewel to my neck and placed the heirloom on the table between us. "Each daughter of Roanfire is endowed with the power to defeat her."

She seemed perplexed. "But you just admitted that you did not destroy her."

"That is true. I didn't. During the battle with the Leviathan Pirates, she fled from this jewel," I tapped the table with my finger for emphasis, "and into the mind of Ikane Ormand, the very man who stood to defend me from the Leviathan Pirates."

Upon receiving a nod from the new queen, I slid the jewel across the wide table so that she could scrutinize it. The queen plucked my rough leather cord from the table, her deep golden eyes boring into the jewel that was tethered to it. It swayed before her. "I've heard tale of a jewel among the nobility of Roanfire."

"I must go after Ikane." I turned my attention to King Sander. "He needs my help, and Rion will only grow stronger as this issue is ignored. You know I speak the truth."

The queen lowered the jewel and nodded. "You cannot do this alone."

King Sander sat upright. "She cannot go at all," he quickly countered.

Lonacheska bristled as she slid the necklace back to me. It was a little rougher than intended, for I barely caught it before it slipped over the edge of the table.

"You think to undermine my advice?" she snapped at Sander. "We are king and queen. We share all responsibility equally."

"That is not my intention," he said hurriedly. "But Shazadeh Leander has offered us help in recovering from this brutal war with the Leviathan Pirates in return for Keatep

Brendagger's hand in marriage. The Glacier Empire can't provide the food that Roanfire needs. Toleah can."

The queens face hardened as she bit her cheek.

Before she could reply, the door opened, and Master Chanter returned with a very drowsy looking man whose hands were splotched with ink. I instantly assumed him to be King Sander's personal scribe. He was a willowy man, with slender fingers and thin shoulders. I could not tell if his eyes were bloodshot from the lack of sleep, or from spending hours reading documents under the meager light of a candle.

Master Chanter closed the door behind them and motioned for the scribe to be seated around the table. He sleepily chose a chair beside Ropert and sat down.

"Thank you for joining us at this hour, Penmaster Eugene," King Sander greeted the man.

"How may I serve you, my king?" the scribe answered, clearly trying to blink his eyes awake.

"Have you discovered any more information about the Phoenix Stone in your transcribing of the ancient documents in the library?" Sander asked.

The man squirmed uncomfortably. "I have, but my transcriptions were destroyed in the fire that consumed half of Meldron's Library. I can only recount what I have in memory and I fear it may not be accurate. Writings are essential to keep details honest."

"Nonetheless," Sander urged. "Tell us what you do recall."

The scribe gathered a deep breath and let it out through his lips noisily. "Apart from the White Wardent's journal entries, there was an account of a very important document that was sent to Emperor Skarand of the Glacial Empire. It was implied that this document held critical information on how to overcome the magic within the Phoenix Stone. The parchment was badly damaged over time. I could only glean a few words from its faded ink."

King Sander nodded to him, urging him to continue.

"Some rumblings of the princess needing to rely on the union of the four kingdoms' of Kelperah. She must draw on the virtue and valor of a sword, seek guidance and learning from a prince, find love in both friend and foe, and develop the compassion and forgiveness of a child," he said. "Forgive me, my king, but that is all I can remember. It was nothing more than a riddle."

"And perhaps it could mean that uniting her in matrimony with the Prince of Toleah is another step closer to uniting the kingdoms," King Sander said.

"Where would that leave the Leviathan's or the Glacial Empire," the queen asked. "Perhaps searching the archives in the Glacial Empire might help," Lonacheska suggested to me. "We have an extensive library and certainly the cold would have prevented anything from harming our documents. I would stake my life on finding the letter to Emperor Skarand completely intact."

I was eager to take this opportunity, but Sander shook his head and Ropert rubbed the back of his neck in skeptical disbelief of everything.

Eamon, though, rubbed his chin thoughtfully at the scribes' words. "Love in both friend and foe..." he mused, reciting a portion of Penmaster Eugene's account.

"Eamon?" King Sander tipped his head to the master warrior in question.

"Do you think it could be referring to Ikane?" Eamon asked.

I pursed my lips in thought. Perhaps Eamon was on the right track. My nightmares hadn't begun until Ikane had set foot in Daram.

Chanter cleared his throat and King Sander straightened.

There was a momentary time of silence throughout the chamber.

"Nonetheless," Sander said. "We must think of the survival of Roanfire. I see the union with Toleah as our only option. I'm sorry, Keatep. But you must put this mystery behind you."

"With all due respect, my king," Eamon interrupted. "As matters of the court go, Keatep Brendagger is still my daughter. You may be her blood father, but you've yet to claim her as your own. I will be the one to decide on whom she shall wed."

King Sander's expression was that of disbelief. "You would sacrifice Roanfire?"

"No, my king. Roanfire is strong. She will endure."

The king turned to Master Chanter for council. After some brief whisperings, Sander sighed and ran his fingers through his hair with a look of tired resignation.

"Go, Keatep. You have two weeks to find Ikane. When you return, we will discuss arrangements with Toleah."

An air of relief flowed through the room and I released breath I hadn't known I'd been holding. Gratitude filled my heart for Eamon who finally acted the part of my guardian. I rose quickly, not wanting to give the king time to rethink his decision and bowed. Eamon stood to escort us from the chamber, but King Sander cleared his throat.

"Eamon," he said. "I would like to discuss this matter with you further."

Eamon's expression hardened, but he gave the king one respectful nod and sat back down. He then turned to me. "Be careful, Keatep."

"I will," I assured him. Then to the king, I said, "I will return as soon as I am able," and turned to the door.

"Keatep," Sander called after me.

I halted reluctantly.

"I know you have feelings for Ikane. Please remember that one's virtue is priceless." The king looked at his queen as he continued.

I took in Lonacheska's eyes that held a bitterness that verged on madness.

"I will remember your counsel, my king."

65

As I stepped into the cold, barren hallway of the castle, I let out a shaky breath. It was almost uncanny how all the events of my life kept me from finding the White Wardent. A part of me was tempted to not return—to instead head directly for the Glacial Empire after finding Ikane. The threat of wedding the Tolean prince felt like an axe over my neck.

Ropert strode past me, harshly shoving into my shoulder on his way. I was about to retaliate when I felt a hand grip my arm from behind. I turned to see Master Chanter holding a scroll between us.

"Read this once you have left the castle," he said in a hushed tone.

My hand stretched out to take the scroll, but Chanter abruptly pulled it away. The old servant gripped my wrist with startling strength and whipped my arm around to pull it behind my back. I went rigid as the scroll came to my throat like a knife. Master Chanter truly was as dangerous as I thought.

"Sir Ropert!" Chanter bellowed after my bodyguard.

Ropert turned reluctantly, but upon seeing my state, whirled, with his blue eyes wide in alarm. His hand strayed for his weapon at his hip.

"If I were a true assassin, Lady Keatep would be dead," Chanter chided my new bodyguard. He released my arm and I shook it out before he placed the scroll in my hand. "You have much to learn, boy. This woman is your charge. Any harm that befalls her will be on your head."

Ropert's eyes narrowed at the abrupt lesson, but nodded nonetheless. "Yes sir," he said.

"Now go," Chanter ordered, waving for me to hurry to Ropert's side. "Make haste. Roanfire depends on you, Keatep Brendagger."

5

FIRESPRITE

The servants had already cleaned the disarray from my scuffle with Ikane. The window had been shuttered and a rather unattractive tapestry hung over the patchwork of wood. With the sunlight thusly blocked, the chamber held a gloom that even strategically placed candles couldn't brighten.

I changed from the red and gold gown into some warm traveling trousers and woolen tunic as Ropert headed to his quarters to pack. It felt strange not to don a uniform of Roanfire. I did not feel like a Lady of Meldron, nor did I feel like a soldier. I didn't know what I had become.

Ropert knocked on my door before entering. "Ikane has been spotted," he said as he shrugged his pack higher onto his shoulder. "Scouts say that he's headed for the Dead Forest."

It didn't surprise me. Ikane knew the area well. As did I.

"It's about four day's ride to the Dead Forest," I said as I swung my cloak over my shoulders and hefted my pack. "Are you ready?"

He stood silently for a moment, looking at me sternly.

My brows narrowed in return.

"Tell me something, Kea," he said. His chin rose a little, indicating that he wasn't going to drop the subject until I gave him a truthful answer. "Why him? Why a Leviathan? Why not a man of Roanfire? After you fled the castle, I was dragged from my quarters and tossed into the dungeon. I was questioned about King Myron's assassination, and you, and labeled a traitor. All because of him!" The emphasis he gave to Ikane was tinged with venom. "You and I trained together, Kea. We grew up in the same battalion. The thought of you falling for a Leviathan... sickens me."

I wanted to be angry with him, but I remembered my own hatred and fear of Ikane when I'd first discovered that he was a Leviathan Pirate.

"We can't judge others by what they are labeled," I said.

"He tried to kill you!" Ropert groaned. "What more proof do you need that he's a monster?"

"He wasn't himself," I said and moved to exit my room, but Ropert blocked my path.

"We're not done discussing this," he hissed and grabbed my shoulder. "I need to know why you are risking everything to save him."

"Because he risked everything to save me!" I snapped and slapped his hand away. "Because he was there for me when all of Roanfire was against me. He was there for me when you weren't! Because he risked his own life to save me! Because he turned against his own brother, and killed him, to save me. Shall I go on?"

Ropert's jaw clenched. "No."

Satisfied, I pushed past him and stepped into the hallway. Morning light was just beginning to filter in through the windows on the far end, silhouetting a few scattered people emerging from their quarters. At least it wasn't crowded with the people of Roanfire anymore.

My feet stopped upon seeing a familiar woman in the hallway. I hadn't seen her since the day she assigned me and three others to escort her niece to Meldron. Lady Caitelyn, the Duchess of the Daram Keep.

Her thin eyebrows narrowed when her eyes fell upon me. Her deep auburn hair and slender features were just as striking as I remembered, though now her beauty was marred by an abhorrence for me that dripped from her soul and spilled into her countenance. She stiffened.

"Lady Keatep Brendagger," she said hotly. I felt the sting in her voice.

"Duchess Caitelyn," I said, trying to keep my voice as neutral as possible, and bowed deeply as Ropert came up behind me. "You look well."

She scoffed and rolled her eyes. "You needn't pretend to care. I see that you've been given another mission." She jerked her head to our travel packs.

Ropert, knowing that the lady was just as bitter with him as she was with me, stiffened. "The Leviathan prisoner has escaped," Ropert said. "We have been sent to retrieve him."

Discreetly, I bumped my elbow into his abdomen. She didn't need to know.

"Let us hope that you two fools can actually complete your task this time," she hissed. "You were assigned to escort my niece to Meldron, and you failed. You were to bring her servant, Illorce Maque, to Meldron, and you failed." Her voice grew louder as she went on, and a deep red grew from her neck to her face. She jabbed one of her fingers at me. "You were to represent Daram to the crown prince and beg for aid, and you failed! Not only this, but you have betrayed us by aiding a Leviathan Pirate! I warned you that you would not go unpunished!"

I stood my ground as her finger harshly poked into my collarbone, feeling like a blunt dagger. "I will see that you pay for letting Daram fall!"

Ropert stepped up, forcing the lady to rethink her actions. She may be superior to his title, but he was my bodyguard, and he was required to keep me from any harm, even if it was inflicted by a noblewoman's finger.

Seeing as she had crossed a line, she turned her nose up and stormed off with her gown rustling loudly.

It took every ounce of energy to keep the lump in my throat from overtaking me. I sorrowed for Daram as much as she did.

A pair of fine horses were already prepared for our departure. The stable-master presented me to a graceful chestnut colored horse with a black mane and tail. He introduced her as Shade Ranger, named as such for her tendency to gallop across stretches of the road in search of shady areas along the way. Furthermore, Shade Ranger, he said, was the only horse that Beast was not threatened by.

As the stable-master had placed the reins of a black stallion into Ropert's hand, I soon realized why this massive warhorse was named such. Beast was temperamental, spirited, and strong-willed – unless bribed with a slice of dried apple, which the stable-master supplied us with.

Depressing gray clouds covered the sky as the cold breeze chilled my bones. The rhythmic clapping of our horse's hooves against the cobblestone streets couldn't overpower the churning of my stomach as I took in the gut-wrenching sight of black soot clinging to destroyed homes and shops of Meldron. A loud argument ensued to my right as a woman shouted at another, accusing her of stealing a sack of grain from her pantry. These squabbles would only grow, and surely turn violent, if we didn't get help – Prince Leander was right. We had about a month before things turned gruesome.

I swallowed hard, realizing that King Sander would be faced with this scene on his doorstep every day. The longer he delayed, the more the people would suffer. He would be hard-pressed to arrange the marriage by the people.

Once we reached the outskirts of the city, Ropert and I spurred the horses into a harsh gallop towards Fold.

"**I**'ll take first watch," I said as we sat by the large fire Ropert had built up. My hands burned against the mug filled with hot stew between them. The steam warmed my face momentarily as I sipped the strong broth.

Ropert lowered his mug from his lips but did not look at me when he spoke. He simply stared at the fire. "How do you plan to help Ikane?" he asked. "I mean... he's not exactly going to let you simply bring him back to Meldron."

I swallowed my meal, feeling the warmth race down to my belly. Ropert's question was valid. What could be done when a witch infested the body of another? Rion seemed to no longer desire my body for rebirth, and that made her all the more dangerous for me.

"Would killing Ikane destroy her?" Ropert asked, taking my silence as uncertainty. I could tell he wasn't jesting in the least.

My skin prickled at the idea, and I had to refrain from pummeling Ropert simply for the suggestion, but it sparked a thought nonetheless. Perhaps he was right. I couldn't destroy the jewel that had been Rion's safe-haven for centuries as it had been protected by magic, but Ikane was flesh and blood. He was not indestructible.

I cursed myself for even toying with the idea.

A roguish smile stole across Ropert's lips as he lowered his mug again. "It would certainly make me feel better."

Lips pursed, I glowered at him. "I don't think we are on good enough terms for you to jest that way. Especially if you still don't believe that Rion exists."

His smile faded quickly, and he took another hasty drink to hide it.

We finished our meal in silence, watching the flames lick at the logs and shift hues from violet, green and blue, to orange and red. As the moments stretched, the tension between us thinned. Eventually, Ropert placed his empty mug on the ground, stretched his back, and stood.

"I'm going to bed," he announced.

I nodded once, absently watching the fire. Ropert's suggestion continued to nag at me like the itch of a healing scab. The fact that I was even considering his suggestion made my stomach churn. No. I needed to find the White Wardent. Who is to say that once Ikane was dead that Rion wouldn't simply flee into another form and resume her tyranny.

Ropert hesitated a moment at my silence. "Are you sure you want to go first? I'm not that tired."

"No," I said quickly. I knew he was lying anyway. He was always exhausted at the end of the day. I, on the other hand, could stay awake for hours, even after the moon was high. "I have some reading material anyway."

I drew the scroll that Master Chanter had given me from my belt pouch and waved it at Ropert.

He nodded, not the slightest bit curious, and ducked into the small tent. Ropert hadn't had the opportunity to learn his letters, and therefore the mystery of books and literature wasn't all that fascinating to him. He hadn't discovered the vast worlds that writings could open to him. I had offered to teach him once... but that was before.

Not wanting to dwell on the past, I broke the seal of red wax, unrolled the parchment, and tipped it toward the fire to see the black ink more clearly.

Lady Keatep Brendagger,

This letter comes to you as a warning. I have heard of many schemes against you within the walls of the Meldron Castle. In spite of defeating the Leviathan Army, there are some who fear you. They see you as a witch and someone who must be stopped.

Among these is the former Duchess of Daram, Caitelyn. I can only presume that her bitterness lies in the fact that Daram was destroyed, and that her husband, Lord Adair, was killed along with it.

My scouts have reported secret meetings with those of a dangerous profession. Actively employ Sir Ropert's skills as your bodyguard. Never leave his side and keep no secrets from him.

In spite of the convictions of many in Meldron, I know the truth behind your actions. Know that King Sander and I have your best interest at heart.

Take caution, Lady Keatep Brendagger.

Master Chanter

I shivered briefly as I re-read the contents of the scroll. It did not surprise me in the slightest to hear of Caitelyn's conniving. Our brief, unpleasant encounter in the hallway was only a taste of what she felt.

My eyes darted to the white canvas of the small tent where Ropert slept. The letter may have been a warning for me, but Ropert was just as guilty in the eyes of the duchess. He was not in any less danger.

As if a drop of highly flammable grease had fallen into the fire, it suddenly flared, catching the scrolls edge. I jerked the yellow parchment away and hastily shook it out. The flames quickly died away, but it had already eaten nearly half the letter. A brittle, brown scorch mark remained on the end.

It was then that I heard a soft whistle, like that of a flute, coming from the fire. The flames seemed to dance with the tune, swaying as if pulled by the wind. And that was when I saw her. A tiny humanlike figure, no taller than my forefinger, sitting amidst the burning logs. Her skin glowed every bit as brightly as the fire, and flames, resembling hair, roiled off her head like a candle. Her nimble fingers held, what appeared to be, a little black flute to her lips.

Her abnormally large red irises rose to meet mine, and she lowered her charred instrument, revealing a crooked, mischievous smile.

A firesprite!

It was said that they were flighty creatures, with unpredictable and fickle temperaments. Tales of encounters with these magical sprites usually ended with the human receiving severe burns that left terrible scars.

I rubbed my eyes with one hand. I couldn't be asleep. I was supposed to be watching the camp!

When I looked at the fire again, the tiny creature leapt into the air like a massive spark. Fearing that she meant to burn me, my body arched backwards, and my hands flew up to shield my face. The movement sent my body off the edge of the rough log I had been sitting on, and I landed hard on my back. With my legs stuck over the edge of the log, fierce heat radiated from her fiery form as she hovered above me.

"How are you doing that?" she asked in a high-pitched voice that somehow held an air of smokiness.

"Pardon?" I asked, barely daring to look at her flaming body through the gap in my arms that were still thrown over my face. She was thumping her charred flute against her thigh, as if pondering her own question.

"I don't understand," she said. "You are repelling the shadow."

Seeing as she wasn't intent on burning me, yet, I lowered my arms a little. "Shadow?"

"Yes, the shadow," she nearly groaned, irritated. "You know, that horrible darkness that bites at your soul? You don't feel it?"

I moved my hands even further from my face and shook my head at her.

Now she folded her arms across her chest. "How can you not feel it? It's so thick around you... then again, you are repelling it. Perhaps you truly can't sense it," she shrugged and darted back into the fire. The flames went into a dancing frenzy as she played another tune on her black flute.

Hastily, I moved my boots from over the log and pushed myself to a sitting position, cautiously peering over the log at the fire. The firesprite, unfazed by my watching eye, twirled and danced on the stones about the fire. Her feet left hot-red streaks on the rock which slowly faded to ashen markings behind her. I had seen these markings in my campfires before but had no inkling of where they had come from. Until now.

An agonizing cry of a wolf split the silence of the night, causing my hair to stand on end. I resisted the urge to spring to my feet, knowing instantly that it was Ikane. I was no longer searching for a man, but for a wolf.

At the noise, the firesprite shivered as if a block of ice had run down her spine. Her eyes grew wide, and the glow of her body flared and sparked with panic. Her wings buzzed like that of a honeybee as she zipped across the log and to my side, like a child seeking safety by its mother. The sprite hovered over my shoulder, her red eyes scanning the dark shadows of the trees for the source of the howl.

"Thrall grows," she whispered fiercely. "The darkness in that wolf is so black, it swallows everything that is good."

My eyes narrowed. "Thrall?" I asked. It seemed to me that her reference to Thrall was known to me as the Phoenix Witch.

Her head jerked around to look at me, causing her candle-like hair to flicker. At first, I sensed fear in her eyes, but she quickly squared her shoulders. "Don't look at me like that," she barked, placing her fists, one of which curled around her flute, on her tiny hips. "You have an aura of light that repels Thrall... much like that of the White Wardent."

I should've known that the elemental sprites would know where to find him. It was said that they are drawn to his aura.

"Do you know where he is?" I eagerly asked. "Do you know how I can find him?"

"If I knew where he was, I wouldn't bother staying with you, now would I?" she retorted.

I pursed my lips at her sassy reply and sighed.

The haunting cry of Ikane sounded again and I could feel the sprite shiver.

"You are far from being safe with me, little sprite," I said.

"It's better than-" she stopped abruptly and darted directly into the fire, sending out an explosion of embers.

The canvas tent flaps flew open. Ropert rubbed his eyes groggily as he stepped out, dragging his cloak with him.

"Kea? Is everything alright? I thought I heard something."

I glanced at the sprite in the fire, but she shook her head, warning me to keep her presence a secret.

"Did you hear the wolf?" I asked.

He yawned loudly as he came to the fire. "Is that what the noise was?" He tilted his head at me. "Why are you sitting on the ground... and away from the fire? Aren't you cold?"

My eyes glanced at the fire again, trying to find a way to explain my situation without giving away the sprite's presence. My eyes fell upon the half-burnt scroll from Master Chanter beside the log, and I quickly picked it up.

"I had a little mishap," I said, showing him the burnt edges of the paper as I climbed back onto the log.

His brows rose with a crooked smile. "Too close to the fire?"

I nodded. "Everything is fine. Go back to sleep Ropert. You have a few more hours yet."

He swung his cloak over his shoulders instead and sat by the fire. "I can't get the noise out of my head," he said as he grabbed a stick to prod at the logs. "I might as well take watch now."

I suppressed a flinch when he moved one of the hot logs, nearly pushing it on top of the little sprite. She ducked and curled under the glowing wood beside it, disappearing from my view.

"What did the letter say?" Ropert asked, jerking his head to the half-burnt parchment on my lap.

I picked it up and looked at the remainder of the words. "Master Chanter simply sent us a warning. It's nothing new, really. We have enemies in Meldron, and Duchess Caitelyn may have something up her sleeve."

Ropert nodded thoughtfully, not taking his eyes off the firelight. "Alright then. We had best be vigilant."

I nodded.

Ropert set the stick back down beside him and pulled his cloak around his shoulders tightly. "Go get some rest, Kea."

I stood, hesitated a moment, then dropped the parchment into the fire. There was no need to carry it around and it was gone in a matter of seconds. I scanned the logs for any sign of the firesprite. She had either left the fire or blended in so well that I couldn't see her.

"There is extra firewood over there," I told Ropert and motioned to my left before heading for the tent.

"Kea?" he called after me.

I stopped and looked back at him.

"I... I still care, you know."

I pursed my lips and bit them between my teeth. I wanted to believe him, but his actions thus far had proven otherwise. "Goodnight, Ropert." I told him.

He seemed a little disappointed that I did not respond the way he had hoped, but he smiled soberly. "Sleep well."

I thought I heard another agonizing howl from Ikane as I ducked into the tent.

White frost covered the landscape when I emerged from the tent in the morning. My breath puffed in the frigid air and the chill already tried to sink into my bones.

Ropert had woken me a few minutes prior, announcing that he'd already packed most of our gear. All that was left was to secure the bedroll to the back of Beast's saddle and collapse the tent.

"Which way?" Ropert asked.

I scanned the black trunks of the trees that towered behind him. Evergreens stretched their green needles out like fans, and their tips pointed to the violet morning sky like directional markers. Beyond these dense trees, I knew, stood the dead forest.

A lump grew in my throat as my chest tightened at the memory the place held. The old arrow wound in my back seemed to take on a new ache. Nonetheless, I nodded to the woods soaring behind him.

He briefly looked over his broad shoulder. "We are headed into the heart of the Dead Forest, aren't we?"

"Yes," I said. If he noted the rigidness in my body as I moved around the tent, he didn't indicate it.

"I don't want to go there as much as you don't," I said as I stooped to pull one of the stakes from the ground. The fabric of the small tent slackened.

Ropert moved around to the other side. "Then why are we doing this?" he asked.

A frown pulled on my lips as I jerked the last stake from the cold ground. The tent collapsed. Ropert's antagonism towards Ikane had no end. His words about still caring the night before seemed empty now.

"You know why," I grumbled.

Ropert crouched to gather the tent with a sigh. "Don't be that way, Kea. I'm simply wondering if it is worth all this effort."

I tossed the stakes at his hands, and he was forced to pull them back before the metal struck his knuckles.

"Ikane was my ally when all of Roanfire turned against me. Even you. He has earned my loyalty and friendship," I repeated. "How many times must I say it?"

Ropert's eyes lowered. But I couldn't tell if it was shame or defiance. Either way, I didn't care to help him with the tent any longer. I turned on my heel, marched towards Shade Ranger, and snatched her reins.

"I'll scout ahead," I grumbled and swung my legs over her back. She danced momentarily under my hasty mount and tossed her head.

"Kea," Ropert sighed as he stood. "Don't."

Ignoring him, I spurred the chestnut mare forward.

"Kea! We need to stay together!" Ropert called after me.

He was right, but I disregarded his warning. I needed a break from him.

Shade Ranger trotted through the trees until I came upon the shallow dirt trail leading towards the Dead Forest. Why did he insist that Ikane held no value? Before he knew that Ikane was a Leviathan Pirate, they had been friends. I reminded myself again that I had felt the same antagonism towards Ikane. Ropert simply needed time.

It wasn't long before I heard Beast's heavy hoofbeats on the dirt. I slowed Shade Ranger's pace.

"Kea," Ropert called out to me. His voice seemed angry.

I gathered a deep breath. Apologizing wouldn't be easy.

"Dagger!" he called again, and this time it was filled with urgency.

I knew there was something amiss, but I froze. He hadn't called me by that name since I had been branded a traitor.

Ropert groaned in pain behind me, and I whirled to see his broadsword fall from his grip and land in the dirt at Beast's hooves. With his face contorted in agony, Ropert brought his arm to his chest to cradle it. It was then that I saw the glint of a knife protruding from his leather armguard.

"Run, Dagger! Go!" he bellowed as he jerked the knife from his arm.

The distinct whirr of a knife flying through the air whistled in my ears. Instinctively, I ducked low to Shade Ranger's neck and caught a glimpse of the silver spark as it twirled past my shoulders. A deep thud sounded to my left, and I glanced up to see the knife lodge in the trunk of a tree there.

My sword made a gentle hissing sound as I drew it from its scabbard and pulled Shade Ranger to my right. Three hooded figures, with black paint on their faces, scrambled from the underbrush with weapons ready. My eyes narrowed as I recalled the warning in Master Chanter's letter. I had placed myself in this position. And by failing to stay with Ropert, I had placed him in danger.

With his sword drawn, one of the hooded figures rushed for me, crashing through the underbrush like a charging bull. Before I could block his weapon with my own, a harsh snap to my upper right alerted me to another assault. I turned in time to see a fourth assassin leap from his perch on a high branch in the trees.

I did not have time to bring my sword up before his body fell against mine. I felt my neck whip forward at the impact. My legs tensed around Shade Ranger's body, trying to keep myself upright as the assassin's arms wrapped around my torso. He used the momentum of his fall to try and pull me from the saddle, and he almost succeeded.

Frantically, I gripped Shade Ranger's mane with one arm as she reared with fright, and simultaneously blocked the first strike of the assassin on the ground with the other. I heard the harsh clang of metal as our swords connected at her flank.

Unexpectedly, the assassin at my back roared in agony, right into my ear. His grip became lax. I seized the opportunity to twist in my saddle and allowed my elbow to fly up into his face. It connected sharply with his nose and his head rocked back at the impact. His body slipped from Shade Ranger's back and he crashed onto his side, revealing the hilt of a knife sticking out between his shoulder blades.

I pulled myself back into the saddle and barely caught sight of Ropert's outstretched arm, indicating that he had been the one to relieve me of my attacker.

The glint of metal forced me to react to the weapon of the assassin at my feet. With a harsh twist of my sword, the weight of his blade jerked his arm wide, opening his face to a strike. My boot quickly collided with his head, knocking him back. Before he could recover, I pulled Shade Ranger around.

Ropert didn't need to say anything as he dug his heels into Beast's sides. Shade Ranger's body tensed and burst into a gallop after him.

Trembling with adrenaline, I risked a glance backwards to see three assassins crowd around their fallen comrade. One of them turned to face us, his gaze boring into our backs as we galloped away.

Only after a few minutes of hard riding, and no indication of immediate pursuit, did Ropert and I slow the horses. I sheathed my weapon and glanced at Ropert's arm which bled heavily, spilling onto Beast's black coat and Ropert's trousers.

"How deep is it?" I panted.

"I don't know," he admitted, just as breathless. "It burns like fire though."

My brows furrowed. It was poisoned. I pulled Shade Ranger to a halt.

"What are you doing? We can't stop now." He pulled Beast to a standstill anyway.

"It's poisoned, and it will kill you if it's not addressed," I said as I rooted through the saddlebags on Shade Ranger's back for my herb box. "Take your armguard off."

He did as was told, revealing an ugly gash on the back of his wrist. I grabbed his arm so that he was forced to lean over the horse. After pulling the cork from his water-skin, I poured the cool liquid over the injury.

"You called me 'Dagger'," I said as I worked, hoping to keep his mind occupied. The last thing I needed was for him to be rendered unconscious.

"Should I have called you 'Broadsword'?" he asked through his teeth.

I smiled a little at his dry humor. At least his mind was still sharp. I pressed down on his forearm, forcing the blood to erupt from the injury in an attempt to flush the poison from his system. He grunted as the blood ran down his arm and dripped to the dirt at our horse's hooves.

"It's just nice to hear you call me that again," I said.

He looked back to the road as I tended to his injury. "Those weren't mere bandits."

"I know," I admitted. "They were assassins, undoubtedly sent by Duchess Caitelyn."

I opened the corked pot of charcoal, took a pinch of the black powder, and dabbed it evenly over Ropert's wound. He watched curiously.

"You seem to have experience with medicine."

I nodded once. "I learned much in my time as a fugitive, especially with..." my voice trailed off. The White Fox Resistance had once been family to me. Hala Whitefox, the leader of the band, had been the closest thing to a sister. And that was why her betrayal had cut the deepest.

"The charcoal will help draw out any poison remaining close to the surface of the skin," I said, trying to keep my thoughts as far away from Hala as possible. "And this," I continued as I placed some dried comfrey leaves over the area, "will aid the healing process. But you will need sutures to close the wound completely. I will tend to it when we make camp this evening."

Using his armguard as a means to tie off the injury, I stuffed the sleeve of his bloodied shirt over the wound and secured his armor. "If you feel lightheaded or nauseous, let me know right away."

He sat upright on Beast's back and cautiously tested the movement of his hand. His fingers worked, but stiffly.

"Thank you," he whispered.

Hastily, I rummaged through my herb box and pulled one last vial from it. The red dust inside glowed vibrantly, in spite of the sunlight breaking through the trees. It was hot against my fingers, and I couldn't help but remember the firesprite from the night before.

Using my teeth, I pulled the stopper off the tiny vial.

"What is that?" Ropert asked as I tipped it into his water-skin. Just a pinch would do.

I stopped it again and placed the vial back into my box. "Firesprite dust," I said and handed him his water-skin. "Drink. You'll sweat a bit, but it will help flush the poison from your body."

He held the mouth of his water-skin to one of his eyes to peer inside. Satisfied, he took a large gulp and proceeded to cough. Water sputtered everywhere.

"Hot," he panted with his tongue hanging out comically.

I couldn't help but laugh as I replaced my herb box into the saddlebag. "Take another drink," I said and gently kicked Shade Ranger's sides.

Ropert drank again, but more cautiously this time. He lowered the mouth of the waterskin as a deep frown pulled on his lips.

"Curse them," he hissed as he wiped his mouth with the back of his sleeve. He looked over his shoulder. "My sword is back there. I am useless as a bodyguard without it."

"I wouldn't say useless," I said. "You make a very good human shield."

He seemed startled at my statement at first, then slowly a smile spread across his lips, and he chuckled. "Did you just make a joke?"

I shrugged with a little smile of my own and urged my horse along. He was right. We could not go back for his sword. It wasn't as if he could hold it right now anyway, but we both felt a sense of our old relationship returning, and it felt right.

The slightly sweet, peaty smell of rotting wood struck my nostrils before I could see the Dead Forest.

And then it appeared. The soft fans of evergreen trees stood as sentinels before the dry, ashen spears of dead trunks, warning us to turn about. The distinct border between the living woods and that of the Dead Forest was still evident: a deep line of foliage and greenery, separated by minimal tufts of vegetation. Even though saplings, grasses, and small patches of moss and mushrooms sprouted from rotten logs that littered the ground, the forest held an air of an abandoned boneyard. Dead tree trunks scattered across the vast expanse, standing out like broken banners on a decimated battlefield.

As our horses stepped over the threshold, the regular soft thud of their feet changed to a harsh clap, indicating that the ground was as brittle as the trees. But there was life! Bugs zipped across the way and pestered Shade Ranger's ears. A squirrel chirped to my right, birds sang in the stumpy-treetops, and the bright gurgling of a river carried through the air.

Just a few yards ahead, I spotted a familiar tree. There was no way I could forget the tangled roots that twisted into the barren soil, or the knot in the trunk just at head height. Here, I had taken an arrow to my back. Here, I had fallen.

My body involuntarily shuddered at the recollection of the permanent injury.

Ropert must have taken my shuddering for something else.

"I know," he said. "It still feels haunted." He almost flinched at the loudness of his voice, seeing as there was no foliage to absorb the sound.

I nodded soberly. Rion had drained every last drop of life from these woods for over four hundred years. Life was finally returning to the place, though it would be a long recovery.

A harsh crack echoed through the Dead Forest. My head jerked to the left in time to witness a tall, pole of a tree, tip to the side and crash harshly to the ground. A whirl of dust and debris exploded from the impact, and a flurry of startled birds leapt to the sky. Our horses flinched, snorted, and stomped their hooves.

After the dust settled, Ropert voiced just what I had been thinking.

"We had best be careful. If we stick to the wider gaps between the trees, we'll have a better chance of not getting squashed."

"There is a river up ahead," I suggested. "If we follow it, we'll only have one line of trees to worry about."

"Lead the way," he said.

By the time we reached the small river flowing towards the ruins of Fold, the late afternoon sun cast an orange-red glow across the gray trees. It struck the running water in such a way that the river itself seemed to be on fire. The river had been further away than I expected, probably due to the fact that sound seemed to be warped here.

We dismounted at the riverbank to allow our horses a few minutes of rest. I knew we still had about two hours' worth of riding before we'd come to the Dead City. We wouldn't make it before nightfall, and I dreaded camping out in the open in these woods.

"Would you fill up the waterskins?" Ropert asked, pushing his at me. "It hurts my wrist to open the top. I'll take the horses downstream for a drink."

"I should really take a look at it again," I said and nodded to his wrist as I took his waterskin from him.

Although he had a natural pink flush to his pale complexion, he seemed a little more flushed than normal, and I could see the shine of perspiration on his brow.

He took the reins of both horses. "In a minute," he said, and led the horses into the shallows of the river. The cool water sloshed against their legs as he guided them downstream.

I searched the riverbank for a good spot to fill up the waterskins and found a decent place a little further upstream. Even then, I determined that I would purify our water with firedust. Who knew what sort of filth floated in this river with decaying trees surrounding it. The last thing we needed was to become ill from bad water.

As I knelt by the shallow river, a light tune caught my attention, flowing with the wind. It was barely audible over the gurgling noise of the river. But I recognized it.

I glanced up to see the little firesprite hovering above the glistening water, playing a melody on her charred flute. Her glowing body almost blended with the reflecting orange burn of the evening sun.

My smile was crooked. "You came back."

"I said I felt safe with you," she answered and fluttered closer.

I chuckled and shook my head as I placed the cork on the top of Ropert's waterskin. "I told you before, I'm not the safest person to be around."

"I know," she declared as she placed her hands on her hips. "Did you know that there were five of them? You wouldn't have escaped without my help."

My brows furrowed. "Five what?" I asked and dipped my waterskin into the river. I watched carefully for debris as the bladder slowly began to fill and bulge.

"Five what?" She rolled her eyes, groaning as she repeated my question. "Five assassins. One was hiding in the underbrush with a bow. He would've shot your companion straight through the heart if I hadn't intervened. They threw the knife at him instead. Though, I have to admit, I was impressed how quiet he remained when I burned his neck. Most people scream so loud it can be heard for miles."

There was a dangerous hint of pride to her last statement and my eyes widened as I looked up at her. She was smiling mischievously, studying her fingernails.

I glanced over my shoulder to see Ropert just beginning to lead the horses from the river. He continued to cradle his injured arm at his abdomen.

A frown pulled on my lips. This wound really must be paining him, for he rarely favored an injury.

"I suppose a 'thank you' is in order," I said as I turned back to the sprite, but she was no longer there.

"Dagger," Ropert called. "Are you done?"

I pulled my waterskin from the river, popped the cork on top, and jogged over to him. After hanging our water over the pommel of Shade Ranger's saddle, I grabbed my little healers kit from my saddlebag and turned to him.

"Let me take care of that while the light is still good." I nodded to his arm.

He hesitated, rubbed the back of his neck, and searched the thick, dead trunks for a moment. "Do it quick. We are completely exposed out here. I don't want to risk those assassins sneaking up on us."

"We'll be fine," I assured him and moved to a fallen log nearby. I patted the area beside me, indicating that he should be seated.

"How can you be so sure?" he asked. Ropert's entire body seemed to sigh as he sat down beside me.

Assassins were the least of my concerns. What I worried about were the people who lived in the Dead City. Ikane and I had personally trained them to become expert in their trade – as raiders. If they still held to the same pattern, a scout may have already spotted us.

"The assassins have as little cover as we do. We'll see them from a mile away through these dead trees. And they know it."

"True," he sighed and rested his arm across his knee. He began to fumble with the latches of his bracer.

I slapped his hand away. "Let me do that."

He easily surrendered.

After removing his damaged bracer, I couldn't help but cringe as the injury was exposed again. My initial treatment didn't seem to do much. The wound was red and severely inflamed.

"I'm sorry," I muttered as I pulled the only needle I had from my box and threaded it in the orange light.

"For what?" he asked.

"I shouldn't have run off like that," I said as I wiped the blood from his wound. "It's my fault you were injured. Master Chanter warned me... but I was just so angry... I shouldn't have... I should've been watching your back."

"Stop it, Dagger," he said quickly. "It's not your fault. That knife could've hit you all the same."

I didn't believe him, but I nodded anyway.

"If I had some waterdust I could numb this," I said as I prepared to stick the needle into his skin.

"I don't need it," he assured me. "Get on with it."

He didn't even flinch as I drove the point of the needle through his skin, but I did see the muscles in his jaw tighten.

"What's for supper tonight," I asked, trying to keep his mind otherwise occupied as I worked.

He took a moment before answering. "The same thing we've had for the last three nights. Bread, cheese, and some dried fruit."

"Hmmm, the bread is getting hard. Perhaps we should make a stew tonight instead."

He nodded thoughtfully. "What sort of herbs do you have with you? I'm not particularly fond of bland bread stew."

I hid my smile. The suggestion of a warm meal was merely to keep him talking. He recognized it too.

"I have some dried oregano, garlic, and onion," I replied.

"Mmmm," he said and licked his lips. "Now you've got me hungry for stew. I think I even saw some small portabella mushrooms around here. Those would make for some tasty morsels."

I chuckled. "If you like mushrooms."

"You don't?"

"I thought you knew that about me," I said.

He shrugged, causing my needle to miss its mark.

"Hold still," I grumbled and pulled his arm back into place across my knees.

"Sorry."

When I finished, Ropert flexed his hand experimentally and frowned deeply when his ring finger didn't curl with the rest.

"The knife went deep," he mumbled. I could hear the worry in his voice. "The muscles don't want to move."

I stood and returned my box to Shade Ranger's saddlebag. "Give it time. And you shouldn't move it too much anyway or you'll tear the sutures."

He nodded, stood, and dusted his trousers off. "Now then, let's see how far we can get before dusk. We've got about an hour of daylight left."

6

THE CLIFFS OF FOLD

The night was cold, and without the shelter of trees to hold in some warmth, the fire did little. Ropert, in spite of crawling into the shelter of the tent, complained that the earth seemed to sap the heat from his body. We decided instead, to fold the thick canvas tent underneath us, with our bedrolls stretched across our legs. Then, sitting side by side, with our backs against a fallen log and feet outstretched to the warmth of the flames, we were able to stay somewhat warm.

Ropert slumbered first, occasionally resting his head against my shoulder. I had to push him away several times in order to place more wood on the fire, which was quite frequent. The wood was so brittle and dry.

The noise of falling trees startled me twice before I became accustomed to the gentle creak and harsh snap followed by a heavy bang as it struck the earth. Although the people of Fold were not prone to attack in the night – their tactic was at first light - I still worried that they may have changed their approach. But I heard little in the way of footsteps.

When the stars reached a certain point in the sky, I woke Ropert for his shift. After briefing him on the typical attack of the Foldeans, I curled up beside him.

I was warm, comfortable, and extremely well rested. The steady throb of a heartbeat pulsed beneath my right ear and my head moved ever so slightly as Ropert's solid chest rose and fell with his soft snoring.

Long shadows stretched across the barren landscape as I blinked my eyes open.

For a moment, I didn't comprehend that Ropert's arm was around my shoulders. Nor did I realize that he shouldn't have been snoring.

I shot upright, throwing his arm away. "Ropert!"

He woke with a startled jerk, grabbed my sword lying beside him in reflex, and leapt to his feet, nearly tripping over the bedrolls that were draped across our legs. He searched the dead trees for an enemy, then looked at me with a dazed expression.

Realization flashed across his face and he groaned. "I fell asleep, didn't I."

I scrambled to my feet and massaged the back of my neck to ease the tense muscles there. "You know to wake me when your eyes grow heavy!"

"I know, I know. But you had already had your shift," he said and rubbed his eyes. "You were sleeping so soundly. I thought I could manage."

"You know better," I grumbled and snatched my bedroll from the ground. "You even let the fire burn cold." I motioned to it for emphasis.

"I'll build it up," he said quickly and tucked my sword into his belt beside his empty scabbard.

My eyes narrowed as he moved to the firepit.

"Give me my sword," I said.

He looked down at our only weapon by his hip, then back at me. "I... think... not," he said slowly. "If your expression could wield this sword, you would have impaled me by now."

My frown deepened. "It's my sword, Ropert! Besides, you're accustomed to the broadsword. You'll send this one flying halfway across Roanfire if you try to wield it."

A crooked grin spread across his lips. "That sounds like a compliment."

I stooped to fold my bedroll and harshly flipped the woolen fabric. "It's not," I said. "And don't bother with the fire. We've got to keep moving."

His face pulled into the familiar whimper of a puppy. "But... breakfast?"

My eyes rolled to the sky. "Ro-"

"Drop your weapon!" a male voice shouted at us from behind.

I chided myself. I knew their tactics. I had taught them myself. I should've been on the lookout when I first opened my eyes.

Ropert whirled and whipped my sword out in defense. As predicted, he was unaccustomed to the weight. It didn't fly from his hands like I thought it would, but whipped across his body in a clumsy manner that left him dangerously exposed. It was pure luck that our ambushers did not intend to kill us.

Slowly, I stood and turned to see a dozen crippled men and women straining to hold their timeworn weapons with the exactness Ikane and I had taught them. The long shadows of the trees matched their withered frames. They were all far too thin.

"You are not welcome here," a tall man barked, jabbing his sword in my direction. A tattered, gray cowl covered his head and hid most of his features, but his severely deformed left hand exposed him as one of our best pupils, Torquin. In spite of his deformity, his skill rivaled even the most educated Phoenix Soldier. He was much thinner than I remembered, and I instantly thought of his wife and son. Were they just as malnourished and sickly?

I took two steps back to Ropert's side and pushed the blade of my sword toward the ground. "Put it away, Ropert," I whispered.

"But Dagger..." He hesitated.

"Drop it," I hissed firmly.

He released the sword and it clanged against the hard earth at his feet. His hands rose to show that he was now unarmed.

Torquin seemed satisfied, but he didn't lower his sword. "Go back to where you've come from," he said. "There is no room here for another mouth to feed. Especially those with no physical taint."

"You don't recognize me?" I asked him and took a step forward.

"Not another step closer!" he snapped, the point of his weapon now only a hands width from my face. It trembled under his exertion. "Go. We do not wish to harm you."

"Torquin," I said calmly. "How are Malese and Pan?"

He was caught off guard and his sword wavered a little. "H... How do you know my name? And my wife...?" His eyes narrowed as he scrutinized my features, paying particular attention to my eyes. Then a glimmer of recollection flashed across his countenance. His sword dropped quickly, mostly due to the weight pulling down on his weakened muscles. Then he pulled the cowl from his jaw and pushed the hood from his head to reveal his masculine features. The ragged beard and wild, dark hair seemed to age him greatly, even though he was only a few years older than I was.

"Paige? Paige Ormand?" he asked, near whispering the name I had given myself while in hiding among these people. His eyes were wide with disbelief.

My smile was as weak as my nod. He looked terrible.

He quickly stepped forward and wrapped his short, withered arm about me in an embrace.

"What are you doing here?" he asked, though it didn't seem that he cared what the reason for my visit was. He was simply grateful to see me.

He pulled away and motioned for the rest of his bandits to lower their weapons as he sheathed his. "They are no threat," he informed them. "Go home. We will scout for another caravan tomorrow."

With shoulders slumping in pure exhaustion, and small sighs of relief and disappointment sounding through the Dead Forest, weapons dropped. The withered men and women almost seemed to use their weapons as crutches now.

Ropert warily retrieved my sword from the ground and tucked it into his belt again.

"You're all starving," I said to Torquin as the band of thieves slowly retreated.

Torquin nodded soberly and stroked his thick beard. "When the Leviathan Pirates attacked, they scared off the caravans and nearby farmers. There is nothing to hunt in the woods. And even though rain now falls in Fold, the soil is so depleted of nutrients that the simplest of crops won't grow," he said. "Flashfloods are a weekly occurrence, and Fold itself has become a very dangerous place. I'm sure you've heard the trees falling in the woods? The same is happening in the city. The stone of the homes has turned brittle and crumbles at the slightest touch. We've had more than a few accidents."

Ropert stepped up beside me as he spoke. "What do you have for food?" he asked.

Torquin shrugged. "We've managed to survive off of fish and a few crustaceans from the sea."

"But that isn't enough to keep your bellies full," I said, not trying to hide my frown. Then I turned to Ropert and placed a hand on his shoulder. "Torquin, this is Ropert."

Torquin extended his hand out to the tall warrior, and Ropert clasped it. The bandit's dark eyes flicked to the blood on Ropert's wrist.

"You're injured," he stated.

Ropert shrugged and retracted his hand.

"I may have some decent bandaging for that back at my home," the bandit said. "We may have nothing in terms of food, but we have abundance in clothing and blankets."

"I would appreciate that," Ropert said.

"So, what brings you out here?" Torquin asked. A small smile stole across his lips. "Certainly, you haven't come for the atmosphere or the delicacies."

I couldn't help but chuckle at his good humor. "No, we've come in search of Ikane. You haven't seen him, have you?"

Torquin shook his head. "I wish I had. How is he?"

"He's been better," Ropert grumbled and reached back to grab Beast's reins. He rummaged through his saddlebag as if on a mission.

"Perhaps you've seen a wolf then?" I asked. "Black?"

Torquin didn't need to think. He knew exactly what I was talking about. "Yes, a large black wolf ran through the city just last night. Startled half the people, it did. Its howl was heard for miles. The beast was headed for the cliffs."

It was Ikane. I was sure of it. And I was just as sure that he was headed for the small homestead cut into the side of the cliffs. He and I had taken refuge there while hiding among these bandits.

"If you're thinking of going after that creature, I wouldn't." Torquin said quickly, realizing that it was exactly my intent. "It was larger than a horse. And its fangs were the size of daggers."

I reached over to Shade Ranger's reins and gently guided her closer. She snorted and shook her head briefly.

"Can we leave our mounts with you? I should like to check the old homestead anyway."

He frowned. "Paige, that place is nearly impossible to get to. If the homes in the city are crumbling, surely the pathway along the cliff has disintegrated. Besides," he said and held his hand up to shield the morning light from his eyes, "do you see those clouds there? We're in for a storm today."

My eyes darted to the small balls of fluff in the sky, noting how they seemed to build at the top. They were tiny, and non-threatening, but I trusted Torquin's judgement.

"If we hurry, we should be able to be back before the storm hits," I said.

Torquin let out a rough breath. "It's dangerous, Paige. The storms here can brew up faster than a pot of tea."

"She won't relent," Ropert said as he stepped back to us with our bundle of rations. "We'd best check it out and satisfy her curiosity before the storm really does hit. Here," he said and jerked our sack of old bread, cheese, and dried fruit at the bandit. "It's not much, but we've got enough meat on our bones to go without for a while."

Torquin's eyes widened. "You... I... it's not... I mean, you need to eat too."

"We will," Ropert said with a wink. "Some fish, maybe?"

The bandit smiled broadly. "You can have all the crusty, salted, dried fish you can carry."

At the edge of the cliffs the vast Rethreal Sea crashed into the precipices below. Sticky ocean spray floated through the wind, reminding me of my home back in Daram. The wind was fierce and dark clouds, as Torquin had predicted, loomed overhead in preparation for a great storm.

It did not take long to find the crumbling pathway that hugged the face of the cliff like a deliberately placed vine. Last season it had been wide and sturdy enough for a wagon and a team of horses. Now, just like the homes in the Dead City, it was dilapidated and crumbling since the curse had been lifted.

My boot slipped on the first step around the rocks that opened to the pathway, and I clung to the cliff-face for support. Treacherous as it may be, I pressed forward. If Ikane were here, I'd find him.

We descended slowly, keeping close to the edge of the cliff for balance. The further we pressed on, the harsher the wind became. It seemed as if nature itself was against us, for the waves of the sea took on another attitude entirely. A blue flash of light darted across the gray clouds hanging over the water, followed by the rumbling of thunder that vibrated against my chest. Even the rocks themselves seemed to tremble.

The cold splatter of fresh rain struck my forehead.

"I don't like this," Ropert shouted over the hammering waves and brutal wind. "We should've searched the ruins of the garrison first."

I gripped a solid fissure behind me and hollered back at him. "All the more reason for us to search here! Ikane would have expected me to go to the garrison!"

We pressed on, wary over the road's mounting slickness as the rain fell.

And then the road narrowed. It was only wide enough to allow one person to pass with their back flattened against the cliff.

As a gigantic wave struck the bluffs, another flash of lightning split the sky. The loud crack of thunder vibrated through the rock. Ropert and I clung to the cliffside until the water receded.

"It's not much farther now," I said. "See the rift over there? That's where the homestead is."

Ropert grabbed my arm. "You're insane! Ikane couldn't have come here!"

I surveyed the rest of our route. An entire segment of the four-hundred-year-old road had completely crumbled away. We would be forced to jump over a five-foot gap. Ropert was right. Ikane didn't come this way.

A giant swell gathered and crashed against the cliff, showering us with cold water. We hugged the crags like barnacles on a ship as the water tugged on our clothing, threatening to pull us into the sea.

It pulled on the ledge as well, and a large segment of rock broke free beside my boot. I hastily stepped toward Ropert to more solid ground. He grabbed my hand as another wave struck the cliffs.

As soon as the water fell away, another brilliant shock of white light forked over the towering cliffs. Even the noise of the roaring waves and pelting rain could not mask the unbearable boom that nearly crippled my hearing and sent a shock of pain through my skull.

"Dagger!" Ropert roared, though I barely heard him through the ringing in my ears. He grabbed my arm as several large rocks, the size of cauldrons, came barreling down the side of the cliff.

With a quick jerk, he pulled me out of their path, nearly casting himself over the ledge in the process. The large rocks crashed into the fragile road beside me, tearing the pathway to shreds. Ropert scrambled back, dragging me along, as the slick pathway disintegrated beneath my boots. The weight of my falling body jerked his arm, causing him to drop flat onto his belly. My ribs struck the edge of the newly formed ledge. Sharp pain raced up my right triceps as my arm scraped along the edge. I jerked to a stop as Ropert's grip was all that spared my fall.

Ropert shook his drenched hair out of his eyes and proceeded to try and pull me up onto the ledge. A deep vein popped out on his forehead and neck as he strained. But he couldn't get enough leverage on the narrow passageway.

I swung one leg up to the pathway beside him, but as soon as my boot found the ledge, the section of rock broke free. I yelped as my body swung back and Ropert's grip on my arm slipped.

"Hang on!" he yelled over the raging wind and rain. The wound on his wrist must have torn open, for blood began to run from beneath his bracer down to our hands.

The next surge was even larger than the last. Ropert was forced to clutch my arm with one hand and a fissure beside him with the other as the water dashed against the cliff and sprayed us with needle-like foam. The water ripped another section of rock from under his chest. He pitched forward momentarily and then struggled to inch his body back to more solid ground. More rock crumbled away as he did so.

It was futile. We would both end up falling if he did not let me go.

He knew my thoughts.

His brows narrowed with warning. "Don't even think it, Dagger!"

"You know there is no other way!" I yelled back at him. My voice trembled. "Find Ikane and kill him!"

It would only delay Rion's design, but at least it would give Lonacheska's future children—mainly female—a chance to learn about her power before Rion would be strong enough to try and take her body.

Salt water and rain dripped from Ropert's lips. "Don't let go, Dagger! I can pull you up. But I can't do it without your help. My hand..."

His grip slipped again. After seeing him work his fingers the day before, I knew his muscles couldn't hold much longer. In spite of my acceptance of the situation, I whimpered in fear. I could hear my heartbeat in my head as I anticipated falling into the roiling waves of the sea. Tears burned my eyes as I felt his strength give way.

"No, Dagger!" His own tears mixed with the seawater upon his face.

I let go.

"Dagger, don't!" he roared as another section of rock broke free, exposing the left side of his chest.

Desperate to spare him, I twisted my wrist from his grip. He roared as I slipped away.

Time seemed to stand still.

My body plunged down the side of the cliff, through the bitter wind, then cut through the roiling surface of the sea.

Icy needles pierced my skin. The shock alone caused me to gasp, and I got a mouthful of water.

The noise of the currents and swells became a muffled roar beneath the churning waves. In an instant, my cloak became a threat to my survival as it tangled with my arms. I struggled to release the clasp and swam upward.

As my head cleared the water, chilling wind whipped my skin. Water burned my nose as I gasped at the air before a wave washed over me. My body rolled and pitched forward as the water drove me into the cliffs. I felt the impact in my back, and the old arrow wound flared up my spine and down my left leg. All air I had consumed exploded from my lungs in a violent burst.

The water receded, dragging me with it. Franticly, I tried to find my bearing. I swam blindly, desperate for air. Breaking to the surface again, I gasped. No sooner did I fill my lungs, another wave washed over me, tossing my floundering body towards the sharp cliffs a second time. Bracing for impact, I sheltered my head with my arms. Sharp pain ignited through my shoulder and hip as the sea slammed me into the bluffs and pulled me away again.

I swam upward a third time, and frantically gasped just as another wave pushed me down once more. I choked as I had inhaled water. The sea buffeted my flailing frame until it struck the rigid cliffs again, and this time a stinging pain zapped through my knee.

The water withdrew, pulling against me harder than I thought it should have. I suddenly realized that my body had become lodged in a hidden fissure in the cliffside.

Gasping, I broke free of the waves, and searched hysterically for a way out.

There. A cave-like shadow in the crevice ahead.

I struggled to shimmy my body from the sharp rocks as the roar of the sea grew louder behind me. Like a battering ram, the sea shoved me through the crevice, shooting me through the fissure like a badly aimed arrow. I dropped into a shallow pool below as ocean spray rained down on my back. A harsh echo blasted through my ears.

With trembling limbs, burning lungs, and aching bones, I pushed myself from the shallow pool. Another wave burst through the chasm and showered me with a last angry waterfall of cold saltwater before I forced my body to climb onto a slick, stone bank of the cave. In the darkness, I collapsed on my back, gulping air of musty, metallic scent.

"Let me out!" a small voice cried. I felt thumping against my waist where my firedust pouch was secured to my belt. "Help!"

Hastily, I opened the pouch. Bright light burst from the opening, and then the elusive firesprite climbed from the leather, dripping wet and shivering. She tumbled out of my belt-pouch and collapsed on the cold, slick surface of the black stone bank. Her hair, usually a long flame roiling off her head, was small and weak. Her wings were drenched, and one was horribly bent.

I flopped back against the bank as another wave of water rained harmlessly, but loudly, into the shallow pool. My chest heaved as I gasped. My body ached... almost worse than after the battle with the Leviathan Pirates.

"I told you that you were not safe with me," I panted, though I did find myself very fortunate to have her here with me. The light from her body, though dim, allowed me to see hundreds of spiraling stalagmites and stalactites protruding from the rock like the white and green teeth of a dragon. The ocean thundered outside, and shot through the crevice at regular intervals, masking the noise of dripping water from the tooth-like rocks on the ceiling.

Beyond them, a dozen openings of dark tunnels offered promise of escape.

"Y... you l...let go," she scolded through chattering teeth.

"I had to," I said. "Ropert would have been hurled into the sea with me." It was nothing short of a miracle that I was still alive.

The firesprite fluttered her wings, and a hint of heat wafted from her body to me. She stomped her foot in frustration when the broken wing failed to lift her.

"Look what y...you've done!"

I rubbed my hip where it smarted the most and sat upright again. The sprite shivered violently, her wings trembling. My brows furrowed, worried for her.

"You'll have to carry me," Mina said. "Don't look so worried. I won't burn you. Don't you know that I can control how much heat to give off?"

"I do now," I said as I held my hand out to her.

The warmth of her tiny body radiated into my skin as she climbed into my palm, yet she continued to tremble with cold. She took a deep, shaky breath, then looked up at me with her big, red eyes.

"I cannot survive long w...without sunlight."

"Then we had best get you out of here," I said and staggered to my feet. But upon placing weight on my right leg, horrible pain flared through my knee. I stifled a groan and glanced down at a large gash in my trousers. Blood soaked into the brown fabric from the injury, but there was nothing I could do for it now. I gritted my teeth and headed blindly down one of the large tunnels with the firesprite's luminous form lighting our way.

7

THE WHITE WARDENT

The copper and salt of the cavern's environment burned into my injuries, and the moisture maintained in my boots caused my feet to blister. I wrenched my body through narrow crevices and climbed over strange, gaping rock formations. The cave was cold and wet, ever pricking my face with the kisses of dripping water.

At one point, I thought my hips would never squeeze through a narrow hole, but the rock broke and I slithered down the rugged ripples of stone to splash into a shallow pond of green, metallic reeking water.

The sprite shrieked as she was once again drenched, and her brightness dimmed alarmingly. I snatched her from the water as quickly as I could, but the faded light from her body indicated that she was running out of time. Or was it my eyesight that was diminishing? The color of the rocks changed from the myriads of reds, whites, greens, yellows and blues until the mystical and unnatural beauty of the caves blurred into nothing but gray obscurities. In the sprite's waning light, all sense of direction became meaningless as I hovered between sleep and wakefulness. My frustration grew. Fatigue sapped motivation. Hunger drove the cold deeper into my belly.

Disoriented and hopelessly lost, I curled up on a slab of rock, shivered as tears stained my scraped cheeks, and slipped into uncomfortable sleep.

Green vines cascaded down brightly painted walls adorned with white, flowing curtains. Colorful pillows scattered upon a large bed within a chamber filled with the sweet scent of lilies. In the midst of this serenity stood a tall, graceful young man. His marble skin was wrapped in white fabric and his long frosty-white hair cascaded down his back like the flowing branches of a willow tree. And his eyes... his eyes were as red as rubies.

He stretched a slender hand towards me as if he would stroke my face.

"Daughter of Roanfire," he said with a tenor voice as smooth as cream over warm milk. "Wake. Walk. You must continue on."

The vision of the White Wardent vanished, bringing me back to the cold aching limbs of a battered body. I rose to my feet, immediately disoriented, and shivered with such intensity that my teeth chattered loudly. Stepping from the slab, my boots slipped into a puddle, and I stumbled into a wall where I scraped my hand against the sharp rock. I barely noted the bleeding.

After what seemed like hours, I found myself hunched over and convulsing. When my stomach finished straining to expel what wasn't there, I attempted to continue.

"Keep going," the firesprite encouraged as she sat upon my shoulder. She touched my cheek with one of her warm hands.

I hadn't even realized that I had halted.

Numbly, I climbed, wriggled, slipped, and crawled through tight, slick cavities of rock. Eventually, I gazed upon a spacious, stalactite-filled cavern with a placid lake of gray water. The ashen colors blurred and shifted as meager light beamed from a crevice high above. A soft tremor in the earth caused the tranquil lake to ripple. I blinked as a fantastic creature emerged from the far end of the expansive chamber.

The majestic body of a white, wingless dragon seamlessly slithered by impeding rock formations with a long, sinuous tail trailing after it. A cascade of webbed horns protruded from its head and down its lean neck. The creature, seemingly no bigger than a grand warhorse, approached.

"What is that?" the sprite whispered into my ear.

I rubbed my eyes, certain that I was hallucinating. "He's beau'iful." My speech slurred as bad as the blending colors of the rocks.

"He... he has the essence of... it can't be," the sprite stammered.

"What?"

"The White W...wardent," the little sprite whispered in awe through her shivering.

The creature's webbed ears twitched upon hearing her voice. His massive head turned to face us, showing the redness of his eyes... the same eyes I had seen in my vision. The white drake moved through the expanse of the cavern so effortlessly, he seemed to be floating. As he halted before me, the scent of lilies overpowered the rusty, metallic stench of the caves.

"The cold is draining thy life," he said in a milky, tenor voice.

I tried to calm my shuddering. Was I truly seeing this creature? Was it the White Wardent... or a drake thought to be extinct?

Slowly, my hand reached up to touch his scales, but he backed away.

"Follow me, child," he said and turned about.

The passages through which this creature moved were level and spacious, but my pace was sluggish as I limped after his sinuous tail. I stumbled over my own feet, even when there were no rocks to trip me up. I halted often to rest, standing in a daze.

Finally, the white drake paused to see what my delay was. I leaned hard against the rugged, cold wall as my vision blurred.

"Kea?" the sprite said in alarm. She clutched the collar of my shirt to keep from falling to the ground as I bent down and placed my hands on my thighs to rest.

"She is near delusional," the drake's voice rumbled as he approached.

I shook my head. My shivering had stopped. "No, I'm jus' tired."

"She has a fever," the sprite told the drake after placing one of her painfully hot hands on my neck. "And she's starting to look blue."

"It's hot in 'ere," I said and began to unlace my tunic. It was stifling, and my boots were burning my feet. I sat on the edge of a rock and began to unlace my boots.

"Thou hast been here too long," he said, a nervous glance spreading across the white scales that formed his brow. "We must make haste." With those words, he nudged me with his enormous nose, which distracted me from the task of removing my boots. I looked at the incredible beast and reached out to touch him again. He was so stunning.

"Lean on me, Daughter of Roanfire," he said as he slid his head under my arm. But my hands did not respond to grasp his horns. I slipped from his neck instead.

Everything darkened when my head collided with the ground.

The first thing I felt when my mind returned to consciousness was the sharp sting behind my eyes. And then the rest of my body screamed in accord. Muscles tensed, wounds bit, and the deep ache in my bones forced me to lay still. The smell of lilies was gone, replaced with a stench far worse than the brittle metallic pong of the caves.

Was he real? Did the White Wardent actually come to my aid? Was he still here?

I needed to know. I forced my eyes open, feeling a crustiness around them that seemed to glue them shut. When I moved my arm to rub the sleep away, I groaned as a sting of a knife seemed to sear through my shoulder.

"Oh, good!" I heard a light, smoky voice to my left. "You're waking up!"

After flinching at the bruise on my cheek, and my eyes were finally rubbed of sleep, I blinked at the source of light and warmth. At first, I saw vague shapes of orange I knew to be a fire. Gradually, my eyes took in the flames and the tall tower of logs surrounded by the gray stone of a hearth.

Something about the hearth was familiar.

Two, half spent candles, unlit, stood on the mantle. A wooden trunk, open, stood by my feet and a small stash of firewood sat beside it.

"Where are we?" I asked, hoping that the sprite's voice hadn't been my imagination. "What happened?"

The spark of the little sprite appeared on the burning logs as she leapt from the center of the fire down to a lower perch. She sat cross-legged on the glowing wood, looking much better than I remembered.

"You were dying," she said. "Not that you didn't deserve it. You shouldn't have let go of his hand in the first place."

"No, I mean... the white drake. Was that real?"

"Sure he was," she said with a grin that reached clear to her ears. "It was the White Wardent himself... well, sort of. He came in the form of a drake to help. After you fell unconscious, he carried you here." She waved to the chamber.

I turned my head to follow her motion, recognizing the doorway that was covered by an old woolen blanket. Upon seeing that threadbare curtain, memories flooded back to when Ikane and I had taken refuge here nearly a year ago. I then realized that the horrible stench was that of the rotting corpses in the tower. It festered as the windows were sealed shut with rock and mortar.

"It was mesmerizing to see him," the sprite continued, her voice soft and distant. "He moved with such grace and elegance, even when carrying your limp body. He made it seem effortless. After making you that bed of old blankets, he held his hands over your heart—"

"Hands? You mean he wasn't in drake form?" I interrupted.

She bit her lip, as if she wasn't supposed to have revealed that information. But then she shrugged. "Yes, he shifted into a man. How could you expect a drake that size to fit through the hallways and tight doorways of this miserable garrison?"

"Where is he?"

"He had to go. You can't expect him to use his power on that level forever, can you?"

I felt my heart sink, crushing my already bruised and battered body. "Did he say anything? Did he tell you where to find him?"

"No." She shrugged. "He said very little to me. He simply healed you of the fever and faded. If you're up to it, he boiled some water for you right there. Though he didn't need to do that. My firedust will keep it hot enough."

She pointed to a spot by the hearth, but I couldn't see it, and I wasn't brave enough to move my aching body to look.

A small prick of anger arose. He had communicated with me in a vision. He had even come to my aid, but he wouldn't tell me where he was. If he truly wanted me to defeat the Phoenix Witch, wouldn't he have shown me how? Or at least told me?

The sprite continued speaking, unaware of my conflicted emotions.

"He had me put what little firedust I could make into it. And you had better drink it all! That dust could've repaired my wing! Now I have to wait until I can harvest warmth from the sun to heal, so don't you dare turn your nose up at it."

The firesprite lay down on the burning log as if it were a reclining bed and played a tune on her charred flute. I supposed I needed to thank the sprite again. This little elemental creature was beginning to be my lifeline. First, she thwarted the assassins, then she was my light in the caves, and now she had given her firedust in order to heal me.

"Thank you... uh... I just realized that I still don't know your name," I said to her.

She paused her melody. "My name is Illumina," she answered quickly. "But you may call me Mina." She resumed playing her flute.

I smiled as my eyes drifted closed again.

"I like it," I mumbled.

Within moments, I fell asleep, listening to the crackling of the fire and Mina's lilting song.

Mina perched on my shoulder as I limped down the familiar corridor with faded paintings along the walls. I knew this place well. I knew exactly where the flight of stairs was that would lead to the great hall, and from there to the arched doorway framing the wide stone steps that descended into the courtyard.

Even though the White Wardent had supplied me with two cups of hot water mixed with sprite dust, it did little to ease the cramping of hunger in my belly. I intended to head down the old pathway of the garrison to the Dead City. Hopefully Torquin could spare me a little portion of fish, and with any luck, Ropert would be there.

As we emerged from the garrison, we were greeted by thick gray clouds hanging low in the sky. Heavy clusters of white snow swayed to the ground, and already, a thick layer blanketed the earth, dampening the sounds of the forest. The bitter chill from the ocean breeze would've frozen my cheeks instantly, were it not for the sprite dust coursing through my veins. I pulled the tattered, moth-eaten blanket over my head and more tightly around my shoulders and trudged onward.

Mina, seeing as she couldn't glean energy from the hiding sun, slipped back into my belt pouch with a threat to burn a hole in my side if I tried anything reckless. In spite of her disappearing into my pouch, a strange sensation crept up my spine, as if someone were watching me. I glanced over the snow-covered rubble of the courtyard, and warily scanned the road ahead for any sign of another being.

Was the White Wardent still here?

Nothing besides dark trees and stone, surrounded by the white snow, looked back at me.

I slogged on, and the pain in my knee flared as I tried to push through the deep snowdrifts on the road. The injury must have split open again, for I began to see little streaks of fresh blood in my wake.

Finding it too taxing to stay on the snow-laden road, I eventually ventured to my left, knowing that the snow wouldn't be as deep among the scattered stumps of dead trees. But also knowing that I would need to keep extra vigilant for the near undetectable noise of falling trunks.

The soft sound of a crack to my right indicated another tree about to fall. I turned quickly to see it crash into a tree standing beside it. Both of them toppled into the snow, near silent, in spite of only being a few yards away. The lack of sound caused a deep apprehension to well up inside of me. Perhaps I had best endure the pain in my knee and stick to the road.

A soft snap. Behind me.

Before I could turn to see where the tree was about to fall, I felt a sharp sting in my shoulder as a black blur struck into it... from a very peculiar angle. Instead of being crushed under the weight of a tree trunk, my body was propelled to my left so forcefully that I spun about twice before tumbling into the snow. Whatever had struck me, flew overhead, and crashed into the snow only two yards ahead.

A moment later, I heard the thud of the tree and a soft explosion of snow rained down on my back. I sat upright and jerked my head to the fallen tree, and then across the way to see what had knocked me out of the tree's path.

When I saw the black fur and muscled body of a wolf pushing himself from the snow, my eyes widened, and my heart leapt into my throat.

"Ikane," I breathed, barely daring to move. With all my heart I hoped that Rion wasn't controlling his lycanthrope form. I would not have the energy or strength to fight him off.

He shook the snow from his back, then turned his head to look directly at me. His emerald eye glowed vibrantly, like it did when he was in the heat of battle. I thought I saw a hint of relief fill his mismatched eyes, and then fear overpowered them. His ears lowered, his tail sank between his legs, and he took a few cautious steps back.

I knew then that it was indeed Ikane. Rion would have torn my throat out by now. I wondered how he had escaped the iron shackles that I had last seen cuffed about his wrists when he fled from Meldron.

"Don't run," I said quickly. "Please, don't run." My knee groaned as I struggled to my feet. "I made a promise. And I cannot keep that promise if you won't let me."

His eyes darted frantically from my face to my outstretched hand. Then he shook his head wildly, barely calming the hair standing on end at his neck. He didn't like something. It was as if he were resisting his own desire to stay with me.

"Ikane," I said his name fiercely. "I need you as much as you need me. You know that, don't you?"

The black fur standing on end across his back softened slightly at my voice.

I stretched my hand out further, pleading for him to come near. His eyes looked at my fingers as though they were fragile limbs made of delicate glass, and he shrank away, shaking his head again.

Before I could lunge at him and grab his fur, he leapt back, whirled, and darted into the Dead Forest. I watched as his powerful body dashed between the trees, growing smaller as he sprinted away.

"What was that!?" Mina shrieked from the pouch at my hip. An uncomfortable amount of heat radiated through the leather, and I worried that she was about to make good on her threat. Yellow hot light burst from the seams.

Hastily, I opened the pouch to see her bright red eyes glowering up at me. "I felt it! Don't try to deny it! I felt that... that... darkness! That vile anger! That... oh, how could you? I can't stay with you, even if you repel that darkness. It's too strong!"

"He's gone now," I sighed and sat back in the snow to take the pressure from my knee. Blood soaked my tattered trousers there, but I barely noticed it. I glanced back up at the path Ikane had taken.

Something inside me was disappointed that he hadn't stayed by my side. But then again, Ikane had pushed me out of the path of the falling tree. He was still nearby - watching, protecting. In spite of being tormented by the Phoenix Witch, Ikane was still Ikane. The kind-hearted, chivalrous Leviathan Prince that I knew and loved.

My feet trudged through the snow, exasperating the heat of my fever and the sting in my knee. By the time I entered the crumbling city and plodded through the deserted streets, my neck was sticky with sweat. The throbbing of my fever-induced headache pulsed through my skull like the hammering waves of the sea. Upon reaching the familiar dwelling, I leaned heavily in the arched threshold of the doorway and knocked.

I heard scuffling noises behind the wooden door as someone moved to open it. The door creaked open and warm light spilled onto my chilled face as I looked up at Torquin. His brown eyes were turned down with pity at first, and then widened in disbelief.

"Paige!" he cried. His hand shot out to grab my wrist and pull me into the warmth of his home. "Come in! What happened? You look terrible. Ropert said that you were dead... that the sea had swallowed you!" As soon as he closed the door, shutting out the chill of winter, he wrapped his arms around me. "I told you it wasn't safe. The storms here come so swiftly."

My eyes darted over his shoulder to the frail looking woman trying to rise from her chair by the fire. Malese. She was weak and struggled to move her starved limbs.

"Paige! Come sit by the fire and warm yourself," Malese waved, giving up on trying to rise.

Before I could protest, Torquin steered me to the vacant seat beside his wife. My body sank into the chair as I felt the heat of the fire penetrate my frozen clothing.

"Torquin," Malese began as she reached out and grabbed my hand. "Be a dear and fetch some hot tea for her. She's burning with fever."

"I don't mean to be any trouble," I told them, though Torquin had already stepped into the tiny kitchen and pulled a mug from a shelf.

"Not at all," Malese said quickly. Her smile was sincere, though it was hard not to pity her due to her sunken cheeks and eye-sockets. Perhaps it was the light of the fire that made her look so frail. Her long hair was stringy and thin, hanging over her bony shoulders like straw.

To keep from staring, I averted my gaze to the interior of their tiny homestead. It was then that I noted the vacant cradle sitting below the window. I searched the rest of the home for the little boy, Pan. He would be about two years of age by now. There was no indication of a child at play on the dry floorboards. Two little toys, a wooden horse and a ball made from colorful scraps of cloth, sat on what was otherwise bare shelves. My heart caught in my throat, thinking the worst.

"Where is Pan?" I asked, my voice cracking.

There was a sudden clatter in the small kitchen as Torquin accidently dropped a mug onto a plate. Malese lowered her gaze and her smile faded.

"You don't mean..." I couldn't finish. "When?"

Malese hugged her shoulders, rubbing her bone-thin arms with fingers that could do little to warm her. Torquin was the one who finally spoke as he came from the kitchen.

"Two weeks ago," he said in a whisper as he handed me a mug filled with hot peppermint and lavender tea.

I took the mug from him but barely felt the heat seep into my hands. Hot, angry tears burned my eyes.

I felt Malese's hand on my arm. "It's alright," she whispered. "He is in a better place now."

I shook my head fiercely. "I should've been here... I could've helped..."

"No," she said quickly. "No one could have changed what happened. If it wasn't hunger, then it would have been the illness in his bones eventually."

My eyes were blurry as I looked up at her for an explanation.

Her smile was soft and sympathetic as she looked up at her husband. "We assume that Pan was afflicted with the same illness that Torquin had as a boy. Torquin was left with a withered arm, but Pan was too pure for this world."

I swallowed hard. "I am so sorry."

"It wasn't your fault," Torquin said. "Now drink your tea. I will fetch some dried fish for you."

"Is Ropert here?"

"He left two days ago," Malese told me. Her already sunken eyes deepened with worry in the light of the fire. "He was sure that you had perished. The poor man... for one as strong as he, he deeply mourned for you. How did you survive?"

I groaned inwardly at the fact that Ropert had a head start to Meldron. I would need to hurry to catch up to him before he declared my death to King Sander.

"There is an expansive cave system beneath the city," I answered as Torquin moved back to the kitchen. "It was sheer luck that the waves drove my body into a crevice hidden in the cliffs."

"Luck indeed," Torquin stated as he set a plate of dried fish on the small table between the chairs. "To survive three days in a cave is unheard of, but clearly you are suffering from hypothermia. Stay and rest until you are well again."

I sipped at the tea, grateful to have something other than firedust as a meal. "I deeply appreciate your offer, but I must find Ropert as soon as possible."

"At least allow us to dress your wounds and outfit you with proper gear for this horrid weather," Malese said. "We may have little when it comes to food, but warm clothing and blankets we have in abundance."

I lowered the mug of tea and smiled. "That would be most welcome."

8

THE WOLF

The young couple graciously tended to my injuries and sutured the gash in my knee. I washed briefly and was provided with a thick pair of trousers, a woolen tunic, extra stockings, and a long cloak trimmed in soft, grey fur. They even gave me some fur-lined gloves that had most likely belonged to a noble, for the workmanship was exceptional. The couple also supplied me with a woolen blanket as my bedroll, and a heavy sack of dried fish. After long embraces, they bade me farewell.

As the sun set behind me, I barely crossed the threshold to the living woods beyond the Dead Forest. From the deep throbbing in my head, and blurred vision, I knew that my fever was soaring.

"You'll never reach that grumpy blond warrior with that fever," Mina said from the pouch at my hip. "You need more firedust... not that I'd be happy to part with it again even if I had managed to make some. You need to rest."

As much as I wished to object, sleep sounded terribly inviting. "You're probably right," I grumbled.

"I know I am," she declared. "Over there." She leaned out of my pouch and pointed to my right. A tall, majestic pine tree towered overhead, its thick needle-covered fans blanketed with snow. "There should be shelter inside."

I didn't have the energy to argue. Crouching low, I did as instructed and pushed past the heavy branches. Snow fell from the pine needles and down the neck of my tunic. But I didn't flinch. It actually suppressed my headache for an instant. After crawling inside, I discovered that the large, snow laden branches of the pine tree became a flawless, warm canopy. It was tall enough for me to sit upright, and wide enough to stretch my body. I spread out the woolen blanket, tucked my arm under my head, and curled up on the soft pine-carpeted earth.

The full moon broke through churning mist, illuminating the snow cloaked landscape with a hostile grayness that leached all warmth from the world. A lonely tree reached skeletal fingers towards the ashen sky with the weight of countless obscure creatures clinging to the branches.

The howl of a wolf penetrated the dusky atmosphere.

Howling.

I heard it before the dream fully faded from my mind. My eyes darted open to the dark canopy of the pine tree tent, with the little candle-of-a-firesprite curled up beside me. Ikane must have woken from the same nightmare... and he was nearby.

I was grateful that the sprite seemed to sleep through his howling. Surely, she would have scolded me again for even considering helping him.

Cautiously, I moved away from Mina, and ducked outside. I flinched as the snow crunched under my feet. The night was far colder than I expected, realizing just how much the pine tree-tent was holding in warmth. The thick clouds had moved from the sky, revealing a few specks of stars and the bright silvery light of an almost full moon. My breath plumed in the air... reminding me too much of the dream, and I shuddered.

I heard the snap of a branch to my left and whirled just as an emerald glow appeared through the branches. Not wanting to startle me, he had purposefully allowed that branch to break. Though it still baffled me how his footsteps could remain so silent.

"Ikane," I whispered.

His ears were lowered as he came into view, but he approached nonetheless. I reached my hand out to him. He hesitated barely a blade's width away from my fingers. I could feel the hot breath from his moist, black nose against my skin.

I longed to close that distance between us. However, the choice needed to be his. I couldn't force him to stay, as much as I willed it. Aching to support him, my mind searched, opened, and beckoned for him to accept my help.

And then his nose touched the tips of my fingers.

I slipped into his mind by accident. My awareness was suddenly pummeled with his frenzied thoughts. *I can't believe I am here. My beautiful little Brendagger— how much danger she is in with me. I do not even know if I will stay in this form for much longer. I am a monster... a beast... my brothers were right. I deserve to die.*

Impressions of a family screaming in terror scorched my mind as two children and a young mother scrambled to a far corner of their cabin. The father lay dead on the wooden floor, with the dinner table turned over. His vision then morphed into the murder of an elderly woman out collecting firewood.

But I cannot face this demon. And if I keep her from it, it will only come after her again when I am gone. I will stay with you, little Brendagger. But oh, how I wish you knew the danger you are in.

His memories dashed through me like a panic-stricken herd of deer until his thoughts began to mingle with my own. We were unable to discern our own thoughts. We feared Rion and longed for the simple life of our homes. We remembered sailing the Rethreal Sea on vast Leviathan Pirate ships, and reminisced of feasts at the Daram Keep after a victory of a Leviathan attack. We saw faces of brothers, caretakers, and friends. We tasted the sharp, sea-like victuals eaten on the Leviathan Isles and the tantalizing, earthen diet of the Roanfireiens. We grew, trained and fought for our homes... until we met in Daram.

We recalled the unease of strangers facing each other on Daram's training arena. The crispness of the autumn air that day filled our thoughts with that moment. I had admired the impossible swiftness in his arms as he manipulated his twin swords, the same way he had respected my bold attempts to surprise him.

When we recalled his green eye sparking with every stroke of his weapon, we were driven apart.

The delicate power that I had used to battle against the Phoenix Witch grew, swarming through our minds in the form of warm, white lights. Like fireflies in the night, they fused together to form a veil between us so that we were no longer entangled in our thoughts.

Finding my body, I gasped and stumbled back. Ikane too, gathered air into his lungs. Our thoughts had been so knotted that we had forgotten such a simple task as to breathe.

Ikane's sapphire and emerald eyes blinked up at me, wide and somewhat startled. *What just happened?* I heard his voice so clearly as if he had spoken it.

A little smile stole across my lips. "I can hear your thoughts, Ikane," I whispered.

He didn't seem impressed. *Then you know what I have become. You know that you are not safe by my side. This form of mine is the only thing keeping her at bay. When I am human, I am completely at her mercy. And it is only a matter of time before she discovers a way to manipulate my wolf form.*

"I know," I said softly and reached out to him again.

This time he ducked under my hand and pressed the top of his head against it, his eyes closing in conflicted enjoyment of my touch. My fingers curled into his rough, black fur. And then I stepped forward and embraced him. His head slid up to my neck until I could hear a soft whimper at the back of his throat.

Kea, he said. *I am so sorry for hurting you. What I have done is terrible, but what pains me the most is what I did to you.*

"It wasn't your doing," I said softly.

I had hoped that the sun would be shining today, but sometime in the night, a thin layer of clouds had rolled in. They were thinner than the snow-filled ones of the previous day, but they were clouds nonetheless. Mina was delayed yet another day in fashioning her firesprite dust, and I knew she would have a fit once she realized that Ikane was just outside.

I looked down at the sprite still curled up on the blanket Torquin and Malese had given me. Her body brightened slightly at every intake of breath, but it was the burn mark on the blanket that made me marvel. She had managed to scorch a perfect mark of her tiny fire body into the wool.

Ikane stirred outside, and I suddenly recognized that the fortune of communicating with Ikane came with a price. Our thoughts and feelings were no longer private. I felt his jaw open in a wide yawn as he stretched his large body and splayed his massive paws. I felt the cold snow beneath his paws and the way the pine needles brushed against the fur on his back. His lungs took in the crisp morning air of the woods, and along with it, the scent of a deer not far from our location. His ears twitched as he listened to the hoofs tenderly walking through the snow.

We didn't have time to hunt, though the thought of venison made me salivate. I had enough dried fish and time was of the essence.

I turned to my task at hand.

"Mina," I said, gently at first. When she didn't stir, I repeated her name more loudly. "Mina, wake up."

Her body flared as she startled awake, actually catching the blanket on fire. She jumped out of the way to let me pound it out.

"Well, that's what you get for waking me like that," she folded her arms across her chest, not the least bit apologetic for the new hole in my bedroll.

"I suppose I did deserve that," I grumbled as I rolled it up.

One of her fiery brows rose. "What do you mean?"

"Well... uh... I..."

"I feel it! Him!" She suddenly roared, her body igniting again. "He's here, isn't he?!"

I flinched.

What's going on in there? Ikane's thoughts broke into my mind. He probably sensed my fear of getting burned by an angry firesprite.

"That wolf is filled with Thrall!" She roared. "Shadows billow from him like the black smoke of a green pine needle campfire! How can you endure his presence?"

"He needs my help," I told her. "You don't need to stay with me."

"You think I have a choice?!" she turned her back to me, showing off her bent wing. "I would have left you long ago if my wing wasn't broken!"

For some reason her words stung.

Kea, are you alright? Ikane felt it too. It was a little annoying how closely we were linked.

"I'm fine," I told him quickly. "We'll be out soon."

"WE?! Don't tell him that I'm here!" Mina barked, and this time several sparks leapt off her hair, nearly catching the pine needles on fire. A spot on the ground smoldered for a moment before I stamped it out.

"He already knows, Mina. I can't hide you from him," I told her. "And to add to the bad news, the sun still isn't shining."

"Gah!" she groaned with clenched fists. She stomped her tiny feet like a miniature bull. "I will stay until you find dust for my wing or the sun returns, but the darkness around him is unbearable! I will be on my way as soon as I am healed."

I nodded. "I understand. And I will do what I can to find you some sprite dust."

"You'd better," she grumbled as she marched towards me.

I hesitated to place my hand down for her to climb into it. She must have sensed my apprehension and her fire dimmed. After I tucked her into my belt pouch again, I climbed from the shelter of the tent, feeling my stiff knee ache.

I was taken aback at how clearly I could see through Ikane's eyes. He looked upon me with fondness for my messy hair and flushed cheeks. To him, I appeared beautiful and strong, though I felt anything but.

*G*et on my back, Ikane ordered when I paused to catch my breath for the fifth time. The muscles in my legs burned and so did my lungs. The fever drained every ounce of energy from my body and the very fabric of my clothing burned my tender skin. The throbbing in my skull eased only momentarily after I grabbed a handful of snow to place on my forehead.

"We will be too slow," I told him.

Not any slower than we are going now. He came to my side and leaned his heavy body against my hip. *Don't think that I do not feel the dull pain in your stomach, the way your knee smarts with the sutures, or the fever that causes your muscles to ache and skin to burn. Just as you feel my senses, I feel yours. Get on.*

My face was splotched with melted snow and feverish perspiration as I reluctantly swung my leg over his tall back. Seeing as he was about the size of a small horse, I was forced to shift my body to his center, leaving my feet a few inches from the snow. It took Ikane a moment to alter his center of gravity under my weight, and I felt his legs strain; not only beneath me, but through our linked senses. As I gripped the fur at the side of his neck for balance, I felt the tug on my own skin. The sensation of being both rider and mount made us clumsy, but we soon found a balance that was both comfortable and effective.

I crouched low to his neck, feeling his fur tickle my cheek as he rushed past the trees with natural effort. Nonetheless, it did not take long before the muscles in his legs burned as he carried me over the drifts of snow.

Stop it, he scolded me. *Your thoughts are making me tired.*

Sorry, I mumbled.

Ikane halted. *How did you do that?*

What? I asked, before realizing I hadn't vocalized the words.

It was at that moment that I detected a rigid thread slither into my mind and grab hold of my thoughts. Not a second later, the familiar zing of lightning struck my mind. The burning sensation caused every fiber of my being to feel as though it were engulfed in an inferno. My jaw seized, and my lungs refused to gather breath. I barely noted the warmth of blood trickling from my nose through the intense redness behind my vision. My body convulsed, expelling the meal I had eaten but an hour before. I slid from Ikane's back and landed hard in the snow.

The instinct to protect myself drove my body and soul into summoning my power. The magic simmered through my body, slowly quenching the pain one drop of water at a time. Fragments of energy sluggishly mended to form a mirror-like shield against Rion's assault. Before the ringing in my ears ceased, I heard the excruciating howl of a wolf echo through my mind.

Kea! Ikane cried out in agony, beckoning for my aid.

Get away from him! I growled at the Phoenix Witch as I wedged myself between her and Ikane's mind. Like a spider clinging to its prey, her unyielding thread snared to his mind, feeding him with a constant stream of unbearable fire.

Without a second thought for my own safety, I took hold of her fiery thread to yank it away from the man I loved. But the pain of her searing heat was only diverted to me. I cried out in agony as her power burned through my mind.

Kea, Ikane called to me again. I was relieved to no longer hear agonizing torture in his voice. But now, it was filled with fear for me. I was barely able to resist her fury, and my shield did little to deflect her power.

Kea, Ikane said again, pushing into my mind. *Use my strength!*

He did not give me an option. He drove his energy into my thoughts, fueling my power with a love that overwhelmed all other emotion. It was the same love and self-sacrifice that Rion had ached to devour on the day she first sensed him. Slowly, our energy drove her fire from my hands. Like a terrible ice-storm, our shared power gradually expanded upon her thread, nulling her blaze so that it hardened like steel in a smithy shop.

Rion's roar was earsplitting. *Don't think that you've triumphed, Phoenix Daughter! The Leviathan is still mine!*

As quickly as she struck, she was gone.

I gasped for breath but got a mouthful of snow instead. Coughing, I pushed myself from the snow-covered ground and blinked away the redness in my vision just as Ikane came to my side. His cold nose pressed up against my cheek and I quickly wrapped my arms about his neck to bury my face in his black fur.

"I'm so sorry, Ikane," I whispered.

His wolf-body shifted to nuzzle across the back of my neck in the best possible embrace a wolf could offer. He too, was trembling with fear and weakness.

You drove her back, he said without hiding his tone of awe.

I pulled away and searched his mismatched eyes. "WE drove her back," I replied. *I did not have the strength to contend with her. I could not have done it without you.*

Quiet sobbing caught my ringing ears. Mina! She wasn't in my belt pouch! Hastily, I searched the snow to discover the little sprite sitting in a puddle of melted slush a few yards away. She hugged her knees and tears steamed off her cheeks as she rocked back and forth in hysterical fear. She looked up at me, her red eyes wide with horror. She sobbed all the harder when Ikane came into her view.

"Get away!" she shouted at him and scrambled back until her wings brushed up against the shallow snowbank. "Don't come any closer!"

His ears lowered as he shrunk back.

"I can't endure the misery that seeps from that wolf any longer!" the firesprite sobbed. "It eats away at my heart. It burns! I can't stay!"

I scooped her from the wet snow and cradled her in my hands like a wounded butterfly. "I will find firedust as soon as I can, and you shall be free to go your own way."

She sniffed loudly and looked up at me with a deep pleading in her wide, fiery eyes. "If only the sun would return... I would be on my way this very moment. Can you not shelter me with the White Wardent's power? It is said that he does it for the sensitive nature of the elemental sprites."

"Believe me. I would do it if only I knew how," I assured her.

She wiped at the tears that had already evaporated from her cheeks and took a deep breath. The candle-like flame that resembled her hair lengthened with her oxygen intake. "I suppose I have no choice... The darkness nearly consumed you, but you repelled it."

I looked over my shoulder to Ikane. "And I shall continue to do so until I find a way to destroy it."

The sprite nodded with reluctant satisfaction and allowed me to slip her back into my pouch. Wearily, I turned back to Ikane.

"Let's keep moving," I said.

His ears perked slightly as he turned about and guided the way to Meldron again. The shame and dread that soared through him was deep, and although I attempted to reassure him that it was not his doing, he struggled to believe it. Eventually, we resolved to spare our energy to communicate and focus solely on haste. Our bodies were both spent from the confrontation with Rion.

I smell fire, Ikane said late into the evening. I smelled it too, but it was through Ikane's nose that I could detect it. Not long after, we caught sight of a campfire flickering through the trees. I cautiously approached the little campsite as the wolf slinked away into the nearby underbrush.

A single tent was pitched in the snow and two horses lazily hung their heads in sleep. Only after nearing did I recognize the animals as Shade Ranger and Beast. And then I saw the man sitting by the fire. His shoulders were slumped. Why was he not closer to Meldron by now?

He must have heard me approach, for he suddenly leapt to his feet, drew my sword from his belt and whirled to face me. The tip of the hardened steel halted at my throat.

My heart ached at the sight of his bloodshot eyes and tear-stained face. "Ropert," I said.

As I stepped into the firelight, his face went white.

"You're dead," he stammered and fell back two steps. "You fell from the cliffs. I watched the waves smash you into the rocks."

"There is a cave under the cliffs," I said. "The waves pushed me inside."

He wildly shook his head in disbelief and he took another step back. "You've come to haunt me, haven't you? I'm sorry, Dagger! I never meant to shun you as a friend. Please, leave me in peace!"

"Ropert!" I snapped. "I'm not dead!"

He blinked, still pointing his sword at me with a trembling hand.

I groaned inwardly. I did not have the energy to fight him, but I saw no other way. With all the strength I had left, I pushed the sword away and rammed my fist into his elbow, forcing him to arch up in order to keep his arm from breaking. This also left his ribs wide open. In a real battle, I would have stepped forward and rammed my elbow into them. But, because he was my friend, I whipped his arm down, wringing the sword from his hand instead, and pulled his wrist behind his back. He groaned and arched forward against the strain on his shoulder.

"I am not dead," I repeated, breathing harshly into his ear. With that, I released him. My fingers could barely hold my sword.

He rubbed his shoulder as he stared at me, and then his blue eyes shimmered with tears of joy and relief. He took two steps forward and pulled me into a suffocating hug, burying his face into the nape of my neck. A small sob escaped his throat as I dropped my sword into the snow and returned the embrace.

"You idiot," he whispered as he crushed me to him. "I told you it wasn't safe." He was warm and solid... but trembling. He pulled away. "You're burning with fever!"

As if my body wanted to confirm that statement, a shiver raced down my spine. At this, he removed his cloak. The warmth of it seeped into my body as he added it to my shoulders. Then Ropert crushed me to him again, wrapping me in his warm arms. After a moment, he pulled me down to the fire with him.

"Here," he said and reached around the log to retrieve a mug filled with something hot and steaming. He pushed it into my hands. "It's not much. But it should warm you. You need a healer."

I gratefully took the mug from him. "I thought you would be in Meldron by now."

He looked down at his hands. "I needed time... I thought..."

I understood. He didn't need to explain.

I took a sip of the contents of the mug, finding that it was a simple concoction of peppermint tea.

"Hold on." His head jerked up. "How did you get here so quickly? You couldn't have walked all that way. Not in your condition."

I swallowed a spicy mouthful of tea, feeling it race down my throat at warm my belly. "I found Ikane," I said and turned to the underbrush where the wolf was hiding. I waved for him to come.

Slowly, the large, black wolf slinked closer, keeping his head low in an attempt to appear non-threatening. Ropert stiffened and snatched the sword from the ground.

My had shot out and grabbed Ropert's arm before he could get to his feet. "This form of a wolf is the only thing keeping Rion at bay."

Ropert's blue eyes darted from me to the wolf. Then his eyes narrowed at the animal. "I was looking forward to killing you, Leviathan," he hissed in a tone that bordered on threat.

Ikane's ears flattened. *I don't understand,* he said to my mind. *I've been nothing but a friend to him.*

I'm sorry, Ikane. I replied as he sat down a few paces away from us. I smiled bitterly, remembering the time I first discovered that Ikane was a Leviathan. I had treated him in the same manner. *He just needs time.*

Ropert stood abruptly. "Come," he announced and extended his hand to me. "You need to rest to break that fever."

I took another sip of the hot tea and took his hand. He pulled me to my feet. My eyes glanced down to my little belt pouch where the soft glow of Mina's light escaped between the worn seams. Surely, she would enjoy resting within the warm flames of the fire tonight.

"You look as though you could use some rest too," I said to Ropert. "Ikane can keep watch for us."

But the look of distrust that Ropert blatantly gave Ikane spoke for him. "I would love to get some rest," he said. "But I don't trust a traitor to watch over me when I sleep."

My jaw clenched as I withdrew my hand from his. "I trust him, Ropert. And you should too."

Discreetly, I slipped my hand into my pocket and felt the heat of the little sprite against my fingertips. She latched onto my forefinger so that I could withdraw her. I turned me back to Ropert and crouched down by the fire.

"Perhaps I should keep watch instead," I said and held my hands out to the flames as if to warm them. The little sprite leapt from my hand into the fire. I cringed as she tumbled into the smoldering ashes, then scrambled to hide beneath the glowing coals of the logs.

Ropert groaned and gripped my arm to pull me to my feet. "I'm sorry, Dagger. But he is the reason we've failed every mission given to us by the Lady Caitelyn. I just... I can't trust him."

His words bit deeper than they should have. I stood and whirled to face him. "The only thing I do not trust about him is that accursed soul residing within his mind. If he does anything to betray or hurt us, I can assure you that it is not his doing." Without waiting for his reply, I pushed by him and ducked into the tent.

I waited to see if Ropert would reconsider allowing Ikane to take watch, but his shadow retreated to his perch by the fire. Disappointed, weary, and aching, I curled up into the warm bedroll.

He really doesn't like me, does he?

It sure seems that way, my thoughts grumbled. Even so, it was a good sign that Ropert had reacted to Ikane the way that he did. It meant that he was beginning to believe me about Rion.

9

ASSASSIN

"Kea," a small voice hissed angrily into my ear. "Kea, wake up."

I forced my weary eyes to open and turned to gaze directly upon the form of the firesprite standing on my makeshift pillow. Although it was clearly early morning, her glowing body seemed more subdued than I recalled, and she was shivering. Her wings trembled and the flame roiling from her head was short and flickered like a candle struggling to stay alight in the wind.

I sat upright in alarm. "What's wrong? Are you alright?"

"That l...lout of a man dumped s... snow on the fire!" she grumbled, trying to keep her voice down as she shivered. "I was still sleeping!"

Ropert is breaking camp, Ikane's voice sounded through my head as he was clearly aware of my conversation with the firesprite. I couldn't help but chuckle at the thought of snow falling over the sprite. Gently, I scooped her into my hand.

"Is the sun shining today?" I asked.

"It looks p... promising, but the clouds s... still hang low," she replied as she rubbed her shoulders. The friction caused little sparks to fly across her skin.

"Dagger?" Ropert's voice sounded from just beyond the tent. I tucked the sprite into my belt pouch just before he pulled the flaps aside and stuck his head in. "Good. You're awake. How are you feeling?"

"Better," I said as I pushed the blankets from my legs and reached for my boots.

Liar, Ikane interrupted. *You are aching all over, and your fever still hasn't broken.*

He doesn't need to know that, I warned him sternly.

"Kea?" Ropert asked, obliviously disturbing our conversation. "Are you well? You look dazed."

"Yes, I am fine," I said, shaking my head. "I was talking to Ikane."

Ropert looked back at the wolf over his shoulder. Ikane stood just beyond the tent and his ears lowered at Ropert's glare. "How?" he asked.

I stuck one foot into my boot. "Well, we sort of have a link. I can hear his thoughts and he can hear mine."

"You two can communicate... telepathically?"

"I suppose," I said and pulled my other boot on. "But it's a little deeper than that. We share each other's senses as well."

Ropert's dark blonde brows furrowed as he bit his bottom lip. "Could you smell the burnt fish this morning?"

I gave him a crooked smile. "What?"

He didn't just burn it, Ikane said. His mind replayed Ropert frantically trying to blow the flames out as the fire engulfed the fish he had placed on a stick. The fish turned black and disintegrated.

Ropert shrugged and scratched his chin. "With that answer, I suppose you didn't. I was trying to warm some of the dried fish and it simply caught fire. It makes for excellent tinder if you ask me. Tastes like it too." He wrinkled one side of his nose in disgust.

I laughed, and it was the first time I had done so in months.

Ropert couldn't help but smile in return.

"You certainly seem to be in better spirits," Ropert finally said. "Let's break camp. We've got a few days before we need to be back in Meldron. We've got time to keep the pace slow." He began to slink back out of the tent.

My smile faded. "Wait," I said in a low voice, knowing that what I was about to say would test his limits.

He paused and looked up at me.

"I can't go back... not yet."

His brows furrowed in disbelief. "What? You were ordered to return to Meldron once you found Ikane."

I nodded fiercely. "I know. But you know as well as I, that once I return, I will become a prisoner in the court. I need to search for the White Wardent. I need his help. It is the only hope I have. He can teach me to defeat this curse once and for all."

Ropert rubbed the back of his neck, clearly struggling with the decision to disobey the king. "Tell me this," he finally said. "*Where* will you look?"

"The Glacial Empire," I said, happy to finally have a destination to begin my search. "A letter was sent to Emperor Skarand centuries ago. I think it will hold some answers. If I can find that letter, then I'm sure I can defeat Rion."

Ropert sighed and crawled into the small confines of the tent. His broad shoulder bumped up against mine as he sat down beside me.

"King Sander trusts me," he began. "I can't simply disobey, even if I want to support you."

My brows rose, and I purposefully pulled them together to mimic his puppy face when he wanted a meal. "Please?"

He chuckled and put his arm around me, squeezing me to his side. "Don't look at me that way," he said. He then continued in a weighty tone. "I know the thought of returning to Meldron frightens you."

"It's more than that, Ropert. I need to get to the Glacial Empire. If King Sander has his way, I'll be sent to the desert kingdom instead. Please, help me... help Ikane."

Ropert's smile faded at the mention of Ikane. His eyes turned to the tent flap, and his sidelong embrace slackened. He couldn't see past the thick, white canvas, but I could feel his eyes burrowing through it as if to glower at the wolf standing at the tree line. "All this for the Leviathan Prince..."

I waited patiently, knowing that he was wrestling with a painful decision. Finally, his arm dropped from my shoulders and he shook his head. My heart sank as he lowered his eyes. "I can't, Dagger. I will not betray my king."

Ikane felt my despair and the thought of simply running away together crossed our minds at the same moment.

"But," Ropert continued, bringing hope back into my thoughts. "I will not leave your side. Even if you are forced to wed the Tolean Prince, you shall not go to Toleah alone."

I turned to him, startled. "What? No, Ropert. You can't come to Toleah with me! You will become a slave!"

"A slave or not, at least I will know that you are safe," he said. A grin stole across his lips. "Perhaps I shall even learn the art of their fine Ridarri Warriors." He moved his arms in a strange manner that made me want to laugh. I couldn't, so I opted for a smile instead.

The Tolean Ridarri Warriors were known for disarming any opponent with their bare hands. I had seen them do it before, when I had been a member of the White Fox Resistance.

"And, I've heard, that the Tolean Prince is a curious man. He may even travel to the Glacial Empire with you, if you ask."

I wasn't satisfied, but I swallowed hard. "You've done some research on him?"

"I've asked around," Ropert shrugged.

"Very well," I whispered, feeling a lump of fear well up in my throat. The thought of marrying the Tolean prince frightened me.

"Now," Ropert said brightly and bumped my shoulder with his. "Let us be on our way. I don't think my stomach can handle much more of the dried fish. We should at least make a stop in Toltak for some bread."

I got to my knees and began to roll up the bed as Ropert slinked out of the tent.

Kea? Ikane asked. *What did Ropert mean about Toleah? Is there something I don't know about?*

I frowned, feeling the apprehension turn to knots in my gut. *You must have realized from our conversation that there is talk about me becoming the bride of the Prince of Toleah. Because most of our crops were destroyed by the Leviathan Pirates, Roanfire needs the food that Toleah can offer. King Sander is eager to accept.*

The Tolean Prince... Ikane's voice drifted off as worry pounded into his chest. I felt it radiate into his throat. His hopes trembled in his mind, revealing a long-dreamed-of wedding on the bow of a grand ship.

Stop it, I grumbled and pushed his thoughts away. Ikane and I could never be, though I felt that in his heart he held out hope for unity between Roanfire and the Leviathan Pirates.

After tossing our meager belongings out of the snow-covered shelter, Ropert and I collapsed the tent in a matter of minutes and secured our gear to the horses.

It was not long before our mounts trotted through a vast field laden with snow. Ikane was forced to keep a good distance from the horses. Beast, in particular, didn't like the wolf around.

Warm sunlight broke through the scattered clouds and rained down on our shoulders. The balminess caused the snow to turn to slush beneath our horses' hooves. And Mina, the little spitfire-of-a-candle, was finally able to absorb sunlight. She perched her tiny fire-body discreetly upon my saddle horn and turned her face towards the golden rays. The flame on the top of her head grew and trailed after her like a brightly burning torch in the breeze.

"I'll be able to heal my wing tonight," she sighed with a smile, and her wings trembled with excitement.

I smiled down at her. Although I was just as eager to see her healed, I knew I would miss her.

Kea, Ikane called my attention to him, jarring me from my reverie. His voice was quiet and far off, but it didn't detract from the urgency and alarm that filled it.

"Dagger!" Ropert's warning followed. "Get down!"

Out of instinct, I ducked low to Shade Ranger's mane. The whistle of an arrow zipped above my head. I watched the dark shaft as it lost momentum a few yards ahead and fell, tip down, into the snow. Black and red fletching protruded from the whiteness.

I whirled to see Ropert already charging towards the five assassins on horseback with dark paint smudging their faces. The archer already held another arrow between his fingers and pulled it against the string of his bow. Before the archer could release his second arrow, a black blur slammed into his side, knocking him from the saddle. The arrow spun from his grip as the bow was ripped from his hands by the teeth of the wolf. A strangled scream broke through the snowy landscape as Ikane bit down on the assassin's neck, killing him instantly.

Alarmed by the abnormally large wolf, the assassins quickly shifted their attention to Ikane, jabbing the points of their weapons at the snarling beast at the feet of their horses. One horse, obviously well-trained, turned under the direction of its rider and began to kick and paw at the wolf. Ikane leapt out of reach and snapped at the horse's legs.

Watch out! I roared, seeing the rider prepare his sword for a deep swipe at the wolf's back. Ikane lunged to the side and the blade of the assassin swept by his left shoulder. I didn't know if it was through Ikane's ears that I heard the sharp hissing noise as it cut through the air, or if it really had been loud enough to carry across the open landscape.

Ropert reached the cluster of assassins just as Ikane landed a harsh swipe of his claws across the flank of the nearest mount, causing it to rear and whinny in startled pain. The assassin sitting in the saddle was forced to lower his weapon and grab onto the horse's mane to keep from being thrown.

Ropert engaged another, and the brash ring of swords thrummed across the snow-covered field. With three assassins occupied by the warrior and wolf, the fourth took advantage of the situation and steered his mount around the chaos. Sunlight glinted off the sharp edge of his battle-axe as his horse charged for me.

I reached for my sword— but felt nothing at my hip. Frantic, I looked down. My heart sank at seeing my empty scabbard clinging to my belt and painfully remembered that Ropert still had my weapon.

The bright glow of the firesprite sitting on my saddle caught my eye as I drew my boot-knife instead. A small smile spread across my lips. She was a weapon.

"I'm going to need your help, Mina." I warned her as I turned Shade Ranger about and spurred her headlong toward the assassin.

Mina squeaked and clutched the saddle horn. I thought I could smell a hint of burning leather.

The assassin waved his axe over his head, and I suddenly realized a grave error on my part. I had no shield to protect myself if he chose to throw it. Either it would hit me or Shade Ranger, and I didn't like the thought of either. I was reminded again at how unfamiliar I was with the battle-axe.

The assassin neared. I could see his eyes now, even beneath the hood of his cloak.

I found it strange that he hadn't taken the obvious move and tossed his axe at me, but I brushed the confusion aside. It was luck on my part, and I wouldn't squander it.

He was close enough now to toss the axe, and I was close enough to toss the firesprite. Mina's body singed my hand slightly as I snatched her from the saddle and pitched her at the assassin's face. Her red flame soared through the air and collided into the collar of his shirt. She immediately flared, startling the assassin. His horse veered to the left and slowed as he frantically shifted his body to get away from Mina's fire.

The edge of his hood burst into flame before he managed to bat the little sprite away. I cringed as she was hurled into the knee-deep snow and disappeared.

With the assassin distracted by trying to put out the flame on his cloak, I brought Shade Ranger close enough to whip my knife across his shoulder. Realizing my intent, his arm flew up, blocked, and grabbed my wrist. Our horses danced in a circle until he managed to twist my arm in a way that forced me to lose hold of my knife. Just before our horses came so close that our legs were momentarily crushed between their massive bodies, the knife dropped between them.

With smoke still streaming from the collar of the assassin's cloak, he wrenched my arm across my back, catching me in a hammer-lock. Pain raced up my shoulder, forcing me to lean my body forward to keep him from breaking my arm.

I expected him to sever my head with the battle axe. My position was perfect for an execution. I closed my eyes, prepared for the inevitable.

Startled, I felt the heat of his breath against my cheek instead. "Don't run. I'm here to help you," he whispered into my ear.

My eyes ripped open. I had heard those exact words over a year ago before fleeing Meldron. I had been ambushed in my bedchamber by Archduke Goldest and his assassins. And again, I heard the same words in the Judgment Hall, when a hooded man had vouched for my innocence in the case of King Myron's murder.

This was Master Chanter's agent! An ally!

Before I could reply, something solid rammed into the assassin, jerking him from the back of his horse. The force behind the blow took me down as well, and I felt my neck snap violently to the side. I crashed hard on my shoulder beside Master Chanter's agent.

I heard a cry before I could push myself from the snow. Ikane already had his teeth plunged deep into the man's shoulder. The assassin pounded Ikane's face with the shaft of his axe in an attempt to free himself.

"Let him go, Ikane!" I cried. *He's an ally!*

Ikane's mind registered my words, but it was too late. The assassin took matters into his own hands. His axe raced across Ikane's chest, cutting into the same mortal injury that would have claimed his life weeks ago. My scream mingled with Ikane's yelp as I felt the blade rend his flesh. Blood spurted from the injury, drenching the assassin before the wolf stumbled away and collapsed onto his side.

A surge of rage, surprise, and fear swept through my entire being. My hand searched for anything to retaliate but found only a handful of snow. Clenching it into a tight ball, a tingling sensation burned my fingertips. I didn't care. My only objective was to protect Ikane. With a harsh swing of my arm, I hurtled the ball of snow at the assassin's face. I thought I heard it crack against his skull as it smashed into his forehead. I barely noted his eyes as they rolled back into his head.

The tingling sensation in my hand fled with the snowball, and energy with it. I felt drained and startled as I watched the assassin fall into an unconscious heap a few paces from Ikane. Looking down at my hand, I wondered if seeing my limb could explain the power that had escaped my body.

I had used magic. It was not Rion's doing this time. It was mine.

"Run!" Ropert roared in the distance, tearing me from my startled state. "Run you cowards and do not return! Or my blade shall sever more than your pride!" Ropert stood in the stirrups of Beast's saddle and waved my sword menacingly after the fleeing assassins.

Ikane whimpered as I fell to my knees beside him. The pain in my chest flared when I placed my hands over his hemorrhaging wound to stay the bleeding. His chest heaved.

Kea... I... the pain took over and I felt his mind grow weak.

I had no choice but to thicken the barrier between us to keep from falling unconscious myself.

"Ikane," I said quickly. "Hang on, Ikane!"

Ropert, upon hearing my voice, turned and nudged Beast to trot towards us. He quickly dismounted and knelt beside me.

"What happened?" he asked as he dropped my sword to his side. His bright blue eyes were filled with surprising concern.

I groaned. No matter how I held the injury, blood dripped through my fingers and pooled into the melting snow beneath the wolf. With each passing moment I felt Ikane's consciousness fade. Fiery tears blurred my vision and my voice cracked with fear and urgency as I spoke.

"We need to stop the bleeding. He's fading."

Ropert's fists clenched in helpless frustration. "By the time we build a fire hot enough to cauterize it, he'll have bled out."

Fire! Heat! Inspiration jolted through me as I recalled the little firesprite. Surely, she would have the ability to sear his wound shut.

"Mina!" I called out to her, hoping that she hadn't already fled. "Mina! Please! If you can hear me, I need your help!"

"Who are you talking to?" Ropert asked, clearly thinking I had gone mad.

I ignored my bodyguard. When she didn't reply, I called out again.

"Please, Mina!"

The hope that had provided me with vigor moments ago began to wane with her silence. Perhaps the firesprite had healed her wing and had already parted ways. I wouldn't hold it against her if she had.

Ikane slipped further into unconsciousness and my mind seemed to slip with his.

"Mina," my voice broke as my throat tightened with hopelessness and his pain. Ikane was dying. Where was Rion? Surely, she wouldn't allow her host to perish this way?

"Over here," a familiar, high pitched voice carried across the open field.

My head jerked up.

Ropert too, glanced up in alarm. "Who said that?" he called.

It was then that I noted a faint red glow coming from a dent in the snow beside Beast.

"Over there!" I nudged Ropert with my elbow as I nodded towards his mount. "In the snow! It's a firesprite. Hurry. Bring her here."

"A firesprite?" he asked.

"Just get her!" I snapped.

Ropert jumped to his feet and hurried to the red glow in the snow. He hesitated as he looked down at the fiery creature.

"I won't burn you," I heard her little voice declare as if she were offended by his reluctance.

Ropert crouched down and I watched in frustrated urgency as Mina climbed into his outstretched palm. With the firesprite in hand, he returned to my side and knelt down.

"Please help me, Mina," I plead with her. "We need to cauterize this wound now... or he will die."

She frowned. "I would prefer to let him die. If I help him, I cannot heal my wing."

I bit my lip and blinked away the burning tears in my eyes. She had sacrificed much already to see that I made it safely from the caves beneath the Fold Garrison. I was asking her, yet again, to sacrifice her freedom and heal the man who radiated Rion's darkness to the point that it actually pained her. Tears burned my eyes. "I understand."

She groaned and rolled her eyes. "Very well. Who knows where that Thrall inside of him will go once he's dead. I'll do what I can, but I cannot guarantee that he will live."

My heart throbbed with gratitude and hope. "Thank you, Mina."

The sprite ignored me as she climbed from Ropert's meaty palm. Her tiny legs worked quickly as she walked along the length of my arm to my wrist. She seemed to ponder a moment as she attempted to step closer to Ikane without getting her feet in the blood that nearly drenched the sleeves of my shirt.

"This wound is deep," she mused as she crouched lower to scrutinize it. I could barely discern the warmth from her fiery body versus the warmth of Ikane's blood on my hands. Mina stretched her little hands out towards Ikane's hemorrhaging gash.

"Move your hand... slowly," she directed me. "I don't need a shower of blood all over me. That's it. Just there."

Fire roiled about her glowing body like a whirlwind of flames until it came to her outstretched hands. From there, it flowed from her little form to the wolf in a steady stream. The stinging heat of her fire burned through my chest like the scalding bite of a branding iron. Even though I had thickened the barrier between us, it took every ounce of energy I had to keep from withdrawing my hands in surprise. I hadn't expected my link to Ikane to permit me to feel his pain to this extent, but I feared to build the barrier too thick, that perhaps I wouldn't be able to reach him again.

I gritted my teeth against the agony.

Mina stopped at my reaction.

"Dagger?" Ropert asked.

"Don't stop," I breathlessly exclaimed. "Keep going."

"Dagger," Ropert protested. "What's wrong?"

"I'm fine," I assured him, weakly. "Ikane and I share a link. We can communicate through it, but in turn, I can also feel his pain. It's alright. I have endured worse."

If he could, I'm sure Ropert would have taken over the task of holding Ikane's injury shut. But it was too risky to swap positions. Instead, he steadied me and nodded to Mina. The sprite continued to cauterize the wound. Scorching pain slowly stretched from my collarbone to the bottom of my ribcage as Mina's fire sealed the wolf's skin. The terrible smell of burning flesh and fur filled the air. But the bleeding stopped.

Before my hands fell from Ikane's fur, Ropert held his palm out for the sprite. She gingerly stepped back into his hand and I nearly collapsed into the blessedly cold snow beside the wolf. He was weak, and his heartbeat was faint.

"Thank you, Mina," I whispered to the firesprite. "I am in your debt."

"Four times now," she reminded me. "And I can't believe I just helped you save that beast's life."

Ropert's brows rose. "You don't like him either?" he asked her with a crooked smile.

She nodded. "For other reasons than you, to be sure. But, yes. I don't like him at all."

Ropert smiled mischievously. "I like her," he said to me.

I was too weary to argue or laugh. Instead, I began to wash my hands in the snow.

Ropert's head whirled to his left as he heard a loud groan. Master Chanter's agent was coming around to consciousness.

"Put her in my pocket," I whispered quickly to Ropert. He quickly dropped her to my waist where she found my belt-pouch and ducked inside.

Ropert snatched my sword from the snow and marched towards the assassin. I got to my knees when Ropert pressed the tip of my sword against the man's throat, preventing him from rising from the snow.

"Ropert!" I barked before he could press the blade into his skin. "Wait!"

My bodyguard glowered at the assassin's poised deep blue eyes as he blinked up at Ropert.

"Why? He's meant to kill you."

"Do with me as you please," the assassin said. His voice was strong and held a musical pitch that made his boyish nose, and slender jaw seem a lie. The thin beard upon his jaw seemed the only indication that he was mature enough to fight the way that he did. "I assure you that I mean you or the Lady Keatep no harm."

"Rubbish," Ropert hissed, pressing the blade against the assassin's neck again. "Just look at her!"

The assassin chuckled, unfazed by the blade against his throat. "She looked terrible before I got to her."

If Ropert caught the joke, he didn't indicate it. He grabbed the assassin by his unruly brown curls and jerked his head back. "You think to make light of the situation?" he hissed.

My legs trembled as I rose from the bloodied snow. Ikane's breathing was shallow and weak, and our link caused my energy to lag. Or was it my use of magic that had drained me so? Either way, I could only hope that Ikane's lycanthrope curse was enough to heal him quickly.

I stepped up to Ropert's side before the assassin could reply. "Let him go, Ropert."

Ropert's face contorted from rage to disbelief as he turned to me. "What? Have you gone mad?"

"Let him go," I said again.

Ropert's brows narrowed, but he did as I asked, albeit very roughly. He stepped back, but kept my sword pointed at the assassin.

I crouched down beside him. Some of the black paint that had shrouded his face had been washed off by the snow, revealing his pale skin beneath. Although his tunic was black and hid the color of blood well, there was a lot of moisture around his shoulder where Ikane had bit him.

"Are you the same assassin who ambushed me in my bedchamber?" I asked.

He blinked. "By the order of Archduke Goldest, yes."

I admired his honesty. "Were you the same assassin who vouched for me in the trial of King Myron's murder?"

"As Sir Ironshade, yes," he replied.

"Can you prove it?"

A glint of recognition flashed across his eyes. He knew what I was asking of him.

"Can you get him to lower his sword first?" the assassin asked, jerking his head towards Ropert.

I looked up at my bodyguard, but Ropert shook his head, unable to fathom what I was asking.

"At least give him some room to sit up completely," I said to Ropert.

Ropert took one small step back but didn't lower the sword. A small flinch radiated through the assassin as he sat upright. He briefly checked his shoulder before unlacing the top of his tunic. I could now see the redness of blood on his pale skin as he opened his tunic to expose his muscled torso.

As I suspected, a horrific pink scar stretched from his lowest right rib to the top of his collarbone, a similar injury to the one Ikane had just sustained.

I couldn't contain my smile. "You work for Master Chanter, don't you?"

He nodded and closed his shirt against the cold.

After standing, I extended my hand out to him. But before he could take it, Ropert slapped the assassin's arm away with the flat of the sword and stepped between us. "What do you think you are doing, Dagger?! This man is a trained killer!"

"He most certainly is," I agreed. "But he's on our side. Let him up."

"He just ripped into Ikane! That doesn't seem like he's a friend."

The assassin looked at the heap of black fur lying in the snow behind us. "I didn't know what else to do," he mumbled. His thick brows furrowed briefly with regret as his hand came up to cover the injury on his shoulder. "My instincts just kicked in—"

"You expect me to believe that?!" Ropert bellowed.

"Back off, Ropert!" I snapped.

Ropert's mouth clamped shut, and the muscles in his jaw tightened.

"That scar on his chest," I began and pointed to the young man, still sitting in the snow, for emphasis. "I gave him that. It was the night King Myron was assassinated. This man helped me escape, knowing that the archduke would've had me killed on the spot. And again, this man stood at the head of thousands of nobles, showing that exact same scar. He is not our enemy."

Ropert lowered my sword a little.

The assassin, who I knew as Sir Ironshade, took the opportunity to stand, and brushed the snow from his stark black attire.

"I'm not happy with this," Ropert grumbled. "If he makes one move against you, I will not stay my blade."

"I wouldn't expect any less," I told him.

"However," Ropert declared as he turned to face the assassin. Ropert's large frame towered over Master Chanter's agent by a full head. "I cannot allow you to be in Lady Keatep's company while armed."

Undaunted by Ropert's powerful frame, the assassin shrugged his uninjured shoulder and began stripping his knives from his belt with his good hand. "I needn't weapons to kill," he said as he handed the blades to my bodyguard.

Ropert glowered at him as he took the handful of knives. "This cannot be all you carry," he sneered.

Without a word, the assassin revealed an additional five knives tucked away in his boots, gloves, sleeves and belt, several of which harbored poisoned edges. He removed his bandoleer that held a conspicuous sum of vials filled with deadly herbs and mushrooms. Even with my assurance that I could trust this man, Ropert grew more and more suspicious with every weapon of death the assassin revealed. After exposing a hidden pocket sewn to the inside of his shirt, Ropert snapped.

"Enough!" He grabbed the assassin by his wrist and wrung it back sharply to detain the deadly mercenary. "I'm sorry, Dagger. But I cannot risk your life this way. Master Chanter made it clear before we left that I need to be on guard constantly."

With those words, he pulled both of the assassin's arms behind his back. The young man tried to suppress a groan of pain as his injured shoulder was strained.

I meant to protest, but the assassin shook his head at me. "It's alright. Sir Ropert is doing his duty. I hold no ill will against him."

"At least let me look at his shoulder," I said to Ropert.

"Only after he's bound."

I watched as Ropert wrapped a rope around the assassin's wrists and was sure to bind it tight. Even with the dangerous man thusly restrained, Ropert remained uneasy. Leaving the man kneeling in the snow, Ropert took my arm and steered me towards Ikane and our horses.

"What more secrets do you have to tell me?" he demanded in a hushed tone.

"Pardon?"

"You failed to tell me that your link with Ikane is so strong that you can actually feel his pain. You have a firesprite tucked in your pocket, and now this?" His grip unintentionally tightened on my elbow as he waved his hand at the assassin. "What more is there? Are there any more dangerous companions I should know about?"

I glanced back at Master Chanter's agent who was still on his knees. His head was bent towards the snow, allowing his brown curls to fall across his forehead... his forehead... where my snowball had struck him. A soft, powdery snowball that had knocked him unconscious.

I had one more secret.

Magic.

I curled my fingers, flexed them, hunting for the sensation that had burned my fingertips earlier. How? What power had I used? Was it even my own? Was it something dark like the magic Rion used? Surely the firesprite in my pocket would've had a thing to say about it if it was. But why now? Why did magic suddenly manifest physically?

"There is something else, isn't there?" Ropert pressed.

I turned back to him. What would he think? How would he feel if he knew that I had managed to actually invoke some magic of my own? I dared not tell him. Not now. Perhaps not ever.

I wrenched my arm from his grasp. "No," I told him.

Turning on my heel, I made my way to Shade Ranger and stuck my hand into my saddlebag. "Let me see to the assassin's injury. And then we must find a safe place to make camp. Ikane cannot travel in his condition and the other assassins know where we are. They might return."

Ropert looked at the black mound of sleeping fur in the bed of white snow. After a moment, he pinched the bridge of his nose and scrunched his eyes shut.

"You're lying, Dagger," he whispered. "I feel something in you. Something you are not telling me." He dropped his hand. "Don't keep secrets from me, Kea. Especially if it could place you in danger."

My body sagged against the saddle, both with exhaustion and defeat. He was right. I sighed and turned to face him. "Alright. I will tell you. But not now. Let us find a good place to make camp, and I will tell you then."

That seemed to satisfy his curiosity, for now. And secretly I hoped that he would completely forget about the question by the time camp was set up.

The assassin's injury was deep and beyond my skills to heal. He would surely develop an infection and a fever within the next day or so. Mina had also done some pretty decent damage to his neck, right above the bite-mark.

Ropert was elated to discover that the assassin's horse had his lost broadsword strapped to its saddle. Not only this, but the assassin had a decent amount of provisions. We could actually fill our bellies with some bread and dried meat tonight. Ropert was surprised to discover a lute securely wrapped in a soft blanket beside his sword. The hint of a melodic tone to his voice made me suspect that he had a great musical talent.

About five minutes south of where we had been attacked, we discovered a shrouded site surrounded by thick pines heavy with snow. Warmth touched our flushed cheeks as the enclosure sheltered us from the bitter cold wind of the early winter. In spite of this, and a roaring fire in the center of our encampment, cold bit at my nose and my fingertips as thick white lace began to descend from the clouds that had rolled in.

My discomfort couldn't compare to that of Ropert's prisoner. My bodyguard had bound Sir Ironshade's hands and feet and left him to fend for himself at the edge of our camp with a single bedroll between his body and the frigid earth.

"Dagger," Ropert tore me from my thoughts as he thrust the tent into my hands. "Help me with this."

Obediently, I followed him to an open space by the fire where we unfurled the canvas.

"Now," he began as he plunged the ends of tall, sturdy sticks into the frozen earth to create the base for our shelter. "Tell me. What is going on with you?"

I frowned and crouched low to drive stakes into the rings of the canvas. He hadn't forgotten.

"Well, I cannot say for certain," I began. "But I feel... well, I'm not quite sure... it just happened. Perhaps it was a one-time thing..."

Ropert remained silent, waiting, without pausing from his duties. He skillfully tethered the tent poles together and proceeded to heave the canvas over the sturdy base. I was scarcely assisting.

"I think I may have used magic," I eventually said.

He paused from his task and looked at me with furrowed brows. "You've used it before. Against Rion, or the Phoenix Witch... whatever you want to call her."

"No, not that." My eyes strayed to the black-smudged face of the assassin lying upon his bedroll. A light dusting of snow covered his black attire as he hadn't moved since he had laid down. He looked terribly cold in spite of his heavy, fur-lined cloak.

"It was different. It wasn't a power in my mind. It was here, physical. I felt it burning in my fingers."

Ropert followed my gaze to Sir Ironshade. "Is that how you brought that assassin down? With magic?"

I shrugged. "'Tis the only explanation I have. All I did was throw a snowball at his face. My whole being was on fire. I thought I was just angry at first, but my hands tingled with energy and the sensation was gone as soon as I pitched the snowball at him. I've asked myself over and over again if it was Rion's doing, but I know it wasn't. She would have drained his life to feed herself."

Ropert looked at the assassin for a moment and then resumed his work on the tent.

"Well?" I asked. "Aren't you going to say anything?"

"What would you have me say?" he responded. "I know nothing of magic."

I frowned and picked his bedroll up from the ground.

Ropert sighed as he finished with the tent. "Dagger, I don't know what to say. I don't even know how I feel about it. In a way, I am in awe of your power, and in another, I fear it. You, yourself, seem startled by it. My only advice is to refrain from it. You don't know anything about it."

"That is why I need to find the White Wardent. It's getting stronger." I tossed his bedroll into the shelter of the tent. "It's as unpredictable as Rion's magic."

Ropert stood and placed his hand on my shoulder. "Just try not to use it, alright?"

I nodded, although I knew it wouldn't be that simple.

"I'll take first watch," I told him, glancing back at the wolf that lay beside the fire.

Ropert nodded as he dropped his hand. "Don't let the fire die out. It's going to be cold tonight." With that, he grabbed his satchel and slipped into the tent.

My mind reeled as I wandered back to the fire and placed a pot of water over the flames. I propped myself up against the log beside Ikane to wait for the water to warm. With my feet stretched out towards the fire, my hand slipped through the coarse fur of Ikane's head. His breathing was labored and shallow, but I felt life still fighting within him.

It was not long before I heard Ropert's soft snoring come from the tent.

"I used all my power to stop the bleeding, you know," the sprite suddenly declared from within the flames. "I would have been able to heal my wing if it weren't for him." She motioned to the wolf at my side.

"I can't thank you enough," I whispered to her. "If the sun doesn't shine tomorrow, we will reach Toltak shortly, and I will purchase firedust for you, even if it costs all that I have."

"I'll hold you to that," she said and closed her eyes as she curled up on a smoldering log.

The water bubbled in my pot. Carefully, I poured the hot liquid into my mug and held it between my hands to warm them. The noise must have woken the assassin, for he lifted his head to watch me.

"Sorry," I whispered. "Go back to sleep."

His head fell back upon the blanket and the dusting of snow upon his hair fell from it. But his eyes did not close. Clearly, he was too uncomfortable to sleep.

I set my mug down beside Ikane, got to my feet, and walked around the fire to the assassin. "How is your shoulder?"

He shrugged, and then winced.

I knelt down and began to unbind the cords on his wrists and feet. "Ropert would have my head if he knew I was doing this," I mumbled.

Sir Ironshade sat up, rubbed his limbs, and glanced back at the tent where Ropert was snoring. "He has his reasons."

I stood and rubbed my shoulders. "Should I be worried too?" I asked as I returned to sit beside Ikane.

The assassin struggled to stand on blood-starved limbs and followed, bringing his bedroll with him. He sat down on the log beside me and wrapped himself up.

"I will not harm you," he assured me. "How is he doing?" he asked, bobbing his chin towards Ikane. Although black paint remained on his face, I could see genuine concern.

"He's weak," I answered, stroking Ikane's fur again.

"I'm truly sorry," he said. "Is he the Leviathan, the one you were branded for?"

It shouldn't have surprised me at how much he knew. "Yes," I answered. "He has risked much for Roanfire."

We were silent for a moment.

"I did not intend to hurt him so," he said.

I shifted to sit beside him on the log. "Let me take a look at your shoulder."

He slowly loosened the collar of his tunic and pulled it down to reveal the deep u-shaped row of red, angry teeth marks, surrounded by shredded skin. It was terribly inflamed and oozing with infection. Mina's burn mark didn't look any better, and I actually thought I heard her chuckle from the fire. He would need the cooling properties of watersprite dust to sooth Mina's magical burns.

I bit my lip. No matter how I cared for him, it wouldn't be enough. "We'll have to find a healer once we reach Toltak."

"Thank you for trying," he said and pulled his shirt back over his shoulder. He re-tied the lacing on his half-burnt tunic, and then wrapped the blanket around his shoulders again.

I repositioned myself beside Ikane when I felt stabbing pain in my chest and gently inspected his injury. A deep blue color had formed behind his skin, pressing against the cauterization. The tightness in my chest made me suspect internal bleeding, and I worried all the more. Ikane may not live through the night.

The assassin leaned forward on his knees, knitting his hands together as he watched the fire.

"I meant it when I said I could help you," he told me. "You will need my support to tip the scales in your favor."

I leaned back against the log and couldn't help but clutch my chest. It did little to alleviate Ikane's pain. "What do you mean? The arranged marriage to the Tolean Prince? Or Rion?"

His deep blue eyes pierced mine through the darkness and the firelight flickering on our faces. "All of it, Keatep Brendagger," he stated sincerely. "All of it."

I was taken aback by his deep insinuation. Could he really help me with Rion's curse?

"You were introduced as Sir Ironshade back in Meldron. Is that what I should call you?" I asked.

He shook his head. "That was an alias. You may call me... Broderick," he said after a moment. "Broderick Ironshade will do."

"Broderick the Assassin," I mused, knowing that it wasn't his true name. I accepted it nonetheless. "How long have you been working for Master Chanter?"

"Thirteen years. I was apprenticed at age six."

"I was brought to the Daram Keep at age six and began my training as a soldier," I said. A little smile stole across my lips at the memory. "Ropert was eight at the time and took me under his wing when I tried to pilfer a slice of bread from Mayama's kitchen. He headed off the cook with the stale bread itself!"

Broderick smiled. "He's always been your protector, hasn't he?"

I nodded. "Yes, yes he has. There was a time when he didn't seem to care, but that-"

"Dagger!" Ropert bellowed, making me flinch. I hadn't even noticed that his snoring had stopped. He burst from the tent and stomped over to where we sat with a hostile flare in his eyes. "What do you think you are doing?" he demanded as he grasped Broderick by the nape of his neck and jabbed his head down to his knees. The young man winced at the rough treatment but did not resist.

"Ropert," I groaned. "If he wished to harm me, he would have done so already."

"You can't be sure of that!"

I tapped Broderick's boot near the toes where I had seen the trigger earlier, when I had unbound his feet. Instantly, a small blade appeared at its front. I pulled the weapon out and held it up for Ropert's scrutiny. "He's been armed all along."

Ropert released Broderick's neck harshly and grabbed the front of the young man's tunic. "Any more weapons on you?" he demanded, hauling him to his feet.

"No, sir."

Ropert looked at me. "Is he telling the truth?"

"I think so."

"Don't abuse her trust!" Ropert snapped at the man and released him unkindly.

Broderick stumbled back, nearly tripping over the log we had both been sitting on. He rubbed his neck, then looked at me. "It's confirmed. He's your protector."

I pursed my lips together to keep from smiling.

Ropert irritably tossed more logs into the fire and one nearly collided with the sleeping firesprite inside. Startled, she leapt from the fire pit and glowered at my bodyguard as her body flared with heat and intense anger.

"Watch it!" she cried, her body igniting for a moment.

Ropert flinched and stepped away as Broderick's eyes went wide. He absently touched his fingers to his collar where the blisters festered. "So that's what burned my neck. You have a firesprite!"

I looked at him sheepishly, but Mina raised her chin and folded her arms across her chest as she looked at Broderick. "I think it suits you," she said. "I should've singed a bit higher though, taken that open-mouthed gawking right off your face."

Broderick couldn't decide whether to frown or smile, but his mouth clamped shut.

"Dagger," Ropert claimed my attention as he sat down at the opposite end of the fire and glowered at the assassin across the flames. "Get some sleep. I'll take watch from here on."

"Are you sure?" I asked. "You've barely slept."

Ropert nodded firmly. "For one, I don't trust him, and second, I don't trust you to keep him in line. Go get some sleep. You're still recovering."

I looked back to Ikane, feeling the deep, throbbing pain in his chest. I rubbed my own in an attempt to soothe it, but once again, it did little. It was getting harder to breathe under the pressure.

"I'll watch over him," Broderick whispered to me.

Reluctantly, I stood. "You two be nice now," I told them before walking to the tent.

"I can't promise anything," Ropert grumbled, glowering at the assassin.

Broderick looked at me with a feigned expression of worry. Then he winked. I tried to hide my chuckle as I ducked into the tent. I think I liked Broderick.

Within moments I was asleep on the soft bedroll that still held the heat from Ropert's body.

10

FIREDUST

I awoke gasping for breath that I feared would never come. My chest burned, crying out for air, as if I had been crushed beneath a boulder. Pain radiated across my ribs like the prick of a hot iron... and then precious, cold, soothing air filled my lungs. I gulped deeply of the air again and again, until the fear of not being able to breathe abated. But this was not Rion...

Ikane!

I leapt from under the covers and scrambled from the tent to find Ropert asleep by the fire and Broderick kneeling over Ikane.

"What are you doing?!" I roared and leapt over Ropert. I nearly barreled into Broderick, knocking him away from Ikane's side. He landed on his rump as Ropert startled from sleep.

"He was dying," Broderick said as he pushed himself up off the snow. "I had to do something."

Hastily, I knelt beside Ikane and scrutinized his wound. Mina's cauterization held, but a new puncture had been delivered to the left of it. Deep red blood oozed from the new injury.

"What's going on?" Ropert groaned as he rubbed his face and sat upright. His eyes drooped terribly.

"He is bleeding internally," Broderick explained. He held out the smallest knife I'd ever seen, as if beckoning me to take it from him. "I had to relieve the pressure in his lungs. He wasn't breathing."

I sat back on my heels, realizing that Broderick had indeed, spared Ikane's life. Nonetheless, I found my frustration rising. Ikane was a lycanthrope. He had healed so quickly before Rion had entered his mind. And why she did nothing to help him now, boggled my mind. Did she not fear losing her host? And why did Ikane not change form? Surely it would be easier for us to assess his wound in human shape.

My fingers ran through the black fur at his neck.

"He'll live," Broderick assured me as he sat upon the log again.

I nodded, but tears burned my eyes nonetheless. "I'm sorry," I whispered as I drew my knees up to my chest. "I thought—"

"I know what you thought," he interjected. "I would have done the same, if not worse."

Ropert seemed dazed. He blinked heavily and rubbed his eyes again. Before he had even removed his hand from his face, his head bobbed against his chest.

"Ropert," I said.

His head lurched up.

"Go, sleep." I jerked my head towards the tent.

He stood sluggishly and stumbled around the fire. Sleepily, he removed his cloak and placed it over my shoulders. His hand rested on my shoulder for a moment, as a silent way of telling me that he felt my worry. Without another word he ducked into the tent.

I pulled Ropert's cloak around my shoulders as Broderick placed more logs into the fire, careful to avoid hitting the sprite. He leaned back and sat beside me with the log at our backs.

My body trembled from the cold and the aftermath of unused adrenaline. I looked at Broderick, noting that he had washed his face from the black paint. He was actually quite attractive, with chiseled features and a handsome smile.

"What happened between you and Ropert?" I asked.

He looked at me, perplexed.

"He was asleep," I stated. "He would've never allowed you to watch over us."

Broderick smiled and looked back at the fire. "I slipped something into his tea," he chuckled. "He's grumpy enough as it is. We don't need him sleep deprived as well."

I shook my head with a snicker of incredulity. "I suppose we don't."

"Lady Keatep," Broderick said my name softly.

I still wasn't used to the name, but the awful pinch in my neck forced me to stir. My eyes blinked open to the pale glow of orange sunlight radiating across the gray clouds in the sky. Startled, I looked up at the assassin, realizing that I had fallen asleep against his shoulder. I sat upright quickly and rubbed the sleep from my eyes.

"How long was I asleep?" I whispered, rubbing my neck to ease the stiffness there. The morning chill did little to help.

Broderick smiled at me in spite of the dark circles that had formed under his eyes. His breath hung in the frigid air as he spoke. "For quite some time, actually. Your body needed rest to heal all those bruises and scrapes."

I brushed my hair from my face. "It looks as though you could use some rest yourself."

"I will rest once we reach Toltak," he assured me and shifted to add another log to the fire, but his body was stiff. I knew instantly that it was the infection in his shoulder causing him to move so poorly.

My eyes strayed to my left where Ikane— Ikane! He was gone! A deep imprint and bloody snow where his body had lain was all that remained. Frantic and wide eyed, I turned to Broderick.

"Where is he?" I cried.

The loudness of my voice startled the sleeping birds from the trees, and a squirrel darted from one branch to another, knocking a clump of snow from the heavy pine needles.

"Calm yourself," Broderick said quickly, but it was too late. Ropert burst from the tent with his hair and tunic in complete disarray, and fists ready to pummel something.

"What's going on out here?" he grumbled.

"Ikane is gone!" I cried as I jumped to my feet. "Where is he, Broderick? You were the last- "

Keatep, Ikane's soft, tenor voice resounded through my head. *I am well. And I have the assassin to thank.*

I immediately opened myself to him, hoping that by thinning the barrier between us that I would be able to sense him more clearly. "Where are you?"

In an instant, I found myself seeing through his eyes. He cleared the thick cluster of trees and emerged into our camp to see me standing over the assassin, with my hand gripping the hilt of my sword. I hadn't even realized that my fingers had strayed to my weapon.

Ropert turned to look at the black wolf emerging from the trees, and pure astonishment fell across his countenance. "Dagger," he whispered, barely daring to lift his voice.

Trembling, I turned about, scanning the trees for the black wolf. My eyes fell upon his obsidian fur and his prominent green and blue eyes staring back at me. He lowered his head to drop the two dead rabbits he had caught into the snow.

Disbelief and wonder filled my mind. He had been so near to death.

Good morning, beautiful, he said as he lifted his head. I thought I could see the wolf smile.

"Ikane," I breathed and sprinted to him. My knees dropped to the snow, briefly irritating the sutured one, as I threw my arms about his thick neck. He smelled terrible, but I did not care. He was alive.

He awkwardly tried to return the embrace. *When I came to, the assassin was kneeling beside me. He did something, Kea. He has an uncanny gift for healing,* he told me.

I looked back at Broderick who was now standing beside the fire. That man intrigued me. He was a skilled killer, a musician, and a healer. What more could he do?

I couldn't agree more, Ikane said, validating my thoughts.

The great city of Toltak was once a prosperous settlement. Built near the Karn River in the center of Roanfire, heaps of commodities arrived weekly by boat and land. It was really no wonder that merchants made Toltak the bartering center of the kingdom. Businesses had flourished here for so long that Toltak rivaled even Meldron in size.

But Toltak was no longer the thriving metropolis it had been. After the war, merchandise was not easy to come by. The scant market offered only a few basic necessities now. Most of the buildings had been damaged and a handful of craftsmen labored to repair the large well in the center of the marketplace.

As we walked, I became increasingly nervous. Not because Broderick had developed a fever due to the infected bite on his shoulder, but because I could sense Ikane less and less the further we ventured into the city. We had left him outside the city walls.

The brightness of my vision darkened, sharpness of my hearing dulled, and even my energy lagged. By the time we reached the market square, my link with him had completely vanished. Ropert, who kept a tight grip on Broderick's arm, pulled the feverish assassin to a halt when he realized that I no longer followed.

"Dagger?" he asked.

I blinked at the men through my darkened vision, marveling that I had even functioned with my average abilities before. With quite some effort I approached, and Ropert steered us on.

It wasn't long before we found a war-torn but well-kept building with the words 'Pepper Malia's Healing and Herbs' etched into a wooden sign hanging from the doorway. Ropert climbed the three wooden steps to the entrance and knocked. An old woman, ailed with some sort of uncontrollable muscle spasm, opened the door. Her head twitched

"What might I do for you?" she asked with a voice so shaky, I thought she was sitting in a wagon.

Ropert tipped his head to her. "Are you Pepper Malia?"

"Who's asking?"

"I am Sir Ropert Saded," he replied and motioned for Broderick to step forward. "This man was bitten by a wolf. The wound is infected, and he just began a fever this morning."

The woman looked at the assassin, her head jerking wildly. She then looked back at Ropert. "I am Maggie Briar, Pepper's assistant. Come in. I will see if she has time for you." She opened the door wider for us to enter.

"Wait here," she ordered after we entered the large room crowded with makeshift chairs occupied by a few sick townsfolk. A braided rug lay in the center, its bright colors dull with age.

The old woman disappeared into an adjoining room which was curtained off with brown fabric. Soon after, another woman appeared. She was much younger, with plump lips and a womanly figure of motherhood. Deep wrinkles adorned the corners of her eyes from obvious years of warm smiles.

"Welcome," she greeted us. "I hear you are in need of some healing? An animal bite?"

Ropert gestured to Broderick and she came to his side.

"Let me see," she ordered.

Broderick pulled at the collar of his shirt.

"No. I can't assess an injury like that. Take the shirt off."

Broderick blushed horribly once his torso was bare. I was stunned to see that he not only bore the scar from my sword across his chest, but many others across his back and arms. Even Pepper was taken aback by his many injuries.

"You've been through much in your young years," she said as she examined the inflamed wound on his shoulder.

Broderick said nothing.

"What sort of animal did this?"

"A wolf," Ropert answered.

"Hmmm..." she mused. "It is much larger than any wolf bite I've ever seen."

"It was a monstrous beast," my bodyguard answered, folding his arms across his chest. "You might want to alert the townsfolk of his presence in the area."

I glowered at Ropert, but he returned it with a playful wink.

"That I shall do," she said. "And what are these blisters above it? These cannot be from infection... they look like burn marks."

"A firesprite," I said.

Pepper's eyes widened. "He needs watersprite dust immediately!" She turned and disappeared behind the curtain again. Moments later she returned with a wooden bowl filled with vials, small containers, and some clean linen. My gaze was instantly drawn to a box labeled, Firedust. I thought of the little firesprite sitting in my pocket.

I watched with interest as she applied a paste of herbs and waterdust to both of his injuries. She bound Broderick's shoulder with clean dressings, and then turned to Ropert.

"Put this on his injury morning and night," she said and handed him a small wooden box filled with the ointment. "And here is some watersprite dust. He must drink it two more times to flush out the infection in his blood. If the fever hasn't broken by morning, come see me again."

Ropert's eyebrows rose at the instructions. "We can't leave Toltak?"

"Unless another healer knows my recipe and how to properly use it, no. Using too many herbs can cause more damage. And blending the wrong elemental dust could be catastrophic."

"Well then," Ropert declared gleefully. "We'll move on tonight!"

"Ropert," I grumbled and folded my arms across my chest.

"I'm only jesting," he chuckled and pocketed the ointment. "How much do we owe you for your services?"

"One moment," I cut in. "I need some firedust."

Pepper frowned. "I do not have much, and you look as though you could use a healer for all those bruises." She reached up to touch a tender spot on my brow.

I hadn't considered my appearance since falling from the cliffs. I may well look like death, but I brushed her hand away. "I just need a warm bath and some firedust."

"Very well," Pepper said. But she was very stingy with her firedust, and the price of her services was outrageous. But pay, we did.

After visiting the healer, we secured two sparsely furnished rooms in a tavern called the Shattered Wagon. Ropert and Broderick chose to share one room while I occupied the other. I dropped my saddlebag to the floor and quickly stripped my cloak and removed the firesprite from my belt pouch.

"I have dust," I told her with a smile as I gently placed her on the single table in the room. I set the small pouch of firedust beside her.

Mina peered gratefully into the small bag. "Finally," she sighed. "There isn't much... and it smells funny. I don't think the sprites were happy when they made this batch."

I began stripping my belt, tunic, and boots as she sifted through the magical powder. "It's the best I could do," I said. My senses were suddenly heightened as I felt Ikane's presence again. He must have made his way around the city.

"I'm going to take a bath," I told her. "Will you be alright by yourself for a while?"

Her wings twitched happily as she climbed into the pouch completely and immersed herself into the dust.

"This won't take long," she said, stirring up the dust until it puffed from the purse. I hurried to brush the glowing embers of dust from the surface of the wooden table. Already, black streaks remained.

"Be careful!" I warned her. "You're going to burn down the inn."

She shot out of the pouch, her wings buzzing like those of a dragonfly. She dashed across the room a few times and came to a hovering halt before me.

"Thank you!" she squealed.

I smiled sadly as I pulled my stockings off and tossed them at my saddlebag. "I suppose you're going to be on your way now."

She folded her arms across her chest. "No, I plan to stay with you forever." She didn't hide the sarcastic tone in her voice.

I gave her a crooked smile. "I'll miss you."

She alighted on my outstretched hand and I felt her comfortably warm feet on my palm. "Before I go, I would like to give you a gift. You seem to need a little extra help anyway."

"But you've given me so much already."

She ignored me as she took flight again. "Hold out both of your hands," she ordered and zipped back to the firedust pouch. She leaned over and scooped a handful of the bright red powder into her hands. I obediently held my hands out to her as she fluttered back to me and sprinkled the dust across my palms and fingers. The warmth of it caused my skin to tingle with heat.

Her body brightened with radiant light and the flickering flame of hair on her head grew longer. "Keep your eyes on me," she demanded.

In that instant, she flapped her wings so vigorously that the firedust flew directly into my eyes. Her body brightened like a brilliant flash of lightning. Instinctively, my eyes closed, but they were already burning. My hands began to prickle as if hot coals had been placed into them. I yelped in pain as I retracted my hands. Frantically, I rubbed my eyes with the back of my wrists as tears surged. But that only ignited the fiery pain further.

"What did you do?!" I cried out and scrambled blindly in the direction of the water basin. I tripped over my saddlebag and sprawled onto the floor instead.

"Dagger?" Ropert called through the door. "Are you alright?"

Fiery tears ran down my cheeks as I cradled my searing hands. The burning would not ease.

"I can't see, Ropert!" I cried. "My hands are on fire! Make it stop! Make the burning stop!"

I heard the door open.

"Dagger!" Ropert hurried to my side and I felt his strong hands grip my shoulders to halt my pain-induced rocking. "What... your hands! What happened to your hands? It was the firesprite wasn't it? Where is she? I'll smash her like a bug!"

He immediately pulled me to my feet and guided me to the washbasin where he poured the cool water over my palms. The burning sensation subsided, but not enough. I plunged my hands into the bowl of water and nearly plopped my face into the basin as well to cool my eyes.

Just then, a scream from outside pierced the walls.

"What in the name of the Phoenix is going on tonight?" Ropert grumbled. "I'll be right back."

Once the door closed behind him, I heard the soft buzz of sprite wings come from the fire. As soon as I felt her radiating warmth against my face, I confronted her.

"What did you do?! I've gone blind!"

"Stop your whining," she groaned. "Keep your eyes closed."

Sniffling, I did as ordered, and tried not to flinch when I felt her tiny hands on my eyelids. Gradually, as if she were a sponge, the burning in my eyes eased under her gentle touch. Only after they felt completely cool, did she pull away.

I blinked at bright shapes visible through my tears. Everything was tinged with red-gold hues. I could not look directly into the fire, for the light was too overwhelming, and Mina's form was almost unbearable to look at.

"Now, hold out your hands," she ordered again.

Reluctant, but eager to have the burning pain stop, I held my palms out to her. Perhaps it was what she had done to my eyes, but my hands appeared to be glowing. I watched as Mina lowered her body to my hands. She crouched on my palms and gently touched my fingers. Just as she had done with my eyes, she pulled the heat from my hands into her tiny form. As the pain eased, I gathered a breath of soothing air and slumped down against the edge of the bed.

"Your eyes will be somewhat sensitive for a few days, but within a fortnight, you will be able to see in the darkness as clear as day," Mina said as she hovered in the air. "The glow in your hands will fade over time. There is power in them. It will come to your protection when the situation is most dire."

I didn't know whether to thank or curse her.

"Farewell, Keatep Brendagger," she said. "It was an honor to meet you."

The door flew open and Mina darted back into the fire.

"Dagger," Ropert said, entering the room. He knelt down beside me and took my hands into his, marveling at them. "Do your eyes still burn? Do we need to take you to the healer?"

I shook my head quickly. "I'm alright. It's getting better."

He helped me to my feet. "Good, because we have a situation outside and I need you."

"What is it?"

"Ikane."

It was full dark outside, and the several dozen burning torches of the townsfolk flickered deep shadows across the market square. And the light, though meager, burned my eyes. A number of the people held pitchforks, swords and axes. Surrounded by the hostile mob, was a wolf, his shoulders hunched in apprehension, and his hair standing on end. His head lifted, and his ears perked when he saw me emerge from the inn.

Kea! Ikane's voice boomed through my head. *Are you well? I felt pain. Burning pain. Is it Rion? Why did I not sense it myself?*

I had forgotten about our link. He had felt every bit of my sweltering agony.

Why are your hands glowing like that?

It was the firesprite, I said quickly. *I finally got the dust to heal her wing and she wanted to leave me with a parting gift.*

By burning your hands and eyes?

She claims that she has given me valuable gifts, I said. *Though I'm still trying to decide if she was simply getting back at me for breaking her wing. But we don't have time to chat. Go! It isn't safe for you here.*

As if on cue, one of the braver townsfolk jabbed his pitchfork at Ikane. He jumped aside, causing the entire crowd to shift, and snarled at the man.

Go Ikane! I am well, I urged him.

I'll find my way back, he replied and bolted through the thinnest portion of the encircling mob. They parted with a shriek.

"After it!" a man shouted, and the entire mob gave chase.

"Will he be alright?" Ropert asked as the dust settled.

I felt Ikane's heightened senses wane as he ran further from me. "They are no match for his speed," I answered.

"What was he doing here?" Ropert asked. "Doesn't he know how much danger he placed all of us in?"

I held my hands up for Ropert to see the glow embedded into my skin.

"Oh, right," he said. "You two have a link. He felt the burning. He was coming to protect you."

I nodded.

"That reminds me," Ropert said, slamming his fist into his palm. "I have a sprite to squash."

I smiled and rolled my eyes. He wouldn't get the chance anyway. Mina was already gone.

The silver-white globe of the moon hung in the sky, illuminating the snow cloaked landscape. Bright reflections of silver light curved around the fringe of roiling black clouds, silhouetting a lonely tree. Innumerable obscure creatures clung to the branches, pulling at the tree's fragile limbs until they hung to the ground.

The howl of a wolf penetrated the thick night. At the sound, the creatures clinging to the tree, unfurled wings of black leather and leapt off the branches. Black arrows darted, spun, and circled through the air in a whirlwind of chaos. The beating of their leathery wings flailed against my arms raised to shield my face.

Kea! Kea! Wake up! We're dreaming! Wake up! Ikane's voice bellowed through my mind. I scarcely knew what was dream and what was real. I felt Ikane trembling. I felt his agony and fear.

My eyes flew open, tearing me from the nightmare.

A sliver of morning sunlight burst through the poorly shuttered window of the inn and fell directly upon my face. It burned my eyes. With a flinch of pain, I scrunched them shut.

The dream again... Ikane groaned, trying to calm his breathing. I felt the panic in his chest ease a bit.

Where are you? I asked.

In the alley behind the inn.

I squinted against the light and sat upright, pushing the blankets from my legs. *Something about this dream isn't right. This isn't Rion. This is something else.*

I wouldn't know, Ikane admitted. *All I know is that it frightens me.*

I agreed.

Your eyes... how long before they won't feel like you're looking at the sunlight reflecting on a polished shield? he asked.

Half blind, I groped for my clothes. *I don't know. Mina said that it should get better, but I'm beginning to think otherwise.*

The wolf's sharp ears twitched at a sound to his left, and I felt him shrink against the wall. *I need to go,* he said quietly, even though no one else could hear him. *I'll meet you outside the city in an hour?*

Yes, we should be ready to go by then, I answered.

I felt the cold of snow beneath his padded feet as he slinked through the alley, and again, the farther he walked away, the less I could feel him. The sharp sting in my eyes eased a little in his absence. Nonetheless, I dressed blindly, and my tunic ended up sitting backwards before I realized that I could not find the lacing. I even put my boots on the wrong feet.

A knock on the door interrupted my task of trying to secure my belt around my waist. My fingers were still tender from the burn of firedust.

"Who is it?" I called through the door.

"It's Ropert. Are you decent? Can I come in?"

I chuckled to myself. If I wasn't decent, I wouldn't know it. "Enter," I said, dropping my belt to the bed... or at least I thought it was where the bed was. I heard the loud clank of my belt-buckle as it hit the floor.

"Are you ready to go?" Ropert asked as he stepped inside. He paused when he noticed me groping along the floorboards to find my misplaced belt.

"Apparently not," he said, slightly confused. "What are you doing?"

I sat back on my heels. My balance was poor as I was unable to see. I wobbled, and eventually landed hard on my rump. I groaned in pain and frustration when I made the mistake of trying to brace my fall with my hands.

"My eyes hurt, and my hands feel like they were left in a furnace," I half sobbed.

"Here, let me see," Ropert said.

I barely saw his broad-shouldered form kneel down before me. His calloused hands were warm and gentle as he took my hands and turned the palms up to look at them. "Well, they're not blistered. But they are glowing."

I tried to look at them, but the glow in my hands was too bright for my eyes.

"I'll pack your things," Ropert announced as he dropped my hands and stood. He reached his hand out and grabbed my wrist to help me to my feet. "Do you think wearing some gloves would ease the pain a bit? If anything, it would certainly help keep curious folk from asking about the glow."

"I can try. Can you find my gloves for me?"

He turned to my pack and rummaged through it. "Broderick's fever broke last night. So, we're good to go," he said as he turned back to me. "Here, let me help."

Carefully, I stuck my hand into the fur-lined opening of the glove. The fine hairs tingled as they brushed up against my skin, but the extra padding helped ease the pain. Ropert helped me stick my other hand into the second glove.

"There," he announced and turned to scoop my belt from the ground. "Hold your arms out a second."

I did as instructed.

"Where is Broderick?" I asked.

Ropert wrapped his arms around my waist for an instant. "I locked him in our room," he said, seeming satisfied with his decision.

"You know he can pick that lock, right?"

Ropert pulled the leather strap of my belt tight and tucked it into the buckle. "I know," he grumbled. "But it won't keep me from trying." Having finished, he stepped back. "Do you need help with your cloak as well?"

I squinted across the room and thought I saw the heavy blue mantle sitting on the edge of the bedpost. After trying to pick it up with my gloved hands, Ropert chuckled.

"Those are the blankets, and we'd best leave those here. I don't want the innkeeper charging us for stolen bedding."

I sighed and allowed my shoulders to sag in defeat. "Fine. Where is my cloak then?"

Ropert stepped around me and reached across the bed. After swinging my cloak over my shoulders, he tightened the clasp under my chin.

"How long will you be this sensitive?" he asked.

I shrugged. "Not long, I hope."

"Well," he announced and stepped back again. "I think you're ready. Why don't you head to the common area and grab a bite of breakfast? I'll see that the horses are saddled and ready."

I felt utterly useless. "Fine."

Ropert tucked the rest of my belongings into my saddlebag and hefted it onto his shoulder. "Do you think you can keep an eye on Broderick for me, if I let him out?"

I shrugged. "What do you think?"

He paused a moment. "On second thought, I'll have him help me with the horses."

11

PHOENIX FIRE

The heat of the winter sun fell upon my shoulders and crisp air filled my lungs. This would have certainly been a day for Mina to feast on sunlight. But it did not bode well for my eyes at all. In spite of hiding my face deep within the cowl of my cloak, it did little. And Ikane's heightened senses only made the condition worse. I had no choice but to ride blindly and follow my companions.

When the sunlight faded, and the sky was left with a bright violet hue, my eyes seemed to breathe a sigh of relief. Just as the sun vanished behind the horizon, Ropert pulled Beast to a halt.

"Broderick, you set up the tents. I'll tend to the horses. Dagger, you get the fire going and tell your wolf-friend to get some supper. I'm famished."

I felt Ikane's annoyance towards Ropert. *We shall see if I get him a rabbit tonight. I'm half tempted to bring him a mouse.*

A smile stole across my lips. *You know Ropert would only eat my rabbit if you got him a mouse.*

Very well, Ikane sighed. *I will hunt for you, but if Ropert thinks that I am merely here as a food supplier, he is sorely mistaken.*

With that, Ikane darted away and I set out to find dry tinder.

The firedust embedded into my hands caused my fingers to throb as I struck the flint together. A spark flew into the kindling but died before it caught. I wished Mina were here to ignite it for me.

Broderick, noting my dilemma, came to my side and crouched by the dry wood.

"Shall I?" he asked, holding his hand out.

Frustrated, I placed the flint into his palm. He struck the stones together twice, and a large spark flew into the dry kindling. A soft gray cloud curled from the wood as he leaned down to blow. When the flames ignited, he rested back on his heels.

"I'd give anything to have a sprite bestow a gift on me," he said, nodding to my hands. I had taken my gloves off, revealing the beautiful yellow-red glow. "Such a thing is rare, and even more so of a firesprite. It is considered good fortune to know a person bestowed with such a rare sprite endowment."

Ropert stepped around the fire and propped his broadsword against the log I was sitting on. "I, for one, am glad the sprite is gone. She did nothing but grumble. Is the burning any better?" he asked me.

"Perhaps a little," I said. "The dark is certainly easier on my eyes, and the light of the fire doesn't hurt so much."

"Sir Ropert?" Broderick asked. "Where is my lute? This seems like a perfect evening for a little music."

Ropert scrutinized the black-clad man for a moment, his face impassive, then he turned and stepped around the fire to where the tent was pitched. I heard a harsh twang of the instrument strings as he jerked it from the pile of saddlebags nearby.

"Careful!" Broderick barked, nearly leaping to his feet. "Those strings don't grow on trees!"

Ropert mumbled an apology and handed the lute to the assassin.

Broderick took his finely crafted lute and set it across his lap, using one of his knees to prop it up.

"Any requests?" he asked and followed the question with a chord as his thumb gently thrummed across the row of strings.

Ropert placed another piece of wood on the fire and sat on the log beside me. "Do you know the Ballad of Amall? Or perhaps the Ode to Kelperah?" he asked.

Broderick's fingers swept across the strings. "I'm impressed, Sir Ropert. I didn't take you for a man of the arts."

Ropert shrugged. "Well, I do like music."

"What about Wardentsong?" I asked. I had always loved the tune when Mayama had hummed it in her kitchen.

The assassin paused a moment and tipped his head at me. He seemed surprised that I even knew the tune. He tweaked a few pegs, then strummed again. Satisfied with the sound, his fingers curled down on the neck of the instrument to change the chords. Then, with a steady rhythm, I recognized the tune of the familiar Roanfirien lullaby I had requested.

His voice, already somewhat musical when he spoke, harmonized with the beautiful melody on his lute. Ropert and I listened intently. It was rare that we had an opportunity like this.

"Fabled horse, one-horned wonder,
Frozen tracks of silver thunder.
Bred of magic on the mountainside,
The glacier lands are open wide.

Stalwart griffon, talons berth,
Hidden sands of barren earth.
Copper feathers, fertile kiss
United ground with nature's bliss.

Leviathan mist, islands rising,
Ships lost in flares of lightning,
Prowl through water, clear and sure,
Alongside the Rethreal shore.

Phoenix fire, burning rage,
Ashes crown a gilded cage,
Fevered friendship, timeless love,
Wings unfurled, warm ne'r enough."

As the song came to an end, I found myself longing for more and I clapped. It only took one small smack of my hands coming together before I flinched.

"Please, can you sing the Ballad of Amall?" I asked eagerly.

Broderick smiled, pleased that I had enjoyed his performance.

I felt Ikane's presence before he appeared with two large rabbits dangling from his maw. He dropped them by the fire.

"Finally!" Ropert declared as he snatched the hares from the snow. Absently, he ruffled the wolf's fur like a pet. "Thanks."

Ikane shook his coat with irritation. *He's getting worse,* he whined at me. *It's equivalent to him ruffling my hair in human form.*

I laughed out loud at the image that brought to my mind, and both Ropert and Broderick looked at me, puzzled.

"What's so funny?" Broderick asked. "Is my voice that humorous?"

"No! No. It's Ikane," I chuckled, wiping my eyes with the back of my hand. I smiled fondly at the wolf when he sat down beside me and wrapped my arm around his neck to pull him close.

Now you're doing it, he said, though he was much less annoyed at my touch than he was with Ropert's. In fact, he seemed to relish it.

Broderick played with a few light chords on his lute, as Ropert drew his boot-knife to work on skinning the rabbits for supper. The evening was almost perfect... almost.

A pang of intense stinging raced through my head... and Ikane's body. I flinched and withdrew my arm as Ikane stumbled towards Broderick. The assassin paused his strumming, noting the shift in Ikane's behavior. It was nothing I had ever felt before. It didn't burn like the fire of Rion.

What was that? I asked Ikane.

The wolf shook his head fiercely as if trying to shake off the bite of a predator. And then he looked up at me with wide and terrified mismatched eyes.

No, a flash of horror raced through his mind. *Kea! Get out of my head! Now!*

Puzzled, alarmed, and curious, I didn't react. And I paid the price for it. I felt his muscles tremble as he strained to keep his composure, and then the overwhelming pain of breaking bones and rending flesh. I cried out in agony and crumbled to the ground. Ikane continued to stumble back as his body snapped and jerked.

In an act of self-preservation, I thickened the barrier between our minds so that Ikane's pain had no more bite than a mosquito prick.

Startled, Ropert dropped the rabbits and the knife to the snow and grabbed his broadsword as he leapt to his feet. Broderick reacted just as swiftly, tossing his lute aside. He took a few steps away from the writhing wolf, and then his eyes darted to me.

Ropert was the first to act. He reached down and grabbed my arm to pull me away from Ikane as the whining of the wolf turned to the anguished cries of a man. Panting and trembling from the aftermath of the pain and adrenaline, I watched as Ikane's body twisted and arched. His face contorted, and his black fur seemed to absorb into his tanned skin. And then, in a matter of a few agonizing seconds, Ikane crouched by the fire in the form of a man. His raven hair hung wildly across his face and a thin, unkempt beard lined his perfect jaw. Confused, he blinked up at us.

Broderick acted quickly and tossed his cloak over Ikane's naked figure.

Grateful, Ikane pulled Broderick's cloak around his muscular form, but his dark brows still wrinkled with confusion. "I wasn't supposed to change form," Ikane said as he looked at me. "Something is wrong..."

And then it began. Ikane grabbed his head and groaned in torture as his body doubled over.

"No! No! No!" I cried, resisting the urge to run to his side. "Fight her, Ikane!"

Ikane's voice roared into the night as he tore at his hair.

She did this. Rion had somehow forced Ikane to change form. My eyes blurred with tears of rage as I watched him writhe under her burning torture. He cried out again as blood dripped from his nose, and then he fell silent. With his head hanging low, his body relaxed all form of tension away, and then swelled with raw power. The silence was earsplitting and thicker than the walls of a fortress.

"It's Rion," I breathed to my companions.

Ikane's head rose in a slow, menacing manner that revealed deep golden-red eyes burning with the color of the phoenix. A dangerous smile spread across his handsome lips as he looked up at me.

Ropert knew the look. It was the marking of a target. When Ikane lunged forward, Ropert reacted, half expecting the movement. With a flash of his arm, Ropert propelled my body behind him while simultaneously stepping aside just enough to allow Ikane to fly past us. He delivered a shocking blow with the hilt of his sword to the back of Ikane's head.

The Leviathan pitched forward and sprawled into the snow behind us.

Ropert whirled, sword ready.

I half expected Ikane to be unconscious, for the resounding crack to his skull still echoed through the trees. But when Ikane pushed himself from the snow, I knew there was no end to Rion's malicious power.

"Dagger," Ropert warned, pushing me behind him again.

Before Ikane could get to his feet, Broderick leapt onto his back like a fabled panther from the Tolean desert. The force and weight of his body drove Ikane to the ground, but the Leviathan twisted just enough to cause Broderick to slip to the side. With the speed of a viper, Ikane's elbow jerked back, catching the assassin square on the jaw. I heard his teeth smash together as his head snapped to the side.

Ikane kept his momentum, twisting around completely until his hand flew to Broderick's throat and drove the assassin to the snow. Ikane's fist slammed into Broderick's face twice before Ropert intervened.

He dropped his sword, not wishing to permanently injure the Leviathan, and wrapped his muscular arm around the Leviathan's neck. Ikane arched back, clawing at Ropert's thick arm. His face turned three shades of red, but he found no leverage to escape. Ropert grunted at the effort it took to keep Ikane from writhing free. I watched Ikane grow weaker with the lack of oxygen. His eyes glazed over and then rolled back into his head. Eventually, he fell limp.

Ropert carelessly dropped Ikane's flaccid body to the ground. "His eyes..." he said to me, trying to catch his breath. "They... they were on fire."

I nodded. "Bind him quickly," I said. "I've a feeling he won't be out long."

Ropert sprinted to our saddlebags and feverishly tore at them to find the extra rope. After he returned and began to bind Ikane's wrists, I cautiously stepped around to check on Broderick who was still lying in the snow.

As I approached, the assassin propped himself up on his elbows, and wiped blood from his nose with the back of his hand. "Well," he said with a small chuckle, and tested his split lip. "I think I like him better as a wolf."

To keep his dignity somewhat intact, Ropert and Broderick managed to slip Ikane's trousers on. But that was the extent of it. He woke shortly after, and Broderick was forced to choke him out a second time. We had no choice but to lash Ikane to the trunk of a nearby tree. I tried to make him somewhat comfortable by placing an extra bedroll under his legs, but the way his head rolled limply on his shoulders made me think that my little act of kindness was futile.

"We need a better way to sedate him," Broderick considered aloud after Ropert tied a thick knot in the ropes. "Especially if we are forced to travel with him in this condition. You might end up breaking his neck."

Ropert tugged on the ropes harshly, making certain that it wouldn't come undone. Satisfied, he stood and dusted his hands off. "I won't lose any sleep over it."

I rolled my eyes at Ropert and returned to my perch by the fire. Ropert and Broderick joined, sitting on either side of me, facing the unconscious Leviathan. Ropert grabbed the half-skinned rabbits from the ground and fumbled through the snow until he found his knife hiding underneath.

"What do you have in mind?" I asked Broderick as I leaned forward and placed another log on the fire. It was strange to not worry about accidently hitting Mina.

Broderick reached back and picked up his lute from the ground. His lips pulled down in a deep frown upon noting a cavernous nick in the finely crafted edge of the instrument. His thumb brushed up against it, as if he were stroking the cheek of his beloved. And then he groaned when his fingers found a broken string dangling from a peg.

"I'm so sorry," I said.

He took a deep breath and sighed. "It's alright. We'll just simply have to make do without music for a time. I'll get another string when we get back to Meldron."

Ropert, almost finished with the first of the rabbits, cleared his throat to keep us on topic. "You were saying that we need a better way to sedate Ikane."

I was a little startled by this. For one, he actually seemed to consider Broderick's warning about breaking Ikane's neck. And then he had actually referred to Ikane by name instead of simply calling him 'The Leviathan'.

Broderick set his lute aside. "I have a tincture..."

"Oh, no you don't," Ropert interrupted, shaking his knife at the assassin. His suspicion of Broderick returned full force. "I'm not letting you near your poisons. You've drugged me once already. For all I know, you'd place some in my water and leave me for dead in the morning."

Broderick gave Ropert a sideways glance with a dangerous, yet playful glint in his eyes. "Don't think the thought hasn't crossed my mind."

Ropert's eyes widened slightly, uncertain if the assassin were actually jesting with him.

At this, Broderick's smile broadened, and then he flinched as the smile irritated his split lip. A bruise was already forming on his jaw.

"I'm joking!" he laughed, then more seriously he continued. "In truth, there is something that will easily keep Ikane sedated. We simply need to get him to breathe it in."

I looked at Ikane's body sitting against the tree. His head still hung low, his long hair shrouding his face. My eyes narrowed, knowing that Rion simply waited for him to regain consciousness, and then the raging beast would emerge.

"Are you sure it won't hurt him?" I asked.

"Much less than Ropert's choking him out," Broderick replied.

I looked back at Ropert who seemed displeased with the idea of giving Broderick full access to all of his potions and tinctures, but he relented.

"Very well. They're in my left saddle bag," he jabbed the knife in the direction of our gear by the tent. "But I warn you, don't try that stunt again, placing herbs in my tea to make me sleep. It was childish and disrespectful, if you ask me."

Broderick stood and walked across the camp to the saddlebags. "You'll have to admit, that was probably the best sleep you've had in months though, wasn't it?"

Ropert mumbled something under his breath as he jabbed the rabbit onto a stick, clearly not wanting to admit that Broderick made a good point.

"Here," he grumbled as he handed me the end of the stick. "Get it roasting while I get the other one ready."

Holding the rabbit over the fire, I watched Ikane sleep. Now, more than ever, I needed to get to the Glacial Empire... and the temptation to disobey King Sander's orders returned. I glanced at Ropert sitting beside me, working hard to get the skin off the rabbit in a single tug. Perhaps I could leave Ikane with him and Broderick. They would take Ikane to Meldron where he would be kept safely locked away...

"Dagger!" Ropert snapped. His hand flashed out to grab the stick in my hands and jerk the rabbit out of the fire. The flesh was burning fiercely and smelled terrible. Ropert frantically blew at it to keep our supper from turning to ashes. The flames died out, leaving a black mottle of flesh on the end of my stick.

Ropert leaned back and shook his head. "Well, that one is yours," he said as he retrieved his other roasting stick.

I sighed. It was only fair.

Broderick whirled, turning our attention to Ikane who had stirred. Ropert and I stood quickly when the Leviathan's head rose, revealing the orange glow of his eyes through the darkness as he took us in. He tucked his legs in as he tried to rise but found that he couldn't. His head jerked down to see the rope lashed half a dozen times around his torso.

It is only a matter of time, Rion's voices said to me. I flinched, feeling my inner barrier rise instinctively to shield myself from her burning essence. But it wasn't needed. She didn't try to attack... at least not now.

I will free him, I told her fiercely.

Oh, I count on it. Her statement caused my will to falter.

Was I playing right into her plans? What was her newest scheme? Or perhaps she had simply said that to throw me off. Either way, there was a calmness about her that made me uneasy. And then I felt her smile.

I told you before that the Leviathan would be mine, and now he is. I shuddered at her innate lust for his soul and all the virtues he upheld. Although she had gained control over his body, I knew that she hadn't taken his soul. He was still there, hiding somewhere inside. I could only hope that she wouldn't reach him before I found a way to draw her out.

Ikane glowered at me, the fire in his eyes sharp and piercing. I had to remind myself again that it wasn't Ikane, but Rion who was scowling back at me. I tore my gaze away and sank back to the fire, hating what Rion had done to him. Ropert, sensing that there was no immediate danger, sat down cautiously as well and resumed roasting his supper. An eerie silence stretched across the camp as we tried to ignore Ikane's burning gaze.

Broderick returned to the fire with a glass vial filled with a clear liquid. He said nothing as he tucked it into a hidden pocket in his shirt.

Silently, I picked at the burnt rabbit on the end of my stick, but my appetite had vanished. Eventually, I set the meal aside and stood.

"I need to go for a walk," I announced.

"You can't go alone," Ropert said and was about to rise.

"I need some privacy," I said, my tone indicating that I needed to relieve myself.

"Oh," he said and turned back to the fire. "Well, don't take too long. We still have assassins on our tail."

I glanced at Broderick who shrugged and gave me a sympathetic smile. "He's right. They'll probably try to strike again just before we reach Meldron."

I groaned and closed my eyes as I turned my head to the sky. I was getting tired of watching my back and watching my thoughts. More and more, I longed for a secluded life, much like the healer Faslight in her little cabin in the woods.

Broderick had taken first watch, Ropert second, and I had taken the last remaining hours into the morning. Ikane had dosed off as well, and it took me a great amount of self-restraint to keep from loosening his bonds, even a little. He looked terribly uncomfortable.

The night gave way to another clear morning, and the orange glow of the sunrise promised warmth during the day. I placed another log on the fire and stirred the embers back to life, then placed the kettle by the fire to warm some water for Ropert and Broderick when they woke.

I felt them. They bored into my back. My eyes narrowed as I looked over my shoulder at Ikane... Rion. Her eyes glowered at me like daggers pulled from the forge.

"Don't look at me like that," I grumbled.

How would you prefer it? She asked, almost sweetly. *Would you prefer this?* The orange glow of Ikane's eyes flickered, flashing between his emerald and sapphire color.

I shot to my feet. *How dare you toy with him like that?!*

She laughed, mocking me further. His eyes flickered again, this time settling longer on Ikane's usual mismatched tone. He groaned and strained slightly under her taunting play of releasing hold on him.

I hurried towards him. "Ikane," I said. "If you can hear me, now is your chance. Fight back!"

His eyes snapped back to their golden burn, as I stood before him. She looked up at me and Ikane's lips spread into a dangerous smile.

Your love for this man will be your undoing, she said.

I smelled the fire before I saw the smoke swirling from the ropes that bound Ikane to the tree. Eyes wide, I stepped back. She had been baiting me. How? How was she able to manipulate magic physically? What new magic had she learned? Or was she simply growing stronger without my knowledge?

Ikane's body tensed against the ropes as he dug his heels into the ground.

"Ropert! Broderick!" I shouted, hoping to wake them before things got too far out of control.

And then the ropes snapped. Ikane lunged for me, his hand racing for my throat. My eyes narrowed. Rion had a terrible addiction to choking me, which had made her moves predictable. I stepped to the side, my left arm flying across my face to smash his hand away from my throat. His arm flew wide across his body. Instantly, my right fist shot into his solar-plexus and I heard the air whoosh from his lungs at the impact. Drawing my hand back, I grabbed his wrist and pulled him into my knee, which dug into his solar-plexus a second time. He groaned and would've doubled over, but Ropert's thick arm wrapped around Ikane's neck again, drawing him back. Ikane's face turned red as he struggled for breath against Ropert's grip.

"Broderick! Now!" Ropert roared.

As if Rion had discovered some new abilities, Ikane suddenly shifted and slammed his elbow into Ropert's chest. I heard him grunt as he pitched forward. At that same moment, Ikane reached up, grabbed my bodyguard's head, and pulled him over his shoulder. Ropert flew over Ikane's body like a sack of grain and landed square on his back. I saw the flash of triumph in Ikane's fiery burning eyes—and the eminent danger for Ropert. With a quick twist of his hands, Rion could easily force Ikane to snap Ropert's neck. Desperate to protect Ropert, I thrust my boot at Ikane's elbow and I heard it snap. There was no roar of pain, no indication of a broken bone, but Ikane stumbled away, losing his dangerous hold on Ropert's head.

Broderick shot forward and grabbed the Leviathan by the hair. With a savage jerk, he wrenched Ikane's head against his chest and covered his nose and mouth with a scrap of white linen. Ikane gasped for air as his arms flew up, but the tincture already soared through his body. His arms dropped. A second breath triggered weakness in his legs, and the third caused his eyes to roll back into his head. Broderick withdrew the cloth before Ikane took another breath and allowed the Leviathan's body to slump into the trampled snow.

Breathing heavily, the assassin crouched and checked Ikane's neck for a pulse. "We have about three hours before he wakes," he said.

Ropert stood and dusted the snow off his trousers. "That wasn't nearly as much fun."

Broderick chuckled. "I'll let you choke him out when I run out of my tincture."

"How did he get out of the ropes?" Ropert asked, turning to me.

My eyes shot back to the tree, eyeing the frayed and charred ropes that lay smoldering around the base of the trunk. I shook my head frantically. Rion was growing stronger and more brazen. "She burned them," I finally said.

Broderick, not quite believing what I had said, walked to the tree and picked up one of the ropes, then dropped it hurriedly as it burned his fingers. He shook his hand out. "It's hot," he confirmed.

Ropert's brows furrowed as he looked down at Ikane. The Leviathan's bare chest rose and fell deeply with each breath, revealing the deep pink scar on his ribcage.

"We'll have to keep him sedated constantly," he said. "We can't afford to have him... uh... to have the witch use any more magic."

Broderick and I nodded in unison.

12

WOLFSBANE

"**W**hy do you keep looking over your shoulder like that?" Ropert asked Broderick.

I wondered how Ropert had even noticed, seeing as Broderick rode behind us. Shade Ranger became Ikane's bearer, as she was the lightest on her feet. In spite of Ikane being invaded by the soul of the Phoenix Witch, we didn't intend to have his ribs bruised by the end of the day by lying across the saddle for hours on end. I rode double with Ropert upon the larger warhorse, Beast.

I turned my head to look at Broderick. Sure enough, his eyes were scanning the sparse trees around us and down the road. His breath plumed beneath his hood as he searched. He didn't seem satisfied when he saw nothing.

"I'm worried about the assassins," he finally said. "It's been far too long since we've had any sign of them, and I don't want to blow my cover."

Ropert slowed Beast a touch so that Broderick's horse could ride along-side us. "What do you mean?" Ropert asked.

"As I said, I am working for Master Chanter. But in order to gather better intelligence, I have gone undercover for many missions," he said and shook his head at himself. "I've grown complacent around you. I am able to be myself with you, more than—" he stopped, feeling that he was sharing information that was far too personal.

Personally, it was nice to hear that he enjoyed our company, in spite of Rion.

"I think it is time to split up," Broderick said.

My brows furrowed. I didn't want him to leave. Not only was I rather fond of him, my hands still ached from the firesprite dust, and I wasn't much good at restraining Ikane. He was pure muscle.

"Don't worry," he said when he saw my expression. "I think I know how I can keep you safe and keep my standing intact with the assassins... as long as they haven't seen me already."

"How?" Ropert demanded.

"You ride ahead. I will follow, and if the assassins find me, I can tell them that I've been on your trail, waiting for the right moment to strike."

"But what if they've seen you with us already?" I asked.

He shrugged. "Then Master Chanter will be quite wroth. We've been working for three years to infiltrate the league of assassins. I don't know what he'll do if I've been made."

It was interesting to note that Broderick was more concerned as to what Master Chanter would do, rather than what the assassins would do if they found out. Once again, I was reminded of how dangerous King Sander's mysterious servant really was.

Ropert looked back at Shade Ranger and Ikane's body lying across her saddle. "How much more time do we have before your tincture wears off?"

"Safely, about an hour," Broderick replied. "I'll give you the rest of my tincture, but I am beginning to wonder about the safety of the repeated use of the narcotic. At the next opportunity, I suggest that you purchase a pair of iron shackles. They won't burn off like the rope."

Ropert and I nodded together.

"We only have two more days till we reach Meldron," Ropert said to me. "Perhaps we can find a small smithy in one of the outlying villages."

I wasn't eager to have Ikane's eyes boring into my back with Rion's fire. But, like Broderick said, I was concerned for Ikane and what the strange narcotic was doing to his body. It was best.

"Alright," I said.

"I will follow you a half a mile or so behind," Broderick said. "If you should run into any trouble, I'll catch up fast enough to help if needed." With that, he tugged on his horse's reins so that she walked at a dreadfully slow pace. He fell behind quickly, continually looking over his shoulder.

"It's good to know he's watching our backs," I mumbled as I settled my cheek against Ropert's back. I meant it in more ways than one.

Ropert murmured something, and I could feel his chest rumble against my ear. "It'll certainly save my neck a bit of aching."

I half smiled, knowing that Ropert was jesting. It was clear that Broderick and Ropert had developed a cautious friendship. It was still fragile and just budding, but it was real.

We rode for another mile before Ropert and I dismounted and walked alongside Beast to give him a little respite. There was a field, a black field of burnt crops that stretched to our right. A small homestead stood at the edge, and the insignificant barn standing near the quaint little house bore black stains across the far corner where the fire had gotten to it. Otherwise, it was intact.

"Perhaps we'll find some iron there," Ropert said, jerking his head to the homestead.

"I doubt we'll find shackles," I murmured. "That looks like a simple farmer's home."

He shrugged. "It's worth a look."

We veered to the right and walked along the worn path that led to the main house. It looked deserted. The door hung from its hinges, and some of the shutters had been damaged. And then I saw the remains of campfires scattered across the yard. Some forgotten items lay scattered around: a pot here, a stocking there, and a few scraps of clothing. This had most certainly been used as a post for the Leviathan Pirates as they had made their way to Meldron. As we neared, the barn doors creaked in the light breeze, causing a gentle clap each time it swayed shut.

Feeling that we had gone far enough, Ropert pulled Beast to a stop and Shade Ranger quickly followed suit.

"I'll stay here with Ikane," Ropert announced as he stepped around the horses to check on the Leviathan. "He may wake again any minute. See what you can find in the barn there."

I nodded quickly and turned for the building. Annoyed by the constant swaying of the doors, I pushed against the one that pendulated the worst. The creaking silenced instantly. I was surprised at how easily my eyes adjusted to the darkness of the building. Piercing beams of sunlight rained through the cracks in the roof and dust swirled in the light, glittering like the dust from a firesprite. I was beginning to see what Mina meant. My eyes were getting sharper in the darkness.

In the center of the barn stood a wagon. Dust and cobwebs clung to the corners of the bed and across the spokes of the wagon-wheels. It wasn't hard to discern the rodent droppings scattered throughout. I always marveled at the way nature took over once man abandoned anything. Along the right side of the wall stood rows of empty stalls, most likely meant for horses or cattle. Some cobweb-adorned tack and saddlery remained hanging along the posts.

Above this, sat a large loft filled with old straw that smelled of rot.

It was the items to my left that caught my eye. I spotted a few shovels, pitchforks, a rake, and a scythe leaning against the far corner. Old barrels and crates held the various tools of a farmer, but nothing that looked even remotely like iron shackles. A dusty chain hung from a peg by the harvest-baskets. I wasn't a farmer, but I knew that chains were sometimes used to help clear the stumps of trees from the land. Doubtful that it would be of use, I grabbed it anyway and made my way back to Ropert.

He looked up at me as I approached. "Did you find anything?" he asked quickly. "He's beginning to stir."

I held out the chain for him to inspect with a shrug. "I don't know how we will secure it around him."

Ropert groaned, then sighed and took the chain from me. "Well, it's a step in the right direction. I should've made sure to grab some iron shackles before we left Meldron. I thought the rope would suffice and it was lighter to carry."

"We'll make do," I told him.

Ikane's head swayed, as if he were trying to comprehend where he was. Surely hanging upside down on the back of a horse made him a bit dizzy. I did not envy the ache he would feel in his ribs when he tried to stand.

Ropert dropped the chains instantly and sprinted to the other side of Shade Ranger, so that he would be right on top of Ikane once his boots hit the dirt. Sure enough, as soon as Ikane slipped back, Ropert caught his arms and wrenched them back. Ikane groaned as his ribs stretched.

"Kea, get the tincture," Ropert ordered. "It's right by that rock over there."

I hurried to pick it up, but upon standing, I looked at the mismatched eyes of Ikane. His emerald green eye was vibrant and true, and his blue one was just as well his own. Rion was not controlling him... at the moment anyway. How long until she did, was the unknown. I hesitated to place a few drops of Broderick's tincture on the scrap of cloth.

"Kea," Ropert snapped. "Hurry up."

"It's him," I said quickly. "Ikane is in control."

Ropert hesitated to slacken his grip on Ikane, but when he did, Ikane shook his head.

"Don't let me go," Ikane said, his voice filled with uncertainty and fear. He looked back at me. "It's better this way. Bind me any way you must. I won't fight you, but Rion... she's planning something... something dark."

"Get the chain, Dagger," Ropert ordered, tightening his grip on the Leviathan again. "We'll secure it with the rope. It may buy us some time if the witch burns it off again."

I grabbed the chain from the ground and stepped around the horses. Ropert shifted to let Ikane's hands come in front of him. Ikane held them, wrists pressed tightly together as Ropert wrapped the chain around them five times. I frowned as I slipped the rope through the links to tie it secure. Ikane had made sure to keep his wrists together, without crossing his arms. It was a trick many skilled warriors used to give a little wiggle-room in the lashing, but Ikane wasn't going to risk giving Rion any advantage, even if his fingers were already turning white from the lack of blood-flow.

He looked at both of us apologetically as we worked. "Is everyone alright?" he asked. "I remember hitting someone. My knuckles still hurt."

"Broderick is fine," I said as I finished with the triple knot.

Ropert held the end of the long chain, watching Ikane warily.

"Do you have any wolfsbane?" Ikane asked.

My head snapped up. Of course! I groaned. "No, and Broderick is probably the only one who does."

"Wolfsbane?" Ropert asked.

"Wolfsbane will force Ikane to change back into a wolf!" I said, unable to contain my excitement. "I should've thought of that before."

"Ah," Ropert nodded. "The curse of the lycan."

Ikane rolled his shoulders and neck to ease the cramping. "Whatever you are doing to sedate me is giving me a splitting headache," he mumbled.

Ropert folded his arms across his chest. "Or it's all the blood rushing to your head. We'll walk for a time. The horses need a break anyway."

Ikane nodded, obviously grateful to use his own body the way he intended.

"Dagger, untether Shade Ranger. You can lead her for now," Ropert suggested.

After I had done so, Ropert tugged Ikane forward gently, until he had enough slack to lash the chain around Beast's saddle-horn. Once Ikane was secure, Ropert grabbed Beast's reins and turned back down the road we had come.

I fell into step beside Ikane, but he seemed to distance himself from me, nearly bumping into Beast's side as he did so. "Not to close, little Brendagger. Knowing this demon inside me, she'll force me to spin around and wrap this chain around your neck once she gets the chance."

My shoulders slumped, and I gave some space between us. "She has a fetish for trying to choke me," I grumbled.

"Perhaps we could run through some scenarios later this evening," Ropert suggested over his shoulder.

"That would be wise," Ikane agreed.

It angered me that we needed to run through scenarios at all. If only I could draw out the witch. If only I could return her to her prison inside of the jewel around my neck.

We cleared the burnt field, leaving the abandoned homestead behind, and the long shadows of the woodland fell across us once more. Although the air was chilled, the snow on the ground was nearly gone, save for the spots where shadows kept it cold. Birds and squirrels chattered in the trees and Ikane looked in the direction of a particularly noisy bird. I could almost imagine him as a wolf with his ears twitching at the sound.

"Ikane?" I asked.

When he looked at me, I continued.

"Do you hear now as well as you do when you are a wolf?" I asked.

He nodded once. "Smell too," he said. "It's not always pleasant and it is sometimes distracting. My eyesight is another matter."

"I thought it was quite sharp," I admitted. "It was doubly painful when Mina first burned my eyes to see with yours."

"True," he admitted. "It is sharp, but it lacks color and brightness. In one way, I can see the smallest movements because there are fewer distracting hues. But then again, I feel like I miss other details."

"So... I could sneak up on you then?" Ropert said from the front.

Ikane chuckled. "Only if you can still your breathing. I can smell you two miles away, especially if you haven't bathed in a while, and hear your tromping footsteps six miles away."

Ropert's eyes widened as he looked over his shoulder at Ikane. "And now you have a witch inside of you, bent on killing Dagger?"

Ikane's smile faded as his eyes turned downward.

"Nice going, Ropert," I grumbled.

"Sorry," he mumbled in return. "I didn't mean to..."

"Hush," Ikane said harshly, his head snapping up. His eyes darted ahead and to the left, as if something had caught his attention.

Ropert halted and Beast snorted lightly.

"What is it?" I whispered.

Ikane's nostrils flared, something I had seen him do before. But it wasn't until I had discovered that he was a lycanthrope that I understood the action.

"Ahead. Three men. I can smell their tanned leather. Armed. The iron has a distinct scent... and," he stopped. A smile stole across his lips as he looked at me. "Wolfsbane. Their blades are saturated with it."

Ropert whipped his sword out instantly and I gripped the hilt of mine.

"They are a mile ahead," Ikane said softly, indicating that the danger wasn't quite yet upon us.

Ropert looked down the road, and I could see his jaw working as he calculated our next moves.

"Normally I'd say let us avoid them by going around, but I am eager to have some of that wolfsbane in my blood," Ikane said.

I wanted that too, but I didn't want it delivered by assassins. One expertly placed weapon could prove fatal and there would be no wolf or Ikane if that happened. Even so, we could not unbind him and let him fight. The risk of Rion overpowering him in the middle of our bout with the assassins could be our undoing.

Ropert stroked the red stubble on his chin as he turned back to Ikane. "Can you smell Broderick?" he asked.

Ikane nodded. "He's about half a mile behind us now and gaining."

"Good," Ropert said. "That means the assassins don't know he's with us. We'll have him on our side. Once he gets close enough, we can charge in and Broderick can watch our backs."

I shook my head. It was just like Ropert to run in and count on his skill and strength to win the fight. "They are skilled archers," I reminded him. "They'll pick us off before we even know where they are. It was Mina who spared us the first time. We may be surrounded by trees, which will limit the use of a bow and arrow, but they are trained assassins. They will hit their mark if they can."

"Then let me go in first," Ikane said. "I will draw their fire."

"That won't work," I said, shaking my head. "They are not hunting you. They are after Ropert and me."

"Then what do you suggest?" Ikane asked.

I bit my lip and looked at Shade Ranger. Perhaps she'd be up for the challenge.

"I'll race ahead and draw them into the open. You two follow behind. Surely you can take one of them out before they overpower me."

"Dagger..." Ropert's brows furrowed. I could tell that he wanted to protest, but he knew I was right. I was their main target. It was the best way to flush them out.

Ikane absently flexed his fingers, trying to pump blood back into them as he processed the idea. Neither one of my companions liked it, but it was sound, and they knew it.

"I'll need a weapon," Ikane said, but there was a hesitation to his voice that I understood. He did not want to be armed.

"We can manage," Ropert declared. "Are you sure about this, Dagger?"

I looked back to Ikane. "If we can get wolfsbane, then it'll be worth it."

"Let's walk a little further then, *quietly*," Ikane said. "We'll make our way closer and I'll let you know when to make your move."

Ropert and I nodded.

Shade Ranger sprinted across the narrow road that cut through the center of the woods, whipping up the fallen leaves of autumn. Her hooves thrummed steadily as the cold wind raced across my face. The long shadows of the trees easily shrouded the assassins in their black garb, but Ikane had said there were two on the right and one on the left. All I could do was stay low and hope that any arrows fired wouldn't hit their mark.

I heard it. It was quiet and distant at first, but the whistle became louder as it caught up to me. Using my knees, I urged Shade Ranger to swerve to the left. I felt the tug against the sleeve of my tunic as the arrow ripped across it and warbled harmlessly away. My heart lurched into my throat, knowing that if I hadn't shifted my horse, the arrow would've sunk deep into my back. Shade Ranger sensed my fear, and I felt the muscles in her body bunch with another surge of energy. I hadn't thought she could go any faster.

And then the expected cry came from behind. I pulled Shade Ranger around, and she reared in annoyance as I interrupted her sprint. Digging my heels into her side, I urged her back the way we had come, drawing my sword.

As planned, Ropert had caught the archer by surprise. The assassin lay prone on the mud splotched ground, unmoving, with his bow beside him. The quiver had spilled over half of its arrows across the assassins back.

Now, Ropert turned to face the other two assassins, who seemed slightly perturbed at how they had been ambushed. They hesitated, keeping their weapons sheathed as they kept their distance from Ropert's longsword. Ikane stood a few paces behind Ropert, still bound and tethered to Beast's saddle. He shifted from one foot to the other, his eyes darting between the weapons at the assassin's belts and the quiver of arrows strewn about.

"Hands up!" Ropert bellowed at them.

That was all the assassins needed to set their resolve. They were not the type to surrender. The one to his right whipped out his sword, while the other took a few cautious steps back in preparation to use his lethal throwing knives. My eyes narrowed at him. He was mine. I roared at him, drawing his attention away from Ropert. He whirled as Ropert and the sword-wielding assassin struck steel on steel.

Hastily, the assassin flicked his wrist at me, and I saw the glint of silver fly from his hand in a dangerous arc. Given that there was enough time to gauge the distance of his throwing knife, I easily swatted it out of the air with the flat of my sword. Another followed almost instantly. This time, it was sheer luck that I managed to fling it away. It spun in the air for a moment, then fell, cutting into Shade Ranger's flank on its way down. She flinched and danced to the side at the sting. Her movement was what spared the third throwing knife from hitting me in the shoulder and it whirred harmlessly by.

Out of knives, the assassin drew a short sword from his belt and readied his stance. A small wave of relief flowed through me. I didn't think I could've managed to evade a fourth knife. It was sheer luck that I had dodged the last two.

Ready to finish him, I kicked Shade Ranger's sides to urge her forward, but she staggered. Her left flank, where the knife had scraped into her skin, twitched convulsively, and her leg nearly buckled beneath her. When she tried to obey my command, her leg folded. She went down hard, throwing me from the saddle as she collapsed. I tucked my head and rolled over my shoulder so that my back easily bowled across the road. Once I felt my heels hit the earth, I slipped them under my body and stood.

In a matter of seconds, I faced the assassin. His face, though smudged with black paint to hide his features, seemed to go a shade lighter as he was forced to draw his long knife from his belt to parry my sidelong stroke. My sword cut through the air with a whistle, marred by the gentle scrape of his knife against my blade. It whipped past him. Seeing as his weapon was smaller and more maneuverable, he managed to loop it gracefully and slice it upwards at my face. I arched back, stepping away.

A cry came from Ropert's attacker, causing the assassin that I faced to stall. This gave me the opportunity to spring forward, driving my sword, point first, at his belly. He stepped aside, trapping my blade between his leather clad arm and side. With an experienced step to the side, he twisted his body so that I was either forced to relinquish my sword or step with him—which would put me in a terribly unbalanced position. As his knife raced for me again, I had no choice but to release my grip and jump away.

Ropert's sword raced at his head. The assassin ducked, dropping my sword. He sprang back into the shelter of the trees as Ropert's blade swung at him again—and lodged in the truck of a tree.

The assassin's eyes flicked to his unmoving companions lying in the road. Without a word, he turned on his heel and sprinted into the shelter of the thick trees.

"Blast!" Ropert jerked his sword from the trunk. "I was hoping to be rid of all of them."

That same thought had crossed my mind, but now I turned back to my horse. Shade Ranger lay on her side, her chest heaving at the effort it took her to breathe. Dropping to my knees beside her, I studied the small cut in her brown flesh. It wasn't deep at all. In fact, it was barely a scratch.

"The wolfsbane," I said, looking up at Ropert who came to her side.

His brows furrowed. "What can be done?" he asked.

I looked back down at Shade Ranger. She snorted, and her nostrils flared. Placing a hand on her neck, I tried to soothe her. "I don't know..."

"Kea, look!" Ropert called, pointing to the road behind us. Broderick came galloping up on horseback.

"I leave you for a few minutes and you're already in trouble," he said as he pulled his horse to a stop. He swung from the saddle. He skirted around the Leviathan, eyeing Ikane warily. Realizing that Ikane wasn't a threat, he sprinted the last few steps to my side.

"Wolfsbane, is it?" he asked.

I nodded.

He pursed his lips. "There is no antidote for it, but..." he slipped his hand inside of his black leather jerkin. Then, he pulled out one of the tiniest glass vials I'd ever seen. A bright blue glow emanated from the contents inside. Carefully, he uncorked the top and tipped the vial over Shade Ranger's injury. Dust spilled from the opening, glowing as it gently swayed down to the small red cut on her flank. Instantly, the injury began to move, as if something had buried itself into her skin. Small white bubbles of foam grew from the wound and slipped down to the road.

"Quickly," he said. "She needs to drink this as well."

"What is it?" Ropert asked as I grabbed my mug that hung by my saddlebag. I snatched my waterskin from the saddle as well, opened the cork, and poured some water into it.

"Waterdust," Broderick said as I held the mug out to him. He tipped the vial again, spilling some of the dust into the mug. "It can flush out the poison."

Desperate to save my horse, I skirted around Broderick and tipped the mug of water to Shade Ranger's mouth. She tried to lift her head, but it fell back again. She was too weak.

"Help me, Ropert," I said.

He dropped his sword and immediately knelt beside Shade Ranger to help support her head. Her tongue licked at the water, but she was quickly losing interest in drinking. Eventually, Ropert and I turned her head so that we could slip most of the liquid into her mouth. Her neck moved as she swallowed. Within moments, white foam frothed across her lips.

"Broderick!" I cried in alarm.

"No, all is well. That is supposed to happen," he said calmly. "Don't touch the foam though. It is filled with the wolfsbane. Wash her skin off with your water. She should be fine."

As suggested, I poured the water from my waterskin over her mouth and watched as the foam was carried away into the dirt. More grew around her lips, but it was quickly lessening. I washed it again and Broderick motioned for me to rinse her injury off as well.

Ikane groaned, putting his chained hands to his head. "Not now." He looked back at us, pleading. "The wolfsbane! Quickly!"

Ropert sprang to his feet, grabbed the knife lying beside Shade Ranger, and marched over to Ikane. Without hesitation, he whipped the blade across the back of Ikane's hand. Ikane flinched and took a step back, his eyes flickering with maddened firelight as he glowered up at Ropert. All at once, he began to shift.

But Beast reared in alarm, jerking Ikane around as he was still tethered to the warhorse's saddle! The massive black warhorse skirted into the trees in an attempt to get away from the writhing man beside him. He whinnied and reared again, kicking his legs at Ikane. Ikane cried out as his body broke and bent, but with his hands still bound, his body couldn't shift the way it needed to.

Ropert tried to grab Beast's bridle, but the horse wanted nothing to do with it. He shook his head wildly and lashed out at Ropert with its front hooves. Ropert had no choice but to leap behind a tree to avoid the blow. One of Beast's hooves smashed against the trunk, splintering the bark. And then he bolted. Ikane was whipped around violently and his body ricochet against a tree as Beast swerved around it. I leapt to my feet, wide eyed and terrified, as Ikane was dragged behind the warhorse. Without a word, Broderick sprinted for his horse, sprang into the saddle, and kicked his heels into his horse's sides. With a sharp click of his tongue, the animal, slightly startled by the chaos, quickly obeyed. Both horse and rider disappeared after Ikane and Beast in a cloud of autumn leaves.

Ropert stepped out from behind the trees, his face pale. "I didn't think that through, did I?"

I didn't know what to say. I would've made the same error. Rion was about to overpower Ikane and I would've done anything to keep her at bay. But we both had forgotten how terrified Beast was of the wolf.

Shade Ranger's head shot up. She rocked her body for a moment, her legs flailing out as she tried to get them under her. I scrambled back to give her space, and soon she was standing upright! I marveled at the effectiveness of the sprites elemental dust powers yet again. The muscles around her flank twitched slightly, but she seemed to have decent use of her leg, though I dared not ride her at full force, nor would I burden her with two riders. Instead, I grabbed her reins and began a hurried pace after Broderick and Ikane.

Ropert hurried to walk beside me. "Dagger, I'm sorry," he said. "I didn't think…"

Realizing that he had taken my silence for anger instead of shock, I interrupted him quickly. "It's alright. I would've done the same thing."

Ropert's mouth clamped shut, possibly thinking that I had only said that to make him feel better.

"Really," I hurriedly said. "I forgot about Beast's fear of Ikane. I simply wanted to keep Rion at bay. Please don't fret about it. I just want to catch up to Broderick and Ikane before something terrible happens."

Ropert's brows furrowed as our pace quickened. "What could be worse than being dragged behind a frightened warhorse?"

I couldn't think of anything.

13

BRODERICK

Breathless, we found Broderick standing beside his own horse and Beast. The massive warhorse's nostrils were flaring, his black eyes were wide, and his ears twitched at every sound of the autumn woods. Frantically, I searched for the chain that I half-expected to be dangling from the saddle-horn. But it wasn't there.

At my expression, Broderick shook his head. "It came off near that bend back there. I don't know where Ikane is."

I turned around instantly, wanting to march back and find him.

Ropert grabbed my arm to stop me. "Hold on, Dagger."

"Ikane needs help! What if he's hurt? His arms—" I cringed at the memory of his arms being jerked forward as he shifted into a wolf. "What if his legs are broken? He can't come after us. I need to find him."

Ropert nodded. "Dagger, calm yourself," he said. "Think about it. You have a link to Ikane, do you not? Breathe. Focus. You'll find him if you try."

He was right. My whole body was still trembling from the event of nearly an hour ago. I gathered a deep breath and plunged into my mind, finding the barrier I had created when Ikane had first shifted into a human. I tore it wide, searching for any link to him. I found it, more abruptly than I had expected, and terrible pain raced up my right arm. It was all I could do to keep from crying out.

Ikane! Are you alright? Where are you? I called out to him, holding my own arm as if it could ease the pain.

Kea, he groaned, and I could hear the high-pitched whimper of the wolf through the trees. It came from my left.

"This way," I said and ran.

I dodged the thick trunks, rocks, and stickery underbrush, feeling Ikane's heightened senses begin to guide me. I could almost smell him now. His whimpering became louder, and then I spotted him. The large black wolf lay in a bed of red and gold leaves beneath a large oak tree.

"Ikane!" I cried, sprinting the last distance between us. A sharp jolt radiated through my knees as I plowed to the ground beside him. But I ignored it. His head came up briefly to look at me, then flopped back down to the leaves with a whimper.

The pain in my arm wasn't imaginary. The chain had slipped from his left foreleg, but his right was tangled in the iron and bent underneath him quite unnaturally. I attempted to remove the chain, but any movement sent jolts of lighting through both of our arms. I gritted my teeth as I tried again, but the pain was too great.

You just... need to set it, Ikane said, gasping through his mind against the agony. *My bones... mend quickly, but not like... this. It needs to be... in the right... position.*

"Dagger!" Ropert called. I turned to look back at him. His eyes weren't quite as sharp as mine with Ikane's heightened senses and Mina's firedust gift, so I waved to him.

Broderick was right behind him, with all three horses in tow. He stopped, keeping a good distance away for Beast's sake.

Ropert, upon seeing me, hurried through the trees and underbrush.

"His leg is broken," I said as he approached. "We need to set it."

Ropert's face went white upon seeing the grotesque position of the wolfs right leg.

I won't bite! Ikane growled. *Just set it quickly!*

Ropert hesitated as he thought the wolfs growl was intended for him.

"Do it quickly," I told him, stepping back.

Ropert's jaw set in a tight line as he knelt in my position, the leaves crunching beneath his weight. Ikane's head stretched out on the leaves and his breathing was sharp and labored. Ropert took a deep breath filled with resolve.

"Alright," he said softly to the wolf and to me. "Three... two... one..."

I screamed as my arm felt as if an axe had severed it clean off, and my cry echoed through the trees. Ikane's yelp was mingled with a growl as the bone broke again. As promised, the pain subsided remarkably as his bones mended at an extraordinarily fast rate.

After a few heavy breaths, Ikane sat upright, then stood. The pain was gone.

Ropert let out a large sigh of relief. "Don't do that again," he said, and ruffled the wolfs fur on his head.

Ikane shook him off irritably. *Here we go again,* he grumbled.

It was the final night of camping out in the cold air of late autumn before we would reach Meldron the following day. Although I longed for the soft warmth of a bed, I wasn't eager to make my way back to where courtly matters would push and pull my fate in whatever direction it willed. This, I felt, was my last night of freedom.

A tune or two would've been most welcome, but Broderick had parted ways soon after we found Ikane lying in the woods. He claimed that he needed to keep up appearances with the assassins and had followed their trail.

My eyes strayed from the campfire to Ikane, who in turn, was already looking back at me. He knew what was going through my mind. He knew the fear. He knew the dread. He knew that I needed to get to the Glacial Empire. And marrying the Tolean Prince would surely kill that chance.

The large wolf sidled up to me, his warm body and fur a gentle comfort. I wrapped my arm around him, leaned my head against his shoulder, and closed my eyes. I didn't want to think about any of it.

Kea! Ikane's voice pulled me from slumber. *Kea, wake up!*

I blinked. The silvery light of the moon lanced through the small slit in the tent flaps, indicating that I had only been asleep for a few minutes after my watch. Irritated, I rubbed my face and rolled over, tucking my arm under my head.

What? I groaned through my groggy mind. I wasn't interested in a midnight conversation with Ikane. It could wait until morning.

Ikane's voice interrupted my sleep again. *It's Rion.*

He had my full attention now, and I sat upright. *What has she done?*

Nothing yet, he answered from beside the campfire, *but I feel her grasping. She's stretching herself. It was the same feeling I had before I changed last time. She's getting better at manipulating my form. I think it must be the wolfsbane. Once it's clear of my system, she can force me to change back,* he explained. *But I can't seem to get Ropert to understand. Every time I nudge his shoulder, he simply pats my head. I'm not a pet!*

On any other occasion, I would've chuckled at the image that brought to my mind, but given the severity of the situation, I pushed the humorous vision aside. *How much longer do you have?* I asked, slipping my boots onto my feet.

That's why I woke you, he admitted. *Minutes.*

I clambered from the tent to find Ropert sitting by the fire with his arms folded across his chest. His head swiveled around to look at me. "Awake already?" he asked. "You've barely been out for thirty minutes."

My eyes found Ikane sitting a few paces away from the fire, and opposite the sleeping horses.

I took a few steps forward, until I stood by the fire. "It's Ikane," I said. "He thinks Rion is going to try and force him to shift again once the wolfsbane is out of his system. Do you still have the knife?"

Ropert's eyes flashed to the wolf as he unfolded his arms in alarm. "I... uh... no. I dropped the knife when Beast took off with Ikane." Ropert quickly got to his feet and dusted his trousers off, his eyes not straying from the wolf.

"Then we'll need to sedate him," I said. Ikane's ears twitched at the sound of my voice and I could feel his apprehension. He didn't like the thought of being slung over Shade Ranger's saddle like a sack of grain again. The deep ache in his ribs was only just beginning to fade. But he quickly shoved the temporary thought of discomfort aside. A little pain was worth keeping everyone safe.

Ropert opened his belt pouch and pulled out the small vial and the scrap of linen. "I still have Broderick's tincture," he said.

"Good," I said and stretched my hands out to the fire. "Now we wait."

You may want to strengthen the barrier again, Kea. Unless you like the feeling of breaking bones.

He didn't need to suggest it twice.

Just as Ikane thought, he underwent the agonizing transformation from wolf to man not ten minutes after his warning to us. We didn't wait to see if Ikane would have control of his body. We couldn't risk it. Ropert immediately pounced on the Leviathan's back and held the scrap of cloth over his mouth and nose until Ikane was unconscious.

Meldron was as gloomy as I remembered. Some progress had been made on rebuilding a handful of homes, but the aftermath of war was still evident. Once again, Ikane lay across Shade Ranger's back while Ropert and I rode double on Beast. A few curious eyes watched as we passed by the main road and through the market square. I glanced up at the library, noting that one of the stained-glass-windows had been shattered. The depiction of Queen Damita, however, was still intact. The beautiful woman, with blazing red hair, looked down at me with fondness... while the crimson heirloom around her neck held an entirely different aspect. I glowered back at it, wishing that the glass of this window had shattered instead of the other.

No sooner did we approach the guards at Meldron's castle gates, did one of the soldiers turn and dart into the courtyard. The other stood at attention, nodding to us grimly as we rode our horses inside. There was a tension in the air that made the hair on my neck stand on end. And it wasn't just the cold or the gray clouds that had rolled in over the course of the day. Ropert felt it too, for I sensed his body stiffen as the horse's hooves clopped along the cobblestones of the yard.

Ropert and I slipped from Beast's saddle and glanced at each other. I led the way as Ropert guided our horses towards the large stables to our right. Promptly, a man appeared in the doorway. I recognized the broad shoulders and salt and pepper hair instantly.

"Kea," Eamon said, his brown eyes wrinkled with worry. He glanced nervously out the door, as if making certain that no one saw him, then beckoned to me with a hasty wave of his hand.

Confused, I picked up my pace. As soon as I was within arms-reach, Eamon grabbed my shoulder and jerked me into the shadows of the barn. He pushed me to the side of the door and pressed me up against the wall there, still scanning the courtyard for anyone who might be watching.

"What's wrong, Eamon?" I asked, keeping my voice low. Clearly, he didn't want to be seen.

"What are you doing here?" he whispered fiercely. "Didn't you receive my message?"

I was about to shake my head when I heard a commotion beyond the stable doors. Ropert had barely stepped across the threshold to guide Beast inside, when he stopped and turned around. Through a crack in the wooden planks that made the walls of the stable, I could make out a dozen, red coated soldiers appear from one of the side doors of the castle. They were led by a man with white hair, Master Chanter.

When three of the soldiers grabbed Ikane and tore his limp body from Shade Ranger's back, I moved to exit the barn. But Eamon pressed me hard against the wall with his forearm, and put a finger to his lips, urging me to stay silent.

"Careful!" I heard Ropert snap at the soldiers who were treating Ikane's unconscious form quite roughly.

"He'll be fine," Master Chanter assured him. "Where is Lady Brendagger?"

Ropert paused and looked around Beast's massive neck to where Eamon had me pinned against the wall. Eamon shook his head fiercely and sighed, knowing that Ropert's obvious look had given me away. Chanter was no fool.

Knowing that his time was limited, Eamon spoke quickly. "You shouldn't have come back... not yet. I meant to warn you in my letter," his brows narrowed. "But now I see that Master Chanter has intercepted it."

"What is going on?" I asked, trying to keep Eamon focused.

There was scuffling beside the door and the soldiers tried to move the horses through. Ropert, sensing that he could at least give me a little time, pulled Beast in the way. But it was of little use. Master Chanter easily slipped his willowy body around the massive warhorse and into the stable. I marveled at how well this old man could move.

"Get that horse under control," he chided Ropert. He then straightened his tunic and brushed his white hair from his face before smiling at me. It wasn't a threatening smile by any means, nor was it terribly friendly.

"Lady Keatep," he said and gave me a curt bow. "King Sander will be so relieved to know that you are here."

Eamon released me and folded his arms across his chest. He openly glowered at King Sander's right hand while the old man gave the war-master a knowing look. "King Sander has ordered all the members of his counsel to convene the instant Lady Keatep returned," he said with a respectful nod. "Come, Lady Keatep," he said and held out his old, scarred hand for me to take. "I shall take you to your quarters."

I glanced at Eamon nervously, but he set his jaw, and gave me one sharp nod. We had no choice in the matter.

The moment my hand touched Master Chanter's, his grip went tight, as if to keep me from bolting. He pulled me out the door and into the throng of waiting soldiers just outside.

"Seeing as you've returned so late in the evening, we will have the counsel convene first thing in the morning," he said as he guided me into the castle with the soldiers on our heels. It felt more like a prison march rather than a welcome home.

We came to a spiraling staircase – not anywhere near my old chamber - until we came to the third floor where I knew nobility was housed. The old man paused by a decorated door with iron hinges and turned to look at me. His gray eyes were filled with an expression of both determination and sadness. At least, that's what I thought.

"Rest well tonight, Keatep. Your life will not be the same after the morrow."

My eyes darted to two soldiers who had taken up their post on either side of the heavy door. "It's already shaping up to be very different."

Chanter's head lowered as a frown pulled on the corner of his lips, but he did not take his eyes from me. "It is for the good of the kingdom, my lady," he said in a low tone, as if that was all that mattered. He then gathered a breath, stood erect, and smiled warmly. "I shall have the lady's maids bring a warm meal and a bath for you at once. Goodnight, Lady Keatep."

With that, the door swung open and he practically threw me into the room.

I barely tasted the meal. And the bath, though much needed, didn't lift my spirits or the confusion. The large room - or more accurately, my elaborate prison - was furnished with a large four post bed, two cushioned chairs set before the fireplace with a small table standing between them, and a finely carved armoire to the left of the bed. There was one window - and it was boarded up, most likely to deter me from trying to escape.

Lying in the soft, feathered blankets of the bed, with the fire crackling loudly beside it, I dove into my mind to find Ikane. Surely, he had woken from Broderick's tonic by now. Carefully, I stretched out, finding that I could actually see auras of the many minds fluttering throughout the castle. Some were hot and enraged, others were cool and weary, some, deep in thought with a white-violet hue, and others were weak and faded in sleep. I had never seen this side of my power before. But, the more I stretched, the more I began to understand Rion.

Each aura held a certain... taste. Some were more desirable than others. And then I saw it. Ikane. His form was mingled with a beautiful emerald blue and vibrant green that held both warmth and strength. It was no wonder she had sought after his soul.

But now, it was mingled with a fog of black and fire. I had never before seen her aura this way. Rion's tasted bitter and rancid—like water that had been sitting in a mug for centuries.

Skirting around her sickening energy, I slipped through a back door into Ikane's mind. I felt him flinch the moment that I did, and then I felt the full effect that Rion's power had on the Leviathan. His body felt distant, like he was groping after something that was just out of reach. Her hold on him dulled his senses, causing his eyesight to blur and his ears to muffle the noises of the dungeon where he was imprisoned.

However, I clearly felt his weariness as he endured the rancid stench of the dungeon cell and the stifled, annoying rhythm of dripping water thrumming through his ears. The cold from the earth beneath him steeped into his skin through the layer of flea-infested hay that had been strewn about. A horrible itch bit behind his right ear, and even though I reached up to scratch my own, it did little to ease his discomfort.

Kea, I heard his startled voice through my head. *What—? How did—?"*

I just wanted to be sure that you were alright, I replied. *I hate seeing you this way. You've done nothing wrong.*

I am dangerous, Kea. You are right to lock me away.

Echoing footfalls and muffled voices reached the Leviathan's muted ears. As they neared, I was able to recognize Master Chanter's voice, which was tinged with disappointment.

"What were you thinking? You were instructed to observe and protect from a distance. This does not bode well for your cover."

"It wasn't that simple," I clearly discerned Broderick's voice as the pair of dangerous emissaries halted beside Ikane's cell. Ikane's blurred vision barely made out two dark silhouettes as they peered down at him.

"Explain," Chanter demanded.

"Duchess Caitelyn's assassins had them cornered. I had no choice but to feign an attack. It was an attempt to spare Keatep and keep my standing with the assassins," he paused. "But... she used her magic. I was not expecting that – I don't think she was either."

There was a slight lull in the conversation. "Magic?" Master Chanter asked.

I barely made out Broderick's nod through Ikane's eyes. "She's growing stronger. She must go to the Glacial Empire, master. You know how dangerous she will become to herself and others if she isn't trained."

"We are here to serve the king, Kavan. Nothing more. We are bound to his will. You know that."

My interest in Broderick was piqued when I heard Master Chanter address him by a new name.

"Yes master," Broderick said. "So, you think he is wrong to marry Kea off to the Tolean Prince?"

"My boy," Chanter sighed. "What I think doesn't matter. And speaking that way of your king is bordering on treason. Do you understand?"

"Yes master."

Rion forced Ikane's body to stir as keys jangled in the lock, and the heavy door swung open. Hot red fire blurred our vision as Rion took full control of Ikane's body and forced him to spring to his feet. He lunged for the shadows, but the heavy chains that were secured to Ikane's wrists held him back. I felt the intense burn behind Ikane's eyes as she shoved his consciousness aside, and with that, she nearly drove me back into my mind. I clung to Ikane, as though I were clinging to a tree in the midst of a raging cyclone.

Undaunted, one of the blurry figures bent down to place a bowl of gruel at Ikane's feet. The door closed and as soon as the lock clicked, Rion released Ikane's mind. He crumpled to his knees, allowing the weight of the chains to drag his arms to the ground.

"He truly is possessed," Chanter mused, and I thought I could see him stroking his groomed, white beard. "Bring him more hay and a good meal this evening," Chanter ordered as they turned to leave. "And be certain to gather some eucalyptus, sage, and yarrow herbs to mix with the hay. It should keep the fleas from bothering him so."

"Yes master," Broderick answered, his voice fading as they left.

Kea. Ikane breathed as if he had been suffocating under Rion's control.

I'm here, I assured him. *I never left.*

I felt him lean forward and sniff at the meal Broderick— Kavan— had provided. There was a familiar scent that I could not decipher. But Ikane knew it.

Clever man, Ikane said as he quickly grabbed the bowl and brought it to his lips.

Rion slammed into me with such force that my magical barrier cracked and allowed her burning anger to zap through my head. She latched onto my thoughts like a hook to a fish.

You cannot keep me here! You know you can't. I will escape. And your rebellion has only sealed the fate of Queen Lonacheska's child!

Desperate to free my mind, I drove my light to repel her. By fortunate accident, I brushed against her link to Ikane. Eager to free him of her grasp, I stretched my thoughts, thrusting Rion away from Ikane as my essence expanded. It seemed effortless to drive her away, yet it was nearly impossible to hold her at bay. My shield quivered under her fiery resistance.

Hold the barrier, Kea! Ikane suddenly shouted through my mind. Something in him was shifting, changing from the complicated awareness of a human to the simple, yet astounding intellect of a wolf. The pain of his changing form pulled on every muscle in my body.

No. No. No! Rion bellowed when she felt her loss of domination over the Leviathan.

It was wolfsbane, Ikane declared with excitement. *Broderick put wolfsbane in the food.*

I tried to distance myself or thicken the barrier between us, so that I was not confronted with the full effect of his pain, but Rion wouldn't let go. I cried out as his transformation burst into full action, and even Ikane groaned under the intense agony. But the painful rending of muscle and bone was brief and faded quickly under the astounding healing properties of Ikane's body. And Rion was pushed aside like a bad meal.

A harsh knock thumped on the door of my chamber. The essence of Ikane's cold, lonely, flea-infested cell was replaced by the warmth of the fire and soft clean nightdress against my freshly washed skin. I reached for Ikane one last time, allowing his heightened senses to fuel my own, and calm the trembling in my body.

"My lady?" came a shout through the door. "Are you alright?"

Kea, Ikane said my name through a distinguishable sense of relief. *It's done. I am a wolf.*

The knock sounded again, this time more urgently.

But for how long? I asked. *Can we keep wolfsbane in your system all the time? Surely it cannot be good for your health.*

It's not, he admitted. *The more I am infested with the poisonous herb, the harder it will be for me to return to my human form... even if Rion wills it. I could be stuck as a wolf permanently. And from the look of it, it won't take her much longer to discover how to manipulate my wolf form as well.*

I did not like that thought any more than the thought of Rion possessing him.

Impatient for a reply from me, the lock clicked, the door opened, and one of the soldiers poked his head into the chamber. "My lady," he began. "You cried out. Are you alright?"

"I'm fine," I grumbled from the bed and rolled away, my back facing him. I didn't want him to see the terror in my eyes, or the whiteness of my face. Eamon was right. I needed to go to the Glacial Empire. I couldn't marry the Tolean Prince. And then it dawned on me what Rion had said. *"Your rebellion has only sealed the fate of Queen Lonacheska's child."* The queen was pregnant... with a female heir.

I had only slept for a few agonizing hours before I woke and banged on the door for the soldiers to open it. After ordering them to bring me a quill and some paper, I sat up by candlelight and wrote. I described everything I knew in detail about the curse. I described the power I had felt and how I manipulated it. I wrote about the White Wardent and the fabled letter given to Emperor Skarand of the Glacial Empire. I wrote everything that I could think of that would help my unborn half-sister in the event that I failed at defeating the Phoenix Witch. I wanted her to know everything so that her chances were better than mine.

There was a knock on the door, and I stretched and craned my neck as I had been bent over the small table by the fire for the better part of the night.

"Enter," I called.

The door opened, and two maidservants came bustling in. They seemed a little startled at first, when they didn't find me sleeping, but carried on without a question. One of them built up the fire, though she didn't have much to do because I had kept it burning bright all night long. The other set a small tray of breakfast items on top of the paper I had been writing on. There was a pot of tea, three slices of buttered bread, and an aromatic spreadable meat substance that tasted a lot like liver. I ate it quickly.

By the time I had finished, the maidservants had laid out a gown of red and gold, with sleeves and a train that flowed longer than necessary, onto the bed. They beckoned for me to come closer.

"King Sander ordered that you wear this for the meeting," one of them announced.

I swallowed hard, knowing exactly what meeting they were referring to. And I recalled the way that he had manipulated me into wearing a fine gown at his wedding, making me appear regal in the eyes of the Tolean Prince.

I shook my head. "No, I will wear my uniform," I said.

The maidservants looked at each other, confused and a bit apprehensive. "But, my lady... it is the king's orders... he, well, it is—"

"I will wear my uniform," I repeated, this time more firmly. "I trust it has been washed and pressed?"

One of the maidservants bit her lip. The other nodded weakly.

"Go fetch it then," I urged.

I was not going to be portrayed as a beautiful lady to the Tolean Prince when I had grown up anything but. I was a soldier, a warrior, a fighter, and I wanted him to see that.

They darted from the room and the door locked after them. It wasn't long before there was another knock. The door opened quickly. I had expected to see the maidservants returning with my uniform, but I was surprised to see Master Chanter enter instead, with a deep scowl on his face.

"What is this about a uniform?" he demanded.

I shrugged unapologetically. "I assume this meeting has to do with Prince Leander of Toleah, does it not?" I said. "If so, I will be presented as the warrior that I am. I am a Soldier of Roanfire after all."

"You are also a Lady of Meldron," he snapped in return.

My reply came just as quickly. "Only just."

He groaned and rubbed his white beard. "Very well, but you may not carry your sword."

I folded my arms across my chest and glowered at him. "That is part of the uniform," I said flatly.

He rolled his eyes to heaven. "Phoenix help me," he grumbled. "This defiant behavior is going to get us both into a lot of trouble."

I didn't care. If Sander was going to peddle me off to the Tolean Prince, I would make him do so with full and open honesty, and a bit of humiliation.

"Very well," Chanter relented and snapped his fingers. The maidservant, who had been standing just outside the door, hurried inside with the familiar red and gold uniform folded upon her arms. The other followed, carrying the deep brown trousers, soft boots, and leather scabbard and sword that would complete the ensemble. A twinge of triumph raced through me. Master Chanter already had the items prepared, even the sword. He knew I couldn't be forced to wear the gown. This uniform, I knew, was brand new: crisp, un-faded, and never worn into battle.

"Now, hurry up," Chanter snapped. "We convene in the next thirty minutes."

He slipped outside, and the door closed.

14

THE TOLEAN PRINCE

The maidservants were trying to do something with my stubborn, shoulder length hair, when another knock sounded on the door. Frustrated, the maids resorted to leaving it free flowing, and went to answer the door.

Ropert stepped into the room, clad in a similar new uniform adorned in reds and golds. It was tailored impeccably to his broad shoulders and muscular frame, something I had rarely seen. Back in Daram, the uniforms were mass-produced and always too snug for the muscular warrior. He constantly popped the seams, sometimes on purpose and sometimes by accident. But now, it accentuated his perfectly built body. The deep crimson of his tunic made his bright blue eyes glow, and the sheen of his strawberry-blonde hair glimmer from oils and tonics.

But all this finery couldn't compare to the smile that spread across his lips. His eyes even shone when they fell upon me. "You've never looked more regal," he said earnestly.

I gave him a crooked smile in return. The crimson tunic and deep brown trousers I wore fit my body perfectly, but they weren't as flattering as a corseted gown. Yet, I did feel like I was respectfully representing my kingdom as well as my position as a Lady of Meldron.

"Oh," Ropert said, remembering something. He fumbled with his belt pouch. "I was told to give you this and that you should know what it means," he said as he handed a little wad of cloth to me.

My smile faded when I recognized the pattern on the fabric. Reluctantly, I took it from him, and the lump in my throat grew when I pulled the cloth away. The mirrored armlet that the Tolean Prince had given me was revealed. I looked up at Ropert, trying to swallow the lump away. This was it. Everything in my life was about to change and my freedom was slipping away. Was I willing to betray my king and leave Roanfire to starve, in order to save Ikane and the Queen's unborn child? Or would I leave Ikane and my half-sister to the mercy of Rion? I knew it was something I couldn't do.

Angry and frightened, my fist curled around the armlet as I felt the first sensation of hot tears ache in my eyes. In one quick step, I wrapped my arms around Ropert's solid waist and buried my head into his chest. His arms instantly surrounded me in return, crushing me against him.

"I won't leave your side," he whispered into my hair.

I whimpered. "I know, and that is what frightens me."

He squeezed even tighter and then released me. He cupped my face in his hands and wiped my tears away with his thumbs. "Dry those tears, Dagger. You are not alone."

I gathered a deep breath, straightened my tunic, and nodded with a heavy sigh. "Lead the way," I said.

The hallway leading to the Council Chamber quickly became crowded with finely dressed noblemen and women. A few aristocrats eyed me curiously as they pushed their way into the room. I followed them inside and caught sight of Master Eamon in a heated discussion with Master Chanter at the other end of the large table. King Sander, standing at the head, was speaking softly with Prince Leander. The prince was nodding at something the king had said, his eyes scanning the rapidly filling chamber. A broad smile spread across his face when he noted me. I couldn't help but notice his honey-colored eyes flick down to my wrists, trying to see if I had accepted his betrothal gift. Fortunately, the sleeves of my uniform covered my wrists, and he couldn't see. I forced a smile in return and tipped my head to him in a respectful bow.

A servant politely held the back of a chair and waved for me to be seated. I was grateful for the distraction, not wanting to keep eye contact with the prince any longer than I needed to. I sat quickly, and once my chair was in place, Ropert took a guarded stance behind it.

Queen Lonacheska already sat quiet and poised in the chair to the right of King Sander's. Her dark eyes scanned the room, observing silently as the other nobles and aristocrats scrambled for seats. I was stunned to see Duchess Caitelyn enter the room. There was a glint of surprise in her violet eyes as she saw me, but she quickly masked it as she made her way around the table. To my dismay, she took the seat beside me. Surely, she was disappointed that her assassins had failed.

Eamon broke off the conversation with Master Chanter, whirling on his heel. He marched to the chair on the other side of me, jerked it out before the servant could, and flopped into it. His fingers drummed on the table impatiently. Master Chanter, just as irritated, turned and took a standing position against the corner wall where he could observe everything.

I placed a comforting hand on Eamon's forearm, and was about to speak, when King Sander's voice rang out.

"Thank you all for coming," he began, and the room hushed instantly. "I've summoned all of you here today in an endeavor to reach an agreement with Toleah. The longer we delay, the more our people suffer. The citizens have begun to pillage their own families for want of food. This meeting will not be adjourned until a settlement is reached, is that understood?"

His gaze was fierce as he scanned the faces of all who sat around the table, and he held eye contact with every one of us until we nodded in agreement – even me. After confirming that we were all in accord, he seated himself in the finely carved chair at the head.

"Shazadeh Leander," the king said, turning to the Tolean Prince who had taken a seat to the king's left. "Please inform the council of your terms."

The young prince stood, straightened his unique sleeveless jerkin, and looked over the table with perceptive eyes. They held a warmth that showed his earnest desire to help our kingdom. His genuine smile returned when his eyes locked with mine. "My father, Shah Malik Polusmed, the King of Toleah, and Father of the Golden Fields, has seen the need of our neighboring kingdom, Roanfire."

His accent was still as heavy as ever.

"We've heard of a great Roanfirien soldier, Keatep Brendagger, who holds power great enough to dispel an entire army." He waved a gentle hand to me, drawing the attention of the room to where I was sitting. I felt a hot flush rise in my cheeks.

"Shah Malik has sent me with an offer to bring food to Roanfire," the prince continued.

"And the price?" King Sander urged, wanting all in the room to hear the stipulation from the prince himself.

"Shah Malik will send food in exchange for Keatep Brendagger," he said and tipped his head to me, the expertly wrapped head-scarf swaying slightly across his shoulders as he did so. "Our offer is not simply to help Roanfire survive starvation, but to build a greater bond between our kingdoms. I, Prince Leander of Toleah, will wed Keatep Brendagger." His bright eyes, shaded by dark lashes and deep, thick brows, searched mine. There was a pleading within them that was impossible to ignore, but also suspiciously genuine.

The room burst into judgments, jarring my eyes from his.

"That seems more than fair," a nobleman said. "Our people can survive the winter and we can create a stronger alliance with Toleah."

"We will be stronger with Toleah as our ally instead of a silent neighbor," Duchess Caitelyn chimed in.

"Hold," Eamon said, raising a hand. "Just because Keatep Brendagger would be the Princess of Toleah doesn't mean that Toleah will become our ally. Have you forgotten the slavery of the kingdom? Or the way they turned their backs to us when the Leviathan Pirates approached? We asked for help, and they turned a blind eye."

Leander's eyes narrowed at my guardian's words. But he knew that Eamon spoke the truth. Toleah had left Roanfire to its fate, and now that we were desperate, it appeared that they had seen an opportunity to strengthen their own kingdom.

"And," Eamon continued even louder, now that he had the undivided attention of the chamber, "Keatep Brendagger spared our kingdom! Without her, we would have taken a devastating blow by the pirates. Perhaps even crumbled under their assault. She single-handedly turned the tides. Is it wise to bequeath our greatest weapon to another kingdom?"

Soft murmurs of agreement spread across the table, and I frowned at his words. I was not a weapon, and he knew it. As much as I didn't want to go to the desert kingdom of Toleah, I suddenly understood the severity of the decision that King Sander was faced with. And I did not envy his position. He could accept Toleah's offer and temporarily relieve Roanfire of its suffering. But he could be gambling with the alliance of a fickle kingdom. Or, he could hold on to me as a weapon that would deter any further attacks on Roanfire, even from Toleah.

Kea? Ikane's voice gently broke into my mind. *Are you alright? Your heart is racing, and your hands have turned clammy.*

I swallowed hard and unclenched my fist that still curled around the armlet that Prince Leander had given to me. Ikane was right. My hands were uncomfortably sweaty. Ropert noted the movement and discreetly placed a hand on my shoulder to comfort me. At that same moment, I opened my mind to Ikane, allowing him to see and hear everything in the chamber. I needed his support, and perhaps his counsel in the future.

"You are correct, Eamon Brendagger," King Sander declared, his voice booming across the chamber to usher it to silence. "You are correct," he repeated as the room quieted once more. "That is why we have come up with another proposition for Prince Leander."

My head shot up as hope raced through me. I searched King Sander's face, but he seemed to ignore me. Prince Leander's brows furrowed, obviously not knowing the alternative suggestion.

"We have apprehended certain members of a resistance group working near the borders of Toleah," King Sander continued. "These rogues have been harboring Tolean slaves, working against the treaty that Roanfire has made with Toleah."

Leander's head tipped, intrigued. "You found them?"

"Not exactly," the king replied, as if this had been part of a previous conversation. "We have captured one of the resistance members."

At this, Sander waved to the soldiers flanking the door. They pulled the doors wide, revealing a disheveled man in irons, standing between two additional soldiers. His gaze lowered to the floor, but his brows were narrowed in a deep scowl. The soldiers shoved him into the room, and my breath caught in my throat.

Ikane felt the fear that slammed into my chest.

I knew the man. His name was Uldar, a member of the White Fox Resistance, and part of my former platoon of the Red Fox Squadron. Memories flooded back to when I had been a member of the White Fox Resistance – or more accurately – a leader of the resistance. I had worked with Hala

Whitefox, driving off the Leviathan pirates with a group of rag-tag men and women from both Roanfire and Toleah. We were successful and strong, but we also did not turn away the fugitives from the desert that came seeking refuge with us, which we were required to do as stipulated in the treaty. It was grounds for war.

I shrank back in my seat, hoping that he didn't see me. If this man revealed what I had done...

"This is my proposition," King Sander began, turning back to the prince. "I will personally see that this resistance group is demolished, and your slaves returned to your lands."

The prince frowned. "That is already part of the treaty. It is not a bargain you can use."

The bearded man in shackles looked up, his dark eyes glowering at everyone within the chamber. His clothes were in rags, but he still looked strong and fit. He couldn't have been a prisoner for more than a few days. And then his eyes fell upon me. I held his gaze, pleading for him to keep my secret. The White Fox Resistance had turned on me when they discovered that I had befriended a Leviathan Pirate.

"Ashia Valhorn," the man said, using the name that Hala had given me as I was living among them. Uldar looked directly at me with narrowed eyes. A devious smile spread across his lips and I knew instantly that he was about to reveal my secret. "It is good to see you again, commander."

My heart raced, pounding so loudly that I could hear it thrumming through my skull. Perhaps I could still bluff my way out of the situation, but Prince Leander was already looking at me suspiciously. The usual warmth in his eyes faltered.

"You must have me mistaken for someone else," I said flatly, turning away.

"Not at all," he answered. "Were it not for your exquisite training, the White Fox resistance wouldn't be what it is today. Did you know that Hala still uses the training techniques that you-?"

"Enough!" I snapped, cutting him off. But it was too late.

King Sander, Master Chanter, and Prince Leander looked at me with open expressions of betrayal.

"You," Leander began, his eyes watching me in disbelief as he shook his head. "You helped them? You are a commander of the White Fox Resistance?" The sting of betrayal in his voice was heart-wrenching.

"I was once," I said and halfway rose from my chair. "It's not—"

But he ignored me and turned to the king. "And you tried to give her to me as a princess?!"

"I didn't know!" King Sander began.

The prince slammed his palm on the wooden table, hot anger rising in his cheeks. Queen Lonacheska, who hadn't said a word, flinched at the loudness of the impact.

I glowered back at the prisoner who was being hauled away by the soldiers. His smile was venomous. I did not blame him for wanting to see me suffer, but he had placed all of Roanfire directly into the path of another war. One that we would not win.

"You think me a fool?! You think Toleah fools?! You broke the treaty!"

"No!" King Sander said, rising to his feet. Queen Lonacheska rose with him when her eyes darted to the curved dagger tucked into Prince Leander's belt. Even though his hand curled around the hilt, he was a prince, and knew that using it now would give King Sander grounds to arrest him.

Realizing this, the prince took a step back. "Ridarri!" he bellowed.

I knew the word. He had called for his personal, elite Tolean Warriors, men that could disarm a fully armored Roanfirien soldier with his bare hands. I leapt to my feet and reached across the table to claim the prince's attention.

"Don't!" I cried. "Please! Take me as a prisoner and slave if you must! King Sander knew nothing of my involvement with the White Fox Resistance. Take me, but do not blame my king for this!"

Within seconds, two Tolean Ridarri Warriors, clad in pitch black, exotic embellished attire, burst through the door. Their bulging, muscular arms, adorned with a myriad of colorful tattoos, easily thrust King Sander's guards into the wall, nearly knocking them unconscious. The chamber erupted in sounds of chairs scraping against the floor and cries of shock and alarm as the nobles scrambled to their feet.

As if the chaos weren't enough, I felt a sharp sting in my shoulder as Duchess Caitelyn rose from her seat. I caught the quick flash of a silver dagger racing from my arm. She didn't even try to hide the weapon as Ropert stepped forward to catch her wrist.

Kea! Ikane barked, feeling the sting. I blocked his mind, unable to handle the cascading events in the chamber.

The duchess smiled at me with a glint of victory in her violet eyes. "I have done what my assassins couldn't," she hissed.

I knew instantly that the dagger was poisoned... most likely with wolfsbane. I could already feel the involuntary spasms of my muscles. Ropert barely managed to twist her arm so that she lost hold of her dagger before Prince Leander roared his next orders to his warriors.

His finger pointed at me. "Take her!"

Ropert shoved the duchess away and drew his sword. "Get behind me, Dagger!"

My head spun as I took the single step. Eamon, noting the injury, grabbed my shoulders to steady me.

"Wolfsbane," I told him quickly.

His brown eyes widened.

"You cannot do this!" Sander hollered in protest, but the Ridarri plowed through the people around me. Ropert, unable to wield his sword in such a crowded room, took a fist to the side of his head. His body flew against the table at the might behind the blow. The Ridarri then shoved Eamon back so forcefully that I heard all air whoosh from his lungs as his back struck the wall.

My hand was going numb now and uncomfortable spasms radiated through my neck. My vision blurred, and I barely felt the Ridarri Warrior's hand as he gripped my arm and pulled me over his broad shoulder like a sack of grain. He marched from the room into the hallway that was already filling with frightened noblemen and women.

"Ropert!" Eamon ordered with a sharp gesture. "After them!"

Ropert, rubbing his jaw, staggered to his feet and sprinted after the Ridarri.

"Put her down," he roared after the Tolean warriors. His voice seemed garbled, like he was shouting through a waterfall. I glanced up, trying to comprehend the events that were spinning wildly out of control. I longed to fight, but my heart felt thick, as if it were pumping hot oil rather than blood.

Ropert pointed his weapon at the Ridarri barring his path. The Tolean warrior merely waited for Ropert to make the first move. Obliging, Ropert's sword raced at his foe in a lethal downward stroke which would have cleaved the Ridarri in half, but the Tolean simply stepped aside and towards Ropert, causing the range of his broadsword to have little effect. Using the momentum of Ropert's downward stroke, the Tolean grabbed his arm and pulled Ropert into a devastating knee strike to his sternum. Almost instantly, the Ridarri pivoted to land an upper-cut fist into Ropert's side, giving my friend no time to recover.

I heard the clatter of Ropert's sword as it fell to the floor.

A low growl mingled with the commotion in the hallway and a black blur slammed into my captor. Both of us fell to the polished floor. Limp as I was, my head struck the ground with a resounding crack. The horrid sound of rending flesh and fabric echoed through the hallway as I struggled to maintain consciousness.

I thought I saw a pair of blue and green eyes looking down at me.

Dull pounding beat through my skull and my lips were thick and stiff. The weight on my eyelids made it nigh impossible to open them. Through heavy blinking, I discerned a room bustling with servants bearing towels, linens, and bowls of water. A familiar, unpleasant man, with a long, graying beard, bent over me. I recognized him as none other than King Sander's private surgeon, the same man who had been given the task of tending to Ikane after the battle with the Leviathan Pirates.

The old man roughly dabbed at my exposed shoulder with a bloodstained cloth, but I didn't feel it against my skin. In fact, I barely felt anything.

"The servant did right to use waterdust," the healer said as he worked. "I do not think I should suture it at this point. We must let it bleed as long as possible to ensure that the poison is flushed out."

I felt a gentle, yet calloused hand, brush up against my forehead. His touch was unmistakable.

"How long?" Eamon asked.

The healer turned to a servant and motioned for another towel to be brought forward. He tucked it under my shoulder as he spoke. "It's up to her. I cannot guarantee that she will fully recover from this ordeal. Wolfsbane can cause paralysis. She may never be able to use her arm again."

Eamon tenderly brushed my hair from my forehead. "Kea," he said softly as my eyes blinked up at his salt and pepper hair. Worry furrowed upon his brow even through his soft smile. "Bless the Phoenix, you are awake." He took my hand in his... but I couldn't feel it.

The surgeon shook his head. "She is still very weak. Let her rest."

I tried to speak, but my lips wouldn't form the words. Eamon leaned forward to try to discern what I was trying to say, but I groaned something incoherent. Frustrated, I closed my eyes. I couldn't feel my body. I couldn't speak.

Kea, Ikane's voice broke into my thoughts.

My eyes flew open. *Ikane. Where are you? Are you well? What happened? How did you get out of the dungeons?* At least I still had a link to him.

Broderick released me when the commotion began, he answered.

I swallowed hard. *Broderick? Where are you now?*

I am here with Ropert. In your chamber, he said. *No, don't try to look. We are sitting by the fire. Ropert has sustained three broken ribs, but he is well. You needn't worry about us. We will remain by your side, as per King Sander's orders.*

"Let her sleep," the healer said to Eamon. "Her body has much recovering to do."

Eamon reluctantly stood. "I wish to stay by her side."

"As you should," the healer said. "Just don't bother her. Go sit by Ropert and the hound over by the fire."

My eyes closed. *What of Prince Leander? Has war been declared? Oh, dear Phoenix, Roanfire cannot endure another battle... not now. We will be crushed.*

Hush, little Brendagger, Ikane interrupted my thoughts. *The healer is correct. Your body cannot handle any more abuse. Rest. Sleep. I will explain all when you wake.*

It wasn't hard to slip back into sleep.

Darkness surrounded our dream, entwining it with flickering stars and threads of moonbeams. The luster had vanished from the earth as the branches of long-dead trees reached toward the sky with pleading fingers. A winged creature soared across the light of the silver moon. It was large in form, and its body human, but the creature was no ally.

15

THE QUEEN OF ROANFIRE

"**O**uch!" I snapped for the third time as the healer pricked at my neck with a tiny needle. "I can feel that just fine!"

"I can see that. And sadly, your lips move just as well," the healer grumbled sarcastically as his hand moved down to my shoulder. He pressed the small needle against my skin as he had on my neck, but here, the pain was severely dulled. I felt the tiniest hint of a prick, as if someone had simply pressed a fingernail into my skin. I looked down at it, my brows furrowing. At my reaction – or lack of it - the healer hummed to himself and then moved an inch further down, just above the black sutures in my arm. The needle pushed into my skin, but I only felt the sensation of pressure. A small pellet of red blood formed on the surface of my skin as he withdrew his torturing device, and he wiped it away with the small rag in his other hand.

"Nothing?" he asked.

I frowned and shook my head.

His lips pursed between his white beard and mustache as he set the needle and rag down on the table beside the bed.

Then he grabbed my hand, turning it palm up as he scrutinized my fingers. His thin, white brows furrowed when his fingers brushed lightly against the embedded flecks of firedust in my skin there. The glow had faded and simply mimicked the appearance of red shards of stained glass.

"What is this?" he asked, tipping my hand toward the candlelight.

"Firedust," I said.

His gray eyes searched mine with clear disbelief. He then shrugged and reached for the needle again. This time he jabbed the point into the tips of each of my fingers, drawing blood from all but one. I almost thought he enjoyed tormenting me so.

"Anything?" he asked.

"No," I admitted, trying to hide my own disappointment.

He sighed and placed my hand back down on the bed beside me. The small gesture of not simply allowing it to drop, spoke volumes. "The wolfsbane has done a number on your muscles, I'm afraid. Everything from your shoulder down is unresponsive," he said as he turned away to place the rag and needle back into his healer's bag.

I pulled my lip to one side. I didn't need a healer to tell me that.

"Will I ever regain feeling?" I asked.

He paused, and although his back was turned to me, I could feel his apprehension. "I don't know," he said and turned to face me. His eyes, that were usually cold and unfeeling, welled with sympathetic emotion. "We've already given you three doses of waterdust. If you were to regain feeling, it would've happened by now."

My chin rose as I swallowed back the lump in my throat, and I straightened my back. "But it's still possible?" I pressed.

The healer rubbed the bridge of his nose, his eyes closing tightly. When he dropped his hand again, the coldness had returned. "I suppose," he grumbled, but I knew he didn't believe it.

"Now, let's get your shirt back on properly," he said and helped me slip my limp, useless, unfeeling arm into the sleeve of my white cotton shirt. He even helped me lace it up, though he was gruff about it. "We'll have to make a sling for your arm to keep it from swaying into things."

Once finished, he turned and grabbed his healer's bag from the floor. "I'll have my apprentice bring it to you a little later this afternoon," he said and headed for the door.

"Healer Bandock?" I called after him, using his name for the first time.

He halted and looked back at me over his shoulder, indicating that he was listening.

"Thank you," I told him.

His eyes closed briefly. "I'm sorry I couldn't do more. It hardly seems fair when a good soldier loses the ability to fight."

He had finally voiced what I knew in my heart. I would no longer be the soldier that I had once been.

His shoulders squared again. "I'll inform King Sander of the status of your recovery," he mumbled and knocked harshly on the door. The soldiers standing as sentry outside opened it and the healer slipped out.

Before the door closed however, I saw the shiny black nose of the wolf push his way into the chamber, and then Ropert followed a little more slowly. Ropert's torso was bandaged, his left arm bound tightly to his ribcage to help keep his ribs steady while they healed. He gave me a broad smile as Ikane stepped up and nuzzled my hand.

Ikane, as we were linked, already knew the verdict and this was his small attempt at comforting me.

"Well?" Ropert pressed. "What did he say?"

My jaw tightened as I swallowed. "It's not good," I admitted as I stood. I held my left arm with my right to keep it from swaying as I walked from the bed over to the chairs that stood before the fire. I sat down in one of them and jerked my head to Ropert in a motion for him to be seated beside me.

He took a few steps closer but remained standing. "I'd rather not sit. The motion hurts too much."

"You should be in bed," I told him as Ikane seated himself beside me.

Ropert wanted to shrug but stopped himself to keep from irritating his ribs. "I've some news on the matter of Prince Leander."

I sat on the edge of my seat, giving Ropert my undivided attention. "Has he declared war?"

"Well..." Ropert paused, his nose wrinkling to one side. If he could, he would've shrugged one shoulder again, but he resisted. "Yes... but not exactly."

My brows rose, and my one good hand moved to urge him along.

"Prince Leander has declared war, but he and his Ridarri have been detained. So far, his declaration is an empty threat, seeing as he has not been able to contact Shah Milak."

I felt my eyes widen in disbelief. "So, King Sander is holding the Tolean Prince against his will?"

Ropert nodded. "It would seem so."

Sighing, I leaned back in my chair. "Then war is inevitable, and Roanfire will not receive the aid it needs from Toleah." I groaned and rubbed my temples with my good hand. "This is all my fault. I should've been open with King Sander and let him know of my involvement with the White Fox Resistance."

Ropert moved closer to the fire, but still didn't sit. "You can't blame yourself," Ropert said. "King Sander should've known that it was an empty bargain. The treaty states that we were to return any Tolean slaves anyway. And he should have included you before presenting this alternative option to the prince."

Careful, Ikane wanted to warn Ropert. *That sort of talk borders on treason.*

I reached out and placed my hand on Ikane's neck, agreeing with him. "You probably shouldn't speak that way of King Sander," I said to Ropert.

Ropert rubbed his chin. "I know," he sighed. "We all make mistakes though. Take me for example. I shouldn't have opened myself for such an attack from the Ridarri. The overhead strike was a poor choice on my part. I shouldn't have rushed in that way."

I gave him a little smile. "He did a number on you, didn't he?"

"Even though I hate what he's done, and I still feel like hell, I can't help but admire his skill," Ropert said, shaking his head. "Did you see it? He stepped aside and with one small flick of his arm, my ribs were right up into his knee. That was the first break. His final punch knocked the air clean out of my lungs and I heard the crack of two more ribs as he did so. I felt like all my internal organs shifted with that final blow." There was a sense of awe and excitement to Ropert's voice, and I couldn't help but notice the way he placed his hand against his side at the memory of the impact. "I wish they would be willing to train Roanfiriens in their art."

I was barely holding onto consciousness when Ropert was attacked, but I recalled Brent of the White Fox Resistance fighting in the same devastating manner. Ropert was right to admire them, but with the news of Prince Leander now a prisoner of Roanfire, I doubted he'd ever get the opportunity. I dreaded going to battle against such lethal warriors.

Kea, Ikane said, sensing an opportunity not to interrupt. *Did you mean it when you offered yourself as a Tolean slave?*

I nodded. *Anything to keep Roanfire from war.*

I would've come with you, he assured me.

I gave him a sad smile and Ropert noted the exchange.

"Are we about due for another dose of wolfsbane?" Ropert asked, knowing that I would be able to speak for the wolf.

Yes, Ikane admitted and I nodded to Ropert in return.

"Well, come on then," Ropert said and patted his thigh to get Ikane to follow him like a puppy. I nearly burst out laughing and quickly covered my mouth to keep from letting it out. My lips made an unpleasant flatulent noise instead.

Ikane rolled his eyes. *It's getting worse.*

Inside, I was laughing so hard I could barely keep my thoughts in order. *At least he's not trying to kill you anymore,* I finally managed to form the thought.

Ropert turned back to me, one eyebrow raised. "What's so funny?"

"Nothing," I quickly said, shaking my head. "Go on now."

You're not going to try and talk to him about it? Ikane asked me in dismay.

No, not yet anyway. It was too much fun seeing their awkward friendship. Ikane groaned inwardly, but he was willing to endure it for my amusement. He followed Ropert from the room, leaving me in peace.

Healer Bandock's apprentice brought a sling made of a gray cotton fabric and helped me fasten it around my neck. A few minutes later, a maidservant entered with my small allotment of supper which consisted of a warm cabbage stew and a wedge of dry bread. It was a drastic change in meals that had been provided to me a few weeks ago. King Sander's desperation to find food for his people was bleeding into the noble court. The pressure to find a solution to this problem would surely be mounting.

A soft knock sounded on the door, but there was no pause to wait for my reply before it opened. I was stunned to see Queen Lonacheska standing in the wooden frame, clad in a deep red gown that contrasted against the golden locks trailing down her spine. Her flushed cheeks and rosy lips complimented her pale skin and dark eyes, but her expression was cautious. She toyed with one of the rings on her fingers as she apprehensively looked up at me.

"My queen!" I exclaimed and hastily rose to my feet.

"Sit," she ordered as she stepped inside and closed the door behind her. I was a little stunned by that movement, expecting that the soldiers standing outside would be there to close the door for her.

I did as told, looking up at her as she walked towards the fireplace. I hadn't ever noticed how she seemed to glide along the floor, the train of her crimson gown trailing after her mimicking the feathers of the fabled majestic firebird. She halted before me, looking down as I sat in the chair.

"How do you intend to destroy Rion Noirfonika?" she finally asked.

I was a little taken aback by her blunt demand. "I... well... I am uncertain," I admitted honestly. "I need help from the White Wardent. My best clue as of yet is to visit your beautiful kingdom and seek the letter written to Emperor Skarand."

She waved her hand at me as her eyes rolled to heaven. "Don't bother using flattering words. This is not a formal visit."

My brows furrowed. Why else would she want to see me?

She withdrew something hidden beneath the sleeve of her dress, leaned down, and pressed it into my good hand. "I think I am with child," she whispered fiercely into my ear. "Do what you must to spare my children the agony you face."

She stepped back and nodded to the object she had placed in my hand.

"How...?" I stammered at the news. "It's only been three weeks since the wedding?" I regretted the words as soon as they fell from my lips. It was not my place to ask such questions, much less of the queen.

As expected, her chin rose, and her lips hardened. "That is none of your concern. Just focus on freeing my children from the curse."

I bowed my head, looking down at the object she had placed in my hand. My eyes widened at seeing the ring that held a rolled piece of parchment in place. The band was made to resemble a single-horned black horse, the Icemount: crest, mascot, and guardian of the Glacial Empire. The powerful creature's legs and tail curved into a circle, forming an opening large enough for a woman's finger to slip inside. Tiny diamonds sprinkled across the length of the single horn, and miniature onyx jewels became its eyes. The beauty and detail that had been put into this tiny masterpiece was breathless.

I glanced up at her, and she nodded, indicating that I should read the note. Using my teeth, I slipped the ring from the paper and struggled to unroll the passage with one hand.

Keatep Brendagger, Daughter of Roanfire, Lady of Meldron, and Destroyer of the Leviathan Pirates...

My brows rose at the newest addition to my title.

It pains me to betray my king. Sorrow eats away at my very heart knowing that many will perish from hunger because of my actions. But I cannot, in good conscience, allow the first Daughter of Roanfire in four hundred years to become a slave to a Tolean Prince, when she alone has the power to free Roanfire from war and famine.

My mother, the Empress of the Glacier Empire, holds wisdom passed down to her through generations. It is my deepest desire that you meet with her and glean information to complete your errand. I have arranged for a guide and two horses to spirit you away, tonight. The guide will be waiting for you by the north gate precisely at midnight. Take no thought as to what you may need on your journey. I will arrange everything to be provided.

Speak of this to no one, even your trusted bodyguard. Eyes and ears surround the walls of the castle. All this must be done in silence. Take this ring, for it is an heirloom that the empress cannot refuse.

I pray to the Icemount Guardian, the One-horned Wonder, that you will be successful on your journey.

As soon as I finished reading, she took the letter from my hand, turned, and dropped the parchment into the fire. She pulled her knuckles to her lips as she watched the flames make quick work of her calculated disloyalty.

"How are you mending?" she asked without turning to look at me.

I glanced at my useless hand hanging limply inside of the sling. "I've been better, your majesty."

She turned back to me and absently placed one of her delicate hands over her abdomen. Her dark eyes were filled with hope, doubt, and admiration for me. "I am truly sorry," she eventually said looking at my arm. I heard genuine sympathy in her voice. "Such tragedy should never befall a soldier."

"Thank you, your majesty," I stammered, stunned by her tenderness, as she had only ever shown hostility towards me.

She then turned for the door. "Rest well, Lady Keatep." With that, she slipped out, once again opening the door herself.

Suspecting that the guards were not at their post for this visit, I rose quickly and opened the door. Peering into the hallway, I saw the last trace of Queen Lonacheska's gown disappear behind a corner. Almost instantly, two soldiers appeared and marched for my room. I ducked back inside, shutting the heavy door softly. I held up the delicate ring still in my hand, watching the orange and yellow of the firelight flicker against the black stones embedded into the precious silver. Suddenly, I felt purpose. I felt empowered by the quest given to me by my queen. My fist curled around the priceless heirloom with determination.

With two arms or one, I would not fail her.

16

ESCAPE

Darkness had fallen across Roanfire long ago, and the Meldron Castle was quiet with sleep. My heart thumped wildly in my chest as I peered out of my chamber into the darkened hallway. The soldiers that had returned to their post after Queen Lonacheska's visit, had mysteriously disappeared again. It was at this moment that I found gratitude for Mina's gift of sight in the darkness. Seeing as it was linked to Ikane's heightened sense of vision, I could make out the smallest cracks and chips in the gray stone at the far end of the hallway.

With Ikane's amplified hearing, I could make out the varied sounds of people breathing in sleep behind the doors lining the hallway. Ahead, the flickering light of a torch cast an orange glow on the stone wall, but it was stationary. Peering around the corner, I found what I had suspected—a lone torch sitting in an iron sconce.

It was almost too simple to slip out into the deserted training arena, but then again, I felt that Queen Lonacheska had something to do with that. The crisp chill of a wintery cold night filled my lungs as I darted across the open field and immediately slinked into the shadows beside the weapon's hut. I didn't need to ask Ikane if he was near. I felt him before he had even pressed his body against my hip.

You brought the wolfsbane? he asked. After he felt my assurance that it was in my pack, he continued. *I really think you should've told Ropert about this. He's not only your bodyguard, but your friend.*

I had wrestled with the very thought since the sun had set behind the treetops and found myself more and more irritated with the decision.

I know, I shot at him. I hadn't intended to be so harsh, but because our thoughts were linked, I did not have the luxury of calming my voice before speaking. I gathered a deep breath.

I know, my tone was softer this time. *I want to tell him. I know in my heart that he would follow me to the Leviathan Isles and back, but the queen forbade it. Not only that, but he has three broken ribs. He cannot travel in his condition.*

Ikane lowered his head and nudged my shoulder. *I just don't want to see you get hurt.*

I glanced around the corner of the hut. Seeing as the stable was nearby, Ikane's nose was filled with the stench of horse and manure. I could not rely on it to pick up the scent of another human— unless that human reeked more than the stables. Instead, I focused on sounds. Two owls hooted on top of a pair of the castle's towers, and the steady bang of the blacksmith's hammer rang to our right. I listened for the sound of his bellows pumping before I risked darting across the way to his workshop.

The familiar smell of iron, coal, and sweat soon became the sole scent in our noses. I had labored here in the past and knew exactly where the blacksmith placed his tools. As soon as he turned back to hammering a long glowing rod of iron, I snatched one of his hammers from his workbench. I realized that he wouldn't have noted our passage even if we had galloped through on horseback. He was so engulfed in his work.

Ducking back outside, I turned to the tall, crenelated wall that towered behind his shop. Here, a water drain was set in the back wall with thick iron bars plunging into the stone. I had helped the blacksmith repair it before the Leviathans had attacked and knew exactly which rocks would easily break and loosen the iron bars. Timing the blows of my hammer to match that of the blacksmith's, the bars soon lay on the ground, leaving a clear opening for our escape.

It wasn't long before we were deep in the dark streets of Meldron walking towards the city walls. Just as the queen had promised, two horses and a guide waited in the shadows near the north gate. The man noted my presence and removed the hood to reveal his features. My eyes widened at the familiar salt and pepper hair pulled back in a warriors' tail. The recognizable brown eyes shadowed by thick brows glanced at the large wolf at my heels.

"Eamon," I whispered as I approached.

"Hurry," my guardian said as he knit his gloved fingers together and held them out at knee level so that I might mount the horse with ease. Typically, I would have refused such aid, but without the use of both of my arms, I was inclined to accept his assistance.

"We ride hard tonight," he announced, replacing his hood. He wrapped a dark scarf around his neck for warmth, mounted his steed, and spurred his horse forward. The horse I rode followed close behind, gaining speed as Eamon set a quick and strenuous pace.

For the next three miles, we galloped across the night-deserted roads, passing clusters of trees and open, devastated farmland. I felt the burn of Ikane's legs as he ran alongside the horses, and the sharp sting of glass in my lungs at breathing in the bitter air. Ikane's relief was overwhelming as Eamon slowed the horses to a steady trot.

As the morning sun overpowered the darkness of night, we arrived at the outskirts of a small village.

"Get off your horse," Eamon said as he dismounted. "We'll exchange our horses for fresh ones here. Keep low in the trees. I'll return shortly." With that, he grabbed our steaming horses' reins and headed to the village.

Ikane's ears flicked as we listened to the horses trot away after Eamon. A small cluster of trees off to the right seemed as good a place as any to wait. I wandered to one of the trunks, found its shadow, and sat down. Ikane didn't hesitate to rest beside me.

I think it is time for another dose of wolfsbane, Ikane reminded me. *I can't shake the feeling that Rion is waiting for an opportunity to act. It's almost as if... as if she wants us to get closer to the Glacial Empire.*

My brows furrowed as I rummaged through my pack for the supply of deadly poison – which was made all the harder by the use of only one arm. But I had felt it too. I thought that perhaps it was her conniving way of keeping me from the clues I needed to destroy her. Was it really her goal to have us get to the Glacial Empire? Or did she purposefully allow Ikane and I to feel her desire, in an attempt to sway our resolve?

I found the wolfsbane sitting in a glass vial with a cork on top. It held enough of the green-gray liquid to poison a small army. I sighed, now faced with a dilemma. Since I only had the use of one arm, I would have to use my teeth to open the cork... and that thought did not sit well with me. I did not want to risk accidentally poisoning myself again.

I think we'll have to wait for Eamon to return, I said to Ikane. He felt my frustration rising.

It's alright, he assured me. *I think we have some time still.*

I sighed and put my good arm around his neck, the vial of poison still in my hand. *I hate what we must do to keep her at bay,* I grumbled and pressed my forehead against his fur.

I felt his ache to hold me in his arms and the fear of being stuck permanently in the form a wolf surfaced. An uncomfortable tightness built in his chest, making it hard to breathe. He tried to nuzzle against me, but it was awkward, and I sat upright again.

Don't think that way, I told him, although those fears were real for me as well. *We'll find a way to bring her back into the ruby.*

Do you think it's possible?

If I had the use of both of my hands, I would've reached up to find the thin cord tied to my neck. I knew I would find the small stone hanging there. If I could only reach her, perhaps I could pull her back into the jewel. But her strength always caught me off guard.

Ikane shifted. *She has had over four hundred years to train her power. And she has the life force of thousands at her disposal.*

My head dropped. *That's not helping,* I grumbled.

Kea. The way he said my name in his thoughts was strong and demanding. *You can overcome her. We did it before. Together. Do you remember? We drove her back. I am here, and my energy is at your disposal, whenever you need it.*

A sad smile stole across my lips. He was right. Although I disliked the thought of using his energy the way Rion did.

That was all she needed to feel. A flash of energy sparked through our linked minds. Like the flames roiling from the feathers of the phoenix, heat seared through our bodies. Redness crept through my vision as the familiar burning heat of her power surged through my bones. My intake of breath was cut short by feeling as though I had inhaled glowing cinders.

You think yourself to be righteous? Her voices echoed through my mind. *You think me to be a murderer when you have slaughtered countless with your sword! Do you not think of their families, and those that they were only trying to protect as you struck them down? The lives I have taken survive in me and live on! I have granted them eternal life!*

It was different, and she knew it. Her fire intensified, causing my body to involuntarily convulse.

And the man who you think to be your guardian, Eamon Brendagger. She continued. *Do you truly think he cares for you? He was nothing but a wine-bibber. It was only after you were brought to Meldron that he assumed his role as guardian and a father figure. Now that you are of some worth to him, he sees fit to resume guardianship.*

That too was a lie. Eamon had already promised to give up drinking, and in return I was to sever all contact with Ikane. Eamon already knew that Ikane was a Leviathan Pirate, and even in his drunken state, tried to protect me from him. Even now, he was trying to help me defeat a curse that I knew he barely understood.

And what of Daram? You were the cause of the destruction of your home. You fell for a Leviathan Pirate. A viper prince of the isles, no less. Roanfire burns because of you!

Her words cut deeper than I thought they should... but that was not the least of my worries. My vision began to blacken due to the suffocating ash in my lungs.

Yes. Lady Caitelyn. She suffers because of you. Her husband was lost. Shame came upon her because you failed to protect Daram. And now you have betrayed the man called Ropert. He too will suffer because of your actions. His back still bears the mark of the driver's whip, and now he will face the wrath of the king for losing track of his charge.

Stop. It was all I could drive through my mind.

You think that I am a monster? She asked. *In time you will see that you are no different.*

At that moment, I felt her gather energy together, devouring several dozen souls. She held their life in her hand like the shaft of a spear. Bracing myself, I waited for her to plunge this destructive power deep into my mind. She recoiled for an instant, and I gathered a desperate breath. And then she expanded like the taught string of a bow, propelling her power forward with such speed that I barely had time to lift my shield.

It did not strike. I felt nothing. Startled and confused, I lowered my defenses to see what she had done. I felt her power rumble through the sky like thunder, bolting across Roanfire and into darkness that I could not trace with my mind. She released us and retreated into Ikane's sub-consciousness with an aura of triumph.

I gasped. My lungs groaned.

The wolf's soft whimper caught my attention as I struggled to push myself from the cold ground. Ikane's legs trembled as he pushed himself up. A small trickle of red blood hung on the tip of his black nose, and his green eye flashed with worry.

Propping myself up against the tree trunk, I wiped at my own blood hanging on my upper lip. Ikane whimpered as he sidled up to me. Shaking, I wrapped my arm around his large form again. He didn't need to convey his horror, for I felt it.

I felt my rage growing against the Phoenix Witch. But neither one of us comprehended what Rion had done to feel such victory.

On the eve of the third day of this strenuous pace, we finally arrived at the outskirts of the lakeside city of Kaltum. Soft, gray smoke billowed from the chimneys, causing a thick haze to hinder my view of Glacier Lake which lay beyond the glowing, snow-covered rooftops. Masts of fishermen's ships swayed behind the buildings like blades of spring grass in a gentle breeze.

"We made excellent time," Eamon huffed and pulled the scarf from his chin. His breath hung in the frigid air. "Queen Lonacheska has secured rooms for us at an inn near the docks. We can rest there for the night and board the ship to Shear in the morning."

My body rejoiced at the thought of sleep—and a bed!

Eamon dismounted and groaned as he stretched out his back. "We'll leave the horses in Kaltum. Lonacheska has provided me with the money needed to purchase new mounts once we are in Shear."

I nodded wearily and slipped from the horse's back. My exhausted knees buckled, and I scrambled to grip the saddle before I fell over. Slowly, my muscles found another ounce of strength, and I was able to follow Eamon through the city gates. The soldiers standing guard barely paid us any heed as Eamon and I entered the city. That was a good sign.

I'll find a way around, Ikane told me as our link slowly faded. I didn't like the thought of losing contact with him again, but perhaps it would ease my sense of weariness. I wouldn't feel his fatigue along with my own.

My legs slogged through the cold marketplace that was nearly drowned in snow. It was clear that Kaltum had been spared the brutality of war. The fact that Glacier Lake was abundant with fish, kept bellies full and spirits high. The market was bustling with merchants and patrons, but I barely noted the bright colored fabric, candles, and pottery that were displayed for purchase. All I wanted was to sleep.

Numbly, I followed Eamon down a narrow alley where the stench of fish and lake became stronger. We emerged from the alley to a breathtaking view of snow-capped mountains bursting from behind the vast expanse of water, casting massive reflections upon the crystalline surface. Hundreds of grand ships and slighter vessels bobbed in the frigid water. Seagulls cried overhead, fighting over scraps of discarded fish from the fishermen's nets as they reeled in the days catch.

It brought to mind my childhood home of Daram, and I suddenly felt homesick.

As Eamon followed the bustling shoreline towards a questionable part of the city, I felt my link with Ikane grow stronger. The smells and sounds intensified as we came upon a run-down inn. The name 'Drowsy Dreamer' was etched into a rickety wooden sign hanging overhead. The timber frame of the inn was crooked, and parts of the honey-colored plaster was peeling off. I did not hold out hope for a decent room. As long as the bed was warm, I wouldn't care anyway.

Eamon spoke to an errand boy nearby and gave him a few coins to care for our horses and bring our gear up to our room. I tried to ignore a group of young sailors loafing beside a stack of wooden barrels. Eamon hefted his bag and moved to the door of the inn where warm, welcoming light spilled into the street. But with Ikane's strong senses overpowering me, I could smell the wine and heavy body odor wafting from the sailor's sweat-stained tunics and shirts.

"Hey," one of the sailors whispered to the other while backhanding his shoulder several times to get his attention. Once he had it, he jerked his head my direction.

The other man, with a thick, black beard, turned to look at me, his eyes darting up and down. A little smile spread across his lips, but it wasn't a warm smile. It was a devious and pining smile that made the hair on the back of my neck stand on end.

The third sailor, with a blue bandana covering his long dark hair, dropped the murky bottle of sloshing red liquid from his mouth, wiped the stubble on his chin with the back of his hand, and then followed the gaze of his distracted companions. His smile was broader than the others as he stood and shoved his bottle at the first man.

My guard went up, knowing that he was about to approach. I was startled at how clearly I could hear his breathing, and then it became evident that Ikane's attention was directly focused on him. He saw a threat there, and his animal instinct was to bristle and snarl. I found myself mimicking his reaction.

The man paused, rethinking his approach.

That's it, Ikane's thoughts swarmed into mine as our link strengthened. *Cower, you louts.*

Ikane, I warned him, feeling slightly overwhelmed by his protective impulse.

Ikane backed off as Eamon turned from the door to see what was keeping me. He eyed the men suspiciously and then narrowed his brows dangerously, realizing their intent.

"Get inside, Kea," he told me, handing me his bag.

Taking it quickly, I ducked into the warm inn and was pleasantly surprised to note that, in spite of the uneven walls and warped floor-boards, the inn was pristine. It wasn't hard to discern the sweet feminine touch to everything. Embroidered curtains hung in the windows of the main tavern, and the five round tables that stood throughout, held autumn branches with golden leaves inside a decorative wooden vase. Even the large hearth on the far wall had autumn décor and candles beautifully arranged on the mantle.

I thought I could smell roasted cabbage and peppered fish from the inn's kitchen, but it was tainted with the smells from outside. Ikane, focused on the three men with Eamon, pulled my senses in two directions. Through his eyes, I watched as Eamon folded his arms across his chest and scanned the young sailors. By now, the other two had stood, flanking the man with the blue bandana. Perhaps it was the fact that Eamon looked like an easy target after three days of hard riding. He was as weary as I was, and they wouldn't let this man, who was past his prime, spoil their evening fun.

Feeling the need to help out my guardian, I turned around and headed back for the door.

Don't Kea, Ikane warned me, knowing my intentions. *For one, you are their target. Second, we need to keep your identity a secret. You know that the Phoenix Soldiers will be on our tail soon enough. We can't leave any clues. Third, you haven't trained enough with one arm to know your limits in combat. And lastly, I've got Eamon's back. Don't worry about him.*

My hand dropped before it reached the lever of the door. Ikane was right. I moved to the window instead and pulled the curtain aside. Ikane was closer now, and I could see Eamon stroking his groomed salt and pepper beard through the wolf's eyes. My guardian eyed the bottle of wine, and then shrugged his shoulders. I could hear his voice clearly through Ikane's ears.

"Do you gentlemen have a room here at the inn?" His tone was flat.

"What do you care, old man?" One of the young sailors said, no respect in his voice whatsoever. I couldn't tell which one of them had spoken, though I assumed it to be the man with the blue bandana, as he seemed to be the frontrunner of the trio.

"I don't," he said and turned slightly as if to leave, but I saw the stance. He was prepared to defend himself.

"Oh no you don't," the sailor snapped and reached out to grab Eamon's shoulder. "We're not done—" The man was cut off as Eamon whipped his hand back into the sailor's sternum. He grabbed the sailor's wrist with his other hand and jerked him forward, catching him in an arm-bar. The man groaned angrily.

Eamon knew the others would try to come to his aid. He jerked the sailor around, causing the man to stumble awkwardly as Eamon used him as a human shield. The young, inexperienced sailors couldn't strike at Eamon for fear of hitting their friend instead.

Ikane found it humorous and a smile spread across my lips.

"Come now," Eamon said, easily dodging another blow. "There is no need for this kind of behavior."

The man with the full beard attempted a full-on charge. Eamon whipped his captive around, causing the barreling man to plow right past him. Using the momentum of the sailor already in the arm-bar, he whirled him around to collide into the back of the full bearded man. They crashed into each other, and then into the rain barrel beside the inn. It toppled over with them, dousing them in icy water.

The third man stood dumbfounded for a moment, and then attempted the same, ill-fated maneuver. Eamon side-stepped easily, swinging one arm around to catch the young sailor's neck. He then pivoted and shoved the final sailor towards his comrades. The man tried to catch himself against the wall of the inn but lost his footing as he tripped over the leg of one of his friends, slamming his nose into the plaster wall. He cupped his face in his hands, groaned, and sank down beside his mates.

Eamon hadn't even touched the hilt of his sword. The three humiliated men sat on the ground, wet, cold, and defeated.

"Now," Eamon said, dusting his hands off as if he had touched something filthy. "I was simply asking if you had a room at the inn. My daughter and I haven't had supper yet, and I thought you looked like you wanted a bit of conversation. Are you up for sharing a meal, or not?"

What? Ikane and I exclaimed at the same time.

I dropped the curtain and ripped the door open, fearing that Eamon had lost all common sense. Eamon smiled at me, gesturing towards the three sailors who were beginning to shiver as their breath hung in the frigid air.

"Gentlemen, may I introduce my daughter, Freya."

My brows rose as I looked at Eamon, and then down to the three ruffians. What was Eamon thinking? These men had something completely different in mind only a few moments ago, and Eamon was now conversing with them like equals?

"Hello," the bearded man mumbled as he staggered to his feet. The one holding his bloody nose gave me a partial nod through his hands. But the young man with the blue bandana seemed to hesitate and stood cautiously while keeping a wary eye on Eamon.

"Supper, you say?" he asked.

Eamon nodded firmly. "I can smell cabbage and a fine roasted fish. You really should eat something to keep that wine from fermenting in your gut. Nasty thing that."

The young man tried to process the strange turn of events but realized that Eamon wasn't jesting in the least. Humbled, and slightly humiliated, the final sailor gave me a little wave. "Hello, Freya," he murmured.

Eamon stepped forward and clapped the young sailor on his back, who flinched terribly. Clearly, he still viewed Eamon as dangerous.

"Come now, I'm famished," Eamon said, steering the young man by his neck into the inn. The other two followed him inside, nodding respectfully to me as they passed.

Still dumbstruck, I closed the door after them.

The three young sailors turned out to be quite adept at pranks. After easing up from the encounter they'd had with Eamon, they told a few entertaining tales of switching skiffs from the larger fishing vessels. This resulted in the captain's arguing for quite a few weeks before they realized what had actually happened. The stories they told of placing random items inside of the mouths of large fish on the market were hysterical. They even told a tale of hoisting their captains' undergarments on the sail, but they blushed quickly when they realized that they had voiced this in front of a woman. To their surprise, I laughed.

"She's been around hooligans like you all her life," Eamon chuckled as he finished his meal. He shoved his goblet of water to the center of the table, pushed his chair back, and then slapped his knees.

"Well, it's been a wonderful evening, lads. But we had best get some sleep. We've got a long journey ahead of us."

I rose with him, suddenly feeling the bone-deep exhaustion again.

"Thank you for the meal," the young man with the blue bandana said to Eamon.

"My pleasure," Eamon said and waved for me to head to our room. "Now eat up the last of that fish. I don't want anything going to waste."

The three young men dove back into the supper as Eamon and I walked down the small hallway lined with doors. He opened the last door to his left and heaved a sigh of relief once he stepped inside. I didn't take particular notice of anything in the room besides the two beds sitting on opposite ends of the walls.

Eamon immediately went to work building a fire in the hearth as I closed the door after us. I immediately sank down on the nearest bed.

"Eamon?"

"Hmmm."

"Why did you invite them to supper?" I asked. "I mean, I'm glad you did. They were a fun group, but they were so hostile. How did you know that you could trust them?"

He shrugged. "I didn't. I just assumed they were bored and needed something to do. Suppose we had simply ignored them, they would have targeted someone else." He sighed ruefully. "That's the problem with young men these days. They have no guidance and no sense of responsibility."

I heard the tinder ignite in the fireplace and Eamon placed a log over the flames. My back groaned as I flopped back onto the soft mattress. It was then that I noticed the crooked walls, and large cracks showing through the shuttered window, but the place was clean.

"You did the same for Ikane, didn't you?" I asked.

He shrugged again but didn't reply.

I don't think he's ready to talk about me, Ikane said.

My eyes closed, and I felt my body shutting down. I didn't even bother to remove my cloak or my boots. But Ikane's statement made me think.

"Why are you doing this, Eamon?" I asked. "Why are you helping me defy King Sander and go to the Glacial Empire? I mean, in a way, you are doing this for Ikane."

Eamon placed three more logs on the fire before answering. "Queen Lonacheska trusts me to keep you safe... and in line," he said as he stood and dusted his hands off on his trousers. "As much as I love my king, he cannot keep you from fighting this. It will destroy you, and Roanfire, if left alone. And it will continue to plague the princesses born to the throne."

I rolled over and looked at him. "You believe me?"

"I believe *in* you, Keatep." He said sincerely, then cleared his throat before allowing himself to become too emotional. After removing his cloak and draping it over the end of his bed, he sat down and pulled his boots off. He groaned as his head hit the pillow. "Get some rest, Kea."

I believe in you too, Ikane said as I rolled onto my back and closed my eyes.

A smile stole across my lips as I slipped into sleep.

The face of the monster that tormented our dream was different this night. We were thrust into the gloom of hot, stuffy caverns. The stench of death overwhelmed the noise of savage roars and frantic beating of leather wings. A withered man crouched in the darkness, his dreary cloak shrouding his countenance. He turned, revealing yellow eyes gleaming beneath his hood. His decrepit hand rose to expose a tiny jewel dangling from a silver chain...

I bolted upright in the darkness, my heart beating furiously. Frantically, I reached for the stone hanging about my neck. I found it. Relieved, I clutched the jewel in my fist as I lay back against the cot again, still trying to comprehend the nightmare.

Ikane's thoughts were immediately with me. *I saw it too.*

He had the jewel. Why did he have the jewel? Who was he? I asked.

Ikane didn't know. *Rion has something to do with it. Of that, I am sure.*

A troubled silence was my only reply.

Upon waking for the fourth time that night, warm light finally leaked in through the cracked shutters in the window. The fire had burned down to faint smoldering ashes. My cheeks and nose tingled with the bitter chill in the room, so I ducked my head beneath the faded quilt. It wasn't long before a knock sounded on the door.

I heard Eamon groan and stretch, the old bed creaking under his weight.

The knock sounded again.

"We're up!" Eamon growled.

The noise of footsteps scampering away faded behind the door as I pulled the quilt from my head. Eamon shoved his blanket from his legs, swung them over the edge of the bed, and I heard his feet thump heavily against the wooden floorboards. With a groan, he rubbed the silver stubble on his chin, and then pushed his white-streaked hair away from his face.

"Good," he stated when his brown eyes met mine. "You're awake. We had best get moving," he said and reached under the bed for his boots. If the cold bothered him, he didn't show it even though I thought I could see small wisps of his breath hanging in the air.

"The boat will leave in an hour, and we had best not miss it. The next ship won't depart for Shear until tomorrow and by then the Phoenix Soldiers will have caught up to us," he said as he stuffed his feet into his boots.

My body protested any movement and sitting upright was more of a challenge than it should've been. My feet thumped loudly against the wooden floor. Startled at the noise, I looked down.

Eamon gave me a sad smile upon noting that I had slept with my boots on. "You'll have plenty of time to rest once were aboard the ship," he assured me. He stood and stretched out his back. I heard three loud cracks run down his spine before he rolled his shoulders and retrieved his cloak from the bedpost. "The innkeeper said that he'd provide warm porridge for breakfast."

The deep ache in my belly deepened at the thought of warm, soft, filling porridge in my stomach. I stood quickly, ignoring the cold in the room as it tried to seep into my bones.

"I'll join you," I said while trying to straighten my cloak with one good arm. I wasn't too surprised to discover that I had fallen asleep with it on as well.

Kea.

I groaned inwardly. *Not now, Ikane.*

There was pain in his voice. *Kea— the wolfsbane!*

Startled, I turned my full attention to him. It had been too long since his last dose.

...Rion... I'm changing... He pushed me away to spare me the pain of his transformation, but I clung to his mind like a hook to a fish. Even with the agony of breaking bones and tearing muscle, I scrambled to find the bottle of poison in my saddlebag and bolted from the room.

"Kea? Where are you going?!" Eamon called after me.

I sprinted into the snow-covered street and whirled to my right. Ikane's mind led me across the way, into an alley where a pile of crates lay half covered by a burlap blanket beside the wall of the building. I heard the whimpering cries of the wolf coming from the rubble.

"I'm here, Ikane," I said as I crouched down to see him. My hand trembled as it held the small bottle of poison. I hesitated. With only one hand, I would be forced to uncork the deadly toxin with my teeth. All he needed was one drop. One little drop anywhere on his skin.

It's not safe here for you! Ikane cried through the pain. *Get away!* His mind pushed at me so forcefully that my vision momentarily went black.

I rocked back on my heels and lost balance. Seeing as my good hand was holding the deadly poison, I dared not try to catch myself. Instead, I allowed my rump to land hard in the snow. And then our connection was gone. All of his heightened senses vanished, leaving me in a blurry haze of my own feeble awareness. Half dazed, I struggled to my knees in time to catch the familiar silhouette of a shadow walking by the alleyway.

"Eamon!" I called out to him just as he slipped out of sight.

He took a step back and peered down the dark alley. "Kea?" he asked and hurried to my side. "Are you alright? What's gotten into you?"

"It's Ikane," I said, holding the bottle of wolfsbane out for him. "He's changing. We should've given him the wolfsbane first thing."

Just as Ikane's body thrashed against the crates, Eamon grabbed the bottle of poison from my hand. I scrambled back, trying to avoid getting struck by the topmost box that tumbled down the others. My back hit the wall as the crate crashed by my feet and splintered.

Ikane tried to keep his groans still, but the sound of pure agony still escaped in harsh whimpers. His jolting body slammed into the boxes that had formed his shelter but a few moments ago, pitching them across the alley like boulders from a catapult.

Eamon hurried to open the bottle, and I heard the gentle pop as the cork pulled free. But getting a single drop on the body of a thrashing beast was more difficult than I'd anticipated. Eamon stepped around a crate and reached out to tip the bottle over Ikane. Before the small drop of green-brown liquid could drip from the mouth and onto Ikane's back, the wolf writhed again. His leg struck the wooden box, driving it into Eamon's knee.

My guardian let out a deep groan as the bottle flew from his hand and landed in the snow... silently spilling the precious toxin. Eamon's face contorted in pain as he staggered back and gripped his knee.

It was too late.

The wolf's long nose shrank back, and the black fur disappeared to reveal Ikane's olive skin and muscled frame. Trembling and panting, Ikane crouched in the snow instead of the wolf. His dark hair hung in wild strands over his handsome face. The dark stubble of a beard covered his jawline, growing around the x-shaped scars on his left cheek.

Scrambling to my feet, I grabbed the burlap sack that had been stretched out across the top of the crates and tossed it over Ikane's naked form. But he made no move to secure it. In fact, the motion only made his head twitch.

I held my breath.

His head tipped up to look at me. I expected to see Rion's fire red eyes burning with hatred and venom. But his eyes were... hazy. The vibrant green of his eye was dull and lifeless. Rion wasn't there, but neither was Ikane.

My brows furrowed. Did Rion escape? Did she take Ikane with her, leaving this shell of a man? No. Anyone Rion had devoured, she had killed. Ikane was still alive and somewhere in his own consciousness.

"Ikane," I said and took a small step towards him. The movement was much more exaggerated than I would've liked it to be, as I was forced to step around a partially broken crate. Ikane hunched, his shoulders rising as he cowered like a frightened hound.

"What's wrong with him?" Eamon asked, still bent over as he continued to hold his knee.

"I don't know," I admitted, not daring to take my eyes off him.

Ikane's eyes nervously darted between us.

Eamon stood upright and unclasped his cloak.

"It's alright, boy," he said as he took a cautious step towards the Leviathan. "We're here to help. Don't worry." His voice was gentle, deep, and soothing. Like a pup, the tightness in Ikane's shoulders eased as he listened to the older man speak. Eamon slowly pulled his cloak from his shoulders and then took three more steps towards Ikane. It was impossible to ignore the small grimace in his face as he put weight on his injured knee.

"It's alright. You're safe," he said. Gently, he placed his cloak over Ikane.

Ikane shivered, as if he hadn't realized how cold he had been. Slowly, his hands reached up and pulled the cloak around his body. And then I saw the flicker. His green eye sparked faintly. I swallowed hard, wishing with all my heart to have Ikane standing before me – but I knew that once he did, Rion would overpower him.

"Eamon," I whispered. "The shackles." I dared not say more, fearing that Rion would leap at the opportunity the instant she heard my voice.

Eamon nodded once and reached behind him where he kept the metal restraints secured to the back of his belt. Trying not to startle Ikane, he knelt down before him and gently took one of Ikane's hands. Smoothly, he slipped the iron round Ikane's wrist.

Ikane's eye continued to flicker as he looked down at the cold iron. His dark brows furrowed as he looked back up at my guardian.

Eamon smiled warmly. "It's alright," he said as he reached for Ikane's other hand.

Ikane pulled his hand back, his eyes darting nervously to me. He looked back at Eamon and then back down at the shackles.

"This is to protect you," Eamon assured him. "Deep down I know you know it. Don't fight me now, Little Wolf." My brows rose at the nickname Eamon used to describe Ikane, and I was even more intrigued when Ikane seemed to stop resisting as he used it.

"Take a deep breath and calm yourself." As Eamon spoke, continually using a gentle even tone, he took Ikane's free hand and easily slid the second shackle around his wrist. Once bound, Eamon slipped his hand onto Ikane's shoulder. "Come, let us get you inside and into some clothes."

Ikane blinked as he rose to his feet with Eamon. The chain connecting his iron restraints rattled. "I... you haven't called me Little Wolf in years," Ikane said quietly. The full-life of his vibrant green eye returned, and with it, his consciousness.

Eamon gave him a crooked smile. "Don't get used to it," he said, his tone drastically changing. "I don't plan on smooth-talking you every time you do this."

There was something in his voice that indicated that he had done this before. I could only assume that it was when Eamon had taken the young Leviathan under his wing during the battle of Amall.

Ikane looked over his shoulder at me and gave me the most beautiful, heart-wrenching smile. "I'm sorry I pushed you away so violently," he said.

I pursed my lips to try to keep from running into his embrace and swallowed hard. "It..." my voice cracked. I cleared it, and then continued. "It's alright."

Eamon began to steer Ikane from the alleyway. "We've got some warm clothes for you, and you've changed just in time to have a warm breakfast of porridge."

I couldn't help but wonder what Rion was waiting for.

"Ikane," I asked as I came up beside him. "What just happened? What... I don't understand. You weren't there... and neither was Rion. Why were you so... empty just now?"

Ikane nodded soberly, understanding my questions. "It has begun," he said softly. "The wolfsbane is taking a toll on my body."

My brows furrowed. "You mean it's getting harder to change back into a man?"

"Wait? What are you saying? Are you saying that your body can't shift anymore?" Eamon asked.

"Something of the sort," Ikane said. "Did you not realize how long it took me to shift just now?" he shuddered at the memory. Only after he voiced the question did I see what he was saying.

"Not only that, but I felt like I couldn't... find myself," he said, pausing a moment to search for the right word. "It was as if I was locked away in a part of my mind that only related with the wolf."

I frowned. "We can't use the wolfsbane anymore."

Eamon rounded on Ikane. "Are you saying it's the wolfbane that's causing this?"

Ikane nodded. "But I will do what I must to keep Rion from overpowering me."

"Why hasn't she done so yet?" I asked.

Ikane shrugged, Eamon's brows rose, and I was left wondering the same thing.

17

SHEAR

Ikane stood at the bow of the ship with his hands clasped at the small of his back, the glint of iron around his wrists. He had requested to be restrained in this manner. With his arms at his back, Rion would be unable to use the chain connecting his wrists as a noose – seeing as she had a tendency to strangle me. The ship hit a swell and rocked slightly. Ikane merely widened his stance like the experienced seaman that he was. Cold wind rippled his black hair as he deeply inhaled, expanding his chest and straining his new tunic that had been provided by Queen Lonacheska. The last time I'd seen him this serene was when we had traveled upon the ship called the Otaridae, sailing from Daram to Bakka. It should have been clear to me then that he was a Leviathan Pirate, but I had been too distracted by his mysterious charm to speculate his origins.

I, on the other hand, tottered across the deck of the rocking ship like a toddler first learning to walk. When I came to his side, my good hand shot out to grasp the railing for balance.

Ikane laughed upon seeing my clumsiness. "Don't you fret," he assured me. "You'll find your sea-legs soon enough. As I recall, you seemed to find them pretty quick when we were on the Otaridae."

I turned to the wind to allow it to blow my stray strands of hair from my face and chuckled. "By the time I find them, we will have reached Shear."

Eamon wobbled up to the railing beside me, limping heavily on his injured knee. I was about to comment on taking a look at it when he leaned over the railing, his face growing exceptionally pale. It reminded me of Ropert the last time he was aboard a ship.

"You're seasick," I said with furrowed brows.

As if on cue, he heaved, and his breakfast of warm porridge splashed into the water below. In all my years of knowing this man, I hadn't known that he was prone to seasickness. If I had, I would've gladly endured another week of hard riding along the coastline of Glacier Lake to spare him. Then again, with his knee so badly injured, it would have taken us far too long.

"Try keeping your eyes on the horizon," Ikane suggested. "It helps to find something steady to focus on."

Eamon groaned and forced his head up. The vast glacial lake stretched out as widely as the Rethreal Sea to the south, reflecting the meager sunlight that broke through the thin clouds overhead. The only difference were the monumental glaciers protruding from the water to our left. Although there was a coastline to our right, it was already too far to detect.

Ikane and I remained on deck for Eamon's sake, in spite of the biting cold wind that chapped our cheeks and lips. Ikane's suggestion of focusing on the unmoving horizon seemed to take the edge off of Eamon's discomfort, but eventually, the gray clouds built up until icy drops of water stung our faces. The captain ordered everyone below, knowing that these afternoon storms could become unpredictable. Luckily, there weren't very many passengers on board and we were able to have some privacy at the far end of the ship.

Reluctantly, Ikane and I helped Eamon below where he curled up on the bottom bunk and tried to sleep. The bunks were stacked three high and were quite narrow. I couldn't help but think of Ropert, and his broad shoulders, and the way he had complained when we had boarded the Otaridae over a year ago.

Ikane slumped down at the base of the opposite stack of bunks so he could keep an eye on Eamon, and then jerked his head, indicating that I should take a seat beside him. He didn't need to ask me twice. As soon as I sat down, with my unfeeling arm against Ikane's shoulder, I could sense the rumbling hull of the ship against my back and buttocks. I shifted a bit to try and find a more comfortable position. Eventually, I found myself sitting quietly beside Ikane, with my knees drawn halfway up for balance – and to minimize the uncomfortable vibrations on my rear.

But my mind was not thinking of the sturdy build of the ship, or Eamon's wellbeing. I was troubled by Rion. Why hadn't she overpowered Ikane yet? Who had she called on for support? What malevolent force would even fancy aiding her? The vision of the frail looking, deformed, old man, clutching the heirloom haunted my thoughts. Absently, my hand wandered up to the jewel hanging around my neck.

Ikane, with his hands still chained at his back, bumped his shoulder into mine to get my attention. "I'm not sure I like this," he said with a glimmer of tease in his eyes.

"Like what?" I asked, dropping the jewel that I had been rolling through my fingers.

"I can't hear your thoughts anymore," he said. "In a way, I rather enjoyed knowing what was on your mind."

I scoffed and shook my head. "And I miss your heightened senses," I admitted. "Everything seems so... dull without them."

Eamon groaned across the way and rolled over in his bunk. He still looked as pale as before.

"If I had known he would be this sick, I would have insisted on riding along the coast," I said, waving my hand at Eamon.

"A few days of seasickness won't kill him," Ikane said.

I sighed and stretched my legs. "Ropert got seasick, but never like this."

"You miss him, don't you?"

I nodded. "He is a good friend, Ikane." I pulled my knees up to my chest. "He would have followed me, with or without broken ribs. Am I doing the right thing?" I asked looking up at the Leviathan's mismatched eyes. "What if Queen Lonacheska is wrong? What if there is nothing in the Glacial Empire for me? What if Roanfire is plunged into another war with Toleah? What if there was something I could do to stop it? What if I am meant to fail, just as all the other queens and princesses of the past?"

Ikane tried to move to embrace me, but the chains rattled as they kept him from doing so. He resorted to leaning against my shoulder even harder and tipped his head so that his forehead brushed up against my cheek. "Win or not, you are special, Kea. And I am here to help you in any way I can."

He pulled away and smiled, another mischievous gleam appearing in his eyes. "After all, you did manage to drive back the entire Leviathan Army."

I smiled broadly. "It seems I missed one."

He smiled at first, and then his face grew tender in earnest. "You'll never frighten me away, Kea," he whispered fiercely.

My eyes darted to his warm lips and back to his beautiful emerald and sapphire eyes. I felt my heart-rate quicken at the thought of pressing my lips against his. It was something that I had wanted to do ever since I met him back in Daram, but there was always something between us. He leaned closer, desperately wanting to close the gap.

And then his eyes flickered. He flinched and pulled away as redness burned behind them. The chains at his back rattled as he tried to grab his head to stay the burning pain that raced through his skull.

"Ikane," I said, getting to my knees. I pressed my good hand against his cheek and he immediately drove his head into my palm, hoping that my touch would ease the pain. "Let me in, Ikane."

He did not resist. But the instant he opened his mind, Rion overpowered him. His eyes burned with orange flame as he glowered at me. My eyes narrowed in return. If Rion could push her way through Ikane so easily, so could I.

I dove into Ikane's mind, finding his thoughts a tangled mass of webs with each thread connecting to another memory or thought. But his mind wasn't what I remembered. There was darkness growing inside that began to eat away at his memories. At first, I thought it was Rion's doing, but upon further investigation, I discovered the wolf. He hunted. He stalked. He fought for his territory. He resorted to animal instincts. It became clear that it wasn't Rion, but the wolfsbane. It was slowly devouring Ikane's mind.

You are killing him, Rion said. *We are both hurting because of your actions. He was dazed when he changed. The next time will be worse.*

Then let him go, I snapped. *Then I wouldn't need to use the poison.* A thought popped into my head and I thought to use it against her. *You'll be trapped in the mind of a wolf forever.*

And you'll lose the man you love, she retorted, unfazed by my bluff.

With that, she gathered a burning flame to her and pitched it in my direction. My flickering shield of white lights blossomed before me, easily deflecting her assault. But the force of her burning energy drove me back. I collided into a memory belonging to Ikane and found myself re-living a brawl he had with one of his brothers. The man's fist to my gut left me crumbled and breathless. Before his boot could connect with my shoulder, I pulled myself from the memory, gasping.

You cannot destroy me, Phoenix Daughter.

I struggled to regain my composure. *You have called for aid, haven't you?*

I felt a small surge of triumph radiate through her.

Kea? It was Ikane's voice. *What are you doing here?*

Rion's dangerous smile sent a tremor of fear through me.

There you are, her voices hissed. Without hesitation, she lunged for him.

Instinct propelled me headlong into the fray and my magic shot forward like a spear. But my power wasn't strong enough to penetrate her shield. My blow simply knocked her off balance and then disintegrated.

Let him be! I snapped at her.

You can't stop me! She bellowed and reached her fiery threads out to Ikane.

I lunged between them, shielding both Ikane and myself from her burning pain with a sphere of white light. Her darts bounded off the bright surface.

Go, Ikane! I roared. *Hide!*

We're stronger together, Ikane said firmly, and I felt his energy burn at my back. *I'm not going to leave you. Here.* Like the warmth of a fire in a hearth, I felt Ikane's energy seep into my soul. It wasn't overpowering or weak. It wasn't demeaning or vengeful. His love for me surged through my essence with such power that it needed to expand. Rushing through Ikane's mind like a tidal wave, it collided into Rion, thrusting her back like a ship on the waves. In an instant, our combined energy bent and shifted around the Phoenix Witch. Her cry of anger was cut short as the power completely surrounded her in a crystal sphere, sealing her within. It floated through Ikane's thoughts emulating a harmless, indestructible bubble.

Our moment of triumph was immediately overwhelmed by our physical weakness. As I withdrew from Ikane's mind, my body slumped down beside him. This seemingly small battle with Rion had drained me more than an epic battle with the sword. Ikane, just as weak, slumped against the bunk, gasping for breath.

My eyes barely took in his glowing green iris.

"Thank you," he whispered.

It was all I could do to pull my good arm up to rest across his chest. "I couldn't have done it without you."

Eamon couldn't have been more elated to see the small shoreline appear on the horizon. Three days aboard the small ship had left him weak, dizzy, and nauseated. I couldn't help but worry for Eamon as he continued to limp. We had tended to his knee as best we could aboard the ship, with poultices of herbs, but something deep inside seemed to have torn.

Knowing that Rion was secure—for now—Eamon released Ikane from the iron shackles. All three of us stood on the bow, eager to set foot on land and continue our journey.

White plumes of smoke billowed from the rooftops of the snow-covered houses around the port. Behind the port-village of Shear stood a wide landscape of snow and crisp glaciers further beyond. The cold was fierce, tearing at our faces. I thought it was simply due to the wind dragging across the lake, but as we disembarked, I realized that it wasn't the case. The wind was coming from the mountains. Even without Ikane's heightened sense of smell, the scent of snow was unmistakable.

I shivered as Ikane helped Eamon walk the gangway to the solid ground of the port. In spite of Shear being a rather small port-village, it was bustling. Seeing as it was one of the most effective routes to trade with the Glacial Empire, merchants flocked here weekly. At the dock, sailors lugged crates and barrels from the ship where eager merchants stood nearby, with papers and charcoal pencils, to take inventory. I eyed a man with a very thick looking, fur-lined coat. My woolen cloak, meant for Roanfirien winters, wasn't going to be warm enough for this climate. We hadn't even gone through Glacier Pass yet and my legs already stung with cold.

Ikane shivered as well, seeing as he was accustomed to the warmer climate of the Rethreal Sea. Eamon, on the other hand, didn't seem terribly bothered by the cold. In fact, he seemed to inhale it like a man drinking water in a desert. And then I noted the color returning to his face.

We pushed by the crowded docks and into the busy heart of the village. Here, a handful of quaint shops lined the market-square, orange light of warmth spilling from their thick, glass-paned windows. I caught sight of a bakery, a butcher's shop, a woodcutter and carpenter's shop, a brewery, an apothecary and... a shop dedicated to the outfitting of hopelessly cold travelers such as us! Thick, fur-lined coats, boots and mittens were displayed in the frosted window panes.

"Oh, all right," Eamon groaned and rolled his eyes to heaven at my longing expression. "I suppose that is why we were supplied with enough money."

We pushed through the heavy traffic in the square, passing by a stone monument of an unfamiliar merchant-man standing in the center. Three wooden steps rose from the snow-covered ground, leading to the shop's sturdy door. Hurriedly, I ducked inside and was instantly slammed with the heat from the hearth to my right. Just as Ikane and Eamon slipped inside, a short woman with healthy curves, looked up from her perch behind a small desk at the far end of the room.

"Close the door quickly," she snapped from behind the counter, though not unkindly.

Ikane pushed it shut against the wind, shutting out the noise of the square.

The woman stepped around her workbench to greet us. I couldn't help but envy the thick animal hide trousers and fur-lined boots that she wore. Her smile was pleasant, in spite of one rotting tooth at the right corner of her mouth.

"Well now," she stated as she folded her arms across her chest and scanned our pitifully unfit garments with one raised eyebrow. "It seems you've come to the right place. There should be a good selection of clothing over there for you two gallant men," she said and waved her hand to the left of her shop. "You, young lady, come with me. I have just what you need."

Without a second thought, I followed her to the right where she had an assortment of fur-lined coats and boots arranged along the thick logs of the cabin's wall. "These trousers should fit," she said as she grabbed a pair of dark-skinned ones from a pile. "And these boots." She snatched up a pair from a row on a shelf. "Do you have woolen stockings?"

I nodded quickly. "Two pair, and I'm already wearing them."

She laughed openly, deep lines forming at the corners of her eyes. "With my exceptional boots, you can go back to simply wearing one set," she said as she placed the trousers in my good arm. "Go change in that room over there, and then we'll find the right coat for you."

It wasn't an easy feat to change with one arm. It took me twice as long as both Ikane and Eamon to get into my new attire. Once finished, the woman presented me with a luscious, brown colored, fur-lined coat that hung just below my knees. She helped me shrug my arms into the sleeves and buttoned the row of thick, wooden toggles down the front. Already, I could tell the difference in warmth.

"You'll all need mittens," she announced as Ikane and Ropert presented her with their choices. Eamon had selected a simple, yet functional blue-gray coat and boots, while Ikane selected a thick, black coat with a high collar that he could tuck his chin into.

Ikane, with his face already hidden deep within the cowl of his new coat, turned to me and took my limp, unfeeling limb in his. Or was it? There was a little sensation... soft pressure on the back of my hand. I pushed the hopeful thought aside. I did not want to be taunted by false hope.

"Here," he said, making certain that the mitten was secure. He pulled the sling over my head and helped me settle my arm back into it. "We'd best keep an eye on that hand. You won't be able to feel the frostbite if it gets too cold."

The woman nodded approvingly. "And even though these coats have exceptionally warm hoods, the wind always finds a way to gnaw at your ears. I suggest you all get woolen caps as well, especially if you are headed through Glacier Pass."

We accepted her suggestion, and each chose a warm cap sitting in a nearby basket. Eamon nearly had a fit when she gave him the total cost of our merchandise.

"It's either that or you freeze," she shrugged.

Grumbling, Eamon paid the lady with the money from Queen Lonacheska.

The woman thanked us. "Please come again soon," she said as we headed for the door.

Eamon mumbled under his breath.

It wasn't until twenty minutes later that I discovered the reason for Eamon's sour attitude towards the woman who had outfitted us so well. The cost of our new clothing alone had eaten up a large portion of the allowance Queen Lonacheska had allotted to Eamon. So much in fact, that we were only able to afford two horses bred to thrive in this climate. This would slow us down drastically. They were shaggy creatures, with dull colored coats and short, thick legs. The one with the darker snout was called Camp, and the other was named Brick.

But this was not all. We were told that Brick suffered from occasional seizures. He couldn't be pushed too hard or he would collapse in a fit.

All in all, it should have only taken us one day of good, solid riding to reach Gerom Post. Lonacheska's instructions had specifically indicated that we make it in the allotted time, or word would reach the soldiers here of my disappearance. With two small horses, three riders, and Eamon's bad knee, we already knew that reaching Gerom Post today would be slim. Considering how cautiously we would need to travel for Brick's sake, it would take us two days at best.

We stood just outside the village gates, facing the wall of towering glaciers in the distance. The snow-laden landscape opened up to a vast grassy field on my right, while sunlight glistened against the expanse of Glacier Lake on my left. Gray clouds, that smelled of snow, hung over the mountains like an expertly crafted quilt. Scattered pine trees dotted the landscape, but they were sparse and thin, and wouldn't provide much shelter. I was not looking forward to camping out in the open, especially with the wind constantly blowing across the open field.

Other merchants were arranging gear and horses near the road as well, preparing to head to Gerom Post. I counted six merchants in total, three to a wagon. Each wagon was pulled by two horses, the shaggy kind, but they looked much healthier than the two we had purchased.

"I'm faster as a wolf," Ikane offered as we arranged our gear on the back of the small horses. Instantly, I thought of the dark corners in his mind, void of memories that had once been there. Who knew what he had already lost?

"No," Eamon and I snapped almost simultaneously, knowing what he was suggesting.

"Besides," I continued, "we don't have any more wolfsbane."

"Kea is right," Eamon said. "You two take turns riding Camp. I'll ride Brick."

I frowned, knowing that Eamon had elected to ride the horse with potential seizures to spare us. But I couldn't fathom what would happen to Eamon's knee if the horse went into a fit and collapsed on his leg.

"You ride Camp," I told him firmly as I took the horse by the reigns. "Ikane and I will ride Brick. I am lighter, and it will give him more of a respite between loads."

Eamon, a little stunned at my firmness, eventually nodded. He moved over to the dark-snouted horse that stood by Ikane and adjusted the bedroll and tent that was strapped to the saddle. He swung his leg over the shaggy horse's back and both of them shifted until they found a good center. Eamon wasn't accustomed to riding anything smaller than a warhorse. In fact, he looked a little ridiculous on the small creature.

Ikane stepped up to Brick and cupped his mitten-covered hands to help me mount the paler of the two shaggy animals. The annoyance of needing such assistance returned as I placed my boot into them. Grasping the saddle-horn with my good hand, I managed to swing up into the saddle. The short mount staggered under my weight and I could feel his muscles bunch as he struggled to keep his balance.

I frowned. This wasn't going to go well. This horse was weaker than I thought.

"We had best get moving," Eamon said. "Those wagons will overtake us in no time. We're going to need to keep a steady pace."

He bumped his heels into the sides of Camp and steered him away from the port village of Shear.

We quickly learned the limits of Brick's abilities after getting through two seizures before noon. The first time the horse had collapsed, Ikane had been riding him. The second time... Ikane again. Anything more than my weight was too much for the animal. It took Brick nearly twenty minutes each time to recover from his seizures, and the guilt I felt at pushing this animal so hard began to eat at my heart.

The two wagons passed us quickly. They, at least, would make it to Gerom Post by sundown.

By the time the sunlight had given way to the arctic night, we were barely over halfway to our destination. We erected our tent beside a lone pine tree, with reedy branches, in an attempt to block the wind, but it did little. Building a fire, even with the tent at our backs, was next to impossible. The pine didn't want to burn, and the constant wind racing down the side of the glacial mountains destroyed whatever flame we did manage to light. Eventually, we gave up and huddled inside the tiny tent together. There was no need to keep watch. No one would be out in this raw, open landscape, and our body heat would warm the tent that was meant for two in no time.

Ikane checked my limp hand before we settled down to sleep, and I thought I could feel gentle pressure again as he turned it palm up. The small flecks of firedust embedded in my skin glowed faintly in the darkness of the tent, reminding me of glittering stars in the night sky. The meager light coming from them illuminated Ikane's face just enough so that I could make out his high cheekbones and strong jaw.

"Your hand is like ice," Ikane commented as he took it and rubbed it between the palms of his hands.

Eamon, who had already shrugged his shoulders into his bedroll, turned his back to us, bumping against my hip as he did so. "It'll warm soon enough. Just get into your blankets and sleep. We'll head out at first light."

Ikane, with a mischievous little glint behind his eyes, kissed the back of my hand before lowering it. I pressed my lips together, trying not to smile. Ikane hadn't shown any open affection for me in the presence of Eamon, though I knew my guardian wasn't oblivious to our love. But the fact that he had kissed my hand with Eamon lying directly beside me, made it a little rebellious and exciting.

Ikane slid down into his bedroll and I did my best to do so with one arm. Eventually, Ikane helped me settle in, and rolled up against my back with his arm around my shoulders. Stuck between Eamon's and Ikane's large bodies, I was warm and asleep in minutes.

Black rock, slick with pungent slime and writhing with the leather wings of bats, surrounded the obsidian figure hunched by a lucid pool of gray-green water. The hood of his long mantle shrouded his features. His hand rose, bony fingers with skin the color of ash. The glint of the crimson jewel stuck between his thumb and forefinger, burned fiercely against the gloomy surroundings of the cave.

He held it up, his head rising just enough to reveal a hint of his thin, gray lips. He scrutinized the jewel, twisting it between his fingers like a child would do to a terrified pill bug. A small smile pulled on his lips, revealing teeth that were nearly the same ashen color as his skin.

"I need this?" he asked of no one in particular in a barely audible whisper.

"She has it," the voices of Rion hummed together, echoing through the cave.

Bats startled at her voices and darted across the cavern like arrows.

Something crowded into this vision and warped it like the ripples in a still pond. White light drove the gloomy cave into the shadows and a new face appeared, one that had graced my visions before. But his usual serene countenance was contorted with dread, barely concealing the flood of panic that rushed through his entire being. His lips moved, as if to say something to me, but I heard nothing. Thrall intruded on him—as if there was a battle between the light and the dark. Faint glimmers of his colorless dreams simmered to the surface only to be

*drowned out by the darkness. With one final burst of energy,
his vision became clear again.*

"They are coming for you!" the White Wardent warned me.

My eyes flew open.

The faint grayness of morning light penetrated the gray
canvas of the tent, casting odd shadows across our bedrolls. I
felt Ikane stir and looked at him. His eyes were wide... he
knew.

"Who was that?" Ikane whispered to me as he sat up.
"Who is coming for us?"

I didn't know. I had no answers, save that Rion had
manipulated some unfortunate soul into doing her bidding.
My soldier's instinct was to find strong shelter, high ground,
and a place to fortify, but there was nothing here on the open
planes of snow and ice. We needed to move.

I sat upright and shoved my bedroll down to my knees.
"Eamon," I said. When he didn't stir, I shook his shoulder.
"Eamon, we're burning daylight. We need to move."

He groaned but sat upright and rubbed his face. He
blinked at me, then wiggled from his bedroll. "Well," he said
groggily and grabbed his boots that had been pushed into the
corner of the tent during sleep. "I'll see to the horses. You two
pack up in here."

Without needing any further instructions, Ikane and I set
to work, and Eamon ducked outside.

"Who was that man in white, Kea?" Ikane asked, hastily
rolling up his bedroll. With one hand, I held the roll firm so
that he could easily buckle the leather straps around it.

"The White Wardent," I said. "He's real and alive, though
I do not know where he is. But he's looking out for us."

"Why won't he simply tell us where to find him?" Ikane
asked, moving to my bedroll now. I shifted my legs, so he
could pull it out from beneath me.

I shook my head and shrugged. I had asked myself that
question several times before. "I think there is something I

need to do first... but I don't know what. There are keys, I think, that I need to find. Eamon thinks that you are one of them."

Ikane paused a moment and blinked up at me. "Keys?" he asked. "What sort of keys?"

"The scribe in Meldron had transcribed a document before the library was burnt. He said he remembered something about four keys, but nothing is clear. It was in the letter that was sent to Emperor Skarand. Queen Lonacheska thinks that I should find the letter intact in the Glacial Empire."

Ikane's brows furrowed, and his lips pulled to one side in thought as he resumed rolling up my blanket. "It still doesn't make sense," he grumbled. "You think he'd be eager to see this curse gone. Why not simply tell us what we need to do next?"

"I've asked myself that—" I stopped when Ikane flinched and his hand flew up to his forehead. His jaw clenched, and his nostrils flared as he tried to breathe through the pain.

"Not now," I hissed, knowing it was Rion. I gripped Ikane's shoulder, and he grabbed my hand in return, looking as me with flickering eyes. How did she escape the sphere we had trapped her in?

"It burns," Ikane whimpered, his eyes scrunching shut. Rion blasted him with the full force of her power, burning his bones until they felt brittle and hot. Ikane's body arched back, the veins in his neck popping out as he struggled to breathe against the splintering fire in his lungs.

"Eamon!" I roared. "The shackles, Eamon! We need the shackles!"

I heard the chains rattle before Eamon pushed his head into the tent.

Ikane's nose was bleeding now. I wanted to comfort him, to reach out and let him know that I was there, but I remembered the pain well. Any form of touch would feel like the brand of a hot iron against my skin. I could only watch, clenching my fist in anger, as Ikane suffered.

Stop it, Rion! I finally cried, feeling tears burn my eyes. *Let him breathe! Let him be! It's me you want!*

Ikane's rigid body fell back against the earth with blood now trailing from his ears. Why wasn't she simply taking over his form? It seemed that she was purely enjoying the burning torture she was inflicting on him.

"Rion! Stop!" I barked again, my voice cracking this time.

Ikane still couldn't breathe, and redness blossomed up from his neck to his face.

Terrified and angry, it became clear what I needed to do. Rion had built her link to Ikane through a forced kiss. And that was exactly what I needed to do to reach her. Heedless of Eamon looking on, I scrambled up to Ikane, placed my hand on his cheek and leaned down. My lips pressed against his tightly clenched mouth, feeling the terrible heat in his body that could've easily been mistaken for a fever.

Rion's power was driven back by the love and passion I held for Ikane. I heard the quick intake of breath through his nose as the rigidness in his body abated, followed by his lips softening against mine. His hands, that had been clenched into fists against his head, eagerly wrapped around my back and pulled me to him. But it wasn't simply passion that drove him to do so. He was clinging to the relief that I brought against Rion's pain.

His mind opened up to me like Meldron's gilded gates, and I slipped inside. An entanglement of fiery threads reached from one memory to another, searing them as she drew on the power they held. A gaping hole lay in the center of the sphere where we had ensnared her.

Frantic, I followed the burning threads to find Rion at the center. Equal to an insect, she was drinking his emotions like a spider for sustenance.

I was wondering when you'd figure it out, her voices raced at me in the form of fiery darts.

My barrier came up, shielding me from the assault. I felt the burn, the sting, the ache as threads latched onto my soul. Like the spider she had become, burning ribbons dropped from an angle I hadn't anticipated. My power flickered around me like trembling fireflies in the night. But the pain was too intense, rendering me paralyzed.

Through the orange and red threads weaving through Ikane's mind, a figure began to take shape. It bent and shifted at first, like a mirage in the desert. But soon, a solid, almost tangible form, materialized. Never before had I seen her so clearly. White hair contrasted against her bronze skin like snow and ash. The red gown flowed across her body like bloodied silk, vacillating with her figure as she floated across the expanse of Ikane's mind. Like the wings of a phoenix, gold and fire blossomed at her back. But it was her eyes that drove fear into my soul. White, lifeless, hollow eyes stared at me.

You should have given yourself to me when I demanded it. Her voice was more distinct now, no longer humming with the voices of thousands. I could hear her own powerful, modulated tone. *Now it is too late, for you and him.*

My mind could barely form a coherent thought against her burning ribbons.

A knowing, crooked smile stole across her blood-red lips. *His emotions are pure,* she said and reached out to a thread with one of her copper hands. Her slender fingers curled around the end, and then her fist crushed around it as if she had caught a flighty bug. With a harsh tug, she leached all emotion from one of Ikane's memories. I watched in horror as the memory burned along the edge of her thread, leaving nothing in its wake. Her eyes closed as her head turned upward, relishing the energy that filled her form. The golden fire at her back surged.

Through my mortal ears, I could hear Ikane cry out.

Frantic, I struggled against her bonds. Somehow, I managed to gain composure of my mind. *You'll pay for that!*

Her head lowered from her ecstatic moment as her lifeless eyes opened. *You thought to use his strength against me,* she said. Without even looking, her hand shot out and seized the end of another ribbon floating nearby, linked to a recent memory.

Don't! I cried.

Her smile was venomous as she tugged on it.

The sensation of Ikane's warm lips against the back of my hand flowed across the burning ribbon. Pure love, kindness, and longing swelled to the surface and she absorbed it. Her form trembled in ecstasy as the wings of golden fire at her back spread.

This time, I heard Ikane whimper— a sob.

My heart burned with anger. I welcomed the fury. It was power. It was strong and formidable. I could use it. Desperate to release Ikane's fragile memories from Rion's grasp, I allowed the anger to burst from me. It appeared as white-red shards of glass that ripped into the ribbons, causing them to recoil and dissolve.

Free from her threads, and driven by maddened rage, I urged this terrible, tainted power to destroy the Phoenix Witch. The shards flew at Rion's form like lethal daggers— but she laughed when the power absorbed into her, causing her wings to flare with energy.

Startled, my anger dissipated, as did my magic.

Rion laughed. *Anger does not become you, little Roanfirien Princess.* With a burning surge of raw energy, she blasted a thick harpoon of fire at my soul.

My shield of white light blossomed before me, but the force of her power ripped through it, plunging deep into my heart. I heard my physical voice cry out as my mind doubled over in memories that spiraled into suffering.

The thought of my useless arm, rendering me incapable of fighting as a true soldier, became unbearable. Failing to defend Daram against the Leviathan Pirates scorched my heart. The hatred of Duchess Caitelyn, festered. Hala and

Ardon's betrayal, stung like nettle. Queen Lonacheska's bitterness at my existence stabbed into my chest like a lance. The thought of destroying Ropert's trust nearly broke me. But it was the impossible love I held for Ikane that snapped my soul.

Little Brendagger! The voice was faint. *Brendagger! Fight! I'm here! Fight!*

I didn't know if I could. The agony of everyone I had harmed consumed all rational thought.

Little Brendagger!

The voice was clearer now. Ikane!

Don't let her twist the truth, he said. I felt him against me, warm and strong. *You know her lies mean nothing. Listen to me. We've come so far. Don't let her destroy what we have!*

He pushed against my broken mind, driving his power to dull the agony Rion had placed there. It expanded, flourishing into a shield that protected both of us, as if his arms wrapped around me.

Fight, Little Brendagger. His voice was soft, but formidable. *My strength is yours.*

Filled with a new resolve, I faced the Phoenix Witch. Her white eyes narrowed.

You can try, she said. *But it's already too late for you.* In spite of her confident tone, she seemed to retreat, as if she feared what I could do with Ikane by my side. This was all the hope I needed to find strength again. With this hope and Ikane's love, my eruption of magic was pure. White crystalline power flew against Rion like a stone thrown from a catapult. She threw up her defenses, shielding her form so that it simply thrust her back.

My second burst of power slammed into her, leaving her as dazed as if I had actually struck her with my fist.

With the purpose of pushing her back into the broken sphere still hanging in Ikane's mind, the bright, vibrant light surrounded her. But it snagged and warped around invisible cords that were tethered to her frame in a way I hadn't seen before. These new ribbons branched away in hundreds of directions, much like the roots of an ancient tree. At the end of each ribbon, we discovered a soul from which she drew her strength. Her prisoners.

With the vigor of a lumberjack, I sliced the thread. As the bond severed, the soul tethered to the end seemed at peace. It drifted away, disappearing like dust in the wind.

Rion screamed as if she had lost one of her limbs in the act. Encouraged, I severed another ribbon. Another soul peacefully slipped away. But there were thousands. I cut a third, and Rion cried out again.

Fool! She screamed. *Do you not see the waste? These souls could have lived on forever through me, but you've destroyed their chance.*

Only a fool would want to live forever with you, I said and struck at another thread. But my blow was weak. I felt Ikane's strength diminishing along with my own. Even together, we were not powerful enough to finish this. Instead of severing the link, I damaged it instead. The soul at its tip cried out as Rion pulled the last of her energy into her. With this, Rion's golden fiery wings burned.

She released a powerful blow, but Ikane's shield held against her onslaught.

Kea! Let them be. Focus. Trap her. Ikane said.

He was right. We couldn't free them all.

Together, our white magic swarmed around the Phoenix Witch, suffocating her of energy. Her high-pitched scream was scattered again, torn between the voices of thousands. We drove her back, sending her reeling into the sphere of silvery white light floating in the middle of Ikane's mind. Without restraint, Ikane allowed his vigor to pour into my energy, causing the pure lights to gather and repair the shards of the sphere. They sealed her within.

The silence that followed was deafening.

It was hard to breathe.

"Kea! Ikane!" Eamon's voice cried from a strange distance.

I retreated into my body. The feeling was terrible. My body trembled, perspired, and cramped. My head whirled and throbbed like the pounding of a blacksmith's hammer, and a horrible copper taste filled my mouth. Lying against Ikane's chest, I fell asleep before his heartbeat sounded in my ear.

"Wake up, Kea!" the cry was urgent.

I sat upright, and everything swirled. I lay back again to ease the spinning. I was so tired.

"Kea! Now! Get on your horse!" The warm bedroll was ripped from my body and the cold hit me like a waterfall. Still, my body felt sluggish. Rough hands gripped my shoulders and jerked me back to a sitting position. My head lulled. Uncomfortable pressure pinched my jaw, and it took me a moment to realize that Ikane had gripped my face to steady my swaying head.

"Wake up, Kea! Come on! We don't have time for this. We've got to go," he said.

My eyes blinked heavily, but no matter how hard I tried, they would not stay open. My limbs felt as if iron pumped through my blood, weighing me down.

Eamon's voice was muffled through the fabric of the tent, but he was clearly calling for Ikane to hurry. Something was wrong...

"Now, Kea!" Ikane shouted as he shoved our belongings and bedding into packs. When I didn't move, Ikane mumbled something and roughly shoved my boots onto my feet. He barely pulled my coat over my shoulders and took the time to clasp only one toggle at my throat before brashly hauling me to my feet and shoving me out of the tent.

Dusty light filtered through the thick clouds in the sky as I stumbled out into the open. Equivalent to a bumbling drunkard, my feet dragged across the field of snow until I collided into the flank of one of the horses. My body rebounded off its rump, and I tipped back into the thick layer of snow that wrapped me in a comfortable nest. My eyes closed instantly. I could just sleep here.

"Kea!" Eamon cried in dismay. "Get up!"

Willing my body to obey, I rolled onto my knees and pushed myself up with my one good hand. But that was as far as I could get. The exhaustion was too great. Almost instantly, Ikane appeared at my side. With a harsh tug on my shoulder, he forced me to flop back so that he could slip his arm under my legs. He scooped me up and nearly sprinted to Eamon, who was already mounted on Camp. He reached down for me. Confused, I straddled the horse behind Eamon. Once Ikane was sure I had my good arm around Eamon's waist, I heard the harsh slap as he struck the horse's rear.

"Go! Go! Go!" he yelled.

The horse's body bunched beneath us and plunged forward on short legs. My head jolted as the horse bound through the snow. Weak, sleepy, and confused at their urgency, my grip grew lax. Eamon tried to grab my arm but was too late. White lace exploded around me, padding my fall from the back of the small horse. The cold of the snow finding its way into the collar of my tunic jarred me awake.

Eamon slowed Camp and was about to turn back for me when Ikane shouted after him. "Don't stop! I've got her!"

Ikane spurred Brick toward me and I felt my eyes widen in dismay. The way he drove the small horse would surely send it into a seizure. Why would he dare risk that?

I struggled to my feet and glanced back to where our camp had been. The tent remained standing beside the pitiful-looking pine tree, abandoned. It was then that my eyes were drawn to a deep shadow forming in the clouds behind him. My blood ran cold. A condensed cluster of black-winged monsters caused the sky to darken as if a great storm was building in the sky. I could not make out distinct features, nor did I want to. Upon seeing the oily-blackness of their flesh and bat-like wings, panic set in, for I had seen them before... in my dream.

"Kea!" Ikane called. He held his hand out for me to take as he galloped toward me.

Our hands linked. The force of the small horse's speed jerked me from the ground and with Ikane's help, I swung my leg over the horse's back. My one good arm slipped around Ikane's waist, clutching him with all my strength as he spurred the tiny, seizure-prone horse on.

Ahead—far, far ahead—stood a distant line of trees, brimming on the white horizon like delicate lace. We would never reach them in time.

The beating of wings became increasingly louder as the shadows neared, and I could almost feel their breath on my back. A chill raced down my spine as the monsters screeched, a high-pitched noise that grated on my ears. It was a cry of assault. They had found their mark. I jerked my head to the side as one of the creatures swooped at it. Black talons, nearly two inches in length, swept past my forehead. I felt the harsh whip of wind over my head as the monster blew past, leaving a horrible sour stench in its wake.

A dull brushing sound hissed in my ear as Ikane drew his sword from the leather scabbard at his back. In the same motion, he cut downward at an approaching monster. His expert stroke whistled through the air as it sliced into the shoulder of its leather wing. The beast's cry pierced my ears as it went writhing to the ground.

Pain zapped through my shoulder, followed by the sour stench and the wild slap of leather wings against my head as the creature clung to me. Through my peripheral vision, I caught sight of its canine-like jaw, filled with razor-sharp teeth, open wide and bear down into the base of my neck. My cry was cut off as a terrible burn took over. Relying on my legs to keep me on the tiny horse, I released my hold on Ikane's waist and wildly grabbed at the monster. My hand finally curled around a portion of its leather wing and a terrible sting radiated up my neck as I ripped it away. Just as I flung the creature to the snow, the unexpected force of another slammed into my forearm, causing me to pivot to my right. An electrifying bite coursed up my arm as it dug its talons deep into my cotton shirt. Whirling violently at the impact, I was dislodged from the back of the horse and crashed hard into the snow.

The explosion of white powder deterred their onslaught for a few precious seconds, and then the weight of the dark creatures piled upon my body, driving me down. Their flailing wings slapped against my skin. Poisonous talons and teeth plunged into me like daggers. I rolled across the snow, momentarily forcing them to flit away to keep from being crushed under the weight of my body.

A terrible sting plunged into the old arrow wound on my back, sending a wave of agony through my spine and down my leg. The scream that penetrated the evening air didn't feel like my own.

"KEA!" Ikane howled.

Red light seared the sky.

18

HOPE

Sweltering agony tore through my entire being as consciousness returned. I wanted to scream but only emitted a gargled cry. The noise of frantic scrambling to my left immediately brought the poison infested bats to mind. Panic. My eyes wouldn't open—or was it simply pitch black where I was?

"Kea," Ikane's tenor voice radiated over me. "Kea. It's alright."

I wanted to sob.

"Help her," Eamon's voice pleaded to someone. "We will do anything..."

Only one eye responded as it blinked open. Soft firelight flickered upon wooden walls. Lightheaded, I closed my eye again. I didn't even bother to try and move. I knew my body would ache.

"Ikane?" My voice broke at barely a whisper. Searing flames burned my throat.

"Shhh. I'm here, Kea. Don't try to talk," Ikane said. "We are safe. Just rest."

The breeze was warm and gentle, caressing my skin like silken sheets. Tender fingers ran through my cropped hair as my head rested in his lap. Branches swayed overhead. His marble skin contrasted against the azure sky and his eyes were as black as obsidian.

"Daughter of Roanfire, I fear for you," he said softly.

I blinked, curious, yet too entranced to inquire.

"This was the design of the Phoenix Witch. You are dying."

My hand lifted toward his, but halted upon seeing horrid, gaping, black, oozing wounds upon my skin. The White Wardent took my destroyed hand in his.

"I am sending help."

My cry upon waking was weak and gravelly. Searing pain stretched from my neck to my shoulder, making it hard to breathe.

"Hush, hush," a strong, but clearly feminine voice said. My eyes, heavy with swelling, barely caught sight of a middle-aged woman leaning over me. Hastily, she tucked her wild, deep brown hair behind her ear before checking something at my neck. "Those creatures cut your throat. Try not to speak," she warned me.

Satisfied with the way my neck appeared to her, she leaned back and met my one-eyed gaze with her bright, violet eyes. A warm smile spread across her full lips.

"You needn't worry. You are safe with me. My name is Erin Ashbrim. I am no healer to be certain, but I will do my best," she said as she brushed my hair from my forehead. Without waiting for a nod from me, she called over her shoulder.

"Ikane! Fetch some water."

My heart leapt at hearing her call his name. He was safe.

It was too dark to see anything more than the orange flicker of firelight against wooden walls of what I assumed to be a cabin, but I heard movement. Within seconds, Ikane's tall, handsome form was beside her. But the worry on his face as he looked at me made my relief at his wellbeing disintegrate.

He handed the stout-looking woman a mug.

"Thank you," she told him as she took it from his hand. Her hand was firm and gentle as she slipped it under my head to help me drink. She tipped the mug to my lips, but I could not bring my throat to swallow. The cold liquid did nothing more than slide down my chin.

Erin leaned back and dabbed the moisture away with the edge of the blanket that covered me. Her face hardened. "Rest," she told me.

With one last look at Ikane's furrowed brows, my eyes closed.

The crimson atmosphere pressed down on me like brittle boulders writhing with rot. Black leathery hands squeezed the walls of my tiny cocoon. The enormous face looking down upon me was distorted by the spherical surface of my encasing. He twirled me about by the ends of his filthy fingers like a giant admiring his favorite jewel.

"I have the stone," he said. "What now, my beloved Phoenix?"

Rion's voices answered. "Get the wolf."

My one functioning hand crept up to my neck, sliding over frayed strips of fabric that surrounded my throat like suffocating ropes. After scratching at my neck for a few unnerving moments, I realized that all but two of my fingers were wrapped in white linen. And the two fingers that weren't encased by bandaging, were swollen beyond recognition.

Where was the jewel?

Frustrated, the groan that escaped from my throat burned so fiercely that I wanted to cry. Knowing that it would only cause more pain, I pressed my lips together to still any further noise. But that too was a mistake. There must have been a gash on my lip, for I felt a horrible sting there.

I heard scrambling to my right but dared not turn my head to look.

"Kea," Ikane said as he appeared at my side. He grabbed my bandaged hand, gently guiding it away from my throat as he stroked my hair from my face. Something stung near my forehead as he did so. He noted the flinch and quickly retracted his hand. "It's alright. We are safe here," he assured me.

My lips opened. I needed to know. Before I could make a sound, Ikane swiftly pressed his finger against them. His brows furrowed as he shook his head quickly.

"Don't try to speak. Those monsters tore your neck open."

Painfully, I wrung my hand from his and desperately patted my collarbone.

He looked puzzled for a brief moment, then his eyes widened. "The jewel?" he asked in alarm.

I nodded quickly, the gesture aggravating my injuries.

"Erin!" Ikane called, whirling around to look into the darkness of the room. Everything was so blurry. I couldn't make out anything past Ikane's form save for the soft glow of a fire.

"Did you see the necklace she was wearing?" Ikane asked, urgency rising in his voice. "Did you take it off when we were tending to her?"

There was some shuffling before the woman with dark, wild hair appeared beside Ikane. Her thick, cotton shirt had seen better days, but the way it hugged her curves and tucked into her belt was flattering.

"Why are you so concerned about a jewel in a time like this?" she asked and leaned over him to check the bandaging at my neck. I noticed several layers of beaded necklaces hanging around her neck, all crafted from wood. "It's oozing again. We need to clean it."

"The jewel," Ikane snapped as his green eye flashed. "Where is the jewel?"

Erin recoiled, and her brows narrowed at him.

"I'm sorry," Ikane said quickly. "I didn't mean..."

"Never mind," she interrupted, waving a hand. "I saw nothing save for the wounds, and they need to be cleaned again."

Ikane's eyes scrunched shut in despair, his face contorting into pain. The demon-bats had taken the jewel. The man from my dream... he was real. He had it.

When Ikane opened his eyes, I could only hope that my expression showed how truly sorry I was. He gave me a painful smile in return. "It's alright. We'll find a way," he whispered.

"Ikane, go and fetch some water," Erin told him, pushing her way closer to my bedside. "You may need to chip at the ice in the well again."

Ikane moved to leave, but I grabbed his hand, stinging pain racing through my shoulder and back as I did so. His head whipped around to look at me, then down to my hand grabbing his wrist. "Kea," he said, gently prying my hand off him. "It's alright."

But it wasn't. The jewel was gone. And Ikane was the new target of whatever abomination was helping Rion. He couldn't go outside. Not alone. Where was Eamon? I hadn't seen or heard from him since the attack. All I could recall was his back facing me as he galloped away on that pitifully small ice-horse. Was he dead? Had the demon-bats claimed his life?

"Erin will look after you," Ikane said, interrupting my worries. "I'll be right back."

He turned and leaned down to kiss my forehead, but something made him pause. He shifted, moving to kiss my left temple instead. I could only assume that he was trying to avoid an injury. "Sleep," he told me. "That is the best thing you can do for your body right now."

His form blurred quickly before he was out of sight, and my eyes ached as they tried to focus on him. The injuries inflicted by the demon-bats were more than that. I felt as though I had been drugged, or that some sort of poison was running through my body. Everything felt heavy and thick, even my eyes. I closed them, trying to ease the feeling of bruising behind them.

I heard the latch of the door click, and the instant it did, Erin rushed to unbind the bandages around my neck.

"Hurry," a voice whispered fiercely. It was soft and gentle, like a summer breeze in a field of wildflowers. I had never before heard anything so mild, and I knew it didn't come from the sturdy woman standing beside my bed.

"I'm trying," Erin murmured as she worked.

My eyes opened. Who was she talking to?

Erin's attention wasn't on me, but on a distorted shimmer hovering above me. I closed my eyes again, fearing that the poison or whatever was causing my vision to be so bad, was beginning to take a toll. A soft, annoying buzzing noise floated through my ears. Surely, it was from the aftermath of the attack.

The cool air of the cabin rushed to my bare skin as Erin removed the last of the bandages. The deep, burning ache that pressed against my throat seemed to intensify as the air careened over it.

"Wait," Erin said. "Let me wash it off first." She hurried off, and I could hear the gentle sound of water being rung from a cloth.

Who was she talking to? My eyes blinked open again. Something shimmered above me... a light? A cloud? A warbled vapor distorted the timber ceiling of the cabin. I scrunched my eyes shut a third time. Everything seemed to be moving.

Erin returned and gently pressed the cold, damp cloth against my neck. I tried not to groan.

"Why do you keep trying? Your dust is only dulling the pain," Erin whispered as she worked. "She's not going to survive."

"Don't say such things," the tender, airy voice replied. "You are right. I do not have the power to heal her, but a watersprite may. We need to get her to Healer Malcom in Gerom Post, and you know it. Now move away."

My eyes opened again. Was I so ill that I was imagining another voice? When Erin pulled her damp cloth away, I knew there was someone else here with us. And from the sound of it, it was an Elemental Sprite!

"Why do you care so much?" Erin asked. "Those demon-bats have been pounding on my door for the last three nights trying to get to her."

"That alone is the reason," the soft voice replied. "Those beasts have an invested interest in her, and not her companions. There is something about her that they are trying to destroy."

Erin sighed loudly. "Well, get on with it then. Ikane won't be long getting more water, and Eamon should be back from fetching the firewood any moment."

Eamon was alive! The relief that flowed with that knowledge was nearly equal to what came next. A little breeze floated overhead. I could see her clearer now, a body and legs. Transparent wings buzzed at her back. This was a windsprite! The rarest of them all! A sprinkling of transparent-white powder rained down from the little windsprite, gliding to my neck like glittering dust in a sunbeam. As if a cool summer breeze swept across my skin, the deep pain in the wound eased tremendously. I was able to gather breath and swallow without feeling as though a branding iron had been stuck in my throat.

"He's back," Erin warned the sprite just as the door to the cabin opened. The tiny form of a whirlwind darted away, and the constant buzzing noise faded.

"How is she?" It was a breath of fresh air to hear Eamon's gravelly voice. I heard the door close and the stomp of his boots on the wooden floorboards as he entered.

I watched Erin shake her head at him. "We need to get her to Gerom Post," she said. "I can only numb her pain."

Eamon walked to the fireplace, and I heard the crash of wood as he placed the logs nearby. "Then we should go first thing tomorrow, after the bats have gone for the day," he said. "Where is Ikane?"

"Getting more water," Erin said as she turned back to me and began to wrap my neck again. "The well may have frozen over. I'm sure that's what's taking him so long."

"I'll go see if he needs help," Eamon said, dusting his hands off. I heard him approach before I saw his form appear beside Erin, dressed in his warm, fur-lined coat and cap. He smiled sadly at me, then placed his hand on Erin's shoulder. "We can't thank you enough for what you have done for her."

Erin shrugged, but even in my hazy frame of mind, I could see the bright red flush in her cheeks. "I'm happy to help," she said, driving all of her energy into wrapping my neck.

As soon as Eamon left, the woman turned to me. "Don't you say a word now," she warned me.

I half chuckled inside. About the windsprite? Or about her affection for Eamon? Either way, it wasn't like I could say anything anyway.

The wagon jolted on clumps of un-melted snow and muddy potholes, sending sharp jolts through my battered body. Erin's efforts to cushion me with hay and blankets were appreciated, but ineffective. Nothing seemed to alleviate the pain... save for the windsprite dust that occasionally appeared when Ikane and Eamon were not looking.

Ikane checked on me from time to time, anxiety crossing over his handsome features. I once heard him criticize Eamon's driving at every insignificant joggle of the wagon. But Eamon handed Ikane the reigns and challenged him to do a better job. Ikane, a seafaring pirate, was unfamiliar with driving a team of horses, and the shaking became momentarily worse. Humbled, he relented quickly and handed the reigns back to my guardian.

Just as the sun began to set, we arrived at the small, but important, sturdy post of Gerom. I was only able to discern this because we passed under a gate. Buildings constructed of thick timber and white plaster towered on either side of the moving wagon. Heavy glass panes covered partially shuttered windows, and a thick layer of snow coated the rooftops. Soft tufts of smoke lifted to the gray sky from the chimneys.

"We should warn them of the danger," Erin stated from her spot in the wagon beside me. Through my partially closed eyes, I made out the glint of an axe in her hand. She absently ran her thumb along the edge as she scanned the rooftops. "They at least have decent shutters here. If we give them enough warning, they can board up the weaker windows."

I could only assume that the demon-bats were still after me... and Ikane.

Eamon looked over his shoulder from his perch on the front of the wagon. "They would not let us stay if they knew what followed."

Her shoulders slumped as her lips pulled angrily to one side as if she knew he was right. "Here," she eventually said and pointed ahead to her right. "This inn here is good. I know the innkeeper personally. Tell her Erin the Woodcutter sent you. She'll be sure to get you a good room. I'll fetch the healer."

With that, she tucked the axe into her belt, and leapt over the edge of the wagon.

I drifted in and out of sleep between finding myself in the wagon, and then in a soft bed with a warm fire crackling beside it. Another time, an elderly man, with a balding head and a pair of gray eyes, leaned over me with an apprehensive expression. And again, I woke to the sturdy woman wiping my brow with a cool, damp cloth.

Erin dipped the fabric in a basin filled with water, wrung it out, and returned it to my forehead. She smiled upon seeing my eyes blink open.

"Hello there," she said softly. "We are in Gerom Post now. Don't you worry. The healer made a tincture for you. He thought it best that we do not suture your lacerations at this point. There is too much swelling and infection. We are changing out the wrappings regularly though."

I was grateful to her for speaking so openly. There were hundreds of questions rolling through my mind, and her rambling answered a few that were nagging at me.

"You need to drink something," she said as she reached across the way to a table. She retrieved a mug, but I grimaced as she tried to tip it to my lips. The pain in my throat was too great.

"I know it hurts," she acknowledged, "but you've gone five days without a drop of water. You are deteriorating. You need to drink." She put the mouth of the mug to my lips. I felt the cool water on the tip of my tongue. It was heavenly. It slipped into my mouth, moistening my parched tongue... and I tried to swallow. Burning pain ignited as if a lump of hot coal had lodged in the back of my throat. The heaving motion made me aware of stiffness in parts of my body that I didn't know could hurt. Water spewed from my mouth all over Erin's face and the front of her warm-looking leather tunic.

Her mouth and eyes clamped shut against the onslaught, and then she wiped her face with her hand. "Well," she said simply as she placed the mug back down on the table beside the bed. "I haven't been spewed on like that since my son..." she stopped herself and allowed hard lines to crease her face.

She took a rag and wiped herself down, then turned back to me. After checking some bandages on my neck and arms she sighed. "You've just torn three wounds open again... make that four," she added after looking at my legs. "We'll need more bandages."

I heard a door creak open behind her, but my eyes— something was wrong. I couldn't see that far, even though it was a mere fifteen feet away. All I could make out was a shadow of a figure as it approached.

"Good, you're done," Erin said as Ikane came into view. My weary eyes glanced at Ikane's face. I could smell the soap he had used to shave his chin, and his long hair was damp from having recently washed it. "I've got to pester the innkeeper from more bandages."

Ikane frowned as he ran his fingers through his damp hair. "She's not getting any better," he huffed. "That healer didn't do a thing."

"He said it would take time," Erin answered.

"How much more time? It's been five days and she is only growing weaker."

Seven days? We should've been in the Glacial Empire by now. Why hadn't we been accosted by Phoenix Soldiers yet?

I wanted to speak to him, but the burning in my throat warned me that trying to use my voice would only result in pain. Again, I tried to link our minds. Again, Ikane was closed off. I couldn't reach him and the effort it took drained me of all energy.

Sleep.

I awoke to the horrid sound of screeching—the bats! My entire body seized with fear and the movement aggravated my festering wounds. My gargled cry sent Ikane flying across the room to my side. Within moments, his strong arms were around me. We listened to the frightened shouting of men and dreadful shrieks of attacking bats outside in the night.

Over the next few hours we listened. Cries would erupt and then silence would stretch long enough for me to drift back to sleep, only to startle awake by another piercing scream. By morning, word reached us that fifteen people had been attacked by large bat-like creatures.

"They seem to only come at night," Eamon stated as he finished his breakfast of bread and cheese. He wiped his lips with the back of his hand and stood. "I'm going to see if there is anything I can do to help fortify the post."

Erin swallowed her meal quickly. "I'll come with you," she said and tucked her axe into her belt. It was then that I could make out this woman more clearly. She barely stood a head shorter than Eamon, making her near my height, but she was far from frail. Even though her body was wrapped in fur-lined animal skins, she still had an hourglass figure any man would find appealing. She hastily braided her dark, wild hair down her back in preparation.

Eamon nodded to her, unquestioning. That alone indicated to me that he found her quite capable of defending herself.

"I'll stay with Kea," Ikane said looking my direction. I don't think he realized that I was awake. "Perhaps I can get her to drink something."

"I'm sorry I couldn't do more for her," Erin said.

Ikane nodded. "You've done all you can. It's up to her now."

Unaware that I was watching him, Ikane busied himself by first polishing his swords, then his knife, and then by gathering the empty dishes onto a tray. They rattled softly as he balanced the tray on one hand and turned to the door. As soon as he pushed down the lever, the door flew open wide, slamming into the corner of the tray. Ikane managed to catch the edge of the wooden tray before it followed the dishes to the floor.

I had almost forgotten how quickly he moved, for he saw the blur of black before my mind registered that there was anything there. The harsh thud of a knife burying itself into wood caught my attention as Ikane held the tray up as a shield. The Leviathan stepped back and jerked the makeshift shield up as another knife spun from the assassin's hand. The blade thwacked into it.

My mind was as sluggish as my body as I tried to push the blankets from my body – but I barely managed to move it down to my waist. I was too weak. Perhaps Erin was right. I wasn't going to make it.

Now, out of throwing knives, the assassin drew a longer knife, one that was only a few inches smaller than Ikane's short swords. He jabbed it at the Leviathan's gut, but Ikane easily rocked away. The second jab came with a lunge, and this time Ikane allowed it to thud into the wooden tray. With a quick twist, Ikane spun the tray to force the assassin to relinquish his weapon that was still lodged in the wood. Then, using the momentum of the spin, he swung the makeshift shield at the assassin's head. The assassin effectively avoided the blow, but not before one of the small throwing knives spun loose in the movement. It clattered to the ground.

At that moment, another shadow leapt through the open door. Ikane was now faced by two assailants and here I lay, like a rotting sack of potatoes, watching.

But then, the new assassin clobbered his comrade in the back of his head with the shaft of his battle-axe. The hooded figure who had been attacking Ikane froze, his head rolled, and then his body crumpled down at Ikane's feet.

Ikane didn't waste a moment. He snatched the longer knife from the wooden tray and held it out in a defensive manner. A small smile crept around the lips of the new assassin, and then he reached up and threw the hood from his face, revealing a familiar tuft of brown hair. His blue eyes glinted mischievously. "You know I can best you, right?"

"Broderick!" Ikane nearly cheered, lowering his guard.

Relief flowed through me, and with it, exhaustion. I knew it wouldn't be long now.

Broderick tucked his axe into his belt as he stepped around the unconscious assassin. "I've been waiting for a chance to knock him senseless for weeks," Broderick said.

"I can't tell you how happy I am to see you," Ikane said, slouching down against the edge of the table.

"Don't be so pleased," Broderick warned him as he crouched down to be sure his fellow assassin would stay unconscious. Not satisfied, he pulled one of the many vials stuck in the bandoleer that crossed his torso. "There are three reasons that I'm here. And all of them have to do with Kea. One, Duchess Caitelyn sent her assassins after her again," he motioned to the unconscious man at his feet, and then popped the cork off the vial. He held the opening to the unconscious man's nose, allowing him to breathe in whatever substance was inside.

"Two," Broderick continued, "Master Chanter sent me to hunt Kea down and bring her back, per King Sander's orders."

Ikane frowned as he began spinning the assassin's knife through his fingers. "And three?"

Broderick stopped the vial again, returned it to his belt, and then rested his arm across his knee as he looked up at Ikane. "To help you get to the Glacial Empire."

A small smile spread across Ikane's lips and he paused from twisting the knife. His smile faded when his eyes darted to my body lying in the bed, nearly invisible.

Broderick followed his gaze. His eyes shot wide upon seeing me. He nearly leapt over the man lying prostrate on the floor and dropped to his knees at my bedside. Hastily, he removed his gloves and pressed his hand against my forehead.

His expression remained stoic as he then tugged at the bandage around my neck.

"This happened ten days ago," Ikane said. "No one has been able to help. She grows weaker every day and she hasn't had a drop of water."

Broderick unclasped his cloak and allowed it to drop to the floor. "Then there is no time to lose. These wounds are festering with unnatural poison. Even waterdust will have little effect. It can only be healed with magic," he said.

Without waiting for approval, Broderick gently unbound the bandaging at my neck until I felt the chill of the fresh air against my skin. He glanced around the room as if searching for something. Then his eyes fell upon the ash bucket by the fireplace.

"Fetch me that ash pale," he said to Ikane as he began removing his leather bracers.

Ikane set the knife down on the table and retrieved the metal pale filled with gray soot. "Ash is good for drawing out poison, I know. But not to injuries this bad," Ikane said as he set it down beside Broderick.

"You're right," the spy answered as he tugged his sleeves up to his elbows. "Without magic, it won't do a thing."

His hands plunged into the soft, gray-white ash. He pressed the dusty substance between his palms and laced his fingers until the ash covered the spaces between.

Ikane's brows rose, but with his suspicion came a flicker of hope. "What can I do?" Ikane asked.

"We'll need water," Broderick answered. "Lots of it. And more ashes. Fetch the ash from the other rooms of the inn."

Ikane nodded quickly and hurried from the room to run his errands. When the door closed after him, Broderick took a deep cleansing breath. His brows furrowed with worry as he looked at my half open lids. I'm sure my eyes were glazed.

"This isn't going to be comfortable," he whispered to me. He gathered another deep breath and gently rested his palms over the wound on my neck. The added pressure made it harder to breathe. I wanted to swallow... but my muscles didn't respond. Broderick's eyes closed, and his jaw clenched in concentration.

A tugging sensation pulled on the wound, as if something was buried underneath my skin. It writhed as Broderick allowed a grunt of effort to escape his clenched teeth. The pulling intensified. It was uncomfortable at first, and then gradually began to bite as if little razors tried to cling to my skin from inside. My groan sounded more like a gargle.

As if a tangled knot of thread finally pulled through a tailor's garment, the cutting discomfort eased. The pressure that had been crushing against my windpipe was gone, and the constant pain had subsided to the point that I was agonizingly aware of the rest of my injuries.

Broderick pulled his hands from my neck. A terrible smell, sour and foul, floated with them as he sat back on his heels. The gray-white ash that he had rubbed over his palms was no longer soft and powdery, but had grown thick and oozing with blackness, and he took care to hold his hands away from the blankets. Small beads of perspiration had formed on his brow, but he smiled at me.

"Your eyes already seem brighter," he said.

The door swung open and Ikane returned with a bucket of water.

"Took you long enough," Broderick chided him as he plunged his hands inside the clear, cold water and washed. Ikane watched the blackness infest the water, then glanced at me. His mismatched eyes widened.

"She's..." he stammered. "It's working!"

He rushed to me and gently brushed my hair from my face. His hand was trembling.

Broderick finished washing up, dried his hands on the corner of the blanket and grabbed another handful of ash. "Take this water away and dump it where it won't contaminate anything. Bring me a fresh one."

Even knowing that it would mean walking out of the city, dumping the infected water, gathering more snow and ice, melting it, and lugging it back to the inn, Ikane eagerly got to his feet. This time, he grabbed his fur-lined coat and shrugged into it. He paused a moment from buttoning up the toggles.

"It was you," he said, looking up at Broderick. He pressed his hand against his chest. "After you..." he hesitated, not wanting to sound like he was accusing the spy. "After your axe cut me across the chest. I wouldn't have lived through the night if it weren't for you."

Broderick shrugged. "It was the least I could do after injuring you so badly. Now go fetch some water. We've got to work quickly, and I don't want to sit here waiting for you to bring me a fresh bucket of water every time."

Ikane nodded, grabbed the bucket, and hurried off.

19

DEATHBITERS

When I woke, my limbs felt as if the weight of a suit of armor had been removed. I even thought I could feel the fingers of my left arm again. Yes—there. My finger twitched. I felt the fabric of the bedsheet... a wrinkle in it.

My eyes fluttered open to the sound of soft murmurings. It was as if I were seeing the room for the first time. Ikane and Eamon sat on the edge of the bed that sat across from mine, separated by a small, round, wooden table. At the foot of the beds stood a small hearth with a pitiful mantle. But the fire burned bright, and the room, in spite of cold stone, plaster, and wood, was warm. One window sat behind the bed where Ikane and Eamon quietly conversed, but it was shuttered tightly. At the opposite end, nearer to me, stood another small table with a washbasin, cracked mirror, and chair.

I watched Ikane for a moment as he brushed his black hair back with one hand, a motion that I knew indicated some irritation for him. The green in his left eye shimmered slightly confirming my suspicion. Eamon scratched at his salt and pepper beard, trying to keep his composure as they argued.

They paused momentarily when the colorful patchwork quilt stirred behind them. I recognized the tuft of brown locks lying on the pillow as Broderick. And rightly so. I had seen the effort it had taken him to draw out the poison in my body. Sleep was his reward now.

When Broderick stopped his stirring, Ikane looked back at me. As our eyes connected, he crossed the narrow distance between the two beds in a flash.

"Kea!" he said. The smile that reached clear to his shimmering eyes was infectious. He took my hand in his and kissed it openly, unabashed by Eamon looking on. "You're on the mend. You're going to be alright," he said, though it sounded as though he were telling himself these things.

Eamon stood, and in spite of watching Ikane press the back of my hand against his tear-moistened cheek, he smiled. "I'll go fetch some broth. You need to eat."

I wasn't hungry, but that was beside the point.

Eamon made for the door.

"Wait," I said, and immediately wished I hadn't spoken. Pain still burned the back of my throat and my voice had no tone to it. It was bland, dry, and airy. But I wanted him to see. I lifted my hand – my left hand! The arm was withered and thin from weeks without use, but it moved. Both Eamon's and Ikane's eyes widened as my arm dropped across my belly, already spent.

Ikane scrunched his eyes shut and pressed the back of my hand against his forehead. Three harsh whimpers escaped, shaking his shoulders before he gathered a deep breath to compose himself. When he looked up at me again his eyes were red with tears and his smile broad.

"You're going to be more than alright," he said.

It wasn't until two days later that I understood the full extent of Ikane's tears.

Erin, with the tender hands of a mother, helped me wash. I sat by the wash basin, looking at my reflection in the small, cracked mirror hanging on the wall behind it. She wrung out a cloth in a bucket of warm water and wiped blood and sweat from my skin, carefully working around the wounds that would leave a plethora of scars in the weeks to come. The soft cotton nightdress that covered my body seemed to tug on every one of them.

The deepest wounds – on my right forearm, across my left thigh, and beside the old arrow wound on my back - had been sutured with black threads. The injury that irritated my voice sat in the form of a red, ragged star, just above my left collarbone, near my neck.

But one injury in particular made me self-conscious. Three long slashes ran across my face, stretching from the right side of my forehead, over my nose, and ending at my left cheek. I traced one of them, ignoring how tender my skin still was.

Erin, running her fingers through my damp hair to detangle it, saw the movement in the reflection of the mirror. "You'll barely see those in a few months," she told me.

I dropped my hand and turned in the chair to face her, wanting to ask so many questions. How did I survive? How did we get away from that hoard of demon-bats? And why were Ikane and Eamon completely unharmed? And where was the windsprite that had given me some of her dust? How did Erin become acquainted with the rarest elemental sprite known? But most importantly, why did Erin stay with us?

I swallowed hard in preparation to speak. "Sprite," I said and immediately clutched my throat to help still the burning pain there. It was comforting yet discouraging, the way my withered arm reacted. It came up as well but didn't reach my neck before faltering.

Erin sighed, dropping her hands. "You saw her then?"

I nodded.

The woman looked over her shoulder at the small mantle stretching over the fire. "Well, she knows. Are you happy now?"

A small wave of distortion moved just above the fire. It was easy to mistake it for the warbled heat rising from the fire. I wouldn't have seen her if Erin hadn't pointed her out. The soft buzzing noise of her wings grew louder as she neared. Erin held her palm out for the sprite to alight. Her tiny body, almost transparent, stood no taller than my forefinger. It was nearly impossible to make out any specific details.

"This is Alizeh," Erin said. "But I call her Ali. I can't seem to get rid of her."

My brows furrowed. Why would she even want to? Such a sprite was so rare, surely Erin was favored by the elements.

The nearly invisible sprite chuckled. "She hasn't tried hard enough," her soft, soothing voice floated through my ears. I wanted to smile, but the movement tugged at the wounds across my face.

"Tell her," Ali said to Erin.

Erin's face hardened, and a deep line creased between her brows as she glowered at the windsprite.

"If you won't, then I will," Ali said and folded her arms across her chest. The movement sent a new wave of distortion through the air.

Erin dropped her hand, forcing the sprite to employ her wings to keep from falling.

"Do what you will," she said and snatched a clean roll of bandaging that lay in a mound of several others on my bed. She marched back to my side, pushed the sleeve of my nightdress up, and began to wrap the sutured wound with the white linen.

Ali hovered in the air for a moment before alighting on the edge of the washbasin. She stood lightly on her tiptoes, perfectly balanced. "I don't mean to upset you, Erin," she said. If her voice got any softer, I feared she would melt away.

"She thinks you're special," Erin murmured to me, ignoring the sprite's gentle apology. "She thinks you have some sort of magic... like the White Wardent. It's absurd, right? The White Wardent is a myth. There is no such thing."

I looked back at the sprite. She felt it. She felt it the way Mina had. I wanted to ask if she felt the darkness in Ikane as well.

"The White Wardent is not a myth," Ali said softly. "And you know there is something peculiar about Kea. Why did those creatures only attack her and not her companions?"

Erin paused from her work. "I don't know."

"And the man, Broderick, he used magic to heal her. That alone should confirm that the White Wardent is more than a myth," the sprite continued. "Why are you so bent on denying it?"

"I don't know!" Erin snapped.

A knock sounded on the door, sparing them any further argument. Ali zipped back to the fireplace to avoid detection.

"She's decent," Erin called quickly as she finished bandaging my arm. She didn't try to be gentle.

The door opened and Ikane stepped inside, balancing a tray of food in one hand with Broderick on his heels. Both men smiled upon seeing us.

"Set the tray down over there," Erin said, motioning to the small table standing between the beds. Ikane did as ordered and stole a piece of bread from the tray before Erin could inspect the contents.

"I told you to get broth," she groaned at him as she peered into the steaming bowls. "This is too heavy for her stomach."

"She's got to get something substantial in her," Ikane replied.

Erin folded her arms across her chest and was about to retort when Broderick interrupted. "I'll go fetch some."

Her violet eyes looked up at him, remaining impassive. She then gave him one quick nod, and he immediately turned to the door.

"Really, what harm is porridge going to do?" Ikane asked.

Erin rolled her eyes. "It could make her stomach cramp up. The last thing we need is for her to convulse and tear injuries open again."

I didn't like the way they were speaking. Not only were they arguing, but they were acting as though I were still asleep. I openly frowned at them.

Ikane took a savage bite of his bread. "She's tougher than she looks," he mumbled through his mouthful.

Her hand flashed across his cheek. It wasn't harsh enough to make a sound, but it caught him completely by surprise. With his mouth half open, he blinked down at her.

"Don't speak with your mouth full. Not only is it improper, but ghastly to look at. You're not a wild animal, so don't eat like one."

Ikane stared at her, then a small smile tugged on the corner of his lips. He made certain to swallow his mouthful before speaking this time. "No wonder the demon-bats leave you alone."

She couldn't help but smile in return, and then busied herself with arranging the meals on the tray before the smile went too wide. "Now, where is Eamon? He was supposed to bring another pale of fresh water."

I pursed my lips, tired of being ignored, and stomped my bare foot on the wooden floor. Ikane responded to the noise immediately, but Erin was slower to react. After crossing the room, Ikane extended his hand out to me. I took it and stood slowly. This was the third time I had been out of my bed since the attack.

Ikane slipped his arm around me, trying to avoid placing his hand on any of the wounds that had been dealt to my back. He didn't have much luck and resorted to simply holding my hand as he guided me back to the freshly washed bed.

"Don't we make a pair," he said softly, obviously eyeing the new scars across my face.

My smile was feeble, mostly because the motion tugged on the healing wounds, but also because I could not fathom that he found me attractive with them.

Erin sat on the opposite bed facing us. She leaned forward and rested her elbows on her knees to listen.

Pain radiated through the back of my left leg as I sat on the edge of my bed. Ikane released my hand, but I held onto him firmly, wanting his undivided attention. After trying to display the use of a pen and paper with my hands, I touched the wound at my throat and then pointed to my lips.

Ikane's eyes were genuine with understanding and admiration, almost as if I had suddenly become the newest weapon on display in a smithy shop. "You want to know how we got away?" he asked as he knelt down before me.

I nodded.

He took my tender hands in his, and then flipped them over so I could see my palms. "Look," he said, nodding to them.

My eyes dropped, uncertain of what he wanted me to see. My right hand was partially bandaged, and my left had an ugly scratch near the wrist... but something was different. The glow. The firedust! It was gone.

I looked up at Ikane, my eyes wide.

"The dust embedded in your hands ignited in the attack," he said. "The light scorched those vile bats like over-roasted rabbits. We found Erin's little cabin at the edge of some trees not far."

The little firesprite's gift had saved me after all.

Without a knock, the door opened, and Broderick returned with a steaming mug of the promised broth in his hands. Eamon trailed in after him, and then the healer of Gerom Post stepped inside. His eyes widened in disbelief when they fell upon me.

"How?" he breathed and hurried across the room to inspect my wounds. He tugged on my arm and gently touched the sutures there. "How have you managed to tame the infection?" he demanded of Erin. His tone was nigh accusing. "My patients are dying."

Erin took the mug of thin broth from Broderick. "I did nothing," she said flatly.

"Then tell me how?" the healer pressed. "Name your price. Two of my cases have died this morning, and three more will surely die before the end of the day if I don't do anything."

Erin finally looked at Broderick, and she jerked her head to the healer, urging him to reveal his secret. But Broderick hesitated, and I understood why. Magic was quite uncommon in Roanfire, and those who used it were often accused of witchcraft when things went sour.

"Please," the healer begged, dropping my hand. "These Deathbiters are infecting more and more people every time the sun disappears. Aside from the light of fire to keep them at bay, we must find a way to heal those that have been touched."

"Deathbiters?" Ikane asked.

The healer nodded. "That is what the people have dubbed the wraith-like bats. Their talons and teeth are infested with a poison that I do not know how to heal. Once the skin has been broken, even a minor scratch, a fever appears. Most have a fortnight to live."

Broderick was clenching his fists at this point, but it wasn't until Erin placed her hand on his wrist that he stopped. He looked up at her and swallowed hard. She gave him a reassuring nod.

"It's alright," she said. "These creatures have stemmed from magic. Only magic can counter it."

I was startled to hear her say that after being so angry at her windsprite companion. It seemed there was something deeper between the two.

Broderick nodded.

"Magic?" the healer asked.

"I did it," the assassin eventually said. "I can draw out the poison."

The healer took a hasty step forward. "Show me how. I must learn to do it." The fact that he didn't care what sort of healing was used showed the desperation.

Broderick lowered his head. "It is not something anyone can do."

"Then who?" the healer demanded.

I was surprised to see Broderick's blue eyes flick to me. "There are a few others who have a strong link to the elements that can do it. Wardents of magic."

The healer's brows furrowed. "You are referring to the White Wardent?"

"The White Wardent harnesses the power of all four elements and their emotions, yes. But there are some that have become attuned to one element or another. As for me, I am a Wind Wardent," Broderick said. "I will come help you, but I cannot heal everyone on my own."

I watched Erin intently as Broderick spoke. She hid her emotions well.

"Do you know of anyone else?" the healer pressed.

Broderick's eyes darted to me again, but he shook his head.

"Then come," the healer said and grabbed Broderick's arm to steer him from the room. "There is a young mother in need of your abilities."

"I'll come with you," Erin said, snatching her coat from the bedpost. "Knowing you, Healer Malcom, you'll make this poor lad heal everyone even if it kills him."

There was a glimmer of gratitude in Broderick's eyes as the three hurried from the room.

"**D**eathbiters," Eamon murmured as he walked to the table filled with the bowls of soup that were no longer steaming. He picked one up and took a sip. "The Phoenix Soldiers have been alerted to your disappearance, Kea. They are searching for you. I fear our window has closed to get you to the Glacial Empire."

"No, we can still do it," Ikane said. He was as eager as I was to get answers, and it was only a matter of time before Rion could overpower him again. I desperately wanted to delve into his mind and examine the confinement that held the Phoenix Witch, but every time I tried, something blocked me.

Eamon shook his head. "The problem is that the Deathbiters are stemming from Glacier Pass."

I looked at Ikane at this revelation.

"The Deathbiters retreat during daylight," Ikane said. "We can still get through."

"Glacier Pass cannot be traversed in one day," Eamon said. "It takes two days... and that only if we have horses."

I risked speaking, needing to know what happened to the small ice-horses. "Brick?" I said, my voice airy and weak. It actually came out as 'rick', but they knew what I was asking. Both Eamon and Ikane looked at me, but it was Eamon who spoke.

"Brick collapsed soon after the bats attacked you. He's gone."

So now we only had one horse.

"But we can buy another," Ikane said.

"With what money?" Eamon countered. "We've nothing left. I don't know how I'm going to manage to pay for this inn either."

Ikane's handsome face hardened as he folded his arms across his chest. "I can get some."

Eamon swallowed his mouthful of soup quickly. "Oh no you don't. I'll not have you plundering our way to the Glacial Empire."

"We've already defied the king," Ikane excused himself. "You and I are already bound for the dungeons. Why not make it worth our while?"

"Don't," Eamon snapped. His eyes narrowed dangerously.

A thought sprang to my mind and I moved from the bed. My body groaned and protested as I stumbled to our packs and belongings that sat in a corner of the room. I felt my chest tighten when I saw my coat—ripped and stained with blood—lying across my belongings.

"Kea," Ikane said as he came to my side. "What is it?"

I didn't want to crouch, and bending down was out of the question, so I motioned to my hand and slid my thumb and forefinger down one of my fingers to demonstrate putting on a ring.

"Oh," Ikane said, knowing exactly what I was referring to. Queen Lonacheska's ring. "No," he said. "We can't barter that. It is an heirloom and you need it to be admitted to the empress."

I frowned. It didn't matter if we didn't get into the Glacial Empire. I could find another way to access the empress. I motioned for him to get the ring anyway, but he shook his head.

"No," he snapped, and I couldn't tell if his anger was towards me or Eamon. Instead of searching for the ring as I had asked, he reached down and grabbed his twin swords with hilts decorated with twisting sea serpents.

"I am done standing by," he said and moved to snatch his coat from the bedpost... but it was right beside Eamon. Eamon's hand flew out and grabbed the Leviathan by the wrist.

"Don't you dare," Eamon's voice growled.

"Try and stop me," Ikane snapped, jerking his hand free. The movement sent the porridge spilling over the edge of the bowl that Eamon still held in his other hand. Before Eamon could respond to the challenge, the harsh sound of metal on leather slid through the room. In a flash, the tip of one of

Ikane's swords pointed directly at Eamon's throat. "We've come too far to give up now, and you know it!"

Eamon raised his hands, the bowl still in one, but the scowl on his face didn't ease. "I do not approve."

"I don't need your approval," Ikane hissed. "I am going to get us to the Glacial Empire one way or another." With that, he cautiously reached out and grabbed his coat. Without lowering his sword, he inched towards the door and slipped out.

Eamon dropped his hand with a sigh as the latch clicked.

I pursed my lips and gently rubbed my withered arm, feeling as though I was the cause of all this animosity. I cared for both of these men dearly.

My guardian sank down to the bed. "I should go after him," he mumbled and halfheartedly placed the bowl back on the tray. But he didn't move. He made no effort to stop Ikane from pillaging. It was against everything Eamon stood for as a Soldier of Roanfire, but he knew we did not have time to collect money and supplies in an honest fashion.

"I should know better than to allow a man like him to court you," he grumbled.

I blinked up at him, wondering where his train of thought had gone. My feet shuffled across the room and then I sat down beside him. The healing gash in my thigh groaned with the movement.

"What?" my breathy voice asked.

Eamon ran one of his hands through his salt and pepper hair, ruining the tightly bound warrior's tail that hung down his back. "As much as I hate to admit it, I do care for him, Kea. If things were different... if *he* were different, I would give you my blessing to marry in a heartbeat."

My hand flew up to my throat, trying to keep from gasping at his words. The sharp intake of breath irritated it anyway.

"When I first encountered Ikane, he was just a young boy," Eamon began. "Ikane couldn't have been older than fourteen years of age. It was a filthy trick the Leviathan's were playing."

I listened intently, desperate to hear the story that Eamon never told.

"I was commander of the army, charged with defending Amall against the Leviathan Pirates. One night, the Leviathan's sent two dozen children into our camp. Ikane was one of them. Hard as I try, I cannot forget the sight of the boy's mismatched eyes blazing down at me as I woke from sleep. His knife was poised to kill."

My brows furrowed at the thought.

"Did he ever tell you how he got that scar across his cheek?" Eamon asked.

I shook my head quickly but guessed that this was the night it had happened.

"I gave it to him," Eamon confirmed my suspicion and rubbed the back of his neck, clearly still ashamed for having harmed the boy. "He was so destructive... so... wild," Eamon searched for the right words. "The knife was infused with wolfsbane."

My lips parted slightly as my brows rose.

"Yes, he turned into a wolf in the middle of my tent," Eamon smiled slightly at the memory. "He was actually a cute little thing. I found it easier to subdue the wolf than the boy."

"Little Wolf," I said, repeating the name that Eamon had used for Ikane back in Kaltum.

Eamon nodded again. "Over the next few weeks, we came to an understanding. I learned that he was the youngest of the Leviathan Princes, deemed unworthy to rule by his elder brothers because he was a lycanthrope. His brothers had sent him on a suicide mission, hoping that he would be killed. Eventually, trust grew, and I began to tutor him. He was a gifted warrior and a quick study. I have not seen the like... save for you."

I smiled weakly.

Eamon rubbed his face. "He was like a son to me," he sighed deeply and dropped his hands. "Over the next six months he became the ultimate weapon in defeating his brothers. He revealed the location of their fleet and gave the coinciding assaults that flowed with the moon and the tides."

I nodded, knowing that he had returned victoriously from that battle. It was what had earned him the title of Master Eamon Brendagger. But that was also when everything had changed.

Eamon clenched his jaw as he rubbed his hands over his knees, taking a little extra care as he rubbed over his injured one. "I was tutoring a Leviathan boy, a Leviathan Prince no less, when the Leviathan Pirates fell upon Daram and slaughtered my family."

I remembered that siege well. I was barely twelve years of age at the time. Ropert, two years my elder, had been ordered to keep me and two other children safe during that attack. We hid in the barracks, underneath a bunk.

"Ikane, headstrong and reckless, ran into the fray of our last battle like a savage wolf. I thought he had been killed... the Leviathans," Eamon's voice quivered as tears burned his eyes. "They killed my son. My precious two-year-old Leon. And my beautiful wife..." He took a deep breath before he could continue.

"I was treating a Leviathan like my own child when the pirates took what was most precious to me."

I placed my good hand on Eamon's back. He blinked and harshly wiped at his cheeks. "At first my heart ached when Ikane went missing. I vowed to return and search for him after reporting to King Myron. But when I heard that my own family had been killed by the pirates, I felt justified. I wanted nothing more to do with him.

"He is a good man," Eamon said as he stood. "His heart is better than most. But I hate how quickly he turns to his old habits in times of trial."

I finally understood. When I was a child, I could not grasp why Master Eamon turned to harsh drinks after returning from Amall as a war hero. My guardian neglected me, frowning upon all my progress as a soldier. I trained harder, hoping that my skills would impress him enough to say something kind. I received honors and a glorified reputation as Master Brendagger's daughter, but all my advancement earned no respect from Eamon. Mayama, the cook in the Daram Keep, had been the closest thing to a guardian since that time. I wondered how the plump, aged woman fared.

Several hours later, just before nightfall, Broderick and Erin returned. I sat upright when the door swung open. Broderick's arm was slung over Erin's shoulders. His head rocked weakly, his face was the pallor of snow, and he was barely coherent as Erin practically carried him across the way to the second bed. The wooden hinges creaked under his weight as he collapsed into it.

Eamon leapt to his feet from his perch at the foot of my bed. "What happened?"

"Healer Malcom happened," Erin grumbled as she gently situated Broderick's head on the pillow. She brushed his brown curls away from his pale face, like a mother would to her son. He sighed softly and rolled onto his side without opening his eyes.

Eamon's brows narrowed. "What do you mean?" he demanded.

Erin proceeded to pull Broderick's boots from his feet. "I thought I had a handle on Healer Malcom when we decided to take care of the worst of his patients today, but when Broderick saw the others, he insisted that he could help them as well."

Eamon stepped up to help strip Broderick of his belt and knives. "How many others?"

"Twenty-three," she mumbled.

My jaw dropped.

"The last ten had only been scratched two nights ago," Erin said as she and Eamon pulled the heavy quilt over Broderick. "I told him that they could wait until morning, but he's persistent, I'll give him that. He collapsed before he got to the final eight cases."

"Where is Ikane?" Erin asked after tucking the blanket around the assassin's shoulders.

Eamon pursed his lips and sat back down on the edge of my bed. "He's on an errand."

The sturdy woman ran a hand through her wild curls with a sigh as her eyes flicked to the shuttered window. "He'd best hurry. The sunlight is almost gone."

20

GLACIER PASS

Ikane didn't return. Darkness fell and the sounds of leathery wings darting across the sky soon filled the night. Save for that, Gerom Post was silent. All the inhabitants had found a way to remain safe by retreating into boarded up homes before nightfall. But it did little to ease my mind. I berated myself for not stopping Ikane. Rion was after him. The Deathbiters were hunting him now. I shouldn't have let him leave, at least not alone.

Eamon held my hand as he sat propped up on the bed beside me. He didn't say it, but he was worried. I could tell by the way he thrummed his fingers against his thigh.

As soon as morning dawned, Erin threw the shutters open, allowing bitter cold, fresh, free air into the stuffy room. It seemed as if all of Gerom Post had the same idea. All the windows of homes lining the streets were flung wide. Even doors hung open.

But there was still no sign of Ikane.

Broderick stretched and groaned a few hours after the sun had reached its noon point in the sky. Color had returned to his cheeks and the first thing he did was devour the remaining cold porridge and hard pieces of bread that were left on the small table.

Still no Ikane.

Eamon began questioning Erin about Glacier Pass. When was the best time to enter? What were some dangers to be aware of? How were the watch rotations at the entrance? How skilled were the soldiers?

No Ikane.

I graduated to pumpkin soup for supper. I hadn't expected to receive any sort of vegetable in this barren, desolate landscape. But it turned out that gourds were very easy to preserve, especially in this cooler weather. Apparently, merchants brought them regularly. The soup was seasoned with onion and held a hint of sweetness that Erin informed me was maple syrup.

The door opened.

Ikane, refusing to make eye contact, entered the room. He walked across the way to where Eamon was sitting at the foot of my bed and held out a heavy leather pouch bulging with coin. When Eamon made no move to take it, Ikane roughly grabbed his hand, and jammed the purse into his palm. The coins made a distinct 'ching'.

"There is enough to pay the innkeeper and buy new clothing for Kea," Ikane said in a low voice.

Eamon looked up at him.

"Don't do that again," Erin said as she approached Ikane with a bowl of pumpkin soup. "We were all very worried about you."

"Not me," Broderick said, spooning some soup into his mouth as he sat on the edge of the bed. "I slept through it all."

His humor helped to lighten the mood a bit.

"Shut up and eat," Erin said to Broderick, and then she turned back to Ikane, thrusting the bowl at him. "You too."

Ikane took it from her gratefully and cautiously sat down beside Eamon.

"Now that we are all here, it is time to devise a plan to get through Glacier Pass," Eamon announced as he set the heavy-laden purse filled with coin at his back. "According to Erin, the guards posted at the entrance are not very skilled, which will work to our advantage."

"How many?" Broderick asked, barely coming up for air between his spoonfuls of soup.

"Five," Erin said.

Eamon nodded. "What we need is a distraction. Seeing as my knee is bad, and I would only slow us down, I volunteer."

I sat more erect at his announcement. I didn't want Eamon to stay behind. Ikane too, seemed startled, and I'm sure he wondered if it was because of his actions that Eamon was sacrificing himself.

"Seeing as Erin knows the terrain and the dangers of this area, I've asked that she be your guide," Eamon continued.

I did not try to hide my surprise as I looked directly at her. There was a soft rosiness in her cheeks as Eamon acknowledged her. She had no reason to help us any more than she already had. But looking between her and Eamon, I was beginning to suspect that there was a relationship budding that was more than friendship.

"Broderick," Eamon turned his attention to the young spy. "You've dealt with Ikane during his 'episodes'. I think you should accompany them as well. They will need a strong arm to subdue Ikane if it should come to that – no more wolfsbane, you hear?"

Broderick nodded and resumed eating.

"Wolfsbane?" Erin asked.

A small wave of distortion warbled by the fireplace, and Erin looked at the little windsprite.

"Ah, yes," Eamon said. "A minor detail. Ikane is a lycanthrope. Wolfsbane will force him to change into a harmless little pup." To emphasize his point, Eamon reached up and ruffled Ikane's hair.

Ikane prickled at the jab and swatted Eamon's hand away, almost spilling his soup as he did so.

"Is that why your green eye flares?" Erin asked.

Ikane blushed irritably and nodded, a little spark igniting in his eye.

"But, we've tried the wolfsbane route," Eamon continued. "It is making it harder for him to change back into a man—though I do prefer him as a wolf. He gets into less trouble that way."

Ikane shot him a look.

Eamon brushed it off with a knowing smile. He was getting under Ikane's skin. "Kea will be the only one to have a knife tipped in wolfsbane."

I didn't like the thought, but Eamon's wisdom was sound. Should the witch force Ikane to attack me again, it would be my only means of defending myself in my weakened state.

"Hold on," Erin said holding her hands up. "Why would he need to change into a wolf?"

"To keep the Phoenix Witch at bay," Ikane said, looking aghast at Eamon as he spoke. "Why are you telling her all of this?"

"Because, as your guide, she needs to know every little thing that could go wrong. It will be the difference between life and death," Eamon said.

Erin stood and gathered a deep breath. "Eamon and I have already talked about this," she said. "And there is one more thing that you should know."

All eyes were upon her, and with a gentle nod from Eamon, Erin waved her hand at the fireplace, beckoning Ali to approach. The glittering vapor of light flashed across the room, darting to Erin. The windsprite alighted in her hand and with a swirl of air, she became tangibly visible. Even I was taken aback at how much detail she revealed. Her body was just like Mina's in proportion and size, but she was near transparent, and her hair floated in soft wisps of fractured light at her back.

"This is Ali," Erin said. "A windsprite, my friend, and we will need to rely on her help to get through Glacier Pass."

Eamon nodded, as if Erin had already introduced him to Ali.

Broderick gave Erin and the sprite a crooked smile. "I thought I felt something," he said. "I am a Wind Wardent after all. It is a pleasure to meet you, Ali."

The smile on Ali's face was translucent, but evident. "Likewise," she said in her soft, breathy voice.

"Am I the only one who didn't know about her?" Ikane asked when he looked at me. "You've seen her already, haven't you?"

I smiled sheepishly.

Ali turned to Ikane, her smile fading greatly. "There is a darkness, Thrall, inside of you that has probably made it impossible for you to feel anything of the elemental sprites," she said. "It is painful to be around you. But Kea's presence makes it bearable."

Ikane's shoulders drooped as his eyes cast down to the floor. He lost all interest in eating. I placed my hand on his back, trying to comfort him.

"Don't go sulking, boy!" Eamon snapped. "It's the witch inside of you that she feels, not you."

Ikane nodded soberly, but it didn't seem to ease the isolation he felt. I wished, once again, that we could re-establish our link. I wanted to hear his thoughts and reassure him that he was not alone.

"Now," Eamon continued, "as for the distraction of the guards, here is what I have in mind."

The money Ikane had acquired was enough to pay the innkeeper her dues and purchase a new fur-lined outfit for me. It wasn't near the quality we had found in Shear, but it was warm enough. But we were still short two horses.

Erin, taking matters into her own hands, went to see Healer Malcom. Broderick was owed a hefty sum for his healing services, especially after healing the remaining patients. With the money earned from the healer, Broderick purchased provisions of dried fruits, fish, a small wedge of cheese, rye bread, and rented two more horses from the main stable named Dredge and Sprint. As we already knew Camp's temperament, Eamon insisted that I ride that little ice-horse. Camp had already proven not to spook easily, and the risk of being thrown was far lower than with the new horses.

Broderick had arrived on his own bay horse, but traded it in for a smaller, sturdy glacier horse named Mince Meat in order to accompany us through Glacier Pass. We discovered quite early that Mince Meat was named for sniffing through the packs and getting into our provisions.

In spite of flexing my hand at every opportunity, the muscles were slow to recover. It would be at least two weeks before I regained full use of my arm again, and that was being optimistic. Walking was bearable, but the old arrow wound in my back zapped a painful spark down my leg if I moved too quickly.

I double checked the knife tipped with wolfsbane that was carefully wrapped in a cloth and stuck in my boot. My eyes darted to Ikane across the poorly lit stable. The beams that held the roof hid him from my view, but I could see his hands working to tighten the belts and straps holding our gear. Broderick, in better view, was leading Mince Meat and Sprint in my direction.

I swallowed hard. Sprint was for Erin – and we would meet her at the guard-shack at the entrance of Glacier Pass.

The weight of Eamon's hand on my shoulder was barely reassuring. I looked up at him, openly displaying my grief at leaving him behind.

"Don't you worry," he said with a small smile. "I know what I'm getting myself into."

That's what I was afraid of. "Be careful," I managed to whisper.

He pulled me in for a rare embrace. My arms wrapped around his muscled torso as he held me. I wanted to weep, but I swallowed back the lump that began to build in my throat. The pain there was enough to keep the weeping at bay.

"You've come so far, Kea. We can't give up now," he whispered.

The fingers of my good hand curled tightly around the fabric of his coat, as if it would keep him from leaving my side. He pulled away and looked down at me with fondness that I had longed to see in his eyes for years.

"Stay strong now," he coaxed me and gently pushed his finger under my chin to raise my head. "You are the daughter of a king, the ward of a warrior, and one of the strongest women I've ever known."

I pursed my lips together and nodded quickly.

"Good," he announced and stepped back to greet Broderick. "Are you ready?" he asked the assassin.

Broderick pulled his hood over the brown curls on his head and nodded. "Ikane is just about finished."

"Let us be off then," Eamon said as he grabbed Sprint's reins. He looked back at me once more and smiled weakly. "Don't be late now. We only have a small window to make this work."

I nodded and watched as Eamon and Broderick stepped out of the stable and into the bright, snow-reflecting light of noon day. Our timing needed to be perfect, or the Phoenix Soldiers would have time to give chase into Glacier Pass. If all went according to plan, the soldiers would be forced to abandon any pursuit or risk being caught in the dark with the Deathbiters.

Ikane approached with the remaining little ice-horses and smiled at me. "Ready, Little Brendagger?"

I frowned. I wished he wasn't trying so hard to be cheerful. He knew as well as I did that this was going to hurt Eamon's reputation permanently. Perhaps this was his way of dealing with it. Either way, I didn't want him to smile.

He stepped forward and laced his fingers together to help me up onto Camp's back. This was the first time I tried to mount a horse since the attack, and my body protested the movement of swinging my leg up. Instead, my knee slid up on the saddle first, and then I sluggishly twisted my body until my leg slipped over the other side. Ikane practically pushed me onto the saddle. His brows furrowed as I frantically gripped the saddle horn.

"Are you sure you can ride?"

I felt Camp's body shift under my weight, and my own muscles tensed and strained as I was forced to find balance. The wound in my back seemed to be causing most of the discomfort, but I was confident that I could ride. I straightened up and nodded. Still not fond of speaking much, I patted my calf to indicate that he should help me wriggle my boots into the stirrup leather. That alone would help with my balance and keep my back from aching so.

Ikane knew instantly what I was asking of him. "Remember to hide your face," he said as he grabbed the heel of my boots and shoved them through the stirrups.

With only one hand fully responding, I pulled my hood over my head and drew the woolen cowl tucked into the neck of my coat over my mouth and nose. Only my eyes would be visible to anyone searching for me, and the new scars across my face would certainly be a camouflage to those who knew me.

Ikane patted my thigh when he finished. "It's time," he said.

"Let's go," I replied, but my voice was still breathy and weak, and the fact that my lips were shrouded in a woolen cowl, made my reply barely audible. But Ikane, with his enhanced senses, easily made out my words. He nodded, grabbed the reins of both horses and stepped out into the sunlight.

The brightness was nigh blinding, in spite of the clouds overhead. The soft haze seemed to intensify the glow of the sun so that everything held a golden hue. Even the rows of plaster, wood, and stone buildings appeared gilded. The air was crisp and fresh, filled with the smell of snow that already glittered in minuscule flecks across my face. I couldn't help but think of Erin and her windsprite friend. Their part of the plan was only just beginning.

Ikane continued to lead the horses through the main street of the small outpost. We passed a large stable first, and then a smithy. Warm light and tantalizing smells came from the bakery. I inhaled deeply, feeling my palate salivate, and then the memory of working with Mayama in Daram's kitchen flooded through my mind. My heart ached for the simple time. I missed Mayama terribly. The old cook was more than a friend to me – she was my mother figure.

Red coats stood out sharply against the gray stone of the arched gateway of the small village. I did my best not to cower as we walked by. The soldiers watched us curiously but did not intercept us as we passed under the stone arch.

Now we were exposed.

Nothing stood between the gate of Gerom Post and the entrance to Glacier Pass save for a wide expanse of flat snow that reflected sunlight as if a field of fire lay before us. Ahead, I could make out the tall, narrow crevice that was Glacier Pass, stuck between never-ending masses of ice. I had heard tales of the sheer, ice covered cliffs of the northern reaches, but seeing this natural wonder with my own eyes was an entirely different experience. For a moment, I felt as insignificant as a grain of sand beside a boulder. The icy cliffs that created Glacier Pass appeared to have been split by a giant axe, the pathway barely wide enough for a wagon and a team of horses. A faint howl echoed through the pass as glacial winds plowed through the crevice.

Erin had informed us that when the sun sets, winds would blast through the entrance so fiercely that it could knock a man back on his rump. This happened every evening, for nearly thirty minutes, as the temperatures within the pass dropped. This was Ali's domain. And we were counting on the little windsprite to help us.

"Almost there," Ikane said to me as he mounted his new horse, Dredge. The small, dark colored horse danced around for a moment under Ikane's weight, but they soon found rhythm. "I know it's going to hurt but be ready for the sprint."

I gathered a deep breath through the woolen cowl. I was ready.

As our horses trotted near, I could make out the small guard shack standing to the left of the pass. The five guards, in their red uniforms, stood out sharply against the white cliffs looming behind them, but they were not at their posts. Instead of flanking the pass as Erin said was their usual position, they were all gathered by the guard shack, speaking with Erin, Eamon, and Broderick. It seemed friendly at first, and I could hear their muffled voices carry across the wide landscape.

I caught Eamon's quick glance back at us over his shoulder, and then his body language shifted. It was time.

He stepped forward and shoved one of the guards roughly on the shoulder. Erin and Broderick cautiously stepped away, allowing Eamon to become the focus of the soldier's attention.

"What do you mean, I can't pass?" Eamon growled.

"Master Eamon, sir," the soldier replied, trying to keep his composure. He was a younger man, probably stationed here because he was no good anywhere else. "There is no need to become aggressive. I am simply following orders."

"Hah!" Eamon roared. "And what are those orders?"

"Uh... well," the soldier stammered.

An older, more experienced soldier approached, stepping between Eamon and the younger soldier. "We have orders to arrest and return the Lady Keatep to Meldron," he announced. If he was flustered, he didn't show it.

"Are you saying that I look like Keatep Brendagger?" Eamon snapped.

Erin had strategically placed herself behind the soldiers now and watched us closely. When we reached a certain point, I saw her fingers flick downward in a signal to Eamon.

"We were informed that you disappeared from Meldron the same night she did," the soldier said, and now I could see the crease form between his brows. "You cannot pass. By the order of the king-"

Eamon's fist flew at the soldier's jaw. "Are you accusing me of treason!?" he roared as the soldier's head spun about. The man stumbled into the younger soldier, who braced him from falling. Immediately, two of the red uniformed men sprang forward and seized Eamon's arms. The master warrior struggled, feigning the ability to escape, but I knew better. Eamon could've bested all five of them.

"Lock him in the guard shack," Erin suggested, urgently.

In the heat of the moment, the soldiers simply reacted to the order of the woman they trusted. Eamon flailed and jerked about, swinging the soldiers that clung to his arms around like sacks of grain. I heard the harsh thump as one of them was pitched into the doorframe. As the rest of the soldiers looked on, I watched Broderick slip a vial from his bandoleer and cautiously open the cork.

And then Erin barreled into the soldiers. The force of her impact drove one more through the door of the guard shack. Three soldiers, and Eamon, crashed into the small building. Erin slammed the door shut and bolted it just as Broderick grabbed one of the two remaining soldiers from behind and shoved the vial at his face.

"Now!' Ikane hissed and dug his heels into Dredge's sides. His horse lurched. Camp followed without much direction from me, his entire body bunching with energy. The tiny legs plowed through the snow and my body screamed in protest at every jolt. The lightning strike of pain raced from my back down to my leg, forcing me to grip the saddle horn for balance.

The height of the narrow cliffs swallowed the sun, and thick sections of ice clotted the gaping maw above us. The chill of the howling wind against our faces sent tremors through my body, not only from the cold that penetrated my skin, but because the sound was near to that of a Deathbiters' shriek. I couldn't help but look over my shoulder, fearing to see black wings and poisonous talons lunging after me. Instead, I saw Erin racing towards us on the back of her white glacial-horse, Sprint.

"Keep going!" she hollered at us, but her voice was faint as it was pushed back by the wind careening through the pass. "You're almost there!"

I turned back, renewed energy driving me on. I trusted that Erin had already scouted ahead. Ali would be waiting for us.

Ikane and Dredge veered around a corner of ice and found Erin's marker - her axe wedged into a thick section of blue-white ice on the wall. I thought I saw the little fluctuating image of the sprite standing on the eye of it.

Ikane pulled Dredge to a halt and turned him about as Camp came up beside him. The motion jarred the agony in my back again.

"Now, Ali!" Erin shouted as she rounded the corner.

"What about Broderick?" Ikane asked just as a sudden surge of wind blasted through the pass. Erin's hood flew from her face, revealing her flushed cheeks and scrunched eyes. She drove Sprint on until she reached us, seeming to step out of a storm. If I thought her wild curls could get any wilder, I was mistaken. She brushed her hair from her face and looked back at the pass. Monstrous daggers of ice clung to the crags above, sentinels against the continuous wailing of the gale that Ali was creating.

"What of Broderick?" Ikane pressed again. Dredge danced around at Ikane's nervous energy. "We can't leave him behind."

"He'll be fine," Erin said as she yanked her axe from the ice. "Let's keep moving. Ali can't hold them off indefinitely. We need to get as far as we can before nightfall."

21

WINDSPRITE

The waning rays of golden light spilled into the center of the manmade portion of cliffs. Here, the ice had been carved out to make way for merchants to store their wagons for the night. My heart sank at the thought of camping here in the open with the Deathbiters... and then I saw it. A heavy blanket lay across what looked like two bodies on our right. Erin noticed them too and dismounted. She crouched down and cautiously lifted the blanket to inspect them. She shook her head as she gently, reverently, replaced the fabric across the bodies.

"Deathbiters," she confirmed.

I only noted the trembling in my body when Ikane helped me from the horse's back.

"Erin," Ikane said in dismay. "We can't stay here. We are completely exposed."

The sturdy woman stood and rubbed her hands off on her trousers, as if some of the Deathbiters poison had leeched from the corpses onto her skin. "We will be safe enough tonight," she assured us. She grabbed Sprint's reigns and guided the ice-horse under a section of overhanging cliffs. It was strange how I hadn't noticed them before. The white-blue of the ice seemed to blend into each other, making surfaces appear flat when they were not and vice versa.

Ikane and I followed, dragging our horses with us through the narrow pathway. Ikane followed as I trailed Erin. She seemed to disappear around a sharp bend in the ice, and once I rounded the corner after her, a wide, cave-like hollow opened up, nearly the size of the mess hall back in Meldron. Mina's gift of sight in the darkness allowed me to see that half of the cavern had been sectioned off to become a stable. A wooden table and two long benches stood at the adjoining end for cultured meals, while a fire pit dominated the center of the chamber. I pushed my hood from my head and pulled the cowl from my nose as I glanced up to see a small rift in the ice hanging just above the firepit. A small shaft of light rained down on the black ash below. Ventilation... and a way for Deathbiters to enter.

"We'd best hurry and unpack while we have some daylight left," Erin said. "I don't think we should risk drawing the attention of the Deathbiters with a fire... even if it is the one thing they are afraid of."

Ikane nodded and took Camp's reins from me. "What about Broderick?" he asked Erin again. "Shouldn't he have caught up to us by now?"

For the first time I saw concern on Erin's face as she chewed on her cheek. "Yes, he should have. But we can't go after him. It's almost dark. We can only hope that he makes it here in time."

My own concern was mounting. Even if Broderick made it before dark, would he find this hidden pocket in the glacier cliffs.

Ikane seemed to know my intentions. "Go on," he said. "I'll care for the horses."

It was surprising to me how willing Ikane was to tend to the four-legged animals, seeing as he was not fond of them at all. He had learned much about them during his time here in Roanfire, probably more than he thought he ever would.

I turned and walked – limped - back to the entrance and peered out for any sound that might indicate Broderick's coming. The gale through the cliffs was steadily increasing, and my breath puffed in the dropping temperature. The orange glow of the setting sun turned a deep violet, and the shadows in the icy crags deepened. After a moment, Erin appeared at my side.

At my expression, she sighed and leaned her shoulder against mine. I knew it was her way of comforting me. "Ali isn't here yet either," she said. "I've a feeling that she's teamed up with Broderick. They'll look after each other."

My eyes flicked down the darkening pathway. "Why are you helping?" I asked her in as few words as possible. I couldn't seem to comprehend why she had risked her own reputation to help us. Her livelihood was woodcutting – and Gerom Post depended on it since wood was scarce in the area. Not only this, but she barely knew me. She had no obligation or ties to keep, and yet she risked everything for us.

She sighed and began to fiddle with something at her wrist. Between her thick coat sleeve and fingerless gloves, I could only make out a hint of a wooden bracelet there. "Ali believes in you," she said simply, if that was all that mattered. After a few moments of listening to the wind race through the canyon, her shoulders drooped, and her head lowered. "No... that's not the whole truth," she whispered.

When I looked at her, expecting further explanation, she leaned back against the icy wall with a heavy sigh. "I was married once," she began.

My brows rose.

"I know, I know. How could someone as harsh as me ever fall in love?" she groaned.

That hadn't been what I was thinking, but my voice hurt too much to bother giving an explanation.

"I had two beautiful children too," she said in a softer tone. Her eyes lowered, and I could see the soft shimmer of tears in them. She took another breath and squared her shoulders. "I don't like talking about it. It hurts too much."

I nodded quickly, not wanting to force her into reliving something terrible.

"But," she continued. "For Ali's sake, I think you should know."

I gave her my full attention.

"It happened one day while we were out cutting wood as a family. Near the city of Lodwen. The trees there are lush and the wood thick and ready. It was going to be a lucrative trip for us. But, after my husband and I felled our first tree, we heard something from the icy mountains nearby. A crack and then a rumble... I can't ever unhear it," she said. "Galien—my husband—sprinted for the hills, knowing that our children had been sledding there. I wasn't as fast..."

She swallowed hard. "The avalanche overtook them all."

My hand flew to cover my mouth, trying to still my own groan of sympathy.

"I dug. I shoveled. I used my axe to get through the densely packed snow, but when I found Galien... he was already dead. I lost all hope for my children, but I dug anyway. For three days, I searched and half of the city of Lodwen came to my aid, but we couldn't find them." Her voice tightened. "On the third day there was another rumble, this one coming from beneath the snow. It was like an explosion from underground. I ran to see."

She choked, her lips trembled, and tears burst from her eyes at the memory. She wiped at her cheeks frantically. "There... in the crater of snow and ice... lay my two darling children, their bodies frozen." She sobbed harshly three times before being able to continue. After sniffing she gave me a weak smile. "They were beautiful. It was as if they had been frozen in sleep. Their faces were serene, and my daughter even had a small smile on her blue lips."

I couldn't help but feel my own eyes begin to burn.

Erin swallowed hard, sniffed, and took another deep breath. Her voice took on its usual tone. "And that was where I met Alizeh the Windsprite. Apparently, she had joined my children in sledding and was buried in the snow with them. She could have simply flown away and saved herself, but she tried to deflect the snow from my children as it came down— or at least that is her story. She was weak when I found her, and both of her wings were damaged. Did you know that windsprites need air to retain their magic? Well, being trapped in the snow, she had no wind, and she was weak from having spent all her energy to keep the snow from crushing my darlings. She told me that she had thought about using the air initially trapped in their grave to burst from the snow, but she wasn't sure it would be strong enough. So, she waited and comforted my children, hoping that help would arrive in time."

My brows furrowed.

"Yes," she said, her voice hardening. "Ali used the final breaths of my children to free herself from the snowy grave. I know I can't blame her... I wouldn't have found them in time anyway. They were buried too deep. In fact, I may have never found them at all. And yet, my anger still lingers towards her. She has made it her life's mission to protect and aid me.

"I suppose the truth is that I feel an obligation to help you, the way the people of Lodwen helped me. It may be futile, but I won't abandon you," she said.

My smile was genuine but mixed with sorrow. "Thank you," I said. She deserved words for this, no matter how painful it was for me to speak.

A large gust of wind suddenly ripped through the narrow canyon, knocking me off balance.

Erin pushed herself from the icy wall. "It's time," she said. "These winds will keep anyone from traveling tonight. Broderick and Ali are on their own... but I wouldn't worry.

The wind here is Ali's source of power. She won't let any harm come to your friend."

I glanced back at the opening, mildly reassured by Erin's words, before ducking back into the cave.

I pushed myself from the biting-cold ground and sat upright. During the last few hours I had been asleep, I had woken over four times, breaking my sleep into unrefreshing chunks. It wasn't necessarily the cold that made it so – my fur-lined coat, trousers, and boots kept me comfortably warm – but the wind. The howling noise beyond the crooked entryway warped into noises of screeching that made me re-live the attack. Perhaps the noises were, in fact, Deathbiters.

Every muscle in my body felt tight, like the string of a bow, ready to fire. I wanted to spring into action, in spite of my unusable body. My fingers trembled as I pulled the mittens from my hands and flexed my left one. It was still weak and thin. In truth, my whole body was weak and thin, and I hated the feeling of helplessness that came with it.

I glanced up to find Erin fast asleep on my left. But Ikane was as restless as me. After tossing and turning for another few minutes, his eyes blinked open, and he sat upright upon seeing that I was awake. He rubbed his eyes and pushed his hair back from his face. His breath was vapor in the bitter cold chamber and his nose was pink.

"Can't sleep?" he whispered as he shifted to sit beside me.

I shook my head. "I'm scared," I finally said. I hated to admit it. I was terrified of being discovered by the Deathbiters, terrified of finding Broderick dead, and terrified of what Rion had in store for Ikane. "The Deathbiters..."

"I know," he said softly, trying to spare me the task of speaking. His arm wrapped around me to pull me close.

"No," I snapped and pushed my finger against his lips to keep him silent. "Listen."

He pressed his lips together and nodded.

"The Deathbiters came for the ruby," I whispered and tapped my collarbone for emphasis. "Rion ordered it."

Ikane's brows furrowed and his eyes widened briefly.

"Now the Deathbiters are after you," I said. My throat was burning now. This was the most I had spoken since the attack. "Someone is helping her." I reached up to my burning throat, pressing my cold fingers against my neck. It helped to soothe the aching.

His jaw tightened as his arm pulled me closer against his torso. His grip was almost too painful, but I felt fear behind his movement. He wasn't only pulling me close to comfort me, but to draw comfort.

"I had a suspicion," he said in a hushed tone.

I wriggled from his grip, needing to straighten out my back, and jumped at the sound of a screech outside. I held my breath as the flapping of wings became evident. Ikane stiffened. The harsh sound of leather against ice returned, but it was soon drowned out by the rushing wind, indicating that it had flown away.

Both Ikane and I let out trembling breaths.

"How can she sleep?" Ikane asked, jerking his head to Erin.

I looked down at the woman who lay on her side with her back facing us. A twinge of jealousy erupted. She looked so peaceful, and I was exhausted. I was half-tempted to thrust my knee into her back to give her a taste of discomfort but thought better of it. At least one of us would have a sound mind in the morning.

Ikane suddenly gripped my hand, his warm fingers crushing mine. "Kea?" he asked, a sense of urgency filling his voice. His eyes were wide. "Where are the iron shackles?"

I searched his eyes, targeting his emerald one specifically. It was flickering. I felt my brows furrow.

"Broderick," I said simply. Eamon had expected to have Broderick here in case Ikane was overpowered by Rion... and now neither Broderick or the iron shackles were anywhere near us.

Ikane flinched as Rion struck at him and dug his fingers into his hair. "The knife," he groaned. "Get the knife."

I drew my leg up as fast as I could and saw the glint of the small metal dagger protruding from the gray fur lining in my boot. Just as my fingers touched the hilt, Ikane's hand shot out and gripped my wrist with such violent strength that my muscles couldn't respond. The blood in my hand pulsed hot. With a savage jerk, he wrenched my hand back, forcing my body to arc with it. My torso slammed to the icy ground, and I barely managed to keep my head from hitting the ice. In reflex, my withered and weak arm shot up to shield my neck from his grasp, knowing that it was Rion's assault of choice.

In seconds, Ikane's leg swung over my body, straddling me.

"Erin!" I tried to call out to her but straining my voice so forcefully only made it softer and breathy. "Erin!"

My attempt to kick her was thwarted by Ikane's legs pinning mine into place. Ikane grabbed my feeble wrist and easily pushed it to the ground beside my head, then leaned dangerously close.

"I've had enough of you, Phoenix Daughter!" His voice hissed Rion's words into my ear. "I truly believed these creatures would finally destroy you."

"Erin!" I called out to her again. "Erin, help!"

The woman stirred at the noise, then bolted upright in alarm. Her hair whirled wildly around her shoulders as she turned to face us. "Kea!"

"The knife," I told her, wiggling my right boot to indicate the weapon's location.

Ikane—Rion—realizing that help had arrived, whirled to face the new threat. In doing so, she released my left arm. If I had been in prime condition, I would've taken this opportunity to land my fist, followed by my elbow, into his jaw. My feeble attempt to even strike him was met by a backhand to the inside of my wrist. My hand flew back to the ice, hitting so hard that my knuckles zinged with cold pain.

It was enough of a distraction to allow Erin to step around him. She pounced onto his back and wrapped her arm around his throat, locking it with the other. He arched back, freeing my hands. I squirmed beneath his legs, trying to reach the knife, but it was wedged between our legs too tightly.

Erin must have sensed the issue and attempted to draw Ikane back with her small body. But in trying to draw him back, she opened herself up for an attack—a rookie mistake for a soldier. Then again, she was no soldier. Ikane's elbow flew back into her ribs. I heard the air whoosh from her lungs as she released him and staggered back.

The movement was just enough for me to jerk my leg from under Ikane's body. I snatched the knife from my boot just as he turned his attention back to me. His hands flew up to my neck... and I felt their cold strength slither around my fragile throat. Before they could crush, I plunged the knife into the heavy fur coat at his abdomen, and then felt it hit soft tissue.

Instead of crushing my neck, he fell forward, bracing his fall with his hands landing on either side of my head. His face contorted in pain above mine, and I watched as his emerald eye began to flicker with green light. His breathing was shallow and harsh, and his body began to tremble.

"I'm sorry, Ikane," I whispered.

He seemed to smile through his clenched teeth, and then scrambled back with the dagger still protruding from his abdomen. He collided into the single table, knocking one of the benches over in the process. Trembling, he grabbed the hilt of the small dagger and drew it from his body. It clattered to the icy floor.

Erin rushed to my side and hastily checked my neck. "Are you alright? Did he hurt you?"

I shook my head as I watched Ikane begin to writhe. Burning tears sprung into my eyes, knowing that this dose of wolfsbane would make it even harder for him to return to his human form. If only Broderick had been here.

The horrible sound of his shifting body echoed through the expansive cavern, and his groan echoed with it. I turned away as his bones broke and reformed. Erin, like the mother she was, wrapped her arms around me as if to shield me from this horror. Then, Ikane's labored breathing, the whinny of frightened horses, and the wind outside the cavern was all one heard. I looked up at the abnormally large wolf who stood by the table, paws splayed, and eyes wide with surprise.

I opened my mind to him, not realizing how eager he was to communicate. He barreled into my thoughts like a drunkard through a tavern door. Before I could comprehend his heightened sense of smell, perfect hearing, and clear eyesight, his voice sounded through my head. *She was so fast this time, Kea. I am so sorry.*

I was only beginning to note the smart in my shoulder, but I did not blame him. It was all Rion. *I'm fine,* I assured him as I staggered to my feet and over to the table.

But Ikane wasn't comforted. He could feel the pain in my shoulder and the sharp sting across my knuckles. He could sense my fear and the worry that he would be trapped in a wolf form forever. *We can't keep this up, Kea. You can barely fight. It was sheer luck that Rion wanted to toy with you. She could've killed you tonight.*

Erin brushed her hair from her face, not removing her wide, violet eyes from the black wolf. She held her side where he had struck her, and he noticed her favoring it.

Please give Erin my apologies, Ikane said.

I relayed the information to Erin as I stood the bench upright and sat on it.

Erin nodded, though still wary of Ikane. "Now I understand why you didn't want to leave Broderick behind," she said as she watched the wolf. "He was the muscle we were relying on to fend you off. Eamon chose him for this specific situation."

Ikane's ears lowered in shame at her words, and I placed my hand on Ikane's back with the intention of comforting him. I promptly felt his distaste for being touched like an animal, and my hand dropped. Ikane shook his black coat to relieve the sensation.

Sorry, I mumbled my apology to him.

He wanted to ignore it, but his thoughts ran back to Meldron and Ropert. Every time he shifted under the influence of wolfsbane, the harder it was for him to return to human form. And every time he shifted, we seemed to treat him more and more like a pet rather than a human being. Even I was at fault.

"So..." Erin began, eying the horses that were just beginning to settle down. "Are we safe with him this way?"

I nodded to her.

"Good, because I could use a spot of tea," she said and moved to our saddlebags that were propped up against the cold firepit. "I think I saw some firedust in here, and some chamomile. That should get us all back to sleep in no time."

I looked back at Ikane as he sat beside me. His eyes were cast down, and his black ears did not sit at their usual pointed position. Even the hair at the back of his neck bristled with irritation.

Stop looking at me that way. A low growl rumbled through his chest.

Erin looked up at us upon hearing the noise.

I averted my eyes. I had wanted to link my mind with his for so long in order to understand his thoughts, and now that we were finally linked, I wished we weren't. The pity and shame I felt for him was unwarranted. Rion was taking a toll on us. We were both exhausted and frightened.

"Here," Erin said, placing a mug of warm tea between my hands. "Drink up, and let's try to get some sleep. We have a strenuous journey ahead tomorrow. The gorge slopes uphill from here on."

She turned and sat down on her bedroll, crossing her legs.

I took a sip, grateful for the warmth that spread through my body. I focused on it: the sweet floral taste, the mild herbal smell as the steam rose to my nose, the warmth across my tongue gliding down to my throat, the way it soothed my churning stomach. It eased the tension between Ikane's mind and my own.

Erin watched Ikane warily over the rim of her mug as she sipped. "I'm sorry we had to use the wolfsbane," she said to him. "Eamon is very worried about you."

Something about her tone comforted him, as if his friends truly did care. Another spark of jealousy arose. She was able to give him comfort when I could not.

Then again, I was grateful to her for it.

22

THE GORGE

A single beam of golden light shot through the crevice just above the firepit, slamming down into the ashes like the shaft of a spear. Erin had been right about the chamomile tea. The sleep that followed that herbal concoction was bliss. Now, as my eyes fluttered open, I watched as hazy blue light slowly penetrated the icy surface of the walls. The entire cavern seemed to glow.

Ikane, who had fallen asleep beside me, yawned and stretched, splaying his claws in the process. He sat upright and blinked down at me. There was a sensation of fondness radiating from him, and then the picture became clearer in his mind. My hair spread out across my makeshift pillow like a halo of auburn sunshine. My lips and cheeks were rosy from sleep, and in spite of the three massive scars running across my face, he was focused on the way my eyes reflected the blue light pouring through the cavern walls. In his mind, I was the most beautiful creature he'd ever encountered.

I smiled briefly. *Your thoughts are wide open this morning,* I told him.

He shook his head quickly, mildly mortified that I had caught his stare. *I didn't intend to make you uncomfortable.*

Erin rolled over and groaned as she stretched. She flinched a little and placed a hand over her ribcage where Ikane had struck her. Without a murmur she sat upright, brushed her hair from her face, and stood.

"Kea, can you manage the bedrolls while I saddle the horses?" she asked. Without Ikane to help out, I would need to step up to extra tasks. It was a challenge I accepted eagerly. The more I moved, the quicker my body would recover.

I nodded quickly.

"And pull out a few items for breakfast so we can eat along the way," she added.

Within the hour, Erin and I guided the small ice-horses from the cavern. My immediate reaction was to look down the narrow gorge with the hope of seeing Broderick riding up on his little horse. There was nothing but silence and a small breeze.

Erin's eyes flashed down the road as well. "He'll catch up if he can," she said. "For now, we must press on. Do you need help mounting your horse?"

I nodded sheepishly.

She quickly laced her fingers to give me a step up. I was able to mount a little better than I had the day before, but the pain in my back returned as soon as I tried to find my balance on Camp's round trunk. And then the horse danced skittishly around, causing the other mounts to catch the tension.

"Get away!" Erin barked at Ikane who had just pushed his head from the cavern. "You're spooking the horses."

He shrank back inside, allowing Erin to calm the three horses.

"You're going to have to follow behind us," Erin said to Ikane as she patted Sprint's white nose. "You shouldn't have to keep too far behind, seeing as the wind will drive your scent away. But the last thing we need is to have three spooked horses."

I know. I know. Ikane's annoyed acceptance of the situation floated through my mind. Not only was he incapable of helping out, but he was frightening the horses to boot.

Golden sunlight beamed down through the chasm and reflected across the icy walls on either side of us, deepening the shadows of the crags. The clapping of the horse's hooves against the icy ground echoed wildly down the narrow pathway that continuously sloped upward. It was so loud, I was convinced that the Phoenix Soldiers standing guard at the entrance to Glacier Pass, could hear it. Deep grooves of wagon wheels carved into the ice, and the center pathway had been worn slick from frequent use of travelers. Even though glacier-horses were accustomed to the icy terrain, and their wide hooves helped to keep them balanced, they began to slip. We were forced to dismount and walk.

The constant breeze sweeping through the fissure softened the further we traveled, but in return, the cold deepened. Our breath hung in the air like clouds of vapor, and my nose and cheeks burned with an icy sting, in spite of pulling my woolen cowl over my face. My thighs burned at the endless uphill march, and every wound the Deathbiters had inflicted became a gnawing ache on my limbs, especially the one dealt to my back. My pace slowed when the dull twitching of muscle traveled down the length of my left leg and lulled near my ankle. I found myself curling my fingers and toes against the freezing bite that seeped into my palms and feet – and then realized I was feeling Ikane's frozen paws.

You're doing it again, he said when I looked over my shoulder to see his dark shadow following us. For the sake of the horses, he kept a good distance away. I had forgotten that Ikane felt every ounce of constant throbbing in my body.

A shadow blocked the only warmth raining down on my shoulders, and my eyes darted upward to the gap above us. A dark cloud veiled the sun for a few unnerving moments, then swept by. The movement strained the injury to my throat, and I looked ahead again, quickly shifting my thoughts to Erin who headed the way. Her gait was strong and firm, planting her feet solidly on the ice as she walked. The horses followed her willingly, drawing on her solid, confident essence. This woman, near ten years older than I, was as sturdy as any warrior. She paused a moment on the uphill slope to gather breath, and then marched on.

Your paws... I said. *We should wrap them up.*

No, he said quickly. *Wrapping my feet will only make me clumsy. We've got to keep - what was that?*

He halted, his ears twitched, his head whirled to look behind us.

How could he hear anything over the wild ricochets of our horse's footfalls? I strained to hear through his ears... and then I heard it. A rhythmic clapping that did not sync with our horses. It was faster and fell harder, as if the horse was near galloping through the pass. *What fool would drive a horse that fast on this slick road? Soldiers? Had they caught up to us?*

I don't think so, Ikane replied. He slinked ahead a few paces until he found a deep shadow in the crags that nearly made him invisible.

Erin, who had been leading our way, realized that I had stopped and paused her steady uphill march to look over her shoulder. The willing horses that trailed her, halted. Slowly, the wild echoing of their footfalls died away – revealing the clear noise of clapping hoofbeats behind us. Her head jerked up.

Broderick? I asked Ikane.

Possibly, he replied. *It's only one horse.*

We stood in silence. Listening. Waiting.

Another deep gray cloud rolled across the sun, casting a shadow across our chilled bodies. But this time it did not lift. The sky seemed to blacken unnaturally as the hoofbeats drew nearer. My chest tightened when I tried to gather breath, and

I felt the uncomfortable prickle of the hair on the back of my neck standing on end. Something was very wrong.

A small, gray, glacial-horse shot out of the shadows, barreling past Ikane. The rider seemed startled when he noticed us in his path. I recognized Mince Meat as Broderick pulled back on the reins, forcing the small animal to slip as he skidded to a halt. Our horses snorted and shifted at the abrupt arrival.

Broderick threw his dark hood from his head, revealing wide eyes and brows creased with more than worry – it was fear. A small gash stretched across the left side of his lips. "Get on your horses!" he barked, spitting blood as he spoke.

Erin took a worried step towards him as her dark brows creased. "Are you alright? What's wrong?"

"Where is Ikane?" the assassin asked instead, his eyes scanning the road ahead for any sign of the Leviathan Pirate.

"Behind you," I said as Ikane stepped out of the shadows to reveal himself. My eyes were drawn to a dark mist building and swirling through the narrow canyon beyond him. It was followed by a rotten tang that even the glacial breeze couldn't sweep away. My stomach tightened at the familiar stench.

Broderick whirled to look back at Ikane.

"What's going on? Where is Ali?" Erin demanded.

"No time," Broderick snapped. "Get on your horses!"

Before his voice completely died away in echoing patterns, the noise of flapping, leather wings, rebounded through the gorge in reply.

Deathbiters!

Panic made mounting Camp a cinch. The surge of pure adrenaline masked the pain in my back and leg. The memory of being swarmed by these filthy, black abominations, jerked my body into action before Camp even had the opportunity to register my weight. I kicked his sides, spurring him past the rider-less Dredge.

Run, Ikane! Run! My mind roared at him.

The four little horses barreled through the gorge like rampaging boars. The slick road made them clumsy, but the fear of what pursued them drove them onward – and it wasn't the wolf at their heels.

Dredge, rider-less and therefore fastest, bolted ahead of the small herd, bumping into Sprint as he went. Erin released a small grunt as her horse careened into the edge of the glacial wall, smashing her leg between ice and the muscular body of the horse.

They're gaining on us! Ikane's thoughts shot through mine.

I looked over my shoulder to see the gray mist swirling with the wind of the Deathbiters wings. Something was aiding them. They shouldn't have been able to fly in the light of day, but the dark clouds that loomed over the head of the canyon and the mist swirling around them seemed to be brought on by some sort of magic.

They're after you, Ikane! Go! Get ahead of us! I tried to pull against Camp's reigns as I gave Ikane the message, but the terrified horse jerked his head, nearly pulling me from the saddle. He whinnied, a high-pitched noise that conveyed his panic, and veered back into the path to cut Ikane off.

"Where is Alizeh!" Erin cried. "She can help!"

"She can't," Broderick shouted back.

He had no time to explain. The first of the Deathbiters swooped low, hissing by Ikane's head. The noise was as clear as if it had rushed at me, and I hunched instinctively to avoid getting caught by the poisonous talons. Another bat plummeted towards Ikane, heedless of its own wellbeing, and barreled directly into the wolf's front legs. I felt my own arms tangle against the flailing leather wings, before Ikane tripped and pitched onto his side.

Desperate to stop him, I pulled against Camp's reins again as Ikane's body slid across the road and collided into the wall of the cliff.

"Ikane!" I cried, watching in horror as the demon bats swarmed overhead like vultures. With Camp refusing to slow, I grabbed the hilt of my sword and drew it from the scabbard that had been secured to the horse's saddle. I did not have time to be surprised by my body's strength. Ikane was in danger. I jerked my boots out of the stirrups, swung my leg over the saddle and leapt.

"Kea!" I barely heard Broderick cry out.

I expected the fall to feel like hitting solid rock, but it felt harder than rock. My boots hit the ice, and my left ankle gave way at the impact, driving my knees into the ground as I pitched forward and reeled onto my side. Years of training forced my body to curl and roll with the momentum, easing the impact somewhat. But a sharp pang radiated through my skull as my shoulder and hip struck the solid ice. The ashen white walls of the gorge spun wildly as my body rolled across the ice five times before sliding across it.

Another sting cut into my shoulder-blade and I clenched my teeth against the familiar burn of the Deathbiters poison. I whirled onto my back, hoping to crush the creature under my weight... but there was nothing.

Jolting upright, I searched for Ikane. He hunched against the opposite wall, trying to protect his flank while a dozen Deathbiters lunged, circled, and darted at him. His lips were pulled back in a frightening snarl, his ears flat, his hair standing on end. One of the black beasts clung to his shoulder – right where I had felt the sting.

Kea! Ikane's mind barely comprehended that he was calling for me. *It burns! Kea!*

Like an arrow releasing from a bow, I lunged forward. One uppercut strike with my sword struck two creatures, batting them away like the filth they were. Continuing the strike, I arched my sword over my head and sideswiped into another. The bat flew across the way and collided into the wall above Ikane's head. Too many leather wings, filled with rotten stench, flailed around the wolf for me to see if the beast had been stunned. I ran into the fray, ramming my entire torso against the wild bats, crushing them against the icy wall. Three of them dropped to the ground as I turned to swing my sword at the remainder, keeping the ice at my back.

Kea! A surge of relief and renewed hope filled Ikane as I stood beside him.

"Duck!" Broderick bellowed.

I couldn't see him through the wild beating of leathery wings, but I crouched instantly. A sharp burst of blue-white light burst above my head, slamming into the ice. It was a dull sound, and it did not echo like I thought it should have. Ice exploded at the impact and rained biting shards upon us - along with half a dozen lifeless bats.

Startled, the Deathbiters scattered.

For a brief moment I could see Broderick clearly. He stood roughly twenty yards away with his hand outstretched towards us – but there was nothing in it. Magic?

"Run!" he barked at us.

Ikane's massive body vaulted toward the assassin before I had even gotten back to my feet. But in that instant, the Deathbiters fell upon him in a tornado of feral obsidian wings.

"Ikane!" I wanted to scream, but my voice cracked, and fire burned through my throat as if I had torn the injury wide open. Sharp points of searing pain penetrated my skin – Ikane's skin. My body crumbled under the weight of the beasts pressing down on him.

Kea! He cried. But it wasn't a cry for help. It was a cry of agony and defeat. A whimper flowed with it.

My tears were ice burning down my cheeks as I sprinted for him. My blood, thick. My breath, stuck. Before I could step close enough to swing my sword at the cluster of monsters, deep thrumming rebounded off the gorge walls as they flailed their leathery wings, blasting a torrent of foul-smelling air towards me. The gray fog around them swirled and bent.

The Deathbiters were trying to carry him away!

Ikane! My heart screamed as my good hand helplessly clenched the hilt of my sword. Bats circled, dashed, and rushed around me like a hailstorm of toxic arrows, forcing me to shield my face.

Rion! This was her doing! This was all her!

My eyes narrowed as the Deathbiters worked together to lift Ikane's massive wolf body out of reach. With nostrils flaring, I allowed my anger to escalate and bubble through my veins like boiling water on cold skin. Rion would not win! I would not allow it! Hot energy expanded through my chest, feeling as though it would rend my body apart if I tried to restrain it. I did not want to. Rion deserved death!

It exploded. The power expanded from me like a massive iron shield, ramming into the black bodies of Deathbiters around me. A short hissing sound raced through their frames and in an instant, black ash swirled in their place, tossed about by the frantic flailing of wings. In response, the Deathbiters arched away, but did not release their hold on Ikane who was now far above my head.

"Kea," I barely heard Broderick's voice as I allowed the powerful energy of anger to well up again. It filled my chest, ignited it with burning. The monsters flapped their hideous wings, pulling the wolf into the black cloud looming above the crevice of the pass. Our connection was weakening...

His mind flashed to our first meeting back in Daram. He adored the way the blush had arisen in my cheeks, and the way I had frantically tried to tame my hair in his presence. His perception of my strength and skill with the sword was far beyond what I felt I deserved.

Ikane! Don't you dare give up! I roared at him, feeling the surrender in his mind.

I love you, Kea.

Snap.

Our connection was severed as if an executioner's axe had fallen on our thread.

"Ikane!" I shrieked as hot tears of rage burned down my cheeks. Unable—unwilling—to detain the power, it detonated. Flaming hot daggers, arrows, and spears of Thrall ripped through Deathbiters and ice. Specks of ash swirled through the mist-shrouded air. The ground quaked. Ice cracked and burst.

How I hated the feeling.

"Kea! Stop!" A voice rang through my ears. I didn't recognize it. It was garbled and indistinct, as if spoken through a sturdy glass windowpane. "Stay your magic!"

Sorrow and anger coursed through me, providing my power with a new torrent of vigor. Another wave of magic exploded as I dropped to my knees, blasting through the chasm with the sound of thunder. A chaotic whirlwind engulfed me, mirroring the uncontrollable emotions of rage, sorrow, guilt, and resentment. Thrall tore through everything in its path, ripping through the surrounding cliffs and shattering the ground beneath my feet.

Abruptly, the power dropped, leaving me breathless in my own heap of chaos. Through tear-warped vision, my eyes turned to the crevice above. Blue sky and warm sunlight burned down into the gorge—as if the Deathbiters were never here.

"Ikane." My voice shook as my sword clattered to the ice, and I sank to my hands and knees. He was gone. Rion had gotten what she wanted. Now she had both the ruby and Ikane.

"Kea," Broderick's voice broke into my mind as I saw the tips of his boots plant before me. He knelt down, and I felt the weight of his hand on my shoulder. He held a small vial in his other hand, filled with a clear substance I recognized. We had used it on Ikane to keep him sedated when Rion forced him to attack.

The bottle was uncorked.

My brows furrowed. Was he going to use it on me?

"What have you done?" he asked in a low voice.

I looked up at him, startled by the disarray of his clothing and hair. But this did not alarm me as much as the horror displayed in his deep blue eyes.

It was then that I noticed Erin standing far off with two horses. I could not see her face clearly at this distance, but I knew from her body language that she was frightened – and not of the Deathbiters.

Shock drove me to my feet. Instead of the narrow, icy road weaving between the soaring cliffs, Broderick and I stood in the center of a perfect, crystal sphere, with a surface that reflected our image like the innermost part of a globe. Shattered ice lay strewn across the border... along with two of our horses and over three-dozen wraith-like bats.

I had done this.

I staggered away from Broderick. I was a monster. Rion had turned me into a fiend! Anger seeped into my mind, boiling into another fury of Thrall that bulged in my chest. I took another step back, gripping my heart as if my hands could stay the magic. I didn't want to release it! Not on Broderick! Not on my friends!

I shook my head as my eyes went wide, locking with Broderick's. He needed to get away! This power could kill him.

As if he knew, he lifted the small vial of clear liquid. "Smell it," he said.

I nearly lunged at the concoction in the assassin's hand and pressed my nose against the opening. I inhaled deeply— not caring if it would permanently take me from this world. Death would be far easier to face than living without Ikane and the horror my friends now looked at me with.

With one inhale of the sweet sharpness inside the bottle, the pressure in my chest abated as if water had been dumped over a fire. The fumes from his vial burned my eyes, but I gathered a second breath anyway. Now, my mind blurred, and my limbs weakened.

Broderick tried to pull the bottle away, but I clung to his hand, desperate to knock myself unconscious... or more. The third inhale of the penetrating, acrid substance, brought blackness across my vision. Blackness I wanted. I felt Broderick's arm slip under mine before I fell to the ground.

Every muscle in his body felt bruised, even his head. The soreness behind his eyes warped his vision, causing the mottled black and gray walls to writhe. His chest felt heavy, even if the air hadn't been thick with acrid sourness. He gasped, chest heaving, as he lay on the hot, clammy stone. Fire stretched across his skin where the Deathbiters had dug their hooking talons into his flesh in order to carry him away.

A soft whimper escaped his wolf body, echoing through the expanse of the black cavern as he tried to move. The poison already clogged his blood and made him burn with fever.

Through his warped vision, the walls of the cave seemed to come alive with movement. But it wasn't stone. It was a gray cloak, shrouding the figure of a man shambling around obsidian rock formations. The ashen skin of his hands and his exposed chin made Ikane's breath grow shallow and frantic.

Desperately, he tried to move as the hooded figure approached. But Ikane's destroyed body had lost any ability to flee. The man knelt down beside him and one of his grey, shriveled hands reached out to touch Ikane's fur. Ikane's lips pulled back, revealing his sharp rows of white teeth, with a deep growl.

"Now, now," the man said in a voice ragged with age. "Don't you worry, little Leviathan Prince. I have great things in store for you."

ABOUT THE AUTHOR

Along with writing and drawing, CK Miller's hobbies include working in the garden, practicing martial arts, and studying homeopathic medicine.

She and her husband share their home near the Colorado Rocky Mountains with three beautiful boys.

73512171R00217

Made in the USA
Columbia, SC
05 September 2019